"I want you," Ward said. "I haven't been able to get the feel and taste of you out of my mind. I told myself you were just another woman bent on making an easy fortune in the gold camps, one I would forget as soon as you were out of sight. I was wrong. I knew it for a certainty when I saw Otto Bruin with his hands on you. I wanted to kill him, to beat him slowly to a cringing death."

"What you are doing is wrong!" Serena cried.

"Is it? I claimed you for mine, and mine you will be for a day, a week, a month—until this craving I have for you is satisfied. Nothing, nobody, will interfere. . . ."

Fawcett Books
by Jennifer Blake:

THE STORM AND THE SPLENDOR 14282 $2.50

LOVE'S WILD DESIRE 08616 $1.95

TENDER BETRAYAL 04429 $2.25

GOLDEN FANCY

Jennifer Blake

FAWCETT GOLD MEDAL • NEW YORK

GOLDEN FANCY

ISBN: 0-449-14369-4

Printed in the United States of America

First Fawcett Gold Medal printing: November 1980

10 9 8 7 6 5 4 3 2 1

PART ONE

Chapter One

The dry evening wind rustled across the plains. It flapped the canvas of the wagons, the ancient Conestogas, the Pittsburgs and flatbeds, and swirled the dust of the milling horses and livestock, mingling it with the rising blue-gray smoke of cook fires. It ruffled the tops of the sage and buffalo grass, sweeping over the ground to where the girl stood on the slight rise, lifting the curling edges of her blue-black hair, making her narrow her eyes against its grit-laden breath.

Serena Walsh drew her faded shawl closer around her. The wind was from the mountains lying like a soft lavender cloud on the horizon. It was cool and fresh after the heat of the day, holding the feel of autumn in its ceaseless embrace despite the prairie daisies of summer that nodded about her blowing skirts. Soon, within two or three days more of travel, they would reach the mountains, reach the towering landmark called Pikes Peak, the Shining Mountain of the Spanish explorers who were the first white men to see it. At its base was a town, almost a city, filled with normal, happy people; religious people, yes, but not fanatics. There, please God, she would leave this plodding wagon train with its harsh-spoken men, its women with downcast eyes, and its children that never smiled.

Serena flung back her dark hair in a gesture of freedom. Her finely molded features were set in a look of defiance, and there was a determined expression in her blue-gray eyes. She was not a Mormon. She would not be a Mormon. Let them frown at her unbound hair and uncovered head, at her unseemly independence and solitary habits. Let them purse their lips at her bright-colored, close-fitting dresses. She did not care. It was true that her dresses hugged her a little too well; her shape had taken on added fullness in the years since her mother had made them for her as a girl of sixteen. It could not be helped. There had been no way to replace them. Three years. As incredible as it seemed, it had been only three years since she had known a home, a settled way of life. It seemed forever.

From the direction of the wagon train came a call, a shrill demand for attention. At the sound of her name, Serena turned her head a fraction. A woman stood with her hands on her hips, staring in Serena's direction. Even at that distance, Serena thought she could see the spiteful frown that twisted the woman's sallow, vindictive face. Elder Greer's second wife, Beatrice, considered it her duty to chasten the gentile creature her husband had foisted upon her, to recall her to a sense of a place as a woman. She could see no reason why Serena should be allowed to escape her portion of the tasks that had to be done before supper was ready for the men. Doubtless, in Beatrice's tainted view, Serena was making a deliberate spectacle of herself; certainly she had hinted as much often enough. Serena could not see how she could be blamed for the attention she attracted. It was only because she was so different from the drab, submissive women of the train that the men watched her of an evening from beneath the brims of their sober black hats. No idea of enticing them had ever come into her head, no matter what anyone said. Look at Elder Greer, pausing in his task of pouring out a meager ration of water for his saddle horse, shielding his gaze by a pretense of wiping sweat from his brow with a grimy rag. Even the leader of the train could not seem to become used to the sight of her. From all indications, the story of the temptress Jezebel and her bitter end seemed likely to crop up again in the elder's sermon tonight.

Beatrice called again, a goaded, strident shout. Serena gave a small sigh, pretending not to hear. As far as she was concerned, she had no duties to the Mormons, men or women. She had not asked to be one of the Greer party when her father and mother had died of typhoid three weeks out from Missouri. Indeed, she had flatly refused to accept that dubious

8

hospitality. The elders, meeting in council, had ignored her objections. She needed protection, they said. She was not capable of seeing after her own livestock or driving a wagon. She must have someone older and more learned to tell her what she must do, to guide her steps toward righteous womanhood and shelter her immortal soul from evil. They had appointed Elder Greer, or rather, he had appointed himself, since he was the leader of the Saints. She was to join his "family," his aging, gray-haired wife of twenty years, Agatha, humble and soft-spoken; his second wife, Beatrice, with her mousy brown hair and round hazel eyes filled with fear and spite; and his third wife, Lessie, a simple girl with pale-blond, almost white hair, and washed-out blue eyes that held not a flicker of understanding though her body beneath her shapeless gray gown was ripe and yielding. Serena was a year or so younger than Lessie, of the same age as the elder's firstborn son. Despite her age, she was not treated as a child, but as one of the older women, a fact that made her more than a little nervous, especially when Elder Greer sought her out, bending his silver head over her, speaking to her in rich, unctuous tones of how her body and soul were in his keeping, touching her arm with his damp, insistent fingers. As soon as she accepted the tenets of the Mormon faith, he said, she would achieve a oneness with him and his family. She would lie safe in his bosom, sanctified by a holy union. All he had would be hers, all she had would be his. She would be pierced by the divine power of God in man, the flower of her maidenhood would be plucked in its early season, and he would rest at peace in the sweet temple of her womanly grace. In contrast to his fair words and reverent tone, the look in his eyes had been so searingly bestial that Serena had twisted from his grasp and run, leaving him rigid with anger behind her. From that day she had made her own cook fire, cleaned her own dishes, and slept in her own wagon with the canvas ends tightly tied shut.

Still, she was often forced to endure the elder's company as he rode along beside her wagon in the noonday heat, or commanded her presence at a sabbath gathering where he spoke long and with fulsome earnestness, laboring to make her accept the superiority of the Mormon creed. It did not serve, and as the weeks went by there was a growing mood of resentment against her among the Saints for her failure to recognize the honor that was being accorded her.

Serena, compelled by some demon of pride and perversity,

9

had taken lately to doing those things she knew the elders and their wives would not like. Holding herself aloof, apart from the other women, was an example, though by no means all. She had taken to loosening the collar of her dress when the sun was high, to unbuttoning her sleeves and rolling them well above her shapely elbows. Sometimes of an evening she would change into the silk gown that had belonged to her mother, put on her mother's satin slippers with their gilt heels, and sit on the wagon seat, leaning her forearms on her knees so that the firelight played over the creamy curves of her shoulders in the low-necked gown, revealing the shadowed valley between her breasts. Strange how the sly looks of the men and twitched skirts of the women could make of her shy and gentle mother's evening gown a garment of shame.

With her hair dressed high on her head, cascading in shining ringlets over her shoulders, Serena looked not unlike the miniature of her lovely French-Creole mother, painted when she had been a New Orleans belle. The difference was in the willful set of the mouth and in the eyes. Her mother's had been soft sherry brown, while Serena had inherited her smoky-blue peat-bog Irish color from her father. How odd to think that if Félicité Crèvecoeur had not fallen in love with a despised Irish laborer, a mere carpenter on her father's plantation acres, and married him in the teeth of her family's opposition, Serena would not be standing on the prairie at this moment. Sean Walsh, her father, unable to find the respect his soul craved or the wealth he felt his wife deserved, unwilling to stay in one place long enough to earn either, had made wanderers of the woman he loved and his only child. They never complained. Their stability had been in the man who had made of life a wry joke and sang to relieve the monotony of the miles they traveled.

Serena drew a deep breath against the pain of remembrance. They were gone, her mother and father. Her desolation went too deep for easy tears, something the Mormons did not understand or readily forgive, one more thing they held against her. Her father had thought to find all he longed for at the foot of the shining mountain called Pikes Peak, in the new gold-mining town of Cripple Creek. Gold, how it had drawn him, leading him to sell all they owned, pawn his wife's few remaining ornaments, even to beg from his formidable French-Creole in-laws. With his stake in hand he had set out for a new life, not caviling even at the necessity

10

of joining this band of religious pilgrims when he found he did not have the resources to pay the rail fare for his wife and daughter across the dusty plains. How much better it would have been if he had waited, taken work over the summer to make up the difference. They would have arrived nearly as soon, and they would have avoided the contaminated water that had caused the death of himself and his wife. But no, Sean Walsh had been too impatient to stand the delay in setting out; he had ever to be moving.

Swift, noisy, relentlessly modern, the railroad rattled through the evening somewhere to the north of the Mormon wagon train. Serena could picture it in her mind, rumbling, swaying, trailing a dark cloud of smoke that swirled about the lamplighted windows. Aboard would be men and women laughing, eating, drinking, or making ready for the night. There would be merchants, bankers, and mine owners, men who had already made their fortunes in the silver boom towns of Colorado, returning to Denver or perhaps taking the spur to Colorado Springs, then on to Cripple Creek itself to add to their holdings. And with them would be their wives and daughters dressed in the latest fashions from New York and Paris, women petted and pampered and showered with a thousand small treasures.

At the thought of such swift, luxurious travel, Serena knew an onrush of restless impatience with the plodding progress of the wagon train. Little though she might relish the idea, she could not deny that she had something more of her father than his temper and his eyes. If there was any merit in his vision of wealth and respect to be had in Cripple Creek, then perhaps there was a fortune of some design there for his daughter as well.

The figure of a woman left the wagons in the growing dusk and started toward where Serena stood. Ungainly, stumbling on the uneven ground; it was Lessie, Elder Greer's third wife.

Watching her struggling progress, the pure lines of Serena's mouth tightened. Lessie was with child; it was monstrous of the others, particularly that shrew Beatrice, to send her on errands. It was not surprising, however; they all did so, down to the least child. Lessie, with her guileless eyes and vacant smile, was so accommodating, so easily browbeaten, that she was treated more as a servant than as a wife. More than once Serena had intervened in the woman's behalf, sending a demanding child, of which the elder counted eleven

11

in his family, about his business or recommending that Beatrice haul her own water, fetch her own wood, or send one of her own whining brats to do it for her. This had endeared her to Lessie, but to no one else, least of all to Elder Greer. He did not allow bickering among his family, he said, but Serena was of the opinion that he did not like to see the contemptuous expression in her gray-blue eyes when she looked from him to the swollen body of his too biddable third wife.

"Serena? Come to the wagon, do, or you will miss your supper." There was an anxious look in Lessie's eyes, and she flung a quick look over her shoulders as she stood clutching her skirts.

"I'm not hungry, and even if I were, I still have biscuits left over from breakfast. You go on ahead without me, all of you. I don't need supper." Serena spoke quietly, her low voice a musical sound in the quiet.

"Please, Serena. Beatrice will be mad, mad at you, mad at me, because Elder Greer will ask for you, want to know where you are. Please, Serena."

For all her simplemindedness, there were times when Lessie was surprisingly acute. The elder would indeed ask for her. It was one of his rules that everyone in his family should gather for the evening prayer before meals whether they meant to eat or not, whether they were too ill to face food, were being punished by being sent supperless to bed, or, in Serena's case, were accustomed to eat alone. She, in particular, had always been singled out.

"There is no sense in it," Serena said with a lift of her shoulders. "I could as easily pray alone, especially here, away from everyone."

"Elder Greer could not see you praying. How would he know?"

"It's none of his business," Serena snapped. "Who does he think he is, God?"

"I don't know, Serena."

Seeing the frightened puzzlement in the girl's soft, faded blue eyes, Serena sighed. "Don't worry about it," she said. "I don't suppose it matters. Surely I can stand it for a few days more."

"Please, Serena, won't you come?"

"Yes, I will come for now," Serena said. Linking her arm through the other girl's to give her support, she turned toward

12

the flickering orange cook fires that lit the night and the wagons.

Night drew in, the evening meal was done. The Mormon women dried their red, wet hands on their aprons, untied the strings, and laid them aside. Hair was brushed and tightly hidden beneath close-fitting bonnets, and shawls and blanket capes were brought out. The faces of the children were washed and their hair combed, that of the boys slicked back with water, that of the girls braided anew and tucked up under bonnets no different from their mothers'. Men reached for their coats and their Bibles. All began to make their way toward the center of the wagons, which were drawn into a circle, not so much in fear of an Indian attack, not in this year of 1893, as against the stray brave off the reservation who might be tempted to plunder. The day was at an end. It was meeting time.

Serena lifted her head from the book she was reading in the light of a small lamp. Through a slit in the closed end of the wagon canvas, she watched the Mormons gather. With a shake of her head, she returned to her book. An instant later, she jumped as the tailboard of her wagon creaked to an added weight. She looked up in time to see a hard hand whip aside the back flap. She pushed herself bolt upright, reaching for her dressing gown to cover her chemise and petticoats, all that she wore in the privacy of her wagon so near bedtime. There was no time to push her arms into the sleeves. She could only hold it over the swelling curves of her breasts as Elder Greer flung his leg over the tail of the wagon and stepped inside.

He stood surveying the interior, the few fine pieces of furniture, the trunks and exquisitely pieced quilts and coverlets, the cot, spread with the fine linen sheets that had been a part of Serena's mother's trousseau, where she sat. His gaze came to rest at last on Serena herself. His eyes traveled over the tumbled dark mass of her hair, devouring the soft texture of her skin, suffused with a blush like rose-tinted ivory in the lamplight, watching the quick rise and fall of her breasts beneath her pristine white underclothing. For an instant his eyes, silvery, almost colorless in the dimness, met her wide gaze, then he looked quickly away.

He swallowed, his throat moving with the effort. "You do not go to the meeting?"

"No."

13

"You are not unwell?"

"I—I have a headache," Serena answered. It was a good enough excuse, since it made little difference to her whether the elder believed it or not. The truth was, she felt herself unable to bear another lecture, another sermon.

"We will miss you, and I think you will regret not hearing the good counsel that would show you the way you must go, the road your feet must take."

"Perhaps tomorrow night."

"Yes, there is always tomorrow, and yet tonight I was going to speak again of the holy mission that we, the people of this wagon train, have undertaken. There will be great rejoicing when finally we reach Salt Lake City in Utah, the land of Zion found by Saint Brigham Young forty-six years ago. Not in nearly twenty years has any band attempted to duplicate his feat of traveling over a thousand miles across these plains and mountains to reach that promised land. How I long for you to be aware of the majesty of what we are doing in reliving the great hardships of this journey. How much I want you to become one of us so that you may feel yourself a part of it."

"You are—kind to think of it, but I believe I must remain true to my own beliefs and the teachings of my parents."

"You are arrogant, lost in your foolish pride. You look down on my people."

Serena stiffened in alarm as he took a step toward her, his eyes coldly blazing. "No," she said, running her tongue over her dry lips. "No, I'm not. It's only that I must have the right to believe in my way, just as you believe in yours."

"You don't know what you are saying. You don't know what you are disdaining in your ignorance. One day you will regret the glorious future that you are denying yourself from sheer stubbornness. It is possible that you need more guidance, more of a sign. If you are too ignorant to take up the golden cup of divine salvation through Sainthood, then perhaps it should be forced upon you. I shall have to pray upon it."

"What—what do you mean?" Serena inquired as coolly as she could manage. She did not like the trend of his words, still less did she like the glint of triumph she had seen rise in his eyes before he bowed his head in all piety.

"There is no time now. I must go to the meeting. We will talk of this another time, when I have meditated upon what I must do."

14

Swinging around, he left her, left the wagon flap dangling, swaying in the wind. It was a long time before Serena returned to her book, longer still before she blew out her lamp and slept.

She came awake abruptly. Alarm shivered along her nerves as she stared into the darkness. The canvas above her shivered in the wind, billowing, making the wagon creak. From far away came the mournful call of a coyote. A cow lowed from the animal enclosure, and closer by there came the sharp bark of a dog. Then, as she lay straining to hear, came the sound that had awakened Serena. It was the scrape of a footstep at the rear of her wagon.

Moving with silent caution, she sat up. She was not really disturbed. It might be no more than a restless sleeper, or someone moving beyond the wagons to relieve themselves in the darkness. Still, she was uneasy. There seemed something furtive about this sound so near her wagon. Her skin prickling with the chillness of the plains night, Serena pushed the long braid of her hair, worn plaited for sleeping, over her shoulder as she strained to hear.

The ceaseless wind brushed against the wagon, ruffling the canvas beside her. In the dim light lent by the three-quarter moon that brightened the encampment, she could make out the familiar shapes of things around her, the furniture, her father's chest of carpenter's tools, her mother's hidebound trunk, the open wooden box that held the iron pots and pans, the tin plates and cups and other utensils she used daily. The flap at the rear of the wagon shivered, then there came a low, muffled noise, the sound of the rope closing being slipped from its knot.

"Who is it? Who's there?"

Her low-voiced query hung in the air. There was no answer. The bed of the wagon shuddered to a sudden weight on the back frame. The shadow of a man loomed against the canvas.

"Who is there? Answer me or—or I'll scream!"

"No, don't do that," came a whisper, hoarse, urgent, in reply. "Wait—only wait a minute." The rear flap billowed and Elder Greer swung a leg over the tailboard to step inside.

"What do you want?" Serena's fear receded a fraction, and yet an unpleasant feeling remained in the pit of her stomach. The elder straightened, towering over her in the narrow confines of the wagon. "I've come to save you, my dear Serena."

"Save me?"

15

"Verily, to fold you to my bosom and keep you safe from harm and the wickedness of the gentile world. I want you for my wife, beautiful Serena. I have prayed over it, and the answer is plain. I mean to take you to me, to merge your body with mine in divine union."

As he spoke he moved closer, coming up against the side of the cot. Serena edged away from him, drawing her knees up, freeing them from the quilt that covered her. "I have told you I don't want to change my faith. I cannot believe as you do, or acknowledge your prophet."

"Yes, and it is a great sorrow to me. However, you are young and a female. You cannot know your own mind. You need guidance, and I am here to give it to you." There was a rough note in his low voice allied to a quaver, as of some violent feeling.

"Can't—can't we talk about it tomorrow?" The danger in which she stood was not unknown to Serena. The elder's physical appetites were voracious. It was not unusual for him to summon one of his wives with a curt nod of his head and disappear with her into one of his several wagons of an evening. The creakings of the wooden vehicles, their peculiar movements on their rudimentary springs and locked wheels, had been the source of much snickering and whispered comments among his older children, some of whom swore to witnessing the ludicrous rites of conception when they were younger.

"Tomorrow?" The elder swallowed, an audible sound in the tense quiet. "Tomorrow will be too late!"

He fell on her, reaching, grasping for her soft flesh shining pale in the shadow-filled darkness. She twisted away with the sharp edge of a scream in her throat. His arms fastened around her hips, and for an instant his bearded face was pressed against her breasts. As he nuzzled blindly into their swelling fullness, Serena was assailed by the sweaty, animalistic odor of his body, and she pushed at him with the strength of shuddering revulsion, wrenching from his hold. That she would seriously resist him seemed to come as a surprise, for his grip slackened. In that instant Serena slid from the cot, scrambling to her feet.

With a bellow of rage, the elder surged after her, his work-hardened hands snatching at the fragile, much-washed batiste of her nightgown. The fabric gave at the sleeve, but he dragged her toward him so that she stumbled, swaying in his direction. Instantly he pulled her down across him, rolling

16

to pin her beneath him on the floor. With a grunt of triumph, he flung a leg across her knees, pressing the hardened lump of his manhood and the firm bulge of his paunch against her. In horror she realized he wore nothing more than a pair of knee-length underdrawers. She wriggled in panting disgust as his fingers groped over her, finding her breast, squeezing the ripe softness. She gave a cry of mingled hurt and anger, and he hitched himself higher. His mouth, wet and foul in the bristling stiffness of his beard, slid over her cheeks, seeking for her mouth to silence her. Nausea rose on her tongue, and Serena arched her back, straining away from him. One hand was crushed underneath him, but with the other she struck out, catching him on the nose with her small hard fist. He bellowed in pain, then drew back, exclaiming with an incredulous oath as he felt the wetness of the blood that trickled from his nostrils.

For an instant Serena thought he was going to give up the struggle in his rage and chagrin that she did not welcome his advances. She was mistaken. Instead, he drew back his hand and slapped her, a stunning blow to the side of the face. As she gasped with shock, held immovable by the pain, his shaking hand fumbled at the neckline of her gown. He tore at the buttons, ripping them from their holes, exposing the mounds of her breasts to the cool night air, then rending the thin batiste to the hem.

That tearing sound seemed to slice through Serena's brain, cutting away the fear and the last lingering disbelief at this unspeakable thing that was happening to her. She heaved away from the touch of his damp, probing fingers, bringing her knees up. Her fingers curved into claws and she struck for his face with the swiftness of a snake, reaching for his eyes. As he jerked away from the tearing sharpness of her nails, she rolled free with the tatters of her gown swirling around her, hanging from her shoulders like a cape. On hands and knees, she lunged for the rear flap of the wagon. The elder scrabbled after her, catching one ankle. To keep from being pulled backward, she clutched at the nearest thing to hand, the side of the wooden cook box. With desperate strength, she managed to get her arm over the side, raising herself to one knee. But then the elder released her leg, grasping higher, lunging up behind her and jerking at the braid of her hair to twist her head back while he thrust himself against her, grinding his body against the softness of her hips.

17

As she was pushed forward over the side of the box, her flailing arm struck the side of a frying pan. She grasped the handle with both hands and swung backward, connecting with the side of the elder's head. He cursed and released her hair to wrench the heavy iron pan from her. With one arm clasped about her waist, he began to push at the waistband of his drawers.

In frantic haste, Serena flailed her arms around her, trying to find a hold, seeking purchase to wrench herself away from the clammy, musky hardness of the man pressed so sickeningly close. The need to call for help shafted through her mind, but there was no time, and with his arm cutting into her middle, no breath to waste on what might well be a useless exercise. The sound of a woman crying out in the night was not so unusual, after all. And then as the hunching elder pushed her farther forward, her outstretched fingers touched a wooden handle and closed around it.

Her weapon was too light for a knife. It was a fork, a three-tined fork. Her disappointment was like a sickness in her heart; still, she did not hesitate. With the last of her ebbing strength she jabbed the sharp steel tines into the arm that held her, slashing, tearing at the sweaty flesh.

Abruptly she was released. She drew a gasping breath and threw herself to one side, not quite avoiding a smacking swing of the elder's hand against the rounded curve of her hip. In swift, unthinking retaliation, she stabbed at his chest with her fork, and had the satisfaction of feeling it rake across his ribs. As he snatched at her hand with a mighty grunting groan, she threw herself back from him and surged up, leaping for the tailboard of the wagon.

She had one leg over the side when he grabbed her, his fingers closing around her arm. Setting her teeth, she plunged on over, trying to use her weight to break his hold, only catching at the canvas flap to prevent herself from falling at the last minute. He refused to let her get away from him, holding grimly to her arm.

The elder had forgotten his drawers slipping about his knees. He tripped and stumbled forward, pitching head first out of the wagon. They fell together in a tangled heap of naked flesh and lay stunned, staring up at the night sky.

A shrill scream shattered the night. It rose and fell with an edge of hysteria, full-throated in the grip of unreasoning fear laced with wrath. Serena, lying dazed with an intolerable weight across her chest and the sting of buffalo grass

18

beneath her bare shoulders, heard it and turned her head. It was Beatrice who stood with her lashless eyes fastened on their nude, blood-smeared bodies, one hand clutching the flannel wrapper she wore over her nightgown and the other holding a lantern. From her narrow mouth issued that nerve-shattering screeching. Voices rose, a low babble of disturbed sound. Lamplight flared, casting a yellow-orange glow against the canvas of the wagons before men climbed down and came at a run.

Serena pushed at the man lying across her, trying to drag herself from under him. Winded, gasping for breath, Elder Greer pushed himself to one elbow, wheezing. He looked around him, then as if coming suddenly to his senses, he stiffened. A fierce look came into his eyes, and he swung his head toward Beatrice.

"Shut up that noise, woman," he growled, holding to his chest as he struggled to a standing position. As she obeyed with a gulp, he ordered, "Bring me my pants."

Beside him, Serena pulled herself to her feet, gathering the strips of her nightgown around herself with shaking hands, still clutching the fork in one fist. After one quick glance she averted her eyes from the sight of the blood that oozed in bright-red runnels down the elder's chest, threading through the sparse gray-brown hair. She turned her pale face toward the sound of people approaching, then as hot color rose to her hairline, she swung to seek the cover of her wagon, away from the startled stares of the men hurrying in their direction.

"No, no you don't," Elder Greer said, shooting out his hand to catch her wrist. He held to her with a hard grip while with the other hand he tugged his drawers up to cover his limp nakedness.

"Let me go," Serena breathed in supplication, trying to break the hold of his fingers that bit into her flesh. She could not. His strength seemed to grow as he clothed himself, as did the wild and maniacal look in his eyes.

"What is it, Brother Greer? What passes here?" The eager question was asked from a good distance. The eyes of the man who spoke, and those of the others crowding behind him, were on the shrinking white form of the girl at the elder's side. The light of the lantern Beatrice had left sitting on the ground gleamed through the thin and ragged material of her tattered nightgown, outlining the slender yet sweetly curved shape of her body with mysterious golden light.

19

"A piece of wantonness, that is what passes here," the elder replied, his voice rich, steady. "This woman pretended to illness in the night, calling out to me to succor her in her sickness. When I went in to her, she tempted me, tearing open her gown, displaying herself. When I told her to cover herself, she refused."

"No," Serena said, shock and dismay making her voice no more than a thread of sound. "It isn't so."

The elder's fingers tightened, stopping the flow of blood to her hand. "It is so. She offered herself to me for a price, spreading her thighs in invitation, and when I spurned her, she was so angered that she tried to do me an injury."

"With a fork, brother?" came a wondering inquiry as the elder indicated the marks on his chest.

"If a different weapon had come to her hand she might have killed me."

Serena shook her head in negation. She opened her lips to speak. At that moment Beatrice stepped from the shadows of the elder's wagon clutching her husband's linsey-woolsey pants to her bony chest. "Whore," she whispered, her face working as she stared with hatred at the slim figure of the girl. "Slut, to try a good man so. Jezebel! She-dog in heat!"

Her husband held out his hand for his pants, and with a look of seething malevolence for Serena, the woman passed them over.

The first man shifted his feet. "We cannot allow such behavior to pass unpunished, even if she is not one of us. She may be a danger to us all, both to our souls and bodies."

Beatrice, perhaps deliberately, perhaps otherwise, stepped in front of Serena, shielding her from the hot gaze of the men. Serena would have been grateful if the woman had not also curled the talons of her fingers around her arm to hold her while Elder Greer slipped into his pants.

"She is in my keeping," the elder said as he passed his suspenders over his shoulders and fastened them to his waistband. "I promise you she shall feel the weight of punishment until she reaches penitence. I shall personally ply the whip to her back, nay even to her naked skin."

Beatrice stiffened, flinging her head up. "You, my husband? Better to let her face open meeting and be judged as she deserves and punished according to what is meted out. You—you are too good, too gentle to chastise her as she deserves."

20

The elder shot his wife a look of stern rebuke. "She is my responsibility. I am answerable for her sins."

"If that were so," Beatrice said slowly, "then you must needs feel the whip on your own back, my husband. No, let the slut stand before us all in her shame. It is a matter for all to decide, since her transgressions, if they continue, may affect all. She is a poison which must be dealt with swiftly and without mercy."

"Be silent, woman!" Elder Greer shouted, but it was too late.

"What she says has merit, brother," the first man said earnestly.

"Yes," said a second. "She has already affected your reason to the point where you went to her aid in the night without being properly dressed. How might she affect your judgment if you alone undertook the task of her chastisement?"

Staring from one to the other, Serena was aware of an undercurrent of meaning in their words that gave her an uneasy hope. "Nothing happened as Elder Greer has said. He is lying! You must believe me," she cried.

The men glanced at her and looked quickly away. "It may be best," the first said, "if we meet to get to the bottom of her exact crime."

"Crime? I have committed no crime!" For all the attention they paid her, Serena might as well not have spoken.

"Be silent, Whore of Babylon," Beatrice hissed, giving her a shake. "Isn't it enough that you have endangered my weak husband's immortal soul by your wicked ways, enticing him into your place of iniquity in hope of payment? Must you blacken his name also?"

Serena had thought Beatrice must realize she had not called out to Elder Greer pretending to be sick; how could she not know it, sleeping so close in the next wagon, as she did? She had thought that, knowing her husband had sought her out of his own will, Beatrice must know why. It was not so. The names she had called Serena, then, reflected not her jealousy, as Serena had thought, but her actual belief as to the truth of what had taken place. Unable to conceive of her husband's entering Serena's wagon without invitation, she was certain he had expected to find Serena complaisant. Why should that be, since Serena had repulsed him a number of times, unless for the sake of a reward? Marriage, because Serena so stoutly refused to change her religion and accommodate herself to Mormon ways, was out of the question.

21

Monetary gain was left as the only explanation. Because Elder Greer hinted it was so, Beatrice actually considered her a fallen woman plying her most ancient of trades, and it appeared from the stern expressions of the gathered Saints that they were of the same incredible opinion.

This was the crime of which they were accusing her.

Chapter Two

The meeting was convened by the clanging of a cowbell. There was no delay. No precious hours of daylight would be wasted for such a paltry cause; morning must find the wagon train on the move once more.

The leaders of the group, Elder Greer among them, sat at a long board supported by a pair of carpenter's sawhorses. A Bible, the Old Testament, lay in front of them, and a lantern sat at one end. A number of other lanterns hung from wagons here and there, adding their illumination to the cleared space in the center of the straggling circle of vehicles. Serena was given time to cover herself decently, as Beatrice phrased it, by donning a dress, but there was no time to put up her hair or even brush it, no time to don stockings and shoes. The elders must not be kept waiting on her convenience. It was she who must stand alone, pale, bruised, and unkempt, before the board while the men and women of the train gathered around her, whispering and staring. It was an endless quarter of an hour before the bearded elders, clad in solemn, rusty black, filed to their chairs.

Serena stood with her back straight and her gaze fixed on the darkness beyond a gap in the wagons. Though she was aware of the low murmur of voices and the simpering titters of laughter, she did not allow them to intrude upon her notice. She knew when Elder Greer glanced at her then looked away, saw the glitter of barely suppressed lust hidden under his calm and magisterial mien, but she did not betray by the flicker of an eyelid that she realized he existed. Only by maintaining this proud, uncaring pose could she force herself to stand still, to stay instead of running out into the night away from this unjust and humiliating tribunal.

One of the judges, the same elder who had confronted Elder Greer earlier, cleared his throat. "You, Serena Walsh, have been accused of the sin of offering yourself to a man for the purpose of fornication. This is a serious charge. Do you understand its nature?"

"I—yes, I understand," Serena answered, and then as the murmur of condemnation for this truthful reply rose, she went on, her voice rising, "But it is a false charge. I did not invite Elder Greer into my wagon. He entered it while I slept—"

"Lies!" Beatrice shouted from where the women of the elder sat with their children to one side. Agatha, the first wife, sat with her lips folded and her gray head grimly erect. Beside her, Lessie was twisting her hands in her lap with tears standing in her soft eyes.

Elder Greer held up his hand for silence. "For what purpose would I do that, my child?" he inquired, his voice grave and a sorrowing look on his features.

"You told me I must be saved from myself," Serena answered, turning her blue-gray eyes in his direction without evasion. "You seemed to think that if you—if you lay with me I would feel compelled to accept the honor of being your wife. You said the union would be a holy one, that you had prayed over it and—and your presence in my wagon was the answer."

"Blasphemy. This is blasphemy," the first elder said, his face growing red.

"She is a viper filled with wickedness," Beatrice said with a savage nod.

With her hands clenched, Serena turned to her. "If what I speak is wickedness, it is not mine. I am only saying what was told to me, telling what Elder Greer tried to do to me."

"You lie, you lie!" Beatrice screamed, her eyes filled with hate.

"Silence!" the first elder shouted, bringing his fist down on the judgment board with a thud. "Silence at once!" When the babble of voices had died away, he turned to the man beside him. "We have heard what this young woman has to

24

say, Brother Greer. Now let us hear what you have to tell us concerning the matter."

The silver-gray hair of Elder Greer glinted in the lamp-light as he slowly turned to face Serena. "I am grieved at the accusations, deeply grieved. However, I trust my good name can stand worse than the desperate mouthings of a girl who is frightened by the enormity of what she has done. No, my concern is for the state of her soul. Despite everything, I feel she is not beyond redemption. Punishment there must be, some mortification of the flesh to correct and discipline the wrongful thoughts that abide in her mind, but when it is done, she must have a place. She herself has mentioned the possibility of becoming my wife. Perhaps this is what she desires in her heart regardless of her outward reluctance to become one of us. If it is God's will that this be the road to her salvation, then I am not unwilling. I shall make it my most sacred duty to see that she repents of her wicked ways and accepts the mantle of grace as befits her womanhood."

"You are too generous, Elder Greer."

"So he is!" Beatrice declared. "She should be put from us as something unclean, left behind, alone in her sinfulness, when we leave here in the morning."

"That is unnecessarily cruel," Elder Greer rebuked his wife with a dangerous look in his face. "It would be to expose her to great dangers, Indian horse thieves, stray riders and outlaws; to the mercy of the elements, the possibility of becoming lost."

"Better for her to face such danger than to continue as a threat to your immortal soul! Besides, what has such a one as she to fear from men? Will she not welcome them into her wagon, even an Indian? As for becoming lost, why, how can that be when the trail is as plainly marked as a turnpike by the wheels of wagons and old cast-off belongings?"

"She has a point," the first elder agreed with a slow nod.

Serena took a step forward, her hands clenched at her sides. "So she does," she said. "I will leave this wagon train most willingly. In fact, nothing would give me more pleasure!"

"See how little she deserves your concern!" Beatrice exclaimed.

"It cannot be," Elder Greer said, frowning.

"No! No," came a new voice. "She might die, and I don't want her to leave. I don't know what I will do if she leaves!"

The speaker was Lessie. Her voice was thick with tears and her eyes red-rimmed and scared, but she had spoken.

"Keep quiet," Beatrice snapped. "We don't care what you think."

"That is not so," Elder Greer corrected. "We do care. Do you want this woman to join the family, Lessie?"

"Oh, yes, sir, I do."

"She cannot be so bad then."

"No, sir. She has always been good, nothing but good, to me."

"That must be in her favor then, surely."

The first elder began to nod. Beatrice, her spiteful gaze clashing with the hard silver stare of her husband, was silent. Serena, looking from one to the other, saw her chance of escaping the fate Elder Greer had in store for her slipping away. The silver-haired Saint turned his glittering gaze to her with a distinct air of anticipation, one hand absently moving to press his chest where she had wounded him. A look of piety sat upon his countenance, and yet in the depths of his eyes hovered an expression that made a shudder ripple over her skin, bringing with it the memory of his hard hands probing her flesh.

"No!"

The word sprang from her lips unbidden, but she would not have called it back, even if she could. "No," she repeated. "As much as I would like to be a sister to you, Lessie, I would prefer not to be a wife to Elder Greer. I have no wish for such an—honor."

"Your wishes do not count in this matter!"

"Do they not? Then perhaps my sinful nature will? I can promise you, Elder Greer, that you will regret it if you force this—this punishment upon me. I will not be a comfortable wife. You will receive more pain than pleasure from me, as I think you have already found. Far from proving my salvation, it is more likely to be my doom, for I doubt very much that I will be able to resist betraying you at the first opportunity!"

The results of that audacious statement were beyond belief. Voices rose in a confused babble. Women spat vicious epithets while men rumbled in condemnation that was not without a certain furtive expectation.

"She is a slut!" Beatrice screamed in angry joy. "I tried to tell you, but you wouldn't listen. Leave her behind, I say. It is a more merciful sentence than she deserves."

26

The purplish-red hue of rage suffused the face of Elder Greer. "You have made your choice," he grated, "but before you put yourself beyond hope, there is one thing more you should consider. You were given into my protection. I was appointed your guardian, both by the public meeting and at the request of your father as he lay dying. By right, since I have been for some weeks your provider, your possessions are mine, if I see fit to claim them. I do so claim them now as a recompense for the injury you have done both to my person and my good name. If you leave my protection, you go with nothing more than those personal belongings, such as clothes and provisions, necessary to see you to a place of habitation."

"You can't do that!" Even as she voiced the protest, Serena knew that he could. The expressions of those around her, of Beatrice and Agatha and Lessie, of the Saints behind the judgment board and those crowding close, made it all too certain.

"I can! So think carefully, for this will be your last chance. Will you stay with us as my wife and hope that with my help you may acquire a chastened and chaste spirit, or will you be left alone here in this place with nothing?"

He thought he had her. He thought she must accept his terms, because to do otherwise would be madness. Well then, she was mad.

"How good of you to warn me," she answered, lifting her chin. "I believe that after the last weeks spent in your company, I would prefer to be alone. Though you may have my possessions, I will still have my self-respect and something you are more likely to take away than to give me, my chastity. As to the danger, I prefer to risk it rather than remain. In this case, the devil I don't know is infinitely preferable to the one I do!"

"So be it!" Elder Greer surged to his feet with such force his chair overturned. His face dark with fury and frustration, he said, "You will return to your wagon and stay there through the night meditating on your folly. If you do not come to me in the morning and beg forgiveness on bended knees, then we will depart from you at first light, and no amount of pleading and prayers will persuade us to turn back for you. Goodnight to you, Serena Walsh, and if God wills, goodbye!"

* * *

27

Morning came slowly. Serena watched it with wide and burning eyes, watched the sky turn from blue-black to gray, watched the velvet earth turn slowly to prickly, scrub-covered sand. When she could see inside the wagon, she pulled out her mother's small hidebound trunk. Removing the contents, she made a neat stack of her own clothing—her three dresses of printed cotton and gingham, her extra set of underclothing and good high-button shoes. On top of these she carefully placed her mother's silk gown and her kid slippers with the gilded heels. Turning to a small lacquer box, she took out its contents, a gold locket containing a miniature of Sean Walsh, a hair brooch, a necklace and earrings of twisted gold and seed pearls, and a gold thimble set with lapis lazuli. She put these treasures that had belonged to her mother into the center of a small lawn handkerchief, tied up the corners, and pushed them down into the toe of one of the slippers. A look of quiet determination on her oval face, she placed the slippers in the bottom of the trunk with the silk dress. Over these went a quilt, then on top of them went her own clothing. Seeing the trunk was not quite full, she added a mantle of gray merino and a half-dozen of the many books that had belonged to her father. She left the trunk open while she brushed her hair and formed it into a soft knot on the nape of her neck held with tortoiseshell pins, then she placed her mother's silver-backed brush, comb, and mirror inside, lowered the lid, and buckled the straps that held it shut.

"You are ready. That's good, since it means I won't have to spend time seeing to it."

At the sound of Beatrice's voice, Serena swung around to see the woman climbing over the tailboard. "Yes, I'm ready."

"You remember what Elder Greer said. You are to take only your personal things."

"I remember."

The woman looked away, her gaze moving possessively over the furnishings of the wagon, coming to rest on the trunk. "You are taking that?"

"I am," Serena replied, her voice even.

"It's an ugly thing, not big enough to do much good. Let me see what you have in it."

"No."

"No? How dare you be so insolent, a woman in your position? Open it, I say."

Serena did not even look at her. Reaching for her faded cashmere shawl, she swung it around her. "I will not, nor

28

will you. If you try, if you touch a finger to it, I will call the elder, your husband, and tell him I have changed my mind, that I want to stay with him as his fourth wife."

"You wouldn't—" Beatrice breathed, but there was no conviction in her strained tone.

"Try me, just try me."

Beatrice looked away, running her tongue over her thin lips. "Well, what do I care what you take with you, since you are leaving so much else behind? I'm sure I don't begrudge you your fancy clothes and gee-gaws. I doubt they are such that a decent woman could wear anyway."

"If you mean a woman like yourself, I am sure they would not become you."

Beatrice flashed her a dark look, but controlled her ire enough to force a sour smile. "I will send a man to take the trunk down for you, then."

"Don't trouble yourself. I can manage it."

"As you like. I assume you have food and water?"

Serena nodded. There was flour and bacon and dried fruit in a sack beside the door, as well as a frying pan and a large tin flask of water.

"Then there is nothing more to be said. I know you do not expect me to wish you good fortune."

"No," Serena answered quietly, "but I will wish you God-speed—far from me."

The satisfaction of that small victory was short-lived. All too soon Serena was sitting on her trunk in the buffalo grass while Beatrice and Agatha and the other Mormon women rode by her on the seats of their wagons with their faces averted and their eyes fixed straight ahead. It helped but very little to see Lessie peeping from the rear flap of the elder's last wagon with tears streaming down her face, one hand fluttering in a forlorn wave. Indeed, the sight of the girl with her swollen belly was more of a reproach to Serena than all the sternly righteous backs that were presented to her. She felt as if she had deserted a friend, and none of the excellent reasons for it that she gave herself had the power to make her feel less guilty.

The wagon train grew smaller in the distance. When it began to shimmer in a heat haze from the morning sun, nearly disappearing in a prairie swell, Serena pushed to her feet. Setting her supplies on top of the trunk, she picked it up and began to follow in the ruts of the wagons.

The sun advanced, the trunk grew heavier. Serena tried

29

putting her supplies inside and hoisting the load onto her shoulder. The wood frame of the trunk bit into her neck, and she shifted it to her back. Once she stumbled, falling to her knees, nearly wrenching her arm from its socket as the trunk shifted, pitching to the ground. Once she walked to within a yard of a sidewinder rattlesnake and was forced to stand completely still for long, aching minutes before the reptile uncoiled and slithered from her path. She rested for a time when she stopped for the noon meal, but before long she was moving once more, this time dragging the trunk by one handle.

One moment the sun was bright and hot, the next it was setting in a flare of crimson and gold while the sky was still brilliantly blue. Serena trudged on until darkness began to gather, making the trail uncertain. Too tired to make the effort to cook, she ate a handful of dried apples, rolled into her quilt, and dropped into the sleep of exhaustion.

Once in the hours after midnight she woke. She lay for a time staring at the stars above her, feeling the coolness of the night wind on her face. Something moved in the grass, a rabbit feeding. There came the whir of wings as a hunting owl quartered the darkness. Searching carefully, Serena found within herself a small uneasiness, but no real fear. That sense of unease came from her lack of control over her life, and yet that very lack gave her, at least for the moment, a fatalistic acceptance. What she could not change, she must endure. She closed her eyes and breathed deeply, evenly. After a time she slept once more.

The second morning was little different from the first, except that the day was overcast, and when she stopped for dinner she found her water was getting low. She was not making good time, in fact she hardly seemed to be moving at all. She could do better if she left the trunk behind, she knew, and yet when she turned toward the shining mountains again she had the trunk on her back.

By the middle of the afternoon clouds began to gather, lying in a low, dark bank in the northeast. The wind grew stronger, flinging up fine particles of grit, hurrying grasshoppers and prairie birds before it. Feeling it on her face, Serena thought she could feel moisture in its breath, so different from the dry air around her. She broke into a run for a few steps, then slowed once more. What was the use of hurrying? There was no shelter anywhere for her. All around her lay nothing but the treeless stretches of the prairie.

And yet, the storm held off. The evening was turning lavender, drawing in, before the first rumble of thunder rolled toward her. It was followed by lightning, the merest flicker at the rim of the sky. She should stop, Serena knew, perhaps seek a low place, a swale or buffalo wallow, in the ground. Somehow she could not make herself halt, not while there was light in the sky. An anxious frown between her eyes, she watched as the purple-gray cloud spread upward, covering the sky, shutting out the sight of the mountains, bringing darkness close to the earth. The thunder came more often, a continuous muttering that exploded now and then into a crashing roar. Lightning walked the horizon, leaping high into the heavens with terrible grace.

Serena's footsteps slowed and she scanned the darkening plains. Lightning crackled and she smelled the sulfur freshness of ozone and something else akin to smoke. It was smoke, for there in the distance was a pinpoint of light, firelight. For an instant she thought the lightning had set the grass of the plains afire, but no, the light was too close, too constant. Was it the Mormon wagon train then? Surely not. They should be far ahead of her by now. Other travelers, then, it had to be. But of what kind?

Tales she had heard crowded into her mind, of renegade Indians, of men with no liking for towns and the trappings of civilization, men who, as the saying went, had gone to the bad, outside the law. Who else would be out here except men like these? For her own safety she should stay as far from that fire as possible.

Even as she gave herself this excellent counsel, the cheerful blaze there in the storm-filled night seemed to draw her like a beacon. She dropped the handles of her trunk, and leaving it, moved closer.

She approached warily, circling to her left. There were two horses tied on long reins just beyond the range of the firelight, fine-looking animals with a sleek, well-cared-for look. Near the burning embers sat a coffee pot and a frying pan, both giving off mouth-watering aromas, while to one side lay a bedroll beneath an oiled canvas shelter. But though Serena circumvented the campfire at a distance of several yards, there was no sign of the person who had arranged such comforts against the night. She did not think he was in the bedroll, though in the uncertain light she could not be sure. Certainly it made no sense for him to turn in with his supper sitting uneaten before the fire.

31

Lightning crackled, forking viciously across the night sky. Serena swung toward the fiery light, then her nerves leaped and she drew in her breath in a soundless gasp. There close beside her, so near she could reach out and touch him, was a man. Outlined against the lightning-torn darkness of the heavens, he was tall and broad-shouldered. He stood at ease with a rifle hanging as if forgotten from his fingers, and yet there was a tightly strung alertness about him that gave an impression of leashed strength. In his silent stillness and the hard lines of his features, there was something cruel and deadly beyond reckoning.

The white glow faded. Serena took a swift step back, whirled to run. Instantly a hard hand clamped down on her arm and she was hauled back. She stumbled a little, and her shoulder came in contact with a chest as hard, flat, and un-yielding as an oaken board.

"Where are you going in such a hurry?" The soft drawl was in direct contrast to the biting grip that held her. "You must accept my hospitality. I insist."

The lightning flared again, flashing with gold flames in the depths of Serena's eyes as she stared up at him. It touched the pale oval of her face and was caught for an instant in the blue-black, windblown wildness of her hair.

"Let me go," she said, her words nearly lost in the roll of thunder.

"I will be happy to do that, as soon as your friends show themselves."

"I have no friends," Serena said, aware of the mockery that edged his tone.

"You expect me to believe that?"

"You will have to. It's the truth."

"And what do you know of truth?"

Serena strained to see him in the darkness. Her answer came unbidden. "More than I know of falsehood. I am not sure just now if it would not be wiser, safer, for me to claim some friend waiting over the last rise."

He weighed her words without speaking. Tension hovered in the quiet. She was aware of the steady rise and fall of his chest with his breathing. Abruptly he released her and made a curt gesture toward the fire.

With her face set and her hand clenched on the skirt of her dress, Serena walked before him. He had made no move toward her with the rifle he held, had said little to give her the impression, and yet she felt like a prisoner. He indicated

32

a seat on the lower end of his canvas-covered bedroll, and she sank down upon the end, being careful not to dislodge the supports which held the canvas covering open like a low tent protecting the bedding from the weather. As the warmth of the fire reached her, she gave a small shiver, holding her hands to the flames. Until she had felt their heat she had not realized how chilled she had become.

Across the orange-red campfire, the man watched her, his face stern as his gaze rested on her slender form in the faded dress and shawl, and the dark cape of her loosened hair glinting with a sapphire sheen in the firelight.

As she felt his steady regard, Serena raised her blue-gray eyes to meet his hard green stare. He towered above her, his face bronzed by the sun, his frame loose-limbed and powerful. He wore a shirt of linen open at the neck under a tailored jacket of split cowhide, and trousers of rough cotton twill tucked into the kind of supple leather boots worn by men of means. He was hatless, and the rising wind ruffled the dark-brown waves of his hair. A frown drew heavy dark brows together, and thick lashes narrowed his stare.

He tilted his head toward the night beyond the fire. "Do you have a mount somewhere?"

Serena shook her head.

"Alone and on foot. I suppose you have an explanation, but before you start, let me warn you it had better be a good one."

Something in his voice and manner sent a wave of irritation over Serena. "I see no reason why I should explain anything to you. I am no threat to you, I assure you. If you can't or won't believe that, then I will gladly leave you and make my own camp."

"I think not."

"You—what do you mean?"

"I mean that I prefer to keep you here until I find out exactly who you are and why you are out here on the plains without an escort or means of transportation."

"Why?" Serena demanded bluntly.

"Because I value my skin. It wouldn't be the first time a pretty shill had distracted a man while her partners slipped up and took everything he had."

"I have no partners!" Serena said in angry amazement.

"So you say."

"It's ridiculous. Do I look like the kind of woman who would do such a thing?"

33

He surveyed her with slow deliberation. "You are attractive enough to claim and hold any man's attention. If you mean the way you are dressed, why, it fits the part of a poor, innocent girl in trouble well enough. It would be stupid of you to wear your finery, wouldn't it?"

Her blood rising with stinging heat at his appraisal, Serena pushed to her knees. "If that's what you think, you should be happy to let me go on my way."

"No."

The word was quiet. He did not move, but Serena knew that if she made any sudden try to escape he would step in to stop her. To hear him call her attractive in that distant, detached tone, to see the look in his eyes as they moved over her, gave her a distinct feeling of peril. Taking a deep, steadying breath, she said, "You can't keep me here."

"Can't I?"

His assurance was maddening. More maddening still was the realization that he had reason for it. He could indeed keep her there, and with little effort. If she tried to run there was every likelihood that he would be able to catch her, and even if she was more fleet of foot, there were his horses ready to hand to run her down. If his attention wandered, she might try to take a horse herself, but she had little hope of being able to mount it barebacked before he could reach her. At this moment, defiance would gain her nothing and might well be dangerous. She had no wish to feel his hard hands upon her again.

Shielding the rage in her eyes with the dark screen of her lashes, she moved her shoulders in a small shrug. "All right. Perhaps you can. But you are going to feel foolish in the morning when you find that I am still here, and still alone with you."

He watched her settle back on his bedroll, recognizing the stiff reluctance that still could not rob her movements of their grace. His gaze traveled over the firm curves of her breasts that strained against the fabric of her old gown, and lingered briefly on the sweet line of her waist that merged with such perfect symmetry into her hips. "That may be," he answered, "and then again, it may not."

"I promise you that you will! If you had eyes in your head you would have seen that a wagon train passed this way sometime yesterday. You should have guessed that I—that I was from it."

"Was?"

34

Serena looked away. "Yes. I—left it yesterday morning, not that it matters. The important thing is that it shows you are mistaken in me."

"The road I have been traveling only joined the wagon route this evening, but I saw the evidence of the wagons."

"Well, then," she said in triumph.

"I could hardly believe anybody would use the old trail at this late date."

She explained quickly about the Mormons and Elder Greer's determination to duplicate the feat of the earlier Saints.

"You are no Saint."

Serena flashed him a quick look of indignation for the sardonic inflection of his voice, though she could not but agree.

"How does it come about, I wonder, that you decided to strike out on your own here in the middle of nowhere—or was the decision made for you?"

"It was a misunderstanding," Serena said, her lips tight.

"It always is."

"You are determined to think the worst of me, aren't you?"

"In my experience, it saves time and trouble, especially where women are concerned."

"What a disappointing life you must have led. You will not be surprised to learn, then, that I was put off the Morman train for enticing an elder into my wagon?"

"Not at all."

"That is exactly what I would expect someone like you to say! Well, let me tell you, it was a lie, a false charge made by Elder Greer to cover his own crime of climbing into my wagon while I was sleeping and trying to force himself on me."

"I suppose you prevented him?" he inquired, a light that might have been skepticism or consideration in the emerald eyes watching her so intently across the fire.

"Yes, though I doubt you will believe it."

"What did you do? Scream for help? He was a brave man, or a stupid one, if he waited around for it to come."

"I stabbed him with a fork, if you must know the sordid details, and when he wouldn't let me go, I dragged him with me out of the wagon."

He stared at her for a moment, then gave a sudden shout of laughter. "Stabbed him with a fork?"

"Yes," she snapped.

35

"Fascinating. I can almost believe it. What did he do, refuse to marry you?"

Serena sent him a look of fury. "He did not! That was his whole purpose, to persuade me to become his wife."

"A rough courtship, wasn't it? Or maybe you just preferred money to honor? That's the usual reason for women finding themselves in your position."

As she stared at him in chill dismay, unable to find words to refute this nightmarish charge leveled at her once more, the rain began, a scattering of drops shaken from the clouds by the reverberation of thunder.

The man spared a glance for the black sky above them. "We had better get under cover." Flicking a look toward the horses, he bent to scoop up the pan of bacon and pot of coffee, then stepped around the fire. "Don't just sit there," he said in exasperation, "get under the tarp."

Serena moved to obey, then she raised wide eyes to the man who stood over her. "My trunk—I left it on the trail."

"Your trunk?" He might never have heard of such a thing.

She gave a short nod. "If it gets wet it will ruin it." Without waiting for his reply, she surged to her feet and ran into the windswept darkness. In an instant she was lost, disoriented. She came to a halt, dragging the hair from her eyes.

"You'll never find it. Wait until morning!"

She ignored his shout. She had to find it. It held all she owned. Then in the brief glare of lightning, she saw its squat shape. She plunged in that direction.

"Let me."

The man was beside her, lifting the hidebound box as if its weight were nothing. He strode with it toward the fire, and was even able to spare a hand to steady her as she tripped over a clump of weeds in her efforts to keep up with his long steps. His action in coming after her might have been to prevent her from escaping from him into the stormy night. Regardless, he need not have carried her burden. The gesture was so casual, so natural, and yet so at variance with his cynical suspicion of her that she was left confused.

She was given no time to consider it. He flung down the trunk, whipped an oilskin coat over it and weighted it down, then drew Serena with him toward the low canvas shelter.

She ducked into the opening, but found she could not sit up. The only way to take advantage of its protection from the rain was to lie down and push her legs back into the lower section. It was disconcerting to discover that in the darkness

36

she had slipped between the blankets of the bedroll beneath the tarp. Before she could pull herself out again, the man was beside her, the long firm length of his leg pressed against her.

If he was aware of her nearness, he gave no sign. "I rescued the bread and bacon," he said, and resting on his elbows began to pull the load he held apart with strong fingers. Picking a curled slice of thick bacon from the fast-congealing grease in the pan, he put it on the chunk of bread and offered it to Serena. When she took it from him, he stretched to reach the cup and pot of hot coffee he had set just outside, and poured that for her also.

Overhead, the rain splattered against the canvas with wet violence. The overhang of the low lean-to tent shelter flapped, spattering drops of rain in upon them. By the light of the dying fire, Serena could see the horses with their backs turned to the storm, stoically accepting the blowing downpour that washed over them.

It was close inside the shelter, but it was also dry and warm. The food smelled delectable, especially the coffee, since she had not troubled to make a fire and brew any for herself that morning. She would eat first, and worry about the position in which she had landed herself later.

With a stiff smile, she thanked her host. Avoiding his watchful eyes, she lowered her lashes and bit into the crusty bread.

Chapter Three

The fire sank to dark, smoking coals. The man beside Serena became no more than a warm presence in the dark. The rain continued, urged by a wind that seemed to sweep in on them with a cutting edge of ice.

Serena polished off the last of her bacon and threw the rind out into the night. With slow enjoyment, she savored the last of her coffee, enjoying its reviving heat. It was only as she drained the last swallow that it occurred to her that she alone was drinking. Thinking back, she could remember seeing only one tin cup.

"I took your cup, didn't I? I never thought. If you have water I will be glad to rinse it for you."

"Never mind," he said, a trace of amusement in his voice for her stiff self-consciousness. Tipping the coffee pot, he took the cup from her and filled it, then drank from the same place her lips had touched.

That gesture with its suggestion of intimacy disturbed Serena. She stared out into the darkness, and as unobtrusively as possible, tried to ease away from him. She thought he turned, staring in her direction in the dimness, but she could not be sure. For no reason that she could explain, she felt her heartbeat quicken.

"Finished?" he queried. At her agreement, he reached to set the frying pan and his empty cup out into the rain. There being nothing left of the bread, Serena brushed away the crumbs that littered the blanket on which they lay, and the clearing of their repast was done.

"Lie down," the man so close beside her said. "You may as well make yourself comfortable."

"I would rather get my own quilt." She kept her voice steady only by sheer strength of will.

"By all means, if you want to get wet. There's no room for it under here. Of course, I could offer to let you occupy my blankets alone."

"No, I couldn't do that," Serena said hastily.

"I'm glad to hear you say it," he answered, his tone dry. "I will admit it seemed unnecessarily gallant of me, too, under the circumstances."

"I—don't know what you mean."

"Oh, come, don't be coy. There is no need. I've known more than my share of women who live by their wits, taking money from men stupid enough to think they can be bought."

"I'm not! I never—"

"Why keep denying it? I'm not likely to think any less of you, not in my position. The main thing I object to is your trying your tricks on me. If you want to survive at this game, my dear girl, you are going to have to learn to pick your targets better. Not all men are so green as to be taken in by a lovely face and a sad tale."

The patronizing sound of his voice was galling. "I see," Serena said, anger making her careless of the impression he gained. "How kind of you to tell me. I am much obliged."

"You should be. I could have sent you about your business, and probably should have. Next time, don't try to pull the wool over anybody's eyes with that story of being thrown off a wagon train for defending yourself against a sleepwalking old man. It just won't stand up. Everybody around here knows the Saints are strict about such things. If you were the innocent you pretend, they would have prayed over the old bastard and strung him up at daybreak. Since you got the bad end of the bargain, it's even money you had it coming. They would never have left you alone out here without reason, and for them the best one is behavior they consider immoral."

"Much you know of it!" Serena returned in bitter rage. "Though why I should expect you to believe me when no one else did, I can't imagine. But one thing is certain, there's no reason why I should stay here and be insulted. I would rather be wet!"

She rolled to one side, trying to push herself to a sitting position. Before she could begin, he clamped his arm across her waist, pulling her against him.

"You don't get away that easily," he said, his voice grim.

"You ought to be glad to let me go," Serena answered, all too aware of the quick rise and fall of her breasts against the hard surface of his chest, and the strained and silent clash of their wills.

"Now what gave you that idea?"

"If you—if you believe that I am from the wagon train, then you must be convinced that I am alone, that I have no friends to pose a threat to you. That being the case, I am no more than an inconvenience, one you can be rid of safely enough."

"Safely, maybe, but not comfortably."

"You mean—"

"I mean I find having you here very convenient indeed."

His grasp tightened. He lowered his head and his lips touched hers. Warm, firm, their pressure increased, tasting, exploring the tender curves of her mouth with a growing demand. For long seconds Serena was still, stunned by the sudden assault upon her senses. Never had she been kissed like this, never had she felt this burgeoning excitement allied to sweet languor. The glow of pleasure expanded inside her, and yet in its spread there was a bright, cutting edge of fear.

She brought her hands up, pushing away from him, twisting her mouth free. "No," she cried, though the word had the sound of a breathless plea.

He did not release her. "Why?" he murmured against her hair. "It is as good a way as any of passing the time."

"Please, you don't understand."

"I need you, and for now, you need me, need what I can give you. What else is there to understand?"

His voice was low, persuasive. Was he suggesting that she accept his embraces to assuage her own need, or for the sake of a bite of food and a warm refuge from the wild weather? How could he think she would agree? It was not possible for her to be so misjudged again. Still as she floundered in disbelief, she felt the scalding demand of his mouth upon hers once more.

She turned her head from side to side, shoving at him, trying to kick, but she was held tight against him, so hampered by the weight of blankets and heavy canvas that she made little impression. Her struggles caused the tarp to flop back and forth, showering them with cold rain. The man who held her gave no indication that he felt it. He gathered her closer, catching her wrists, pressing her to her back. His lips trailed fire from the corner of her mouth and across her cheek to the vulnerable curve of her neck. He pressed a kiss to the hollow of her throat, dropping lower as he sought the limits of the bare skin exposed by the V-shaped opening of her dress. His breathing quickened and he slid his hand from her wrist along her arm to the soft fullness of her breast. His fingers touched the buttons that held the taut material across them.

"No—no, you can't. I've never done this. I'm—"

Her words were drowned in the sudden change of the sound of the rain around them. It increased a hundredfold, rising to a roar, drumming with stinging weight on the canvas, rattling, pounding against the ground.

They went still. The man stiffened, lifting his head. He shoved himself upright.

"Hail!"

For one brief instant, Serena thought the word he uttered was a curse, then as he flung back the blanket and whipped open the lean-to flap, she recognized the bouncing fall of hailstones. It came down around them with hard-striking fury, bringing with it a freezing chill that made the air difficult to breath. The horses, tormented by the flailing balls of ice, whinnied, plunging on their lead ropes.

The hailstones seemed to gather light in their white descent, making the night less dark. The maddened horses could be seen backing, rearing, dim shapes plunging, bucking stiff-legged as they were pummeled by the slashing storm of ice. Then, even as their owner ducked from the shelter and surged to his feet, the rope that held one of the horses parted. The animal wheeled, lowered his head, kicked up his heels, and broke into a run.

This time the oath was plain. The man dived for the other mount, jerked the lead rope free, and flung himself up onto the back of the horse. In an instant mount and rider had disappeared into the night after the other horse. The sound of hoofbeats was drowned in the drumming of the hail.

Serena pushed herself erect. She shivered as the cold penetrated the warm cocoon of blankets. The canvas over her was growing heavier with its weight of ice. It swayed under the ceaseless pounding and the sweep of the wind.

41

How far would the loose horse run before it could be caught? Was there any chance of finding and coming up to it with the drawback of darkness and its pain-crazed fear? The thought of the man out there without protection from the driving hail sent a shudder over her. The necessity for it was clear enough; even discounting the animal's value, it was needed to carry gear. Moreover, Serena could not ignore the fact that the possibility of her obtaining a ride on into Colorado Springs would come to nothing if the horse could not be run down.

As abruptly as it had begun, the hail stopped. The marbles of ice shifted and clattered together as Serena emerged from the lean-to tent. The rain had come to an end also. The night was still and cold. Nothing moved, there was no sound. The hail lay in piles of white, thickly covering the ground. The sky to the north was clearing; there was the glitter of a star hanging in the hollow blackness.

Serena stood for a moment, a set look coming into her fine-chiseled face. Swinging around, she located her trunk and threw the oilskin that covered it aside. She opened the lid and took out her quilt, then closed it again. With the oilskin in one hand and the quilt in the other, she kicked a space of ground clear on the opposite side of the blackened firepit from the tarp lean-to. That done, she put down the oilskin, wrapped herself in her quilt, and lay down upon it.

At first the thick cover felt damp and chill, then as she lay motionless, it began to take and hold her body heat. Her eyes closed. She did not know what the man would do when he came back and found her there. The thought troubled her, but she did not know what other course to take. Running would be of little avail. She could not leave the wagon trail for fear of becoming lost, of wandering on the trackless plains until she dropped. And as long as she kept to the well-worn wheel ruts, she could be easily overtaken by a man on horseback. Added to that was a belief, not too firm but persistent, that the hard stranger who had shared his food with her would not press his attentions upon her against her will, not when she had made her reluctance plain in this manner. She had been given little reason to form such a belief, quite the reverse, if anything, and yet the strength of it allowed her to acknowledge her tiredness and drift into sleep.

She came awake with a rush. The gray light of dawn smudged the sky. Beside her came a crackling sound, and the smell of smoke was strong in the cool air. Turning her head, Serena saw the man crouching on one knee, kindling the morning fire. His face looked drawn with sleeplessness in its orange light, and there was a dark stubble of beard on the lean planes of his cheeks. Beyond him were patches of hail on the sodden ground, though much of it had melted. The bruised and flattened buffalo grass was slowly rising once more, releasing a fresh scent. The horses, both of them, cropped at the tough blades from the end of their ropes, their tails switching in contentment in sharp contrast to the terrors of the night.

"You caught your horse," Serena said, her voice quiet.

"Finally." Intent on what he was doing, he glanced up only briefly. Reaching for the coffee pot, he dumped the old grounds, sloshed water into it by way of a quick rinse, then filled it with water and fresh coffee. He set the full pot near the flames, then looked once more toward Serena as she levered herself to one elbow.

"Did you sleep well?" he asked, irony edging his tone.

"Yes, thank you." Her answer was given with a lift of her chin.

"Since I am to have the pleasure of your company for breakfast, if for nothing else, I suppose I should know your name."

Serena gave it to him.

He flicked her a strange glance. "That sounds remarkably real."

"Of course it is. Why wouldn't it be?"

"Most women in your position aren't so free with that information."

"What do you mean?"

"Out here, women like you prefer the privacy of a moniker that's simple but easily forgotten. It's not a bad idea, especially in the gold camps. Miners and cattlemen are an irreverent lot; if you don't give yourself some kind of handle they may do it for you, and the results may not be to your liking. Naggy Nell or Sloppy Sal, for instance."

"Two ladies of your wide acquaintance?" Serena gave him a brittle smile.

"Hardly ladies, but real women for all that."

"You, of course, are qualified to know the difference?"

His eyes narrowed in recognition of her sarcasm. "I think so," he agreed.

"I take leave to doubt it."

"Do you," he asked, a fine shading of something near contempt in his green eyes as he surveyed the tangled mass of her hair, the frayed and worn quilt that made her pallet, and the too snug dress she wore. His gaze rested on her neckline, and glancing down, Serena saw she had not refastened the buttons of her bodice undone in their struggles. The creamy swells of her breasts looked ready to strip the other buttons from their holes.

A hot flush of embarrassment and remembrance rising to her cheekbones, Serena snatched the cover higher. "It takes a gentleman to recognize a lady, and you are certainly not that!"

"No. For all the Dunbar name, I am not, but then I don't pretend to be."

"Dunbar?" It was a distinguished surname along the Mississippi River. The Dunbars of Natchez not only lay claim to some of the most fertile and productive acres around that city, they numbered a former governor and several other legislators among their ancestors. Their holdings extended to property in New Orleans, and they were always prominent among the plantation families who came to the Crescent City for the winter season.

"Ward Dunbar, at your service."

"Of the Mississippi Dunbars?"

"No," he answered, his features hardening. He pushed the coffee pot nearer to the fire, then drew back from its glowing heat.

He obviously wanted to close the subject. It pleased Serena therefore to keep it open. "Odd. I could have sworn your accent was from that region."

"You are mistaken."

The more he denied it, the more certain Serena was that he lied. "Am I?" she queried, tilting her head to one side.

"I am a citizen of Cripple Creek, Colorado, the proprietor, with my partner, of the Eldorado Saloon and gambling hell, nothing more."

"A gambler?" She could not keep the blankness out of her voice.

"Just so."

"Not for long, I think. I was under the impression the gold strike in Cripple Creek was under three years old."

"That can be a long time."

"Surely before you came here you lived somewhere else?"

"No," he said, a single, uncompromising syllable.

44

"I see. Can it be that it is not only a certain type of female who finds a change of name expedient in Colorado?"

He sent her a shuttered glance, his green eyes dark. "No," he said shortly. "Stained or unstained, the name is mine. I have no need of any other."

With a lithe movement, he came to his feet. He turned to his gear and took out a nosebag and a sack half full of feed. With them dangling from his hard fingers, he moved off to feed the horses.

Serena threw back her quilt and stood up, trying to shake the wrinkles from her dress. It did little good. They were pressed into the material by dampness and her restless turnings in the night. In her trunk was a hairbrush, and she longed to use it to bring order to her tumbled curls, but she refused to give Ward Dunbar, if that was his name, the satisfaction of thinking she was trying to improve her appearance for the sake of his good opinion. With the increase of daylight it was possible to see a small sinkhole of water a short distance away, half hidden by a swale in the gently rolling prairie. She bent to retrieve her shawl from where it lay tangled in her quilt, swung it around her, and started toward the water.

When she returned, Ward had bacon sizzling in the pan. He looked up at her approach.

"How good are you at mixing flapjacks?" he asked.

"Passable," she replied.

"Good." He nodded in the direction of a can of flour.

They finished eating and wiped out the utensils with sand before rinsing them clean. Serena folded her quilt and packed it away, and shook out the oilskin that had protected her from the wet ground. With swift, competent movements, Ward was packing his gear. Folding the oilskin, Serena stepped around the smoldering fire and handed it to him. He flicked her a quick look as he took it from her, but said nothing.

Serena clutched at her shawl, half turning to look at her trunk. Her gaze moved to the long, winding wagon trail and the distant line of the mountains shimmering in the sun. To one side stood the horses, one of them saddled. They stomped to dislodge a cloud of clinging gnats, blowing through their noses at the delay in getting started.

A determined set to her shoulders, Serena turned back to Ward.

45

"Put your finger here," he said, nodding at the saddlebag he was packing.

She obeyed, and his strong hands knotted the leather thongs that held one of the voluminous pouches closed.

"Mr. Dunbar?"

"Ward. Mr. Dunbar is likely to get tedious before we get to Colorado Springs."

Gratitude, not so much for the implied invitation to go with him as for his generosity in saving her the need to ask, rose in a warm tide inside Serena. "You don't mind if I come with you?"

His movements slowed. He turned to look at her, his green eyes level, his face relaxing into something approaching a smile. "I may not be a gentleman," he said softly, "but I don't leave women stranded."

They reached the bustling town of Colorado Springs at the foot of Pikes Peak an hour before sundown. For the last few miles, Serena had ridden with her eyes on the mountain. It rose up out of the plains, a massive pile of granite, lavender-blue still with distance, its topmost reaches swathed in a soft veil of clouds. Its lower slopes were studded with pines and aspens that had the look, as the aspens began to turn, of green velvet edged with gold lace, sweeping in folds like a lady's train down to the rocky foothills. There, where the ramparts of the mountain range began, stood the red sandstone sentinels, massive wind sculptures, formless works of art in stone that dwarfed the buildings of the town that sprawled in front of them.

The houses of Colorado Springs were of wood, one- and two-story homes set in squares of parched land that could hardly be called lawns. Tall cottonwoods, elms, and maples were planted around the houses and lined the streets on which they fronted. Farther along the straight thoroughfares, on the far side of town, could be seen a few more pretentious dwellings with shingled turrets and cupolas, and wooden curlicues of gingerbreading.

The streets of the business district were spread out over a wide area, a varied collection of general, hardware, drug, and clothing stores, feed stores adjacent to livery stables, and mining-company offices, banks, restaurants, and boarding-houses. There were numerous hotels, including the baroque splendor of the famous Antlers Hotel, one of the few west of the Mississippi, according to Ward, that could boast of electric lights and hot and cold running water.

There was no lack of activity. Horses lined the rails before the stores. Buggies, surreys, and sixteen-horse-hitch freight wagons raised clouds of dust. Businessmen in tweed jackets with leather patches on the sleeves, green corduroy pants, and laced boots rubbed shoulders with miners in dust-covered twill and battered hats, and with their rust-colored underwear showing at the open necks of their shirts. Ladies, their delicately printed sateens and silks buttoned to their throats and protected by dust cloaks, their faces shielded by broad-brimmed hats trimmed with plumes, bows, and veils, drove by in carriages or stepped down before the stores. The gentlemen at their sides wore dark business coats, and a few sported English bowlers with round crowns and narrow brims.

Serena, staring around her, was both enchanted and repelled by this town at the end of the long road west. There was a cool vigor about the place, a sense of thriving life and free-spending prosperity. The setting was such to take the breath away. And yet, the countryside itself gave a feeling of harshness, of arid desiccation which made the memory of Louisiana's lush and moist greenness seem akin to Eden.

"How do you like Little London?"

Serena turned to Ward, sitting his horse easily as they walked their mounts side by side down the powdered rock of the street. "Little London? You mean Colorado Springs?"

He gave a nod. "So called because of the numbers of British subjects that have been persuaded to settle here over the last twenty years. Tea and crumpets at five is a must here in the shadow of Pikes Peak, a compensation, or so the founding fathers view it, for the fact that this is a temperance town."

Serena smiled without replying as they moved aside so that a horsecar filled with passengers could pass them. Her attention wandered to a general store, where just inside its dim, Aladdin's-cave interior stood a man and a small boy in the round hats and dark clothing of Mormons. A thrill of dismay swept over her and receded. The man did not turn, did not seem to see her. Why she should be so affected she could not say. It was not as if she had no reason to suspect the presence of the Saints. As she and Ward had entered town they had seen a wagon train encamped along the banks of a swift-running stream that Ward had called Fountain Creek. She had been hoping they would have passed on by the time she arrived, that was all. It didn't matter, of course

47

it didn't. There was no reason to think that in a town this size she would have any problem staying out of the way of Elder Greer and his followers.

It was difficult to believe that she was here at last. Her thoughts had been so attuned to coming to the end of her journey that she had not adequately considered what she would do when she reached her destination. Ward had recommended a boardinghouse, an economical place kept by a widow in her home. Though Serena had not mentioned the fact to Ward, it would have to be inexpensive indeed, for she did not have the price for more than two days' accommodation. It was imperative that she look for employment at once. Surely in a fast-growing town like this there was something that she could do, no matter how menial. She did not mind hard work; she was strong, stronger than she looked, and most of all, willing.

The scream of a train whistle sounded away to the west, on the far edge of town. Instinctively, Serena glanced at the man beside her.

"That will be the Midland pulling in, I expect. When I left Cripple Creek in June they were laying her track from Florissant to reach the gold camps. I wonder how far they have carried her."

"Is that the train you will be taking?"

"I doubt it. When I left, the odds were in favor of the Florence and Canon City Line out of Denver being the first to reach the town of Cripple Creek itself. The plans were for Pullman cars on a night run that would come through Colorado Springs about midnight, and right now that sounds mighty good to me."

It was not surprising, seeing that the gambler had been in the saddle for the better part of the past three months. It was his habit, he had told her as they rode through that long day, to spend several weeks each summer in the mountains around Cripple Creek and beyond. It was not just a case of gold fever, though he did not deny being stricken by that disease; he enjoyed the peace that he found among the blue peaks and their silent mountain valleys. During the winter months spent in closed, smoky rooms, stifling with heat and the smell of unwashed humans, he built up a terrible craving for fresh air and solitude. He had been forced to cut his pack trip short this year because of a business trip he had to make to the southeast part of the country, though he carefully did not say precisely where, nor for what reason. He had been

48

returning from that trip, intending to make a loop for business purposes by Colorado Springs, when he had come upon Serena.

The gambler turned toward her, a measuring look in his green eyes. "You can still come with me to Cripple Creek, you know."

Serena shook her head, forcing her lips to curve into a smile. She had ceased to try to convince him of her chastity. The task had seemed to be beyond her without plainer words between them than she could bring herself to use. Moreover, she had begun to suspect that if he should believe her, he might feel some misguided sense of responsibility for her. The last thing she needed was to have another man, and a gambler at that, appoint himself her guardian. Experience had already shown her where that could lead. Not that she had anything to complain of on that score. He had not attempted to touch her since she had removed herself from his bedroll the night before. Still, there was something in the way he watched her at times, in the way he helped her on and off her horse, that made her know he was aware of her as a woman. That, and her own response to his nearness, prevented her from trusting him. No, she much preferred to look after herself.

"I suppose you mean to make a play for one of the new mining millionaires? I ought to warn you that the competition there is rough."

Serena ignored his mocking tone. "I'm sure it is."

"If that really is your game," he said, a frown drawing his brows together, "I suggest you invest in a new wardrobe as soon as possible. For all your attractions as a waif, wealthy men prefer a woman who doesn't look as if she needs rescuing from poverty."

"That is valuable advice, I am sure," she said, injecting an arch tone into her voice. "Do you have anything else to recommend?"

"Yes, you might try beginning your hunt at Count Pourtales's Broadmoor Casino and Hotel outside of town. Most men adjourn there for a drink in the evening. And see that you stay away from Colorado City down the road. Most of the red-light district is in that area. Men of means may visit the houses there, but they don't take their mistresses from them. Why should they settle for such well-used goods when they can buy fresher merchandise elsewhere?"

Serena turned her head sharply away as the heat of a

flush rose to her hairline. "Yes, of course," she said in a smothered voice.

He leaned suddenly to catch the rope that served as a rein for her horse. As she swung her startled gaze in his direction, his green eyes stared into hers. "You are blushing," he said, puzzlement blending with the accusation in his voice.

"I—the effect of temper, I assure you," she answered. "I don't need you to tell me how to conduct myself."

"No," he said, easing back into the saddle. "More than likely, not. But you did ask."

They did not speak again until they had come to a halt before the boardinghouse the gambler had suggested. When he had dismounted and handed her down, he unstrapped her trunk.

"Maybe we should make certain there is a room available," Serena demurred.

"There will be one," he said.

He was not mistaken. The widow, a plump woman with a massive bosom, gray-streaked, red hair piled on her head, and wearing a plum-colored dress with an ecru dog collar of lace that scratched her rounded chin, came hurrying from the back regions of the house at the sound of the hall bell. Her eyes lit up as she caught sight of the gambler, and she gave a cry of welcome.

"Ward! Bless me if it isn't good to see you! Where have you been, you devil? It's been too long since you put your feet under my table. I'd much rather it was your shoes under my bed, but I'll settle for the one if I can't have the other!"

A grin banished the darkness from Ward Dunbar's face as he returned the woman's hearty embrace. "If I only had the time I would oblige you on both counts," he bantered. "Still, I wouldn't insult you with a quick sampling of either."

"Go on with you! You always were a dreadful liar, but I know you'll do me the favor of keeping the truth behind your teeth. What brings you back?"

"You, acushla."

"Listen to the man," the widow said with a wink and a heavenward cast of her eyes for Serena. Stepping from the circle of his arms, she patted at her hair, a droll look in her eyes that could not quite disguise her pleasure. "And what else, you terrible man?"

"A matter of business with Nathan Benedict."

"Well, if you're looking for me to help, I'll have to tell you I have nothing to do with the gold gentry, my lad. Besides,

50

I thought Benedict was making his headquarters at Cripple Creek these days, had built a big house up there."

"He's supposed to be in town for a meeting of the mine owners."

"Something to do with this union business?"

"I expect so."

"You get an invitation to sit in with the rest of the millionaires?"

Ward smiled. "Are you trying to find out if I've struck it rich? Maybe you think I'm worth more than a bit of light flirting? Sorry to disappoint you. I've filed a few claims, sunk a few shafts, enough to qualify me for this meeting, but I have yet to strike a vein worth following."

"Never mind," the widow said comfortably. "You will. And then we'll see if you can resist my blandishments! But enough now. I don't know what this young lady must think of us, going on like a couple of zanies. Introduce us now, Ward, if you please."

"Mrs. O'Hare, Serena Walsh. This young lady is the reason for my visit. She is in need of a room."

The widow divided a quick glance between the two of them. "I see."

"I doubt it," Ward said with the lift of a dark brow. "I am not sponsoring her."

"Ah, and of course you are not, you devil! How could you think I ever suspected such a thing for a minute?"

"Easily," the gambler answered, but the widow ignored it.

"Come in, my dear, come in. We will see what we can do for you. I think I have a front room left. It looks like you have been a few days on the road. Just arrived, have you?"

"If you have a place to put Serena, I will leave you to settle her in. I'm sure you can prise the story of her life out of her much better without me standing around."

The widow, leading Serena up the stairs, flung a look of mock outrage over her shoulder. "Indeed, we can do without you, if that's what you mean. Take yourself off to your meeting, since that's where you're raring to go."

Serena came to a halt and swung around, staring down at Ward Dunbar from a few steps above him. "If I don't see you again, I would like to say how grateful I am to you for letting me travel with you, and for bringing me here. I'm not sure I would have made it without your help."

"I enjoyed the company," he answered, his green eyes

shaded with irony and something akin to dark admiration. "But don't be in such a hurry to make your farewells. The gold district, even this town, is not that big. There's every chance that we will see each other again."

He stood gazing up at her long moments, almost as if testing the truth of his own words in his mind, then he gave a curt nod and was gone. Serena stood staring after him until the widow reclaimed her attention with a merry comment and led her on up the stairs.

The front room was pleasant, with scrubbed wood floors covered with woven rag rugs, an iron bedstead with a quilt thrown over the thick, fluffy mattress, and horizontal wood siding walls hung with sepia prints. Serena signified her complete satisfaction with her accommodations, then turned to the widow with a resolute angle to her chin.

"I won't mislead you, Mrs. O'Hare. My circumstances are such that I can't pay for more than a day or two with you at most, unless I find some means of earning a wage."

"There, my dear," the woman said with a motherly pat on Serena's shoulder, "don't worry your head about it. Any friend of Ward Dunbar's will always have credit with me."

"I don't wish to be beholden in any way to Mr. Dunbar."

"Well, now, I don't doubt that's wise of you, a pretty young thing like you are, but if you are worried that he will take an unfair advantage, I have to tell you that I think you misjudge him. Oh, I know I talk a lot of nonsense, but I would sooner trust Ward than any man alive. Why, I could tell you things—but I won't. I'll just say that if it wasn't for Ward Dunbar I would have been scrubbing floors somewhere these two years since my Owen, rest his soul, got himself killed in a blasting accident at the Commodore Lode. We talk a fine tale, me and him, though we both know he could have his pick of women younger and prettier than me, still I know, too, that he could have made this house into something more than a boarding hall. If he had wanted, he could have brought in women and liquor, set me over them, asked for part of the take. He never thought of such a thing! No, he paid out his money, and instead of raking off the profits, he lets me pay for the building out of them."

"Perhaps he knew you would refuse such a position?"

"Bless you, child! What makes you think so? I would have had no choice, none at all. Oh, I might have kicked about it, but in the end, I would have agreed. There's no comfort in virtue when a body is starving to death."

There was something in the woman's forthright way of speaking that appealed to Serena. She found her lips curving into a smile of sympathy and wry recognition of an essential truth. "He—is a strange man."

"He has reason to be. I nursed him through pneumonia his first winter in the mountains—me and O'Hare were living at Cripple Creek then. You learn a lot about a person when he's down. He's a fine man, is Ward Dunbar, a man who sometimes likes to forget all the things that make him what he is, a man who hates what he sees himself becoming so much that he sometimes sets out to prove he is worse than he really is, if that makes sense. No, I can see that it doesn't. Let it go. Sometimes I don't make sense to myself."

Serena lowered her gaze. "About work, Mrs. O'Hare?"

"Now that is something else. I'm not sure there is such a thing now. The few positions that a woman might could take are filled; there's many a miner's wife helping out by doing laundry, working as cook, cleaning woman, and such like. I hear that in the East young women are working in offices and behind the counters in stores, but there are more than enough young men out here, men who found out hard-rock mining is rougher than they expected, to take the jobs like that."

"I would be glad to cook and clean. I'm not afraid of work."

"Your best bet," the older woman said with a quick laugh, "might be to stay here with me until one of these strong young miners notices you and asks you to marry him. It won't take long, I'm sure. Ladies are scarce just now, the marrying kind, that is. There are plenty of fancy women all too ready to take a man's wages."

It was gratifying to be classed among the former, despite the way she was dressed. "I will have to keep that in mind," Serena answered with a smile.

"There's no hurry, at any rate. Now, I hope you will make yourself comfortable. I expect you will be glad of a chance to rinse off the dust; I'll send up hot water to the bathroom at the end of the hall. After that, you may want to eat a bite. I don't usually allow boarders in the dining room before mealtime, but in this case I think I can bend the rules."

When the woman had gone, Serena stood with her hands clasped before her. The widow O'Hare seemed nice, and no doubt she meant well, but she was wrong on one point. There was reason for haste. She might trust Ward Dunbar if she pleased; Serena, however, had no wish to remain for long the recipient of his casual patronage. The expression in his eyes, the tenor of his words before he took his leave, had held too much the sound of a warning fairly given. She did not intend to ignore it.

Hours later, as she walked the streets of the town, Serena was not nearly so confident. She had met with nothing in her quest for employment except curt dismissals, or else leers and attempts to fondle her or cajol her into dark back rooms. The situation was much as Mrs. O'Hare had said. There were too many people for the positions available.

One by one the stores closed as the light faded. The boardinghouses and hotels were still open, however, and Serena had turned her hopes toward their shining lights. The results were depressingly the same. There was nothing for her. One old harridan, standing in the rear door of a rundown rooming house, had eyed Serena's slender frame and asked if she had any experience in warming beds. For one instant Serena, standing in the cool night air, had thought she was speaking of some necessary task, then the meaning of the woman's snide query became obvious. She had lost no time in getting away from that place.

The night deepened. The board sidewalks emptied except for knots of aimless, rough-looking men who called suggestively after her as she passed. As much as it went against the grain to admit defeat, Serena knew she must call an end to her search. As the hour advanced she was becoming more conspicuous. No decent woman ventured abroad this late. Her wisest course would undoubtedly be to make her way back to the O'Hare boardinghouse and take stock of her position.

She was so tired. She must have walked for miles, stood before countless dusty counters waiting for the attention of the proprietors of every manner of establishment. Though the quick bath she had indulged in before changing her clothing had freshened her spirits for a time, the weariness of the long day spent in the makeshift saddle of the pack horse had crept back, increasing her exhaustion. She should have eaten before she set out, as the widow had suggested. She had been too excited, too determined to prove to herself that the woman was wrong. She had been so certain that if she offered herself for hire someone must accept her sacrifice. How wrong she had been.

She had walked far. She had thought the street she was on was the one on which the widow's establishment stood. If

54

so, there was no sign of it. The houses around her seemed far too grand to be its neighbors, in fact. She must have taken a wrong turn.

She halted, slowly swung about. From the dark shadows behind her there came a scraping sound. Serena went still. A moment later a cat meowed and padded toward her to rub against her skirts.

Serena let out her pent breath in a shaky laugh. Giving the thin animal, scarcely more than a kitten, a quick pat, she began to retrace her steps. The cat followed a short distance, then suddenly hissed and shied away, disappearing into the black night at a run. Serena walked on more quickly.

In the dark nothing seemed familiar. She would have to choose another street and hope for the best. Ahead of her was a main thoroughfare with its softly glowing streetlamps. From there she should be able to find her bearings.

She turned a corner. Coming toward her along the board sidewalk was the squat shape of a man. He passed beneath a street lamp, a massive figure, bearded, dressed in a plaid lounge suit, celluloid collar, and a bowler that made his head look small for his body. Most of his weight was in his upper torso, for his legs were not overlong. By contrast, his hamlike hands at the ends of his arms swung near a level with his knees. As he neared, Serena saw that she held his attention. Moving as far to the right as she could, she averted her face. As he came closer, her breathing quickened. It seemed she could feel the intentness of his stare. He came on, a rolling swagger in his stride and his heavy shoes thudding on the boards. He seemed to take up the entire sidewalk, shouldering along with no intention of giving way for her. Skin prickling in some primitive reaction of warning, Serena veered to step into the street.

"Hey, wait, girlie! Where you going in such a hurry?" He reached out to close his enormous fingers around her upper arm, snatching her to a stop.

Serena smothered a small scream as she was thrown off balance. She braced against the pull upon her arm with one hand on his barrel chest. An animal heat rank with the acrid smell of liquor, stale sweat, and Florida-water cologne radiated from him. Her voice tight and a little high, she said, "That's none of your concern. Release me at once!"

"Now why would I want to do that? You're the best-looking piece I've seen all night. Be nice to old Otto and we'll have ourselves a fine time."

55

"No, I can't." Sickness rose inside Serena and her arm felt numb.

"Why? My money's as good as anybody's." A black scowl wrinkled his forehead, pinching his small black eyes closer together. He gave her a shake that jerked her head forward.

Protesting her innocence was useless. Ward Dunbar had not believed her; why should this man? In desperation she cast about in her mind for some other excuse. "Please," she said, "someone is waiting for me."

"Let 'im wait. I ain't had a tasty morsel like you in a long time and I'm right ready to rip into it. I know a place along here that will let us have a room for an hour or two."

"No! No—not now."

"I don't think you heard me right, girlie. I got something for you, and you gonna get it whether you want it now or not."

He took a step, dragging her with him. Serena twisted, digging in her heels, clawing at the enormous hand that held her. Without stopping, the man shifted his grasp to her waist, clamping her to his side so that her feet left the ground. His grip crushed her ribs, driving the air from her lungs. A red mist rose before her eyes as she tried to kick, to drive her elbow into his chest, to draw in enough air to scream. He laughed, and as though her resistance excited him, wrapped his long arms about the lower part of her body, sinking his fingers into the soft curve of her hip.

Through the roaring of the blood in her ears, Serena thought she heard the pound of running footsteps. Abruptly the man who had called himself Otto staggered as he was shoved from behind. He let her go, and she felt herself falling. He stumbled over her legs with a roared curse, flailing around to face his attacker. Serena scrambled from under him in time to see him stagger under a blow to the side of his bullet head. The bowler flew off, revealing a straggling fringe of hair around the bald dome of his skull.

"Get up, woman," came a harsh, well-remembered voice above her. "I have delivered you from this son of Satan, and will now take you back into my fold like a lost sheep."

In disbelief Serena stared into the grimly smiling face of Elder Greer. "You," she whispered.

"When I was told that you had arrived at last, I had to come for you, in spite of the tale that you were with another man. I saw you and followed you to find out the truth. It was God's work that brought me to you in your hour of need."

56

It was a mistake for the Mormon to turn his attention from the man he had struck. With a bull-like roar, the miner charged at the elder, drew back an enormous fist, and drove it with bone-crunching force into his face. The older man was flung back, his arms and legs flopping. He hit the wooden sidewalk with a crash and lay moaning, the blood oozing dark and red from his nose and mangled lips.

Frozen horror gripped Serena for a long instant. Otto, the victor, grunted in satisfaction and swung to take a lumbering step toward her. There was bloodlust in his porcine face and a cruel grin on his formless mouth.

Serena rolled, scrambling to her feet. Vaguely she was aware of an open tilbury coming toward them at a fast clip, running before a cloud of dust. The giant of a man seemed to neither notice nor care in his need to get his hands on her. The chance of help from the driver of the carriage was slim, but it could not be ignored. She angled her retreat toward the street.

Suddenly a long arm shot out. She sprang back, stumbling as her foot left the sidewalk. The sausagelike fingers of the man called Otto snagged the loose weave of her shawl, closing on the thin material of her dress as his hand clamped bruisingly on one breast. With a throat-rasping scream, she threw herself to one side. She heard the rending sound as the bodice of her dress parted, then she was free, spinning to leave her shawl in his clutches. She swung to run.

A man shouted. Carriage horses reared screaming, walleyed above her, their ironshod hooves flashing about her shoulders. Something struck her side, and she was knocked sprawling in the dirt of the street. Before she could regain her breath, hard hands bit into her waist, hauling her upright. With dust in her mouth, she kicked backward, squirming, struggling in a crazed mixture of terror and disgust.

A hard cracking sound exploded over her. The man who held her gave a howl of pain. The sound came again, and she was released, shoved away as with a bellow of rage Otto turned to face this new menace.

It was Ward Dunbar. He stood in the street with his legs spread, a tall figure resplendent in the satin-edged black of evening dress. The whiteness of his shirtfront shone with a pale gleam in the dim light. In his hands he held a carriage whip, while behind him lay a silk top hat, as though he had lost it as he leaped from the tilbury.

The carriage backed as the horses shifted. Ward swung

his gaze to the driver still on the seat, a Negro in a uniform of livery. Assured that he was going to be able to hold the nervous team of matched grays, Ward turned his hard stare once more in their direction.

"Dunbar, what's the idea of you butting in on my game?" Otto demanded. There was rage in his eyes as he nursed a red welt on his face, but his voice held an undertone of respect.

Ward Dunbar flicked the man a glance, his face set in lines of grim contempt. Turning away, he held out his hand. "Serena," he said.

She took a hesitant step toward him, and then as the other man made no move to stop her, moved in a rush to the gambler's side. His free arm closed around her, and at his touch, a racking shudder ran over her. With trembling hands she tried to pull the tattered edges of her bodice over the white curves of her breasts that swelled above her chemise. It could not be done. Though her shawl lay only a few feet away, where Otto had dropped it, she could not bring herself to leave the gambler's protective hold to retrieve it. She crossed her arms over her chest, hugging herself in an effort to still her trembling. With a quick movement Ward tossed the carriage whip to the Negro driver and shrugged out of his coat to wrap it about Serena.

"So that's the way it is," Otto exclaimed, throwing back his head. "Hell, how was I to know? I seen her on the street and figured she was fair game."

"Your mistake," Ward said, his voice like steel. "Make it again and I will horsewhip you within an inch of your life."

An ugly look came and went in the man's eyes. He lifted one hand as if in token of faith. "I got your point, Dunbar. Thing is, I done took me a liking to this girlie here. I gotta know what she is to you. What I mean is, is she something special you mean to keep for yourself, or are you taking her up to Pearlie? If you mean to set her up in the parlor house, I'd be willing to pay big for the first chance at her."

Serena was not certain just what a parlor house was; still, she could guess. Instinctively she pressed closer to Ward Dunbar's side.

"Sorry to disappoint you, but she is mine."

"I'da damned sure never laid a hand on her if I hadda knowed that," Otto said, a crafty sound in his low voice. "I sure hope you know what you're doing, though. This ain't gonna set too well with Pearlie, you coming back with another woman."

"It won't, will it?" Ward drawled, an odd inflection in his tone before he gave a shrug. "You let me worry about Pearlie."

His arm tightened around Serena. It seemed to her that his embrace had become more possessive since he had claimed her as his. She wanted to deny his words, but something in his manner prevented her. The hulking man seemed willing to accept Ward's authority now, and yet there was no way of knowing what he might do if he thought Ward had cheated him of his prey for no good reason.

"I'll do that," Otto said with a slow nod. "But if Pearlie yells too much, or if you ever get tired of that fine piece there—"

"It's not very likely," Ward said, his voice hard and impatient, cutting across the other man's words. He turned back toward the carriage, urging Serena toward the steps. As she climbed up, there came a weak cry from the direction of the board sidewalk.

"Serena!" Elder Greer cried, struggling to one elbow. "Don't go. Come to me! Help me!"

Serena turned to stare at the fallen Saint, seeing his blood-streaked face, the gnarled hand he held out to her.

"Serena!" the Mormon called again, his voice weak. "I tried to save you. Don't go."

The grip of Ward's hand was firm under her elbow. "Don't look back," he said.

An instant later she was on the seat, squeezed between Ward and the driver. The gambler shifted to put his arm around her, making more room on the seat. The driver yelled at the grays, snapping the popper of the whip about their ears. The tilbury jerked forward.

Anger brought the elder swaying to his feet, increased the power of his lungs. "Whore!" he shouted after her, staggering along the board walk. "No-good slut! Temptress! Bitch! Jezebel!"

Serena pressed her hands over her ears, and closing her eyes, pressed her face into Ward Dunbar's shoulder. She did not look back.

59

Chapter Four

They rattled along the dark streets, swinging around corners, bumping over rocks, slowing as they climbed, speeding as they reached the downgrade. The driver spoke to Ward and he replied; Serena did not hear. Her body felt sore, as if she had been beaten, and inside her was a hard knot of apprehension that would not loosen even now, when she knew she was safe. The night air brushed coolly over her face and stirred the dark mass of her hair. The man who held her absorbed the swaying and the jolts, imparting the warmth of his body to her chill skin. Serena did not move.

The tilbury slowed and came to a stop. They sat silent. Serena took a deep, shuddering breath and with great effort forced herself to sit erect. They were pulled up before a small building with the words "Florence and Canon City Railroad" emblazoned across the front, and the initials F&CCRR picked out in gold on its glass door. Despite the late hour, a light shone inside, and men wearing the green eyeshades of clerks moved to and fro. A half-dozen other men lounged on the platform some distance away.

There was no sign of the train. The empty rails stretched away into the darkness beyond the sleeping town. A number of freight cars sat on the siding, however, along with empty ore and cattle cars, and an impressive Pullman-type car colored a dark blue and decorated with brass fixtures and scrolled moldings bright with gold leaf.

"What is it? Why are we stopping here?" Serena inquired, her glance wary and a flush across her cheekbones as she sat stiffly holding Ward's coat about her. She had thought she would be taken back to the boardinghouse.

As she spoke the Negro driver got down, secured the horses at a hitchrack, and moved toward the private railroad car. Taking a key from his pocket, he inserted it in the door, climbed the steps, and disappeared inside. Within seconds a light bloomed, outlining heavy drapes over the windows.

"Nathan Benedict, the man I met this evening for dinner, owns a fair share of the F&CCRR. He offered me the use of his private railroad car on the run up to Cripple Creek. It will be coupled to the train from Denver coming through tonight, and will make the return trip back to Colorado Springs for Nathan's use tomorrow."

"I see. It—it should be comfortable for you." The palms of her hands stung where the fine granite gravel of the road had gouged into her skin as she caught herself when she fell. She stared in surprise at the stains of blood that appeared.

"I can think of worse ways to travel."

"What about your horses?"

"They'll be loaded on a cattle car. I turned them into the corral where they are holding the other livestock bound for Cripple Creek earlier this evening."

"And the carriage?"

"Nathan's property, too."

Her queries had been idle, something to hold him near while she thought of a diplomatic way to put the most crucial question. Before she could find the words, Benedict's driver emerged from the railroad car and came toward them.

"All ready, sir," he said. Face impassive, he stood to one side, waiting for them to alight.

Ward stepped down and turned, ready to assist Serena. She stared at him with her bottom lip caught between her teeth.

"There's no need for me to get down here," she said, a catch in her voice.

"There is every need." The night wind ruffled his dark-brown hair as he stood watching her. The look in his eyes was patient, yet unyielding.

"I—I would prefer to return to the boardinghouse."

"Nathan gave strict orders for his man to return the carriage to the Antlers Hotel at once to take his other guests home."

The Negro man cleared his throat. "That poker game the gentlemens was playing will last another hour or two, sir. Mr. Benedict wouldn't mind if I—"

"There's no need," Ward repeated, his voice hardening. "That will be all," he added, and flipped a coin in the man's direction. The driver caught the spinning disk. Staring down at it, rubbing it with his thumb, he gave a slow nod and moved away to stand at the horses' heads, crooning to them in a soft voice.

Serena's gray-blue eyes were dark as she stared down at Ward. "I don't know what you are suggesting, but I must get back to the boardinghouse. Mrs. O'Hare will wonder what has become of me."

"We will send her a message by telegraph in the morning from Cripple Creek."

"I can't go to Cripple Creek with you," Serena said, her voice thin as she lifted one trembling hand to massage her forehead. "I have no clothes." Her head ached. She could not think straight, and she felt cold all over since Ward had left her alone on the seat of the tilbury.

"We will tell Mrs. O'Hare to put your trunk on the first train up the pass in the morning."

"No, I can't!"

"You will have to," he said, and reached to close his warm fingers around her elbow.

"Why? Why must I?"

"Because," he said roughly, "you need a keeper, before you wind up in a crib somewhere taking on all comers."

Before she realized what he meant to do, he pulled her toward him, placed his hands at her waist, and lifted her down. The instant her feet touched the ground, he bent to put his arm beneath her knees and lifted her high against his chest.

Alarm coursed along Serena's veins. She wanted to cry out, and yet, so strange was Ward's manner she could not be certain she had reason to be so disturbed. He seemed driven by anger rather than lust. Perhaps in her overwrought state she had read more into his words than he had intended. In any case, she was not sure that here, late at night, in her disheveled state, any man who came in answer to her screams would believe her in need of help. She had been given good cause of late to doubt it. That being so, she lay rigid in his

62

arms as Ward climbed the steps of Nathan Benedict's private railroad car and shouldered inside.

Serena received an impression of richness, of thick blue carpet, the soft sheen of brocade and velvet, and the gleam of mahogany. A door at the upper end of the car stood open, revealing a tiny pantry-kitchen. Ward swung in the opposite direction, toward another door at the far end of the main parlor area.

It was reached in a few strides. Ward depressed the brass handle and kicked the panel wide. Inside was a sleigh bed with the gilded and scrolled headboard and footboard of the Empire style. Strewn with jewel-hued pillows, its coverlet of champagne brocade shone in the dim light of the parlor lamp. It seemed to fill the small room, crowding the brocatelle chairs and the small tables with their unlighted lamps topped by milk-glass shades.

Serena stiffened, her hand gripping the material of Ward's shirt. It did no good. He stepped to the bed and dropped her onto its shimmering surface.

The instant she felt the soft brocade beneath her, Serena flung the coat that covered her aside and rolled in a flurry of skirts, sliding toward the far side of the bed. Ward dived after her. He caught her upper arm, hauling her back among the pillows. The weight of his body came down upon her, pressing her into their silken plumpness. She stared up at him, her gray-blue eyes stormy and her breathing quick.

"Ward, no—" she said, searching the stern set of his features, seeing the desire that warmed the green depths of his speculative gaze.

"I know it's not what you want, but it will be better than what you were heading for. Even if I am not a silver baron or a gold king, I am not a poor man."

"You don't understand!"

"I understand that I want you. I haven't been able to get the feel and taste of you out of my mind. I watched you today and told myself you were just another woman bent on making an easy fortune in the gold camps, one I would forget as soon as you were out of sight. I was wrong. I suspected it within an hour, I knew it for a certainty when I saw Otto Bruin with his hands on you. I wanted to kill him, to beat him slowly to a cringing death."

"It's wrong. What you are doing is wrong!" she cried.

"Is it? I claimed you for mine, and mine you will be for a day, a week, a month—until this craving I have for you is satisfied. Nothing, nobody, will interfere, not now. Later, when it's over, you can do as you please. I won't try to stop you."

"No, I can't—"

"You can and you will," he said, his harsh voice cutting inexorably across her words. "It has never been my habit either to force women or to pay their price, but for you, darling Serena, I will make an exception!"

His mouth descended on hers with urgent heat, twisting, searching for a sweet weakness. Serena tried to turn her head, but the piled pillows gave her little room. She struck at him, hard, angry blows that made little impression. The pressure of his lips increased and his tongue slipped past her defenses in an intrusion so intimate it made her draw in her breath and arch away from him, bringing up one knee. This added purchase gave her the strength to wrench herself away from him. With a smothered gasp, she scrambled over the smooth surface of the bed.

It gained her nothing. The tumbled silk of her hair was caught under his elbow. Before she could jerk it free, he shot out a hand, fastening it on her knee, dragging her back as he pushed her skirts higher, exposing the marble whiteness of her thighs. With a sob in her throat, she snatched at that exploring hand. He immediately lowered his head to the full mound of her breast exposed by her torn bodice. He had eased to support himself on his right elbow, at the same time confining her left arm with the weight of his body. She had only one hand to use to stop his ravishing caresses. Clenching her teeth, she released his hand on her thigh and sank her fingers into the crisp, dark waves of his hair. She curled them tightly together and pulled.

As satisfying as was his grunt of pain, she had no time to enjoy it. His left hand, left unhindered, sought higher under her skirts.

Never had she been touched so. It was unbearable. She released her grip, heaving herself upright on a surge of trembling rage. She would not be taken like this. She had not succumbed to Elder Greer; nor would she be brought down to defeat by this man.

But the strength of the Mormon had dwindled the longer she fought. Not so the gambler's. With incredible swiftness he shifted, imprisoning her wrists in his hard fingers and carrying them to the small of her back. Slowly, with iron determination, she was forced back down among the pillows.

His leg weighted hers, holding her immobile. His face, dark with passion, hovered above her, and then his lips took hers once more in a thorough possession that was no less hateful for being gentle. Holding both her hands behind her back with one of his, he pushed aside the chemise, moving his warm palm over her naked breast. She flinched, then shivered at the odd sensation of reluctant pleasure that moved along her nerves. His kiss deepened, his touch grew bolder. Then in panic she heard the rending sound as he finished what Otto had begun, stripping away the remains of her dress. The constriction at her waist loosened. She felt the slide of her chemise straps and turned her head from side to side in silent, hopeless negation.

He did not heed it. The cool air touched her bare skin. Ward's lips felt burning hot in contrast as he trailed soft kisses to the valley between the trembling hills of her breasts. The feel of his mouth on one fear-contracted nipple sent her mind careening through the dark recesses of space, splintering, dividing, one portion unable to bear, refusing to accept what was happening to her, slipped into blackness, while another stirred with heightened sensitivity and increased vulnerability to the assault upon her senses.

"Ward—" she said, a strangled whisper of sound. "No. Don't—"

He stopped her pleas with his mouth while he pushed her petticoats down over hips. She shuddered as she felt them leave her, felt the thrust of his knee between her legs. His hands moved over her, smoothing the curves of her body, lingering in the tender hollows, remorsely invading, ceaselessly caressing.

Her heart beat high in her throat, her lungs strained for air, her skin expanded, glowing with internal heat. A stillness came upon her. Deep inside she felt an opening, stretching sensation.

His touch left her. At the edge of sanity she sensed his swift movements as he divested himself of his clothing. There was a fleeting instant when she might have torn herself free if she had not been so lost in indolence. On the edge of longing, she felt the urge of flight, but there was a stronger need to wait for his return.

It was not long in coming. The hard strength of his thighs was against her. She tensed against the probing firmness of his manhood, arching away from him, spreading her fingers over his chest. His arms encircled her, holding her, molding her along the lean length of his body, pressing her hips closer. A trembling ran over his frame, and with a slow twist of his loins, he thrust into her.

Serena caught her breath against the burning pain, the air constricted in her chest. Tears sprang into her eyes and ran in slow tracks down her cheeks.

Ward went still. "Serena," he whispered, an aching sound threaded with remorse.

As if released by that soft acknowledgment of her anguish, she let out her pent breath on a soundless sigh. Gathering himself, Ward moved deeper, carrying with him a soothing, spreading warmth. The sensation pulsated through Serena, washing back upon itself with a feeling of awakening. Her skin prickled as the slow drive of his desire increased. She seemed to have no will, no more need for resistance. Her mind retreated in confusion before the primitive compulsion to yield, to accept him because it was less hurtful than denial, because in acceptance there was a deep and dark red solace.

He eased from her but did not let her go. With gentle fingers he smoothed the fine strands of her hair from her face, releasing the tension where it was caught beneath him or under her shoulders. For all his nearness, the close rise and fall of his chest and the naked length of his body against her, he seemed remote, lost in thought.

At last he sighed. "I'm sorry, Serena. I have no excuse, except that it has been a long time since I knew a woman who told the truth."

She drew away a small space. "It doesn't matter," she answered, her tone stifled. "If it had not been you, it might well have been Otto."

The seconds ticked past. "A commendable attitude," he drawled. "Am I to understand you see me as a cut above, a small cut above, our apelike friend?"

"If—if you like."

"I don't like! I told you—"

"I know, you don't force women!" Serena rolled farther from him, flinging the dark curtain of her hair behind her shoulders. The action revealed the proud thrust of her breast and the long, supple line of her hips as she supported herself on one elbow.

Ward turned his gaze sharply to the ceiling. "I am beginning to think my mistake was even greater than I realized."

"I would be happy to think so!" Serena replied through gritted teeth.

66

"I'm sure you would. The question of what is to be done with you remains, however."

"Nothing need be done with me. I will take care of myself!"

"As you have so ably done until now? You said it yourself: if not me, then some other man would have taken advantage of you."

"It is so kind of you to remind me."

"Unkind, you mean? That doesn't make it any less true."

That could not be denied. Serena swung from his set face and, pushing to a sitting position, began to search for her clothing.

Ward leaned over his side of the bed and came up with a bunched wad of material. "Is this what you want?"

She sent him a venomous look and snatched the dress and petticoats from his hand, giving them a hard shake. The dress very nearly came apart in her hands, so fragile was the worn material now that it had been torn. Her sharp sound of dismay was loud in the silence.

"Don't worry about it. I'll buy you a new one," he told her, a trace of impatience in his voice.

She flung up her head to throw him a look of sparkling scorn. "Thank you, no. I want nothing from you."

"That's a bit hasty, don't you think?" He lifted his hands to lock them behind his head, turning to lie back with his long form stretched at ease like a huge cat, his interested gaze turned in her direction.

"No," she said baldly.

"I do. In fact, I see nothing wrong with my original idea."

The corner of her mouth curled, though she did not look at him as she turned her chemise to the right side and slipped it over her head.

"You mean to take me with you to Cripple Creek?"

"In part. Since you have been so obliging as to say you prefer me to Otto, or any other man, I think I will keep you with me."

"I never said anything of the kind!"

"You ran away from Otto and your Mormon elder, but you have yet to leave me."

"I tried," she said, her fingers slowly clenching on the torn ribbons she was trying to use to fasten her underclothing.

He reached out as though he would touch her, then drew back. "So you did. I'm sorry. I only meant that you stayed with me after the hailstorm, and earlier today. You sit there and look at me now as if God made no lower creature, but you haven't broke and run."

"I—I can't go naked!"

"You could if you were frightened enough."

"I thought you understood that I—that I wanted to be left alone. As for right now, what good would it do to run away?" Bitter irony laced her tone as with her lashes lowered, she jerked the ribbon of her chemise into a ragged bow, ignoring the jagged rent that outlined the curves of her breasts, and dragged her petticoats on over her head.

"Exactly," Ward said and came up from the bed, one strong hand closing over her fingers. "You have nothing to lose, not now, and everything to gain. With me you will have comfort and safety, two things you will find hard to provide for yourself."

"For how long?" she inquired, lifting her gray-blue eyes cold with contempt to his face. "A day, a week, a month?"

"As long as you require them."

The words were firm, the green gaze unwavering. Still, how could she believe him, or believing, bear such an arrangement? He had not mentioned marriage, and certainly she did not want it, but there was nothing in her upbringing that would allow her to live with him under any other circumstances.

"I don't," she said distinctly, "require anything at all from you."

"Your mistake, I think," he answered, his voice soft and his eyes narrowed.

He might have said more if a discreet knock had not sounded at that moment from outside the railroad-car door that opened into the parlor.

In an instant Ward was on his feet, pulling on his trousers. "There is a bathroom through there," he told her, his voice quiet as he indicated a small door opening beyond the bed. As she gathered her torn dress to her and slipped inside, he was already moving from the bedroom, closing the door into the parlor section quietly behind him.

The bathroom was as luxurious as the rest of the car. The tub was encased in fine-grained mahogany; the seat of the toilet and the water closet high above it were of the same wood. The fittings of the tub and washbasin were of ornately etched brass, though the water that trickled from them was cold. The Turkish towels were a deep blue and carried the monogram of the owner, as did the cream linen washcloths that hung on the mahogany rack. A faint bluish light entered the small compartment through an arrangement of tiny semi-circular skylights in the ceiling, an innovation she had noted also in the bedroom and parlor.

Close attention to the appointments of the railroad car was as good a means as any of distracting her mind from what had occurred. Looking around her made a good excuse for not meeting her own eyes in the oval mirror above the lavatory, not seeing the pale face reflected there.

What was she going to do? The choice was plain. She could stay, or she could go. She could remain with Ward and journey to Cripple Creek as his—call it his companion, for want of a better word—or she could return to the boardinghouse and the near-hopeless quest for a job to keep herself. One way she would have security, food, and shelter, for a time. The other she would have her self-respect, also for a time, a small length of time, until the days of accommodation she had paid for were done. If she went with Ward, she would have to accept his embraces; if she did not, she might well be reduced in a few short days to seeking the embraces of other men. As Mrs. O'Hare had said not so long ago, virtue was little defense against starvation.

Virtue. She felt as if her own had been stripped from her, not in a single act, but by one betrayal after another over the past three days. The injury she had taken was as much to the mind as to the body. She felt herself to be vulnerable, easy prey. In such a state, she was by no means sure she would be able to avoid the peril Ward had envisioned for her, as a crib girl allowing men to use her body in order to survive. If that was what her life was to be like, wouldn't one man be better than many?

No. She was not so weak, she could not be. There must be another way. Mrs. O'Hare would help her. Or would she? She was a friend of Ward's. Would the widow lift a hand knowing the gambler did not want her to be helped? Mrs. O'Hare was so certain Ward Dunbar was a good man, better than he thought himself to be. Poor deluded woman.

She had to do something. There had to be a way out. There had to be.

"Serena?"

Ward's quiet tap came on the door. Serena had not even begun to try to piece together her dress to put on over her ragged undergarments. A considerable expanse of bare skin was still showing through the rents. It did not matter that

69

Ward had already seen her unclothed. At that moment she had an overwhelming, irrational need to cover herself.

On a brass hook on the back of the door hung a man's robe of quilted satin in royal blue with velvet lapels. Serena hesitated a moment, her fingers clenched on the softness of it, then as Ward called her name once more, she snatched it down and pushed her arms into the sleeves, pulling the belt taut at the waist.

"What is it?" she called, her voice breathless.

"You can come out now."

The robe, designed to be full-length for a man, was ridiculously long. It dragged on the floor as Serena emerged. Her attention on the deep cuffs she was rolling up her arms to free her hands, she pretended not to notice, though the color across her cheekbones was high.

Ward's mouth twitched. Reaching out, he lifted the heavy swath of her hair from inside the collar of the robe and spread it out over the quilted satin.

Serena flinched, her nerves tight. Ward let his hands drop, a dark flush coming into his face before he turned away.

"Who—who was it?" Serena asked, swallowing with an effort.

"Nathan's driver. He left a basket with his employer's compliments. It seems my host thought I might enjoy a midnight supper, since I was fortunate enough to have a guest with me for the trip."

Serena ignored the irony of his tone. "That was—kind of him."

"Wasn't it?"

"I suppose I must have looked hungry to the driver."

Ward swung to face her. "Are you?"

Serena had spoken at random. It was a shock to realize that her suggestion was nothing less than the truth. Her eyes were dark-blue with amazement edged with self-doubt as she stared at him.

"It's not an unusual reaction," he said, his voice quiet, and carefully reserved. "It doesn't mean you are depraved."

"I—I never thought it did!" she declared with a lift of her chin, but she could not deny the gratitude that flicked over the surface of her mind.

"How long has it been since you ate last?"

"This morning. Mrs. O'Hare fixed a plate for me before I left the boardinghouse, but I was too anxious to go out and find work to swallow more than a bite or two."

He nodded, the thick lashes of his narrowed eyes shielding his expression. "Shall we call a truce, then, while we eat? Making decisions on an empty stomach never pays."

His grave manner was suspect. Serena had the odd feeling she should be on her guard. The effort was too much, however. What harm could there be in sharing one more meal with this man? She had nothing to fear from him now, had she? She gave a brief nod, and as he stood to one side, swept before him into the parlor with the tail of the blue velvet robe slipping along behind her.

The basket contained a roasted chicken, link sausage, crusty buttered rolls, pickles, dried apple tarts, and to wash down the repast, a bottle of iced champagne. Though plain, the fare had a delectable smell as Serena took it from the basket. Rummaging in the pantry kitchen, Ward found a knife, a pair of forks, plates, and two flat-bowled wine glasses. They set their places on a round table in the parlor section. Ward drew up chairs, opened the champagne and filled the glasses, then held Serena's chair while she seated herself.

"Shall I carve the chicken for you?" he asked in mock politeness as he took his place across from her and picked up his glass.

"I can manage." Serena detached a wing with a large piece of white meat, then glanced at Ward's empty plate. "Aren't you going to eat?"

"Not just yet." He lounged back in his chair, sipping at the sparkling yellow liquid in his glass.

"There's too much for one."

"You forget, I've already eaten." His dark-green glance rested briefly on the blue shadows of the bruises beginning to appear on her wrists where they emerged from the sleeves of the robe. He looked away, drinking off his wine in a single swallow, before he leaned to refill his glass.

Serena tasted the champagne with caution. It was decidedly refreshing. It seemed to tingle along her veins, leaving a surprising sense of well-being behind. Setting her glass aside, she bit into her chicken with renewed relish.

Despite the effects of the champagne, it was not easy to make her meal under Ward's brooding regard. As much as possible, she turned her attention away from his broad-shouldered form with the bronze sheen of lamplight falling across his bare chest. She surveyed the parlor, the blue-and-champagne-colored Wilton carpet, the taupe brocade draperies with their deep fringe and tassels, the Turcoman cloths that

71

covered the tables, and the blue-and-rose brocatelle upholstery on the mahogany-and-gilt-framed settee and chairs.

A familiar object lay in one corner of the settee. "My
shawl," Serena exclaimed. "Where did it come from?"

"The driver rescued it from the street, along with my hat,
on his return trip to the hotel. He dusted both off as best he
could, but I'm afraid being left in the dirt didn't help them."

Serena gave a nod. No matter how dusty it was, her shawl
represented a covering for her torn dress, some means of
sustaining dignity and modesty until she could get to her
trunk for a change of clothing. It was odd to think of such
things while having supper with a man in a state of near
undress, perhaps, but after what had passed between Ward
and herself, that also did not seem to matter.

Clearing her throat, Serena said, "Speaking of rescues, I
haven't thanked you for stopping Otto a little while ago. I
was grateful that you came along just then."

"Was?" he queried, staring at the play of light in his wine
glass. "Never mind. I expect that's an accurate statement of
your feelings, and I will accept it as such. But I didn't just
happen along; I was looking for you."

"For me?" Serena could not keep the astonishment from
her tone.

"I left the hotel early, went back to the boardinghouse.
Mrs. O'Hare told me you had gone out and weren't back yet.
She seemed to think that you were worried about her charges
for the room. I kept thinking about you walking the streets,
seeing you being tolled into one of the parlor houses or dance
halls in Colorado City. I wasn't too happy when I comman-
deered Nathan's rig and set out to find you; by the time I saw
you with Otto I was in a mood to—to take my temper out on
the first person I met."

It was as near an explanation for his conduct as she was
likely to get, she thought. Trying for a less strained mood,
she said, "I appreciate the sacrifice, if you left your poker
game for me. That kind of thing must mean a great deal to
you."

"Because I run a gambling hell?" he asked, a hard smile
flickering across his features.

"I suppose that was what I meant."

"The poker game started after the business meeting. I
wasn't interested enough in it to stick around. Few men
choose to relax in the same way they make their livings.
Besides, my—profession tends to give me an unfair advan-

tage. If a man comes to the Eldorado for a game, he accepts that fact; anywhere else—" He finished with a shrug.

His attitude was understandable, even commendable; it was the irony with which he expressed it that baffled her. She ate her chicken in silence, crumbling a roll as her appetite receded. Her gaze lifted to the ceiling, where the small skylight surrounded a painting of cherubs holding flower garlands floating in a blue sky. In one corner was a radiating sun that looked suspiciously like a rounded heap of precious metal. Noticing it, Serena allowed a smile to curve her mouth.

"What is it?" he inquired, and when she pointed out the resemblance gave a brief upward glance. "It's possible. Nathan has a sense of humor. It would be a fitting emblem, don't you think, for a man who counts a major part of his wealth in gold-mining shares."

"This man, Benedict—is he proud of being rich?" It did not seem unlikely, since his monogram, an ornate set of initials encircled by sheaves of wheat, adorned not only the towels in the bathroom, but nearly everything else in sight, from the linen napkin in her lap to the heading of the draperies at the window.

Ward shook his head. "Not really, though Nathan enjoys his money, or rather the things it can buy. Most of this"—he indicated the furnishings of the car with the hand that held his glass—"was planned by his wife just after they struck it rich. She died before it was delivered. Nathan always hated that."

"You sound as if you have known him a long time."

"Only since I came out here in '91. That was just after his Century Lode was assayed at two hundred eighty dollars to the ton. His wife died a few months later. It can't have been more than three years that we have known each other; it only seems like a long time."

Wrenching himself out of his chair, he moved to a small sideboard that held a cut-glass condiment set and several decanters hung with silver tags. Taking up the cut-glass bottle marked brandy, he removed the stopper, sloshed an inch of the dark spirits into his glass, replaced the stopper, and returned to his chair. Noticing that Serena had emptied her champagne glass, he poured the last of the bubbling wine into it and set the napkin-wrapped bottle to one side.

Serena stifled a yawn. She pushed back her plate, flicking a glance at Ward from the corner of her eye. Her hunger was appeased now, her flash of content gone. All she felt was weariness and a dull alarm at the way the man across from her was drinking. He sat watching her, his green eyes intent on the hectic color that lay across her cheekbones and the blue shadows beneath her eyes. To avoid that narrow scrutiny, Serena picked up her glass and drank.

Abruptly he stretched out his hand and took the empty glass from her fingers. "Go and lie down. Get some rest," he said, his voice harsh. "It will take a little time to send a message for the carriage again to take you back to the boardinghouse. You may as well make the best of it."

She glanced at the connecting door, the longing to do as he suggested plain in her face. She was weary beyond endurance, her body bruised and sore and her spirit beginning to flag. She would not admit it, however, even to herself.

"Now," he grated, "before I change my mind."

It would be stupid to fail to heed the warning. Serena rose on unsteady legs, and with the quilted robe trailing behind her, moved slowly into the bedroom. She put her hand on the knob of the connecting door and quietly swung it shut, pressing it until the latch clicked into place.

Removing the robe, she hung it away once more where she had found it. She turned on the brass tap in the bathroom then and wet a cloth with cold water. She wiped it over her face and arms, and then when she was through, carried it into the bedroom. Taking the coverlet from the bed, she rubbed at the reddish stain that marred its smooth perfection. When she was satisfied that little trace remained, she spread the coverlet over a chair to dry. Only then did she climb into bed and slide between the fresh sheets.

For a long time she lay, her fingers caressing the raised satin stitch of the monogram that marked the linens, staring up at the small, half-closed eyes of the skylights that glowed with the light from the railroad terminal. Her mind teemed with all that had happened to her in the past two days. Elder Greer, the counsel of Saints, her long trek ending with Ward and the hailstorm. Her arrival in Colorado Springs, Otto, his fight with the elder, the ravaging clutch of his hands. Ward again, a tall avenger, possessive champion, passionately tender lover. She closed her eyes as she felt once more the piercing pain that had taken her virginity. She wanted to feel outrage, grief, hate. All she could muster was a sigh of tiredness.

She was jerked from the edge of sleep by a clanking, metallic thud. Brakes ground and squealed, steam hissed, a mighty engine panted. The car was being connected. It began to move, rocking, swaying on its way to Cripple Creek. She had not agreed to go, had not said she would stay with Ward. It was too late now. Too late. Anger stirred and died away. Well then, let the train take her, let the decision be made for her; she could not bring herself to care.

Serena came awake with a start. The train was still moving. They were beyond the town, for there was no light filtering through the skylights. The bedroom was dark and filled with the rush of air. Somewhere a door swung back and forth, banging against the wall with each swing.

She sat up. The door into the parlor was open, also thrown wide, moving in the rocking draft, as was the rear door that led from the bedroom out onto the back platform of the train. Through this last doorway came the noise of the engine ahead of them, the pounding of its great heart and the scraping grind of the wheels on the metal track. Beyond the opening, standing on the platform, was the shape of a man, a dark silhouette against the night sky.

Serena slid out of bed and padded over the vibrating floor to the rear door. It was Ward who stood in the windy, smoke-whipped darkness. He was shirtless still, his muscled arms braced against the guardrail of the platform as he stared up at the pinpoints of orange sparks flying past overhead, winking out as they flew over the top of the Pullman car next in line.

"Ward?" she spoke quietly, allowing nothing of the sudden fear that gripped her to seep into her voice.

He turned, a deliberate movement. Seeing the white blur of her chemise and petticoat, he looked away again.

"Why are you out here? You'll freeze. Come inside." She took a step closer, reaching out to put her hand on his bare shoulder. The contact sent a tingle of shock along her arm, and unconsciously she tightened her hold.

He acknowledged her presence beside him with a brief glance. "Lies, Serena," he said quietly. "How we lie to ourselves. I was a gentleman once—an upright citizen who would have shot without a thought the kind of cur who would take a woman against her will. I told myself, in spite of everything, that I could still make that claim. I was wrong. What, then, do I deserve for what I have done to you, sweet Serena?"

"You—it was a mistake," she whispered, driven by some

75

traitorous sense of compassion to ease the pain she heard in his voice. Though he spoke plainly and stood rock-steady against the swaying of the train, she thought he was more than a little intoxicated.

He straightened slowly, turned. "Are you making excuses for me?"

"No, but neither can I deny the reasons that are there, not if they can be counted as important."

He lifted his hands, placing one on either side of her cheeks, cradling her face. "They are important," he said, his voice soft though his face was unreadable in the dark. "Oh, they are, but can they justify the longing I feel for you, the need I have, knowing that I have destroyed your innocence, to do the same again? And this need to keep you with me, knowing it's not what you want. What kind of man am I?"

"I don't know," she whispered in distress, aware of an ache that began in the region of her heart and rose upward with the press of tears into her throat.

"It might be better if I found out, once and for all—" He set his mouth to hers with the touch of tender fire. It flamed between them as their lips clung, a leaping thing that consumed puny questions of doubt and blame, feeding on itself. He pushed his fingers deep into the dark mass of her hair as he tasted the trembling corners of her mouth and trailed fire along the lovely turn of her jaw to the hollow of her throat. One hand smoothed down her back, pressing her hips to the lower part of his body. Her pulse throbbed as she felt the heat of his desire, and she clutched his shoulders, spreading her fingers over the muscles of his back. She half expected to find him chilled by his vigil; instead his skin held a fevered warmth that made her shiver with her own recognition of the windy chill.

He drew back, turning her toward the open doorway. A quick swing and it had closed behind them, shutting out the noise and the smoky, blowing wind. Her head rested on his shoulder, the black silk of her hair spilling over his arm. He tilted her chin with one finger, kissing her eyelids, then he bent to lift her, holding her close as he put one knee on the bed and eased down with her upon the rumpled sheets.

With slow care he removed her chemise and drew off her petticoat, then stripped off his trousers. His hand cupped her breast, sensing the pounding of her heart, then slid down over her belly to test the muscles of her abdomen tensed in a strange combination of fear and anticipation. He gathered

76

her close then, letting the side-to-side movement of the railroad car rock them in a gentle and steady rhythm while their mouths were sweetly molded together. The taste of brandy was on his lips and the freshness of the night clung to his body. In the flush of growing excitement, Serena felt the thrust of his tongue and shyly, hesitantly, touched it with her own. The pressure of his arms increased, constricting her breathing. His hands clasped the soft swell of her hips in an intimacy that should have been repellent, humiliating, but was not. Her breasts were flattened against the hard planes of his chest. She brushed the fingers of one hand along the strong column of his neck, feeling inside her the slow welling of her own ardor. It was a blooming thing, suffusing her, crowding out all except the sensations that assaulted her from within. She felt a tender soreness as he pressed into her, and then it was as though she had received that which alone could increase the growing, molten pleasure that engulfed her. He penetrated deeper, his movements quickening, and on an upsurge of rapture she clung to him, ascending in a white heat of expanding, limitless exultation, floating, returning to earth only as his movements slowed, finally ceased.

They did not move apart, but lay with their bodies entwined as their breathing eased. And the train roared on, climbing ever higher into the mountain night.

Chapter Five

The Spanish peaks called the Sangre de Cristo, blood of Christ, mountains were tipped rose-red where the light of the morning sun was reflected on their mantles of snow. They lined the horizon to the southwest, distinct in the high, clear air, and yet blue and mysterious with distance. To the north lay the snow-capped purple ranges of the Rockies, while to the east loomed the lavender-gray granite of Pikes Peak. In their journey to Cripple Creek, Serena and Ward had circled around the four-hundred-square-mile mass of the shining landmark. The gold-mining district was on its western slope, actually a part of the great mountain itself.

Cripple Creek township was located in the depths of an ancient volcanic crater, lying like the dregs in the bottom of a wide-mouthed wineglass. At the top of the rim, there were traces of brownish-green grass, a few stands of aspen and spruce, but for the rest, there was only scarred earth and tumbled rock piles of mine diggings. The gold in this region, Serena had once heard her father say, was not found like that uncovered in other strikes. The soft ore had been forced up by volcanic action from deep inside the earth, carried along natural fissures in a chemical salt solution with a number of other minerals, silver among them. As a result, there was little surface gold, none of the fabulous nuggets of pure metal such as had been found in California's gold rush of '49.

Placer mining, panning in the mountain streams of the area, yielded little more than flakes and specks of the mineral. In order to get at enough of the gold to be worthwhile, vertical shafts had to be sunk through the granite following the lines of gold-bearing fissures. Hard-rock mining was difficult and dangerous work, requiring an enormous investment in special tools, machinery, and buildings. It was not an undertaking for a poor man.

The nature of the mining was the cause of the great slag heaps of rock that dotted the encircling hillsides, and the tall and narrow buildings, like the outhouses of giants, that overshadowed the town. Tailings from the mines, the crushed and broken rock left over from the mining process, had been used to fill in the ruts in the streets of Cripple Creek. Some said that the sharp-edged granite still contained ore in quantities too minute to make extraction profitable; still, for this reason it could be claimed in all seriousness that the avenues of the town were paved with gold.

Spread over the rolling interior of the crater, Cripple Creek was a town of up-and-down streets, lined for the most part with jerry-built wood-framed business establishments of unfinished lumber topped by false fronts in a variety of angular styles. Here and there was a structure of brick, such as the Palace Hotel with its ornate veranda, but the many rough, unpainted buildings and houses, interspersed with an occasional log cabin chinked with a mortarlike mud, gave the place a raw look. For all that, it was not completely without amenities. The principal street was strung with telegraph wires. Stores sported striped awnings to protect their display windows containing groceries and clothing, mining equipment, hardware, and drugs from the powerful effects of the sun at that elevation. There were painted signs splashed on their sides advertising the benefits of tonics, shaving creams, and pork and beans. Nearly everywhere one looked in this town of single men, there were signs proclaiming the availability of furnished rooms.

There were two major thoroughfares, named for the two men, Bennet and Myers, who had platted the town on their cattle ranch in the middle of what had become known as the three-million-dollar cow pasture. Bennet Avenue was a street of retail establishments, of stockbrokerage houses, assay offices, banks, hotels, barbershops, and eating houses. Above it, to the north, were the schools, churches, and homes of the affluent and upstanding element in the community. Two blocks below it was Myers Avenue, where the tenderloin began.

The tenderloin. Though Serena had seen the name spelled out in the newspapers, had even heard it applied from time to time to certain sections of New Orleans, she had no clear idea of what it meant. Riding slowly along the length of the street beside Ward, she began to have some idea. At this hour of the morning, when the day should be beginning, little moved. Everything was quiet, though it was not the silence of peace but more the drugged somnolence of exhaustion. Broken beer bottles glinted brown in the sunlight. The smell of stale food and liquor hung in the air, vying with the odor of animal dung from in front of the hitching racks, and from the scavenging burros that rambled here and there, pawing at refuse piles in the alleys like dogs. The rough, uneven sidewalks, with their high sides shored up by rocks and log timbers on the slopes, were empty except for wandering drunks, groping along the walls, and laundry women with straggling hair hefting baskets of soiled linens. There were a few open doorways at the eating places, or at the saloons where barmen swept soggy sawdust into the street and threw the contents of cuspidors after it. But farther along, most of the houses were closed, the places with the neat look of private homes or select hotels, as well as the small shotgun houses with signs carrying crudely lettered women's names above the doorframes. Here, the doors were shut tight, the curtains drawn, the lanterns with red glass shades that hung on poles before them burned out. There was one exception. In the doorway of one house Serena saw a girl leaning on the jamb, her wrapper falling open to reveal a black corset cut indecently low, made lower still as she stretched and yawned and scratched at her tousled, brassy yellow hair with talonlike fingers. Serena looked quickly away.

Nearer to hand, there was a building which proclaimed itself to be the opera house, and another splashed with lurid posters advertising vaudeville offerings of dancing girls in flesh-colored tights and strippers in French underwear. There was a place called the Red Light Dance Hall, and another that styled itself the Mountain Belle. There were saloons in board shacks whose kerosene lanterns revealed sawdust floors, crude wooden benches, and an array of bottles behind a slab of wood for a bar. These had names like Last Chance, the Deer Horn, Hard Rock. And then there were drinking places with brass and amber glass chandeliers, sanded wood floors, and barmen in white aprons standing before mirrors framed in gold leaf over polished mahogany bars skirted with brass footrails. Saloons of this ilk had names like the Abbey, the Opera Club, the Golden Eagle.

The Eldorado was one of the latter. Serena and Ward drew their horses to a standstill before the hitching rack. Serena, holding her shawl tightly over her torn dress, allowed Ward to help her down. As she stared at the rough and rowdy life that flowed along the street around her, trepidation seized her. What was she doing here? She did not belong, could never belong, in such a place.

Ward took her arm. The steps which led up to the wide double doors of the saloon, with their colored glass panes, were before her. There seemed nothing to do but allow Ward to escort her inside.

The barmen turned as Ward entered. One set down a cuspidor he was cleaning. Another slid a mug foaming with beer along the bar and slapped down his polishing cloth. Wiping their hands on their aprons, they came forward with warm smiles and wide grins to pound Ward on the back and make him welcome. The few customers surged to their feet to join the melee, to demand explanations for his absence and a report of his luck on his prospecting trip. Serena, standing to one side, was ignored. Ward made no effort to bring her forward or to introduce her, an omission for which she, catching the sidelong glances slanted in her direction, was grateful.

To one side of the long barroom was a staircase with a mahogany railing and turned balusters. Little by little, Ward worked his way in that direction. At last the time came when he could accept one last challenge at a game of cards, promise once more to be down later on in the day, then sweep Serena with him up the stairs to the second floor.

He moved quickly along the narrow hall bare of carpet or paint to a transomed doorway. Taking out a key, he fitted it into the lock and turned the knob, then swung to glance at Serena.

"Are you all right?" he asked, a frown drawing his thick brows together.

She stood with a hand pressed to her chest. "Yes, I think so," she answered, attempting a smile. "I'm just a little out of breath."

His face cleared. "It's the altitude. I'm sorry, I wasn't

thinking. You will have to take it easy until you get used to it."

"You would think that as slow as the wagon train was moving I would have had time enough."

"Possibly, but you came the last four thousand feet overnight, and that's quite a distance straight up. Cripple Creek, at ten thousand feet, doesn't like much being two miles high."

He stood back for her to precede him into the room. She did so without thinking, concerned as much with finding a place to get away from the men below, to sit down and catch her breath, as with where he was taking her. Just inside the door she stopped.

Before her was a sitting room with a bedroom and other accommodations stretching beyond. There was about them a masculine air, but it was the heavy, over-opulent masculinity of the seraglio. The floors were covered with Persian carpets in gold and black and red. Billowing gold silk draperies, overhung with red and black brocade, edged with fringe, and looped up with tasseled ropes, blocked the sunlight at the front windows. Portieres of the same style hung at the doorway that led from the sitting room into the bedroom, and yards of the same fabrics were draped about the four-poster bed. Instead of settees, long low couches with splayed lion's feet, tight-rolled tube pillows, and piles of silk and satin cushions had been used in the sitting room. Beside them were overstuffed chairs and stools with leather seats worked in gold. Paisley shawls had been thrown over every surface. On one of the low round tables placed near the head of a couch sat a hookah water pipe. On another was an enormous brass urn filled with peacock feathers. Directly in front of the entrance door was a preserved elephant's foot surmounted by a marble tabletop on which sat an enamelware bowl in brilliant colors, filled with fruit.

"My God."

It was Ward who spoke. He stood just inside the room with his hands on his hips and a look of incredulous amazement on his bronzed face.

"You—you live here?" Serena asked at last.

"I thought I did." His voice was grim as he answered.

"Ward! Ward, you're back!"

The happy scream came from the hallway. Hard upon it, a woman burst into the room. As Ward turned, she threw herself into his arms and twined her hands behind his neck. Tilting back her head heavy with a weight of auburn hair

82

and crowned with a broad-brimmed hat of black straw set with pheasant wings, she pressed her red mouth to his lips. She moved her pliant body, clad in a walking costume of black-and-white foulard fitted tightly to her opulent shape, against him, a low sound deep in her throat. For an instant he seemed to respond, then he lifted his hands, closing hard brown fingers around her wrists to prise them loose.

"You are up early," he drawled, "or is it late?"

The woman grimaced. "I had to go down and inspect a shipment of wine for the parlor house that came in on the Denver train. I couldn't believe it when I heard you had just gotten off. I had to come and see for myself. I thought this time you were never coming back!"

"You know I always turn up, Pearlie. But what is this? What have you done to my rooms?"

"Don't you like it?" she pouted, lowering her head so she could just see him beneath the brim of her hat, at the same time fluffing the boa of rust-and-black feathers that hung over her arms. "It's the latest thing from New York. I thought you might like being rigged out like a Persian prince."

"You misjudge me," he said dryly.

"There's no need to get nasty! And there is no need for you to live in stoic squalor either! I thought it would be a nice surprise."

She swung around to survey her handiwork. At the sight of Serena the woman's wide smile vanished. She went still, a blank look in her pale-blue eyes that quickly turned to one of glittering rage.

"It's certainly a surprise," Ward began.

The woman called Pearlie cut across his words without ceremony. "Who is this person? What is she doing here?"

Ward lifted a brow. "Allow me to introduce you," he answered, his tone over-cordial to the point of irony.

"By all means!" Pearlie snapped. She stepped away from Ward, a move that brought her closer to Serena. There was about her the bristling antagonism of an animal that has discovered another of the same species and sex in its territory.

"Serena," Ward said, circling with deceptive loose-limbed casualness to interpose his body between her and the other woman. "May I present my business partner, darling? She likes to be called Pearlie."

"How do you do?" Serena said, her voice even, but the glance she divided between the other two wary.

The auburn-haired woman might not have heard the

greeting. "Not by everyone I don't!" she snapped, throwing back her head, her pale-blue stare icy cold. "You haven't said what she is doing here."

"I fail to see how it concerns you," Ward answered.

"Do you now? Let me make my concern clear, then. I want to know whether she is here for business, or for pleasure, your own pleasure!"

Ward turned to face her, the look of distaste on his face so evident that Serena was not surprised when Pearlie lost a degree of her confidence. "She is not here," he said softly, "for your business."

"You—may want no share of the parlor-house profits, but that hasn't kept you from visiting it now and then!"

The last words were said with a shade of defiance accompanied by a vicious glance in Serena's direction.

"Until now," Ward said, finality in his tone.

Pearlie paled beneath the powder and rouge that close inspection revealed on her face. "How noble, though it does seem to me that the first time you brought a woman in here you could have picked one with a little more class. This one hardly seems willing, much less able, to hold your attention. What did you do? Carry her off and rape her?"

Ward, his face set, moved to the door that still stood open behind them. His hand on the knob, he said, "If you don't mind, we will talk later. Serena and I have had a long trip. We would like to settle in."

The woman looked from Ward's chiseled features to the flush of color that suffused Serena's face to the hairline. Reaching out, she twitched aside the shawl that Serena held around her, exposing the torn edges of her bodice and the ivory swells of her breasts where she had tucked the ragged edges into her chemise.

"Good Lord! I was right!" Pearlie said, and went off into a gale of shrill laughter.

"That will do," Ward said, his voice hard.

"To think of it," the woman gasped, holding a hand to her abdomen. "You, of all people, so fastidious, so aloof from all the crawling vices and weaknesses of other men—and women. Rape, my darling Ward! And I suppose she was a virgin, too. That would appeal to you."

"I said that's enough!"

"Oh, it is, is it?" Pearlie said, suddenly sobering. "Is it indeed? Will it ever—when will it ever—be enough?"

Serena straightened her shawl. It was as though they had

forgotten her, as if the pair of them spoke across some dark void, a meaning beneath their words only they understood. Serena felt a tremor of disturbance move over her that had nothing to do with her embarrassment. Dislike for the auburn-haired woman rose inside her. Swinging around, she moved to the windows of the sitting room that overlooked the street. Her back stiff, she lifted a fold of the gold silk gauze draperies and stood staring out.

"Later," Ward told the other woman, and there was the sound of concession in the grim shading of his voice.

"Yes," Pearlie answered, "by all means, later."

There came the soft swish of skirts, followed by the closing of the door. A heaviness descended over the room. Serena heard the slow approach of Ward's footsteps. He stopped close behind her. Unconsciously, she braced herself, though for what she could not have said.

"I apologize for the things Pearlie said. I never meant your welcome to be like this."

"That man, Otto, said she wouldn't like me being here. I see what he meant."

"There's no need to let it concern you. What Pearlie likes or dislikes has nothing to do with you."

The stern inflection in his voice sounded a warning. There was no indication to Serena that it was for her; still, there was always that possibility. "Perhaps I had better go, if I am going to cause trouble."

It was a moment before he answered, and then his voice was hard. "Go where?"

"Anywhere. There must be something I can do." She made a slight movement of her shoulders, aware, though she deplored it, of a sense of waiting inside her. They had not spoken of his virtual kidnapping of her since the night before. There had been no time, no opportunity.

"I'm sure there is," he replied, reaching out to take up a curling tendril of her hair that had escaped from the chignon low on her neck to curl across her shoulder, "but would you like it?"

She swallowed hard. "I suppose I would have to."

"And what of my peace of mind?"

"I don't know what you mean."

"It would be like throwing a kitten to the hounds."

"I have claws," she said sharply.

"Sink them in me, then," he said, his green gaze level, his voice even. "I intend to be the leader of the pack."

She swung to face him, her blue-gray eyes dark as she scanned the brasslike hardness of his face. "You may have tricked me into coming with you to Cripple Creek, but you can't keep me here."

"Can't I? Forgive me for pointing it out, but you are as near to being naked as makes no difference beneath the shawl. You have no money, no friends. And the one thing you do have, your sweet and fragile beauty, is only a danger to you. I don't doubt you would like to be rid of me—I keep remembering that you did not deny an interest in Cripple Creek's mining millionaires."

He paused as if to give her a chance to do so now. Serena hesitated. The admission he so obviously expected would leave her dependent upon him, his total responsibility by reason of his having forced himself on her. She did not want that. She was no charity case who must be grateful for his support and patronage. As soon as she was decently dressed once more, as soon as she could learn something of the town, she would see to making her own way.

A muscle corded in his jaw. "At least we know where we stand. This may not be what you wanted, but for now, regardless of what you may think, it will be better for you."

"That is, of course, your whole consideration," Serena snapped, "what is best for me?"

"By no means," he corrected, blandly ignoring her sarcasm. "You should know, after last night, that my compassionate instincts are undependable, my good intentions easily overcome."

She opened her mouth for an indignant retort. It was never spoken, for he reached out with his iron grasp and drew her to him, pressing a warm kiss to her parted lips. Just as abruptly as he had caught her to him, he released her.

"I have to attend to the horses and telegraph Mrs. O'Hare about your trunk. You will be all right alone here, so long as you don't try to go below this floor. Keep that in mind, because I intend to leave instructions with the barkeep downstairs that you are not to set foot below the landing of the stairs. No doubt he would enjoy the tussle it might take to put you back where you belong; somehow I doubt you would. Is there anything you need before I go?"

"No," Serena answered, her voice stiff, then as he began to turn away, she changed her mind. "Wait. Is there anything here I can use to make repairs?"

"I doubt it, though you can look around, if you like. You

might start in the dressing room at the back. On second thought, don't bother. When I come back, I'll bring you something to wear until your own things put in an appearance."

"I want nothing from you."

A mocking smile twisted his lips. "So you said once before. It's really too bad. You are likely to get it anyway, though I suppose I will have to resign myself to doing without your— gratitude."

He moved with his lithe stride to the door. It closed quietly behind him. With a frown drawing her winged brows together, Serena stood staring at nothing. He was a puzzling man, this Ward Dunbar. For all the sign he had given this morning when they had awakened together in the gray dawn in bed aboard the private railroad car, his remorse of the night before, the things he had said on the platform outside, might never have been. He had got up and put on his clothes, and then, either from tact or indifference, left her alone. And yet, some time later when she emerged from the tiny bathroom, she had found him standing beside the coverlet where she had left it to dry, a corner of the brocade crumpled in his hand as he stared broodingly at the faint rust-orange water stain that marred its shining surface. He had lifted his eyes to hers for a long moment, and it had seemed to Serena there was an accusation in their dark-green depths. That expression had been so like the glint of contempt in his face just now, when he had mentioned the wealthy men of the town, that she could not help but question if there was some connection with what he had felt then, and just now. Had he suspected her of trying to keep her virginity to barter in return for the affections of a rich man? It did not matter, not really. Still, she hated to have him think that she would sell herself in such a fashion.

Would he actually keep her a prisoner here in these rooms? It did not seem possible, not in this day and age. But beyond the question of why he would feel the need, it would not be an easy task, not if he left her alone like this. She had only to fling up a window and scream for help, and when it came, charge him with his crime.

Would help come? There would be nothing unusual here, she thought, about women crying out, calling in shrill voices, screaming with laughter. What attention would be paid one more? And even if someone came, could she bring herself to speak of what had happened? Supposing she could, would they believe her? Might they not just as easily conclude she had brought her problems upon herself when she refused to accept the place assigned to her as a woman, refused to accept the authority of the man who had her in his keeping, Elder Greer? What was so terrible about her now being in the keeping of another man?

What was so terrible was the loss of her freedom. But Serena, staring at the closed door where Ward had gone out, could not persuade herself that the miners passing back and forth along the street outside could be brought to see it. Nor, in all truth, could she find it within herself to blame Ward. The purpose was to protect her, wasn't it?

Was it? It made no sense otherwise. He had come across her under peculiar circumstances that made him doubt her virtue. He had given her aid and, finding her desirable, had taken the payment he deemed most suitable. The discovery that the price he had exacted was more than he deserved had come as a shock to him; there could be no question of that. Bringing her here was his way of making recompense, but by no word or deed had he suggested that she could expect anything more from him than his protection. The saving respectability of marriage was not a condition one could associate with such a man; she did not expect it. But what, then, did she expect?

Abruptly Serena threw back her shawl, letting it fall to the floor. Swinging around, she hurried to the front window. Her fingers felt numb. She could not discover how the curtains opened. Then she was pulling the gold silk wide, sweeping it back on either side. The sash was stiff from disuse, but she pushed it high, letting the cool mountain air inside. With the palms of her hands on the sill, she leaned out the window.

An instant later, she drew back inside. From where she stood, she could see Ward just leaving the Eldorado, crossing the street. The sun gleamed with russet lights on his dark-brown hair, noticeable since he was the only man on the street without a hat of some kind. He walked with a free swinging stride, avoiding an oncoming wagon with ease, a man with a purpose. Head and shoulders above the others, or so it seemed, he threaded his way through the ambling drunks and sauntering midnight dandies without looking back.

He was gone. She was alone. Serena drew a deep, calming breath. Chin high, she picked up her shawl from the floor, pulling it close around her once more, and swung in the direction of the door that led out into the hallway.

The knob turned under her hand. She stepped outside and drew the panel to behind her. With a quiet tread, she moved toward the head of the stairs.

A lazy murmur of voices came toward her as she walked. She heard the slow brushing sweep of a broom being wielded below, and the clink of glasses being stacked. At the head of the stairs, she paused, one hand clutching the shawl together at her throat while she reached for the stair railing with the other. She descended a step, two, three.

Silence fell in the barroom. The creaking of a chair was loud in the quiet. A man with an apron tied around his waist and wearing armbands on his sleeves came into view. The light of an oil lamp, burning low this time of day, shone on his bald pate with its gray fringe of hair as he tilted his head back, staring up at Serena.

"Would you be wanting something?" he growled, his tone insolent despite the politeness of his query.

Serena halted. "No. I—thought I would take a little walk, see something of the town."

"Expect you had better wait for Mr. Dunbar, let him show you around." The man crossed his arms over his burly chest, his feet spread wide. Once more, the words were civil, but the barman's eyes gleamed with anticipation.

Serena veiled her expression with her lashes. Ward's threat to post a guard over her had not been idle. She should have known it would not be. Indeed, she had known it, but she had to test it for herself. "You may be right," she answered. "I hope he doesn't mean to be long?"

"I doubt that, seeing as how he knows you're here, waiting for him."

With a cool nod, despite the color in her cheeks, Serena inclined her head and, turning, retraced her footsteps with as much dignity as she could muster. The barman did not move, but stood watching until she was out of sight.

Back inside the room, the air was close and overwarm, filled with the musty newness of fabrics and thick-napped rugs, overlaid with the sour liquor smell that drifted up from the barroom. With the sudden energy of fury Serena went through the suite of rooms, opening the curtains, shoving the windows as high as they would go. The apartment slowly filled with light, making it seem less somber, less opulently depraved. By degrees, the air began to circulate, to billow a silk panel, to ripple the fringe on the brocade over-drapes, to move the peacock feathers lightly in their brass urn.

There was dust everywhere, a slow seeping from the streets. Serena could write her name on the surface of the bureau in the bedroom, and wipe cloudy streaks across the mirror in the door of the wardrobe. The rolltop desk in one corner was so thickly coated as to appear covered with gray fur, and the red brocade curtains drawn around the head of the four-poster bed needed a good shaking. Beyond the bedroom was a dressing room, also fitted with a wardrobe and a small, rather feminine-looking dressing table. An alcove of the same room, shielded by a sandalwood screen, contained a claw-footed tub and other bathroom fixtures.

Serena stood staring at them a long minute. She had not expected such amenities, not here. The rawness of the camp, the number of privies seen sitting discreetly at the back edges of the street lots, had not encouraged her to expect it. Was it a part of Pearlie's reorganizing of Ward's rooms? She did not know. She only knew that her grandfather's plantation home on the Mississippi River, a home of much pride and luxury, could not boast of such convenience. On trips with her mother as a young girl, there had been the novelty of bathing in a long tub of lead with soldered seams called a julep tub. It had been filled by Negro servants carrying cans of water laboriously up the back servant's stair from the kitchen. Otherwise, as a child and young woman, she had performed the necessary rituals of cleanliness in the round wooden tub her mother had used for washing clothes. Never had she enjoyed the comfort of a porcelain tub such as the one before her, not even at Mrs. O'Hare's boarding house. The bathing arrangement there had been only a slightly larger edition of her mother's washtub, something on the order of a rain barrel, with the hot water supplied once more from the kitchen.

Leaning over the tub, Serena turned on the tap. It ran cold for a few seconds, then began to grow warm. She drew in her breath. The temptation to make use of that lovely flowing water was near impossible to resist. She longed to wash her hair, to lie back and soak the grime of the long wagon journey, without facilities of any kind, from her skin, things she had not been able to do during her quick ablutions the afternoon before in Mrs. O'Hare's barrel. At the mere thought her skin itched.

She turned off the water and straightened. She could not do it. Ward might return at any minute. They were his rooms, his things. She had no right to make use of them.

As she turned away, she caught sight of herself in the full-length mirror set in a scrolled wood frame attached to the dressing-room wall. The reflection showed a slim girl in a dress that was faded and wrinkled, stained where she had fallen to her knees in the dirt of the street, and with the bodice in shreds. Wisps of dull hair straggled about her face, falling from the few pins left to her after her struggles, and there were blue shadows under her eyes from fatigue and restless nights. It was no wonder Ward Dunbar thought he could do as he pleased with her. She looked like the homeless waif he had called her, spiritless, without pride or strength of will. No wonder she had aroused Pearlie's laughter, even her tolerant contempt.

It was not to be borne. She could not stand to look so another minute. Let Mr. Dunbar come back when he pleased, think what he chose. She had not asked to be brought here, had certainly not wanted to be incarcerated in this place. If she made herself at home more than he liked or expected, that was too bad. There was little he could do about it.

There was a bar of castile soap in the brass holder beside the tub. Serena soaped her hair with it again and again, letting the fine, silken lather slide down over her shoulders and across her rose-tipped breasts. She scrubbed herself inch by inch, then lay back, luxuriating in the warmth of the water, the delicate scent of the soap, the feeling of being fresh and clean.

Once she thought she heard a sound and she started up, splashing water onto the carpeted floor, her heart pounding so that the wet and shining roundness of her breasts thudded with its beat. It was nothing, only the slamming of a distant door, perhaps in the saloon's storeroom somewhere below. It had sounded loud because of the open windows and doorways, that was all. Ward's rooms lay lengthwise of the barroom, which would make the dressing room with its bathing alcove on the backside of the building.

Finally the water began to cool. Serena rinsed the last traces of soap from her hair. She stood up with slender grace and, drawing the dark strands of her hair over her shoulder, twisted it around her arm, squeezing the water from its long length. As she flung it back over her shoulder, the wet ends of the tangled skein whipped against the skin below her waist. Reaching for a Turkish towel from the nearby hardwood rack, she stepped from the tub. She dried herself with slow care, enjoying the feel of the soft, velvet-like toweling.

As quickly as she dried her back, however, her wet hair dampened it again. Drawing it forward once more, she leaned forward from the hips to rub the lustrous tresses.

She did not know what caused her to glance at the mirror on the wall. It might have been no more than an accident; it might have been that unconscious awareness of being observed that comes to us at times. From where she was standing, the angle of the mirror neatly circumvented the sandalwood screen, revealing the interior of the bedroom and the high surface of the brocade-covered four-poster bed. Upon that coverlet was stretched a man. He was fully clothed, propped against the pillows with his hands locked behind his head.

It was Ward. His booted feet were crossed and his eyes were hooded as he lay staring. It was in that brief moment of recognition that Serena realized that if she could see him, he could also see her.

She whipped the towel around her. The heat of a flush warmed her face, deepening as she had some difficulty in finding the ends of the towel to cross over her breasts. To be caught at such a disadvantage once more added anger to her embarrassment, and as she dove to swing the dressing-room door shut, it did not close lightly.

Holding the towel around her, she swung away, pushing at her hair, trying in distraction to force her fingers through the tumbled masses. The nerve of the man, lying like some Biblical king spying on her as she bathed. To know that he had observed her when she thought she was alone, making an entertainment of her private moments, was more enraging than if he had barged in upon her.

Where were her clothes? As much as she might cringe at the thought of putting them, soiled as they were, back on, she had to have something to cover herself beside a length of toweling. She had left them thrown over the bench before the dressing table. They were not there now, nor had they slid to the floor on the far side.

A knock came on the door. Serena did not answer. In growing wrath, she stared around her, then took the few steps needed to peer behind the screen, scanning the bathing alcove.

The knock came again, firmer, more insistent.

"Go away!" Serena cried.

For an answer, the knob turned and the door swung slowly open. Ward lounged against the jamb. "If you are looking for

92

something to wear," he drawled, his tone laconic, "you might try this."

Hanging on the end of one brown finger was a wrapper of deep-blue sateen with shadings of lavender in the folds. It had elbow-length sleeves in layers that were edged with lace, a high waistline that wrapped and tied with a long purple satin cord, and a flowing skirt that spread into a demi-train in the back.

"What is it?" she asked, clutching at her towel though she had almost forgotten her near nudity for the moment.

"I told you I would bring you something to wear."

"Who does it belong to?"

"It belongs to you."

"A bribe?" The word was bald, uncompromising.

He lifted an eyebrow. "Let's call it a replacement for your dress that was—damaged."

Serena raised her chin a fraction. "Let's not. Where are my clothes?"

"You know," he said, his face bland, "I'm not sure. I told Sanchow to burn them—he is the Chinaman who brought our breakfast from the restaurant down the street, which, incidentally, is getting cold. But you know how frugal the Chinese are. They refuse to waste anything. He will probably give them to his wife either to refurbish or to sell for paper rags."

"You mean you gave my clothes away!"

"I didn't know you were so fond of them," he replied in mock apology.

"It's all I have to put on!" she exploded.

"How can you say so? You have this!" Once more he indicated the wrapper.

"You would like that, to have me walk around in front of you dressed as some—some lady of the half-light."

"Such a delicate phrase. I wonder where you heard it? But let me disabuse you of your curious notion about my tastes. If it is me you are studying to please, you will wear nothing at all. It was your feelings in the matter that concerned me."

She was silenced. She felt at a disadvantage, bewildered in the knowledge that she was confronting a man who had stepped outside the line of what was acceptable, yet one who might step back inside at any time. She expected civilized behavior and received enforced intimacy. She braced herself for an assault upon her defenses, and was met with sudden, disquieting solicitude.

93

"Of course, if I was wrong, if you would prefer to stay in your towel, then I have no objections." A smile tugged at one corner of his mouth as with studied slowness he allowed his gaze to move over her, dropping from the line of her shoulders to the curves of her breasts defined by the damp towel, and lower, to the indentation of her waist that flared into a slender hipline, her tapering thighs and calves and small, narrow feet. The bronze of his face paled a shade, and a look of strain came into his green eyes. "I suggest," he added, "that you make up your mind quickly."

It seemed sensible. Clenching her teeth, Serena took the wrapper from his hand, stepped back, and slammed the door upon him. It wasn't her fault that it did not quite hit him in the face.

She tugged her towel loose and flung it over the screen, then shook out the sateen garment and slipped her hands into the sleeves. It was a lovely fit, neither too full nor too tight. There was a small string tie under her right breast, then the material overlapped it and was held together by the satin cord. The only trouble was, this cord was the only closing. The bodice of the wrapper had a small, standing ruffle that grew narrower as it swept forward in a wide, curving neckline shaped like an inverted heart. The effect was an inordinately deep and wide decolletage that displayed more bosom than was seemly. The front of the skirt, caught high in its Empire style, was demurely closed as long as she stood still, but the instant she took a step, it opened to reveal the length of her legs to well above the knee, especially with the drag of the demi-train in the back to spread the opening wider. Though she had considerably more material draped upon her frame, the wrapper was not as protective of her modesty as the towel had been.

A tap came on the door once more. "I hate to rush you, but I can't guarantee the food will be edible once it gets cold."

The amusement in his voice was plain. Serena's lips tightened. Ward Dunbar thought he had put her in a dilemma. So he had, though she would die before she would let him know it. At least the wrapper was secure, she told herself, leaning forward experimentally, not so apt to slip as a towel. However much it might look as if she was going to come out of it, she was in no danger of doing so. The white flesh so artfully exposed belonged to her. It was her body; there was no necessity for her to be embarrassed by it. The only way she could be made to feel uncomfortable was if she permitted the man outside to make her conscious of herself.

"Serena?"

"Coming," she answered and, taking a deep breath, turned to open the door before she changed her mind.

Chapter Six

Ward stepped back to allow her to emerge. Face gravely impassive, he said, "Perfect, but then I knew it would be."

"I don't doubt your experience in these matters," she answered with a fine attempt at composure as she lifted a hand to her hair. "I suppose you also thought to provide me with a comb?"

"No, but I will be happy for you to use mine." Almost as if reluctant to look away from her, he turned to where a pair of silver-backed military brushes lay on his chest. Picking up the matching comb, he handed it to her.

"Thank you." She swung to give him a view of her well-covered back. Dragging the comb through her curls, she moved into the sitting room, where she could see an assortment of dishes left upon a tray on one of the tables. Ward stepped around her, beginning to remove the covers from the food.

Serena stood back, trying to bring some order to her hair, working at a snarled strand. "Don't wait for me."

He made no reply, but watched with his hands resting on the back of the chair he had pulled out for her until her hair hung like a dark, damp curtain about her shoulders.

She put the comb on a stand to one side, then came forward to sit down. The skirt of her wrapper began to part, and hastily she caught the edges together with one hand as she drew the chair under the table. Only as the hanging edge of the paisley shawl covered her lap did she release her hold.

His face unnaturally solemn, Ward took his place across from her. Serena slanted him a suspicious glance, then looked quickly away again.

"Do—do you have no arrangements for cooking here?" she asked.

He shook his head. "All my meals come from the Chinese eating place—it doesn't deserve to be called a restaurant—down the street."

"How convenient," she commented.

"By the tone of your voice I suppose you mean how lazy and shiftless?"

He had read her well. She did not trouble to hide it.

"I prefer to think of it as a matter of foresight. I don't have a lot of time to spend on eating; I'm not particular as to quality except for an occasional binge in Denver, when I happen to be up that way. Moreover, if I have no kitchen, there is no excuse for Pearlie to come in and cook for me, or as would be more likely, hire a cook for her to supervise at odd hours, a woman who would be slamming pots and pans around just when I am trying to sleep after being up all night downstairs."

"Her devotion must be so tiresome," Serena commented in a pretense of sympathy.

"Do you never say what you mean? I agree it probably sounds conceited, but there is more to it than appears on the surface."

Serena picked up a plate, ladled out what looked to be beef stew upon it, and handed it to Ward. She then served her own. "Pearlie is your business partner?"

"Half owner of the Eldorado."

"She lives close by?"

"Next door, in the parlor house she built and staffed with her own funds, since you are so curious. And you needn't look disapproving. There is a great deal more to such a place than the upstairs bedrooms. They offer a friendly drink, warm surroundings, and soft, female companionship to men who lead a hard, cold life far away from their homes."

"For a price."

"True, but one most men are willing to pay. The girls who occupy such places are not, strictly speaking, respectable, but then women of that sort are hard to come by out here. With few exceptions, the respectable women are all married, or too young or old to be eligible. Unless they are holding out for a rich husband, most decent young women, no matter how unattractive, are snapped up the minute they step foot in the district. There are more than fifty-five thousand people in this area. Of that number, better than half, approximately thirty thousand men, are without women, though some may have wives elsewhere. But all of them, married or unmarried, have money in their pockets and loneliness and lust in their hearts."

"You are eloquent in your defense of such people. Or is it in Pearlie's defense?"

"Pearlie needs none; her life is her own choice. As for the rest, perhaps it's myself I am defending."

There was a wry look in his green eyes that was backed by a degree of warmth that had little to do with the beginnings of companionship slowly growing between them. His gaze rested briefly on the marble-tinted expanse of Serena's shoulders, flicked over the glistening lock of her hair that had fallen forward across her breasts, and touched upon the sweet perfection of her mouth. His face tightened as with determination he turned his attention back to his plate.

Serena lowered her eyes also, aware of the flutter of nerves in her stomach. It was ridiculous for her to feel the least urge toward understanding of the reasons behind this man's treatment of her, very nearly as ridiculous as her sensitivity to his shift of mood. He wanted her, she knew it. Something about her must have provoked his desire, or was it just that she was there, available to him?

In the hope of distracting him she said, "I suppose you spoke to—to Pearlie about me, about my staying here?"

He gave a short nod.

"She was agreeable?"

He looked up, his eyes hard. "There was no necessity for her to agree. She may be my partner, but she has no claim on me, any more than I have on her."

"Strange," she commented, tilting her head to one side.

"What do you mean?"

"Her attitude was not exactly disinterested, and then there is all this." She indicated the room with a sweeping gesture of one hand. "It seems unlikely that she went to so much trouble and expense merely for your comfort. It looks to me as if she expected to share her handiwork, more especially since the style seems to be in her taste instead of yours."

"Impossible, not after all this time. You don't understand." Despite the certainty of his words, his expression did not clear.

Serena gave a small shrug. "Apparently not."

"Regardless," he said, his voice soft, tentative, "there is nothing in what is between Pearlie and myself that need be a concern to you."

"Are you telling me to mind my own business?" she inquired, forcing a smile.

"Not at all. I'm telling you that you have nothing to fear from Pearlie."

"That almost sounds as if you think I am jealous." She should drop this line of conversation. Why she persisted with it, she could not have said, but she could not bring herself to leave it alone.

He surveyed the frown between her eyes, a faint smile curving his mouth. "I hope I am not so stupid as to suggest such a thing."

"That is no answer," she said suspiciously.

"Isn't it? I thought it was."

"I am not jealous," she said, her every word distinct so there would be no chance of misunderstanding. "In fact, I would be happy to relinquish my place to Pearlie."

"No doubt, but that would not suit me at all."

"I fail to see why!"

"But then you are not looking at the—situation from my vantage point."

It was impossible to sustain the bright-green mockery of his gaze. There was an edge to it that seemed to scorch her through the blue sateen of her wrapper, a promise that brought the sting of color to her cheeks. "No," she answered, a light quiver in her voice. "Nor you, mine."

He was silenced. The minutes ticked past, filled only by the scrape of cutlery against stoneware. Finally, Ward put down his fork. "You told me when we first met that your parents are dead. But have you no other relatives? Grandparents? Aunts and uncles? Anyone who might take you in?"

"None."

"No one at all?"

"I never knew my father's parents. He left them behind in Ireland when he came to the United States. As for my mother's people, they did not approve of her marriage. My father was not welcome in their home. My mother and I used to return for a visit now and then, before my grandmother died. Afterward, my grandfather made a settlement upon my mother with the understanding that if she gave a penny of it to my father, if she stayed with her husband instead of returning to care for him, her own father, as he thought was her duty, then he never wanted to see any of us again."

"This settlement, I suppose it is long since spent?"

"I'm afraid so. My father worked hard, but he was never able to stay in one place for any length of time. It has been three years since I can remember a home. The last of the money went to finance our expedition into the gold country. He was going to come here to Cripple Creek and make his fortune. He was going to be able to give my mother and me everything he wanted, everything he thought we deserved. There would be riches without end." She looked away, her eyes dark with remembrance.

"I suppose every man—and woman—who comes here thinks the same."

Was his comment directed at her? She did not like to think so, but it was more likely than not. Serena did not reply.

"Most of them wind up working underground in the mines for about three dollars a day, the men, that is. The women are not so lucky."

Serena barely heard. Too late she realized the direction of Ward's questions. If she could have claimed rich and influential relations, grandparents concerned over her fate, then Ward might have thought twice about keeping her here in his rooms. If she could have manufactured some sort of message from them, then he would have been forced to let her go. As it was, she had delivered herself into his hands. He need have no worries, no compunction about holding her as long as he liked. The warm blood receded from her face, leaving it pale. Slowly her hands, resting in her lap, clenched into fists.

Ward pushed back his plate and leaned back with one forearm resting on the table. "Are you afraid of me, Serena?"

Her head came up. Her chin took on a proud tilt. "Certainly not!"

"It would have been easy to convince me otherwise."

"Because I object to—to becoming the object of your affections? I had not realized that was a mark of cowardice."

"You know that isn't what I meant."

She did know it; still, with stubbornness born of pride and fear, she refused to acknowledge it. She sat tight-lipped.

"Will it be so bad, since you aren't afraid, to stay here

with me? I am a man, nothing more. I won't hurt you, or let harm come to you in any form, so long as you are with me. I will not insult you with a pretense of love, but I want you more than I have wanted any woman." A quick frown came and went across his face, as if he had not meant to say the words that had left his lips, and yet hearing them, had recognized their truth.

"You speak as if I had a choice," Serena said slowly, slanting him a blue-gray glance from beneath her lashes. "I was under the impression that I had none."

"I would feel better if you were not unwilling."

"A willing prisoner? A contradiction in terms, surely? You expect too much."

"I was not referring only to your status in this room."

"You—you mean you prefer that I am not unwilling to—to share your bed?"

He inclined his head, a slight smile relieving the severe lines of his mouth. "It could be put that way."

"I am sorry to disappoint you!"

"I doubt that," he said, "though I wonder if you realize you make it necessary for me to try, at least, to persuade you to reconsider."

"You need not bother!" she snapped, a shade of panic in her voice as he got to his feet, moving toward her. She stood up and sidestepped her chair, intending to put the width of the table between them.

He reached out, catching her wrist. "No bother at all," he said. "None whatever."

"Ward, you don't mean—" she began, retreating despite his loose hold.

He followed her, his tone determined for all its softness as he answered, "Oh, but I do."

"You can't, not now, in the middle of the morning." She had to make the protest, though what she saw in his dark-green eyes gave her little hope that he would heed it. And then as the backs of her legs touched one of the couches, she realized the reason for his indulgence of her attempt to avoid his embrace. He had been gently guiding her toward the couch's low, pillow-strewn softness.

"What better time?" he murmured, a quizzical smile in his eyes as he released her wrist to place both hands on her shoulders, forcing her down. "Or place?"

He pressed her back among the cushions. Her wrapper fell open, exposing the curving lines of her hips and legs. Her

101

hair spread around her like a dark and shining cloak. The ties that held the garment she wore proved no impediment to the man who had chosen it. As she lay rosily naked, Ward knelt beside the couch. He took up a long strand of her hair, letting it curl confidingly about his fingers for a moment before he let it fall, watching with bemused eyes as the silken strand with its rainbow highlights covered the tip-tilted roundness of her breasts.

"You are so lovely. It would probably be good for my soul if I could resist your innocent provocation, but I think, sweet Serena, that I would as soon be damned."

"Ward?" Serena whispered, a question in her blue-gray eyes as she searched his face. There was in his words a faint indication that he remembered more of the night before than she had thought. But there was no time to consider the possibility. His arms were around her, holding her against the cold bone buttons of his coat; his mouth took hers in a burning demand. The sudden fierce rise of his ardor swept over them, and he possessed her there among the decadent oriental splendor, in the clear light of day.

Afterward, Serena lay in the curve of his body with her cheek resting on Ward's forearm, and covered at least in part by the flowing skirt of her wrapper. She could feel the steady rise and fall of his chest against her back that made it seem he was on the verge of sleep. She wanted to feel resentment, some vestige of anger. Her limbs seemed weighted and her mind too steeped in languor. Sighing, she closed her eyes. She did not notice that the fingers of one hand were stilled curled around the hard brown hand of the man who held her.

The days that followed settled into a routine. Ward spent the evenings in the barroom below talking, playing cards, acting the part of host to the merchants and miners who patronized the Eldorado. In the small hours of the morning he would seek his bed, and Serena. They awoke, usually, just before midday to the arrival of a breakfast tray brought by the Chinaman. Included with the fare was a pot of hot coffee and a folded copy of the *Daily Miner*. With their second cup of coffee, they perused the news, reading of the political chicanery in Washington, the repercussions of the strike among the miners during the summer just past, the day's ration of mining accidents and freighting mishaps. A sensational item, one that took space for several editions, was the death of a woman from one of the Myers Avenue cribs. She had been

102

beaten in a senseless act of violence. Her hoard of money, no small amount, had not been touched, and as far as anyone was willing to say, she had no enemies, was generally well liked. From reading the articles, Serena received the impression that although it was not too unusual for one of the ladies of the lamplight to give up her life due to pneumonia, tuberculosis, a botched abortion, or an overdose of morphine, for one to become the victim of murder was out of the ordinary. It was discreetly suggested that the most likely culprit was her paramour, if she had one, the man who lived by her ill-gotten wages. The newssheet discounted the idea that the killer might have been a customer. It was of the opinion that there was no need for panic among the women of the town.

The paper finished, Ward might stretch and reach for Serena, or less often, slide naked from bed and pad into the dressing room to bathe and shave. He never seemed aware that Serena lay watching him, or if he was, he did not mind. He moved with the unself-conscious grace of an animal, the muscles gliding fluidly under his skin, rampantly, undeniably male. It was an attitude that Serena gradually began to copy, though with varying success.

The afternoons were devoted by Ward to business matters, though he did not discuss them except in vague terms. He would return after a few hours, well before dinner. Now and then a visitor dropped in to see him, but he never invited the men in, taking them instead back downstairs to his table for a drink in the barroom. It was just as well. Not only did Serena have little desire to be introduced as Ward's kept woman, she still had nothing to wear other than the wrapper he had bought her. Her trunk had not arrived. Ward seemed unconcerned, though Serena worried, as the days went by, that her few belongings might have been taken off the train at another stop, at Canon City or Florence, or even have been left on board to be unloaded in Denver. In the meantime, the result was that for most of the day she wore next to nothing. Sometimes she wrapped herself in a sheet and trailed around the rooms like an imitation Roman goddess. At others, she borrowed one of Ward's shirts from his wardrobe, though more often she lay in bed unclothed, resting against a pile of pillows with a book in her hand.

Her reading material came from Ward's collection. It was piled in a box pushed ignominiously under the bed, doubtless during the redecoration. Among the volumes was a complete set of law books, including the 1825 revised edition of the

Code Napoleon for Louisiana, something for Serena to puzzle over as she turned it in her hands. There were also a number of classics in worn bindings, an assortment of the works of the romantic poets, and a sizable number of the type of literature known as penny dreadfuls. The classics she had already read; her grandfather had enjoyed a well-stocked library in his plantation home, and her summer visits had been long. Poetry did not suit her mood. It was the cheap novels of Western adventure that she devoured. She became so engrossed in tales of desperadoes, of mountain men and Indians and pony soldiers, that often she would hardly notice Ward's footsteps in the hall outside in time to reach for her sheet or wrapper.

When occasionally the books palled, she entertained herself by staring out the windows at the activity along the street. She was rewarded one day by the sight of a pair of nuns in windswept habits making their way among the earth-covered miners and their fancy women. Another time she saw a hurdy-gurdy man and his monkey. Chinese, Japanese, Mexicans, Negroes, and a half-dozen other nationalities passed beneath her windows, nor was it too rare for her to see the somber dressed figures of Mormons pacing along. From her vantage point she saw the parade of a flea-bitten circus, an ancient elephant, a sad bison, and a dyspeptic camel. She also watched the funeral procession of the girl who had been murdered.

It was not an impressive affair, and yet there were flowers on the coffin that trundled past on the black, plume-decorated undertaker's wagon, and the carriages that followed were filled with women dressed in their best, with bodices buttoned to their throats in the current mode, hats shielding their faces, and gloves on their hands. Surprisingly, there were quite a few men riding or walking in the cortege.

It was the women who drew Serena's closest attention, however. Watching them in the bright light of day on this solemn occasion, seeing them dabbing at the tears that ran down their faces, talking quietly among themselves, or staring with set features straight ahead, she could not tell that they were different in any way from any other women she had ever known. The only remarkable thing about them, it appeared, was their occupation.

How hard it was to connect them with the terms she had heard used in whispered undertones these last years since she had grown old enough to hear such things mentioned, to see in them the depraved creatures given over to the pleasures of the flesh that were denounced from countless pulpits. So they used their bodies to gain money? What choice did they have? Would starving have been better, or the slavery of working at back-breaking menial tasks for a pittance, even if such tasks could be found? There would have been no market for their wares except for the strong desires of men, and yet the men who paid over their coins escaped the stigma conferred on these women by society, as well as the dangers of pregnancy and disease. There was no justice in it.

Serena had never pondered such ideas before, never had cause. Nor was she so sanguine as to think it would have occurred to her to do so now if she had not found herself in much the same position as those other women.

As time crept past, the realization of just what had happened to her became clearer. Often at night, sitting at the top of the steps that led down into the barroom, the nearest to the saloon that Ward would permit her, she watched the women at their work, comparing them to herself with a slow rise of fear. As they went about their work, serving drinks, encouraging gaming, high-kicking in a dance that showed their underclothing on the stage at the rear of the barroom, their nervous, overloud laughter and ingratiating smiles made her wince. The brassy ones, with their posturing and posing, the lewd invitations in their bodies and eyes, seemed to have a brittle quality in their hard personalities. It was as if they had yielded up so much that what was left had to be closely guarded against encroachment, because, if their defenses should prove too weak, life itself might be thrown away in a last gesture of reckless defiance. Would she someday come to this, this short-tempered competition for the favors of men, the desperation to please, the eagerness for the forgetfulness of strong liquor? The pathetic pride as some grinning miner was led away out the back door and up the rear stairs of Pearlie's parlor house next door?

Her presence there, at the entrance to Ward's private rooms, did not go unnoticed. The women below sent her glances of curiosity and envy that turned slowly to resentment. They ran their eyes over the wrapper she invariably wore, and a sneer curled their lips. No small amount of their displeasure was caused by the fascination of the men in the room with her silent, demurely provocative, rather wistful figure above them with her feet close together and her elbows propped upon her knees. Once or twice, miners had tried to

105

approach her, but the seemingly casual intervention of a broad-shouldered bouncer at the foot of the stairs had made them veer off in another direction. The most ludicrous thing about that circumstance was the fact that the bouncer was more often than not Otto Bruin. He had returned to town within days of Serena's arrival and had taken up what was apparently his old job. Positioned near the bottom stair as much to protect her as to keep her in her place, he reminded her of a particularly vicious bulldog guarding what belonged to his master. Though she did not like to think of herself as Ward's possession, it was increasingly evident that nearly everyone else around her looked upon her in that light.

The exception was Pearlie. Ward's partner had first seen Serena as negligible, a diversion that would last no more than a night or two. She had been annoyed to find her still in Ward's rooms at the end of a week, an annoyance that had turned to irritation when Serena was still in residence after the second. At the end of the third, Pearlie's displeasure became smoldering anger, building slowly to rage.

One night the woman, dressed in a gown of watered peach taffeta trimmed with pure-white marabou, and with aigrettes in her high-piled auburn hair, strode toward the foot of the stairs. Otto hesitated, as if doubtful whether to step into her path. With a cold look of scorn, Pearlie brushed past him, picked up her skirts, and mounted the carpeted steps to tower over Serena.

"What do you think you are doing, sitting up here on your pretty little behind? Get up from there and put a dress on. We need you down below." She jerked her head in the direction of the barroom in a gesture so curt that one aigrette plume loosened from her curls. With a vicious jab, the woman set its comb back in place.

As Serena turned her head to look up, her dark hair spilled across her shoulder, cascading in curls across her breast. "I couldn't do that, even if I wanted to," she answered. "Not only do I not have a dress, Ward would never let me."

"Don't have a dress?" Pearlie echoed.

"My trunk hasn't arrived."

The other woman's eyes narrowed to slits. "I could have sworn—not that it matters. Come as you are."

"I told you, Ward—"

"I don't care what Ward said, or what he wants. I see no reason why you should take advantage of the shelter and

106

food provided to you by the Eldorado without giving something in return."

Serena colored. "I would gladly pay my way, if I could."

"Mealy-mouthed nonsense!" Pearlie's lips twisted in a sneer as she cut across Serena's words. "I've told you what you can do to repay the debt. You needn't look so reluctant! You may have been an innocent when Ward came across you, but you can hardly make that claim now. If I know Ward, you have been thoroughly inducted into the pleasures of the flesh, and it is time you sampled the methods of other men. Who knows, you might even astonish yourself by enjoying it."

"I doubt that," Serena answered, her voice hard. The suggestion did not surprise her as much as she might have expected. Pearlie, of all the other women, was the only one who seemed to find enjoyment in what she was doing, though admittedly of a macabre sort. It might have been due to her freedom and financial independence as owner of the parlor house to pick and choose, or it might not. Some nights she would refuse all requests for her company with a tormenting glitter of laughter in her light-blue eyes. Others, she would accept the advances of as many as four or five different men. Appearance and style of address had little to do with her choices, or so it appeared. If anything, stamina seemed to be her main criterion. She sometimes disappeared into the night with Otto Bruin. He would return alone after an hour or so, with a swagger in his step and a self-satisfied smile on his fleshy lips.

"Don't be so smug. You will come to it eventually, you know. Whatever Ward feels for you now, it is unlikely to last. It never has before."

"That may be," Serena answered slowly, intrigued by the bitterness in the woman's voice. Ward had denied Pearlie's claim upon him, but he had not said that there had never been one. Had she been unable to hold his interest?

"I know it is. You may as well resign yourself to what I say. Now, get up off your backside and get below."

"I think not."

The words were low and deep, and spoken in a tone so firm it could belong to no man except Ward.

Pearlie whirled, a spot of color blazing on each cheek. "This does not concern you!" she snapped in frustrated fury.

"Doesn't it? You are interfering with my private arrangements, Pearlie, something you know I will not tolerate." As

107

he spoke Ward moved up the stairs toward them, coming to a halt on the tread where Serena sat so that she seemed to recline at his feet.

"Your arrangements! Do you mean this stray you picked up and brought in to batten upon us?"

"Serena is in my care," Ward said, his voice dangerously quiet. "She is no charge upon the Eldorado."

"If that's so," Pearlie cried, her lips trembling, "then you are being cheated. She spends so much time staring out the window, or squatting here on the stairs, that I can't imagine what she does to warrant such tender concern."

"Can't you?"

The suggestion in the soft words could not be misunderstood. Pearlie's hands clenched into fists. "Damn you!"

"My apologies," Ward murmured, inclining his head, "but you seemed so anxious to know, I thought your curiosity should be gratified." He stretched out his hand, and when Serena put her fingers into it, pulled her to her feet. He slipped one arm around her waist, holding her to him, casually sliding his fingers upward over her ribs, almost cupping her breast.

"Ward—" Pearlie breathed on a note of pain.

"You will forgive us if we say goodnight now, won't you, Pearlie? I've been waiting impatiently for closing time this hour and more. Since you have brought me here, close to Serena, I find myself unable to resist the temptation to carry her off to bed."

He did not wait for a reply, but turned, and holding Serena close, climbed the last step and moved away down the hall.

Inside their rooms, Ward moved through the dimness to where Serena had left a kerosene lamp burning with a low flame on the bedside stand. His attention on turning up the wick, he said, "I didn't mean to make you uncomfortable just now. Pearlie has a way of bringing out the worst in me."

"It doesn't matter." Serena followed him into the room, moving to the window to stand gazing into the night.

"It matters to me," he said abruptly.

"As a gentleman?" she asked, her tone dry.

"Yes, dammit!"

She knew when he moved to stand close behind her, but so long as he did not touch her, she could pretend to be unaware of his nearness. Silence, the most suitable answer to his claim, hung in the air. She heard the rustle of his broad-

108

cloth coat as he lifted his hand as though to touch her shoulder, then let it fall again.

"Do you do this kind of thing often?" he asked, his tone grim.

"What kind of thing?"

"Stare out the window, as Pearlie said just now?"

His change of subject was disconcerting. "There isn't much else."

"I hadn't realized. Maybe I should thank her for pointing it out to me."

"I don't believe that's a good idea, not at the moment."

"No. I think something should be done about your lack of entertainment, however."

"There's no need," she answered, keeping her tone carefully neutral.

"I think there is. I wouldn't want you to be too dissatisfied. Besides, you haven't seen much of the town or the mines."

"I'm not a child. You don't have to promise me a treat to keep me satisfied. If you were really concerned, you would let me go."

"Must we go over this again? I thought you understood it is for your protection." He placed his hands lightly at her waist and bent his head to brush his lips along the slender curve of her neck.

She twisted away from him. "Somehow, it doesn't seem like it."

After a moment he began to shrug out of his coat, throwing it to one side, tugging at the string tie under his collar. "Maybe you would rather go downstairs at night, as Pearlie suggested? Is that it?"

"No!" The mere idea chilled her so that she clasped her arms around her, rubbing the goose flesh that sprang up along her arms. The nights were growing cooler, almost cold. Her bare feet were like ice.

"I didn't think you would, but a man can never be sure."

"That doesn't mean that I want to be kept here at your convenience, waiting for you to notice me!"

"Do you wait for me, Serena?" he asked, unbuttoning his shirt, stripping it from his trousers as he watched her with an intent look in his dark-green eyes.

"Don't be ridiculous."

"I was only trying to understand you. I would have expected before now to have been called upon to chase you

109

down. I will admit that I have been surprised that you haven't made a more determined effort to get away."

Serena swung away. "Toward what end? This thing I am wearing, as you well know, makes me look like a walking invitation to be bedded. I've had enough of being mistaken for something I'm not, I thank you! Even if that didn't happen, I have no money, no friends, and without them, no way to leave this place. What it comes to is, this entire town here in the mountains, so far from anywhere, is a prison."

"I can see you have given the matter some thought," he said, his tone laconic.

"How can you expect anything else?"

"Maybe I'm used to women who act instead of thinking."

She paused in her pacing to stare at him, her chin high. "I suppose you prefer that, women who are all feeling and no brains."

"I wouldn't say that." Deliberately, he removed his gold stud cufflinks, then stripped off his shirt and flung it on the bed.

"You don't deny it, either."

"No, I'm far too intrigued with the question of why you are troubling yourself with what type of woman I might like."

"I'm not!" she declared in goaded tones. Moving in a dark swirl of hair, she stepped to the bureau and, picking up the silver-backed brush she had taken for her own, stood twisting it in her hands.

He stepped into the sitting room to use the cricket bootjack that sat beside the cast-iron stove with its long, flat top and ornate nickel-plated grill. Levering off his half-boot of soft brown leather, he said, "No? It sounded uncommonly like it to me."

"Then you are mistaken."

"Possibly," he admitted as he returned to the bedroom.

She glared at him in the shaving mirror, dragging the brush through the silken masses of her hair. "If you think I am studying how best to please you, then you are thick-headed, and thick-skinned, beyond belief!"

"Unkind," he murmured, "when I have been considering this past hour how best to please you."

He meant that in the most physical sense, Serena knew. Her mouth tightened, and she sent him a dark look, though she was aware of a quickening inside her she could not control.

110

"Don't you believe me?" he asked, his voice silky and one corner of his mouth tugging in a smile.

"You—you have been wasting your time," she snapped. In the reflective surface of the shaving mirror she watched his slow advance. The silver-backed brush clattered as she placed it once more on the top of the bureau.

"Somehow I don't think so."

A wild rose flush glowed on her cheekbones, but her blue-gray eyes remained steady. "If you mean—?"

"No, no, Serena, how could I?" he asked, amusement running through his voice. He cupped her shoulders in the palms of his hands, smoothing slowly down over her arms as he drew her back against him.

But he did, she knew he did. He meant to remind her that she did find pleasure in his arms, that try as she might, she could not always remain unmoved under his caresses. Not always, but often, he penetrated her defenses, made her respond to him against her will. With gentle tenderness, or sudden rough passion, he broke through the barriers she set between them, and yet he was never quite satisfied. It was the knowledge that he wanted still more from her that allowed her to meet his green eyes now.

"You could, easily," she answered his question, her voice husky.

Busy with the satin rope tie of her wrapper, he said, "What a terrible opinion you have of me."

"With—with good reason." She tried to inject the proper sting into her voice, but it was difficult while she rested against the hard planes of his bared chest, enclosed in the strength of his arms. Her wrapper fell open and he slid his hands about her waist, spanning its slimness so that the tips of his fingers and thumbs met.

His green eyes grew dark as the wrapper opened wider, and he allowed his spread hands to glide upward to the pink-and-white fullness of her breasts. "I think," he said, "that I must give you even more."

111

Chapter Seven

The knock that fell on the door was sharp, and yet somehow furtive. Serena looked up from the penny dreadfuls she had been turning over without enthusiasm in their box. Ward had been gone only a few minutes. If he was returning for something he had forgotten, he would certainly not stop to knock before entering, but she could think of no one else that the barman on constant duty below would let above the stairs. Almost no one, that is.

She pushed the box of books under the bed and rose to her feet. Gathering her wrapper around her, tying it firmly in place, she moved to open the door.

It was Pearlie who stood outside. There was a wary look in her pale-blue eyes. Opening tight-pressed lips, she said, "I would like to speak to you."

"About what?" Serena stood her ground despite the movement Pearlie made as if to brush past her into the room.

"There are a few things you should know about Ward Dunbar, a few things you should understand, before you get hurt."

It would be foolish not to listen to the other woman, Serena told herself, not to learn everything possible about the man who was keeping her here. Curiosity did not enter into it at all. With a brief nod, she stepped back, allowing Pearlie to enter before closing the door firmly behind her.

Pearlie took a turn about the sitting room, pausing to glance into the open door of the bedroom without troubling to hide her avid interest. Ward's shirt, the one he had removed the evening before, lay over a chair where he had tossed it with his limp and twisted tie. The bed where he and Serena had so recently lain was unmade, with both indented pillows drawn together in the center above the rumpled sheets.

Pearlie swung around. "Well," she said, her voice strained. "Aren't you going to offer me some refreshment?"

"I'm sorry. I have nothing. Ward drank the last of the coffee Sanchow brought up for breakfast before he went out."

"I had in mind something stronger. Considering the location of these rooms, it doesn't seem too much to ask. But don't trouble yourself. Now I think of it, this isn't a social call."

"In that case, I won't ask you to sit down," Serena replied. Clasping her hands lightly in front of her, she waited for Pearlie to state her business.

A flush of anger mottled Pearlie's pale face. She eyed Serena with dislike. "You won't be so calm, I think, when I tell you that the man you are living with, before he came to Cripple Creek, was charged with murder."

Serena went still. She could feel the blood drain from her face. And then she noticed the small, satisfied smile that thinned Pearlie's lips. "You are lying," she breathed.

"No. I assure you it's the truth. Ward was hauled off to jail and arraigned before a judge for the murder of my husband."

"Your—husband?"

"Shocking, isn't it? Even unbelievable. It sometimes seems impossible even to me. Shall I tell you about it?"

Without speaking, Serena indicated a seat on one of the couches. Spreading her skirts with conscious grace, Pearlie settled herself, then watched bright-eyed as Serena took a place across from her.

"They were law partners, you see, Ward and my husband. They had one of the best firms in Natchez. They were the best of friends, too, had been since they were boys together. They practically lived in each other's houses when they were growing up. After Ward's parents died, Jim's people were especially kind to him. Later, as young men, *beaux sabres*, of Natchez, they went courting together, courting—me."

"Then why? What happened?" The horror was strong in

113

Serena's voice. Her fingers were knit so closely together that the knuckles were white.

"Jim, that was my husband's name, proposed first. Ward, ever the gentleman, backed off when he saw how desperately in love with me his friend was. He would do nothing to jeopardize Jim's chances of winning me for his bride, though heaven knows I gave him enough encouragement. Ward was serious about me too, I know he was, but all through their boyhood he had been in the habit of holding back where Jim was concerned. He knew he was stronger than Jim, that his was the more forceful personality. I think a part of the trouble then, and later, was that Jim knew it too."

"If it was Ward you wanted, and you were so certain he cared for you, why didn't you just refuse his friend's proposal?"

"You don't understand. They were both wealthy men, both of the elite of Natchez, both handsome. *How* the other girls envied me, having them both on the string! My name wasn't Pearlie then. Lord, how my mother would shiver if she knew I was called anything so vulgar. We were aristocrats too, you see, but not rich. No, not rich at all. I could not afford to refuse such a good offer for the sake of one that might never materialize. I put Jim off as long as I could, but Ward still would not speak, not even when I led him out into the dark garden alone the night of my eighteenth birthday. In answer to my hints concerning marriage, he only went on about what a good husband Jim would make me. I was so annoyed with him, I gave Jim the answer he wanted to hear that very evening. And so we were married. Ward was best man, and the kiss he gave me after the ceremony was more exciting than anything that happened on my wedding night."

Distaste flickered over Serena's face. "But your husband, how—?"

Pearlie shrugged. "After six years of wedded bliss, he shot himself."

"Shot himself? But you said—"

"Oh, no. I never said Ward killed him. I only said he was arrested for his murder."

The other woman's smile was mocking, hateful. Serena swallowed hard, holding to her temper with difficulty. "I don't understand."

"Neither did I," the other woman answered in deliberate provocation, though there was a small frown between her eyes. "I never refused Jim anything, not anything. His house

114

ran smoothly, our servants catered to his every whim. His favorite dishes were always on the table. I entertained his stodgy parents, and was always awake when he came to bed. Perhaps if there had been children, babies to occupy me and make him think better of himself as a man—but there were none."

Serena could spare little sympathy. "There must have been something."

"You mean I must have done something," Pearlie said, flinging her head up. "Well, all right, though I still think it was childish of Jim to be so jealous. I was bored. God, how bored I was of sitting making lumpy French knots, or tatting lace. Genteel tea parties make me sick with the endless whispers about childbirth and the change of life, or the illnesses of snotty-nosed brats. I wanted to be out and doing, but the only people who lived like that were either whores or men. Women were only allowed to join either group under one condition."

"You were unfaithful to your husband."

Pearlie laughed. "Unfaithful. How quaint, but yes, that is what it came to in the end. It was exciting. I felt alive and wanted and gloriously wicked."

"And Ward?" The words were out before Serena could stop them.

"Ward? He was a gentleman, damn him. He fended off my lures. Once he even told me in plain words that he did not intend to cuckold his friend as everyone else did. That's what makes it funny, the way things turned out."

Her face tight, Serena waited for the woman to overcome her amusement and continue. The woman's harsh laughing died away, and she gave a petulant shrug.

"It was at the harvest dance. Ward and I had had our talk in the library. It was a warm night and the windows and doors throughout the big old house were thrown open. What we did not realize was that Jim overheard a part of our conversation. He went straight to our bedroom, where he kept a pistol, then he had a horse hitched to his buggy and drove himself to his office. He wrote out a careful note explaining what he was about to do, and why, and then he held the gun to his head and pulled the trigger."

"But the note," Serena said, leaning forward with a frown. "If it was found, how did Ward come to be blamed?"

"Sheer bad luck. When Ward left the dance he decided to go by the office for a brief he had been studying. He found

Jim, read the note. He knew the fact that Jim had taken his own life would horrify his parents, people who were like family to Ward, and the reason set out so clearly in the note would cause a scandal that would nearly kill Jim's mother. The effect on my life you can imagine. With everything brought out into the open like that, with Jim's death laid at my doorstep, I would never be able to show my face outside my house again. Ward did the only thing he could see that would better things. He took the note and pistol, and rearranged the office to make it look as if Jim had been shot and robbed after a struggle. It was a good solution; the only thing that kept it from working was that Ward was seen as he left the office that night."

"There was gossip about you and the other men, I suppose," Serena said slowly.

"And of course, quite a few had noticed when Ward and I disappeared together at the dance."

"If he was seen leaving the office later, and Jim was discovered dead the next morning, then it must have looked as though he and his friend had quarreled over you."

"Not only that, the sheriff found the pistol in Ward's carriage."

"He found the pistol, but not the note?"

"How quick of you," Pearlie applauded. "No, he did not find the note, and Ward kept silent, refusing to defend himself. He would have let himself be hanged, I suppose, if I hadn't acted to save him. What Ward hadn't realized was that Jim left two notes. One to me personally, to tell me he loved me in spite of everything, and another for public consumption, to punish me for what I had done to his dream of a sweet, ordered life, for daring to want more than he had to give."

"You made the first note public? You did that for Ward?"

"Was I supposed to let him die? That would have been stupid. Besides, I knew well enough that he would never be able to turn away from me again, not after such a sacrifice. Of course, there were still those who declared that Ward had killed Jim to have me, but a search turned up the other note in Ward's jacket pocket and the authorities were satisfied. But that wasn't the end. It didn't take many days of being cut by our friends, of hearing whispers of the sordid rumors that were floating about, for Ward and me to understand that we were finished in Natchez. There was no one to console us except ourselves."

116

"If Ward was innocent, surely he could have stayed and lived the incident down?"

"He might, except that no matter how blameless he was, Ward could not forgive himself for his part in Jim's death. He wanted nothing more than to get away, to start out new in another place. And then there was the responsibility he felt for me."

Serena gave a slow nod. "What I don't understand is why you are telling me this. If you are bent on showing Ward to me in a bad light, then you are going about it in the wrong way."

"That wasn't what I had in mind at all," Pearlie said, a scowl drawing her brows together. "What you feel about him makes no difference to me. But I did mean to let you see that nothing permanent is going to come of this, of you being here with him. He's not the kind of man who can be tied down, not even if he was free, which he isn't. This thing that is between the two of us, Ward and me, goes deeper than you can imagine. We have shared so much, good times, bad times. We have been together when we were hurt inside, and afraid. We are outcasts, separated from our people and our homes, but no one can separate us from each other. Not you, not anyone."

How much of what the woman said was true, how much concocted on the moment? The tale had the ring of truth with its complications and far-reaching consequences, and yet, how many of the conclusions Pearlie had drawn from it were factual, how many the effect of her own hopes and illusions? It could not be denied that there was a bond between Ward and Pearlie, but that it was based on love twisted by guilt and remorse, as Pearlie had hinted, seemed unreasonable. If that was so, why had she and Ward ceased to console each other? Why did Pearlie give herself in orgies of debasement at night in her parlor house? And why had Ward installed a woman in his rooms beneath Pearlie's very nose, and dared her to interfere?

Serena met the gaze of the other woman, her blue-gray eyes clear. "You need not have gone to so much trouble on my account. I want nothing from Ward Dunbar. I promise you I am no danger to you."

"Danger?" Pearlie jeered with a sharp crack of laughter. "Don't you think I know that? I just wanted to make certain you didn't misunderstand Ward. He sometimes lets his protective instinct run away with him, but it doesn't mean any-

117

thing. The shell he has built around himself in the past few years is too hard to be broken by any feeling so soft as love. I know better than to expect it, which is why we suit each other so well."

Pearlie's words remained with Serena long after the woman had swished from the rooms, leaving the heavy smell of patchouli hanging in the air behind her. She wanted nothing from Ward, Serena told herself, least of all love. There was no need for her to understand him, especially if understanding was going to bring with it this wrenching sympathy. Pity was an emotion she could ill afford, unless it was for herself.

The strange twists and turns of the story she had been told seemed embedded in her mind. She could not stop thinking of it, of Ward as a young attorney with clients in Natchez in the state of Mississippi, but also in New Orleans since the cities were so close, where the civil code promulgated by Napoleon and adopted by the French had complicated legal matters for nearly a hundred years. Ward, of the Mississippi Dunbars, that old patrician family with deep roots in the South. He had denied it when she asked him. Did the scar caused by that abortive charge of murder go so deep? *I was once a gentleman,* he had told her with pain and self-loathing in his voice. Against her will, Serena began to realize his meaning.

She did not have long to consider it. Within an hour of Pearlie's departure, there came a heavy tread in the hallway outside. The door shuddered to the pounding of a hard fist.

"Coming," Serena called above the noise. She swooped through the sitting room, pushing her hair behind her shoulders in a useless gesture of tidiness before she pulled open the panel.

Otto Bruin stood outside with one fist upraised, ready to knock again. He grunted at the sight of her, his gaze dropping like a plummet to the length of her bare leg exposed through the slit in her wrapper by her haste. "Package for you."

Serena twitched the material of her skirt into place, glancing at the fat, paper-wrapped bundle the apelike man held in one huge fist. "For me?"

"That's what the woman from the dressmaker said. Got your name on it and everything. See?"

It was true. Slowly, Serena took the bundle into her hands. "Thank you, Otto," she said, the words of appreciation automatic in her preoccupation.

118

"Is that all I get?" he asked, shifting to lean over her in the doorway, propping one shoulder against the jamb while he reached across to brace his hand on the other. "It's not my job, carrying bundles up and down the stairs, you know."

Serena sent him a cool glance. "I have no money, or I would be glad to pay you for the effort you put out."

"Now you know that's not what I want, girlie."

"No? Well, I expect if you carry your complaint to Mr. Dunbar he will be able to take care of it. He—handles these things for me."

She did not wait for a reply, but swung the door shut upon the hulking giant. At the sound of his muffled curse and retreating footsteps, she gave a small nod of satisfaction.

Taking the bundle into the bedroom, she placed it carefully upon the bed and untied the string that held it. The paper fell back from a mound of gray cheviot embroidered with small satin-stitched chevrons of dark blue. Catching the material up, Serena shook it out. It unfolded to reveal a walking costume with large leg-o'-mutton sleeves full to the elbow, then tight to the wrist. The standing military collar was edged with shiny blue satin, as were the revers of the lapels. The skirt flared out into a bell that was smooth in front and gathered in folds at the back. With the dress went a plain linen underblouse, or shirtwaist, a pair of high button shoes of black leather, and a small toque of gray velvet with an upstanding blue ribbon cockade. As Serena reached for the hat, she dislodged another layer of tissue paper, revealing a set of cambric petticoats edged with lace that was threaded with pale-blue ribbon, a ribbon-trimmed chemise or corset cover, and a pair of lace-frilled, ribbon-trimmed cambric drawers. Beneath these was a cambric corset bag embroidered with a design of purple and yellow pansies. From it she took a tiny, waist-cinching corset in white satin trimmed with Irish lace threaded with ribbon. In the latest style, it had dangling ribbon garters to hold up the neatly folded silk stockings that lay at the bottom of the pile. Taking these up, marveling at their luster and sheerness, Serena discovered a square of thick white paper. The note was signed with Ward's initials.

"Try these for fit," Ward penned in a slashing scrawl. "I will come for you for our promised drive as soon as I pick up a rig from the livery stable."

Serena hesitated, torn by the need to refuse any gift from Ward, especially something so intimate as wearing apparel, and pure feminine delight in the new clothing; between the impulse to refuse to fall in with his high-handed arrangement, and the need to be out in the open air. It was the prospect of freedom that overcame her scruples. She had been confined for so long that she could not bear to miss this opportunity to get out and about.

The dress was an excellent fit. The gray material with its touches of blue complemented her coloring, while the fashionably wide sleeves and lapels, and the high collar, gave her a regal, ladylike appearance. She could have used a buttonhook for the shoes with their scalloped holes. That the buttery-soft, elegantly pointed footwear had been included amazed her. She would not have expected Ward to notice how split and worn her old shoes were.

There was one problem she could not surmount. The velvet toque was designed to sit just forward of a hair style that was pulled sleekly back and drawn into a knot on top of the head. With only the one or two pins left to her, Serena could not secure the slippery silk of her hair in its proper place. The knot she twisted up slid this way and that, the escaping tendrils spilling down the back of her neck. In frustration she searched through Ward's chest of drawers, hoping for a stray hairpin, a ribbon, anything she might use to hold it. There was nothing.

She was standing in the middle of the floor with one hand clamped to the ball of hair on top of her head when Ward swung into the sitting room and strolled toward her. He stopped in the doorway, sliding one hand into the pocket of his lounge coat.

"Not ready yet?" he asked, a quizzical look in his eyes.

"It's my hair!" she exclaimed in despair. "I can't do anything with it."

"It looks fine to me."

"It won't stay. I don't have enough pins!"

He drew his hand out of his pocket. Clasped in his fingers was a small metal box. "I just happened to pick these up at the mercantile."

"Oh, Ward," she breathed, her eyes shining as she moved toward him with her hand outstretched.

"Not so fast," he said, removing the box from her reach. "I haven't heard a word of thanks, or any other sign of appreciation so far."

"I do thank you for the clothes, of course," Serena an-

120

swered, flushing a little as she let her hand drop to her side. "I can't imagine how you arranged such a perfect fit."

"I simply gave the local seamstress a dress of yours a few days ago, with a few instructions for enlarging it here and there."

Serena frowned. "But I thought you said you gave my dress to Sanchow for rags."

Ward lowered his bright-green gaze to the metal box in his hand, shaking it a little to make the pins rattle. "Then I must have lied. No matter. We were discussing the form your appreciation should take for my outlay so far on feminine fripperies."

"You—you are as bad as Otto!"

"Otto?" he asked, his head coming up. "What has he to do with this?"

"He thought I owed him a reward too, for bringing the package from the dressmaker up the stairs." Serena lifted her chin as she spoke, her blue-gray eyes dark with contempt.

"And did he get it?"

"No! No more than you are likely to get yours."

A tight look came and went across Ward's face. "Otto I will attend to later. For now, there is one small difference between him and myself. I still have something you want." Again he rattled the pin box.

Serena released her hair, letting it cascade in a shimmering cape about her shoulders. Her fingers went to the buttons that fastened the bodice of the gray cheviot. "If it is a question of paying for what you have given me," she said, a tremor in her voice, "then you can have it back. All of it."

"No." Coming close in one swift stride, he caught her wrists in his strong fingers, stilling her movement. "That wasn't what I meant, and I think you know it well enough. I only wanted you to come to me for a change, to offer freely what I have been forced to take, until now. Forcing you to accept my every touch gives me no pleasure. I have a craving to find out what it would be like if you were willing."

Another time Serena might have answered his suggestion with scorn. But now in the deep and even timbre of his voice, she seemed to hear an echo of the promising attorney who had tried to shield his friend's good name, and protect that friend's parents from the horror and shame of their son's suicide. She met his eyes with a long and searching look, noticing for the first time the gold flecks that gleamed in their green depths. Slowly, almost without her own volition, she turned her hands in his grasp, and as he released her wrists, reached out to smooth her fingers upward beneath the lapels of his jacket. She pressed closer, and with her lashes concealing her expression, raised herself on tiptoe.

He drew in his breath as her lips touched the chiseled firmness of his mouth, but he did not move, did not stir even as she molded her soft curves to the length of his body, sliding her hands upward to clasp them behind his neck. Then with a low sound in his throat, he caught her to him, his arms closing so tightly around her she could not breathe. He sank his fingers into the silken mass of her hair that tumbled down her back, his kiss deepening, bruising in its strength.

Abruptly he lifted his head. Face shuttered, his breathing ragged, he set her from him. His hands gripped her forearms for a long moment to steady her, then he stepped away. He turned toward the sitting room, before glancing at the pins in his hand as if he had never seen them before. Stepping to the bureau, he placed them on the near corner.

"If we are going on that drive," he said, his voice rough, "we had better get started."

"Yes," Serena said, her voice faint. She did not move until he had left the room and she had heard the springs of the couch in the sitting room creak as he threw himself upon it.

With fingers that shook, she twisted her hair into a knot and secured it with pins, then set the velvet toque over it. So preoccupied was she that she scarcely looked at the set of the smart little hat. In the mirror, her face was pale and her lips crimson from Ward's kiss. Beneath her agitation she was amazed at herself, at the impulse that had made her go to him, and the desolation she had felt when at first he had held himself so stiff and unresponsive. Did he feel the same when she lay unyielding in his arms? It seemed unlikely, and yet he was clearly dissatisfied with the situation between them. Would he expect her to act as she had just now from this moment onward? If so, he would be disappointed. Though she was not certain how she came by the knowledge, she knew well that to continue in that way would be dangerous. Setting her lips in a firm line, she swung from the mirror and moved toward the sitting room.

The sun shone with the bright crystal glare of high altitudes. The air was crisply cool, fresh with the scent of spruce and pine, and yet with an undertone of woodsmoke and dried grass that spoke of fall. They took the wagon road that wound out of town in the direction of Mt. Pisgah. They passed the cemetery with its stark tombstones and blowing grass starred with purple mountain asters, and rattled past an outlying collection of decaying ranch buildings. About a mile out of town, near the turning that swept upward toward the rocky peak of the mountain, they saw a house. It lay off to the right in a small draw where the road forked. An enormous structure of white-painted clapboards with turrets and ornate gingerbread woodwork, it was an imposing residence, built on a rise that backed up the mountain slope, and fronted by a clear-running creek. Serena turned in the buggy to stare at it, and at the arched stone gateway that marked the entrance to the drive.

Ward flipped the tip of his buggy whip in the direction of the dirt roadway. "The stage route to Florissant."

"I was looking at the house."

"Oh, that's Nathan Benedict's place, the biggest and best in the district. It's patterned after the Antlers Hotel down in the Springs, has not one but two rocking-chair verandas, and a bathroom for every bedroom."

"It's rather isolated, isn't it?"

"That's the way Nathan likes it."

Nathan Benedict, the man who had given Ward the use of his private railroad car, a widower with a taste for space and his own company. Nodding in the direction of the smoke that came from one of the numerous chimneys, she said, "He seems to be in residence."

"Would you like to meet him?" Ward asked, an edge to his tone. "I'm sure it can be arranged."

Serena sent him a quick glance. Straightening in her seat, she stared ahead. "Not today, thank you. I wouldn't cut this drive short for anything."

They climbed higher and higher, winding over the mountain road with its dirt and granite gravel bed that fell sheer away on one side. Ward was silent, concentrating on his driving, urging the horses up the steep inclines. Serena exclaimed now and then at the sight of wild flowers, the flight of black-headed bluejays, so much larger and more brilliantly blue than those in Louisiana, or the glimpse of a scurrying ground squirrel that she persisted in calling a chipmunk. Gray squirrels, disturbed by their passing, chattered at them from the tops of spruce trees. The carriage rolled beneath the overhanging branches of bare-branched aspens, the horses churning the fallen leaves, like heart-shaped golden coins, under their hooves. The dust rolled out behind the buggy, settling quickly in the thin air. Wind swept down on them, soughing in the trees, fluttering the manes of the horses, and tugging at Serena's toque hat. She lifted her face to it with a swelling sensation inside her chest. Staring around her at the vast and burning blue of the sky, the rolling green hills and the majestic mountain ranges that edged the horizon, blue and silver with distance, she was aware of a sharp enjoyment bordering on content.

After a time Ward pulled up to rest the horses. The novelty of the scenery and the chilling closeness of the road's precipitous edge had worn away. Serena slanted Ward a long glance and looked away again. She cleared her throat. "It's a beautiful day."

"Yes, it is."

"I—I do appreciate your taking the time to drive me out here." The words were out of her mouth before she realized how provocative they might sound after what had passed between them.

He flung her a quick frown. "There's no need to thank me, not now. It's something I should have done long ago."

It was also something Pearlie had prompted him to do, Serena thought. Grasping at some means of changing the subject, with the other woman on her mind, she said, "I had a visitor this morning."

"Did you?" His eyes narrowed, though he stared straight ahead.

"Pearlie seemed to think it was time I knew a little of your history, and hers."

It was a moment before he spoke. "I trust you weren't too bored."

"No, not at all. I was fascinated, in fact."

"That's hard to believe."

"Why? It explained a great deal that had puzzled me."

"Such as?"

His question, Serena thought, was not idle. "Why you had denied your Southern, Mississippi heritage. How a man like you came to be a gambler."

"There's nothing wrong with being a gambler. It's a profession like any other that happens to be based on mental labor instead of physical."

"You don't believe that!"

"Don't I? From what pinnacle do you sit in judgment, Serena? You are a gambler yourself."

"I?"

124

"You, your father, every man and woman who has come to Cripple Creek. You are all ready to stake your last dollar, sometimes even your lives, on the chance of striking it rich."

"We—we aren't after something for nothing."

"Nor am I. Every time I play I risk losing what I have gained. No man has to play against me. He does it precisely because he would like to gain something without having to work for it: something for nothing."

Mulling over the answer, it was some time before Serena realized he had neatly circumvented any inquiry she might have made into the past he had left behind in Natchez.

To reach the summit of Mt. Pisgah, they had to leave the horses and buggy and climb some distance on foot. The view from that elevation was astounding, a vast panorama. They could see in every direction of the compass. To the southwest lay the Sangre de Cristos. North and west were the ranges of the continental divide. Tipped and streaked with snow, the peaks of a hundred mountains ringed the world, shading into the cumulous-studded cerulean of the sky. Pikes Peak loomed to the east, a massive red-pink shape that overshadowed the cradling walls of the volcanic crater where the gold camps lay. They could see Canon City, fifty miles to the south. Cripple Creek was spread out below them, its shanties and more substantial houses alike with the look of child's toys. Farther away in the folds of the mountain crater lay other gold-mining towns, Victor, Elkton, Alta Vista, Altman, and nearly a dozen more. Large and small, the smoke from the stacks of their homes and smelters stained the sky. And as far as the eye could see, there were yellow-brown scars of individual gold mines, each surrounded by its tailing dumps and framework of buildings, including the supports that held the drums for the hoists that let the men down into the mines. Their names rolled off Ward's tongue as he pointed them out, along with the amount of gold produced. There was the Independence, richest mine in the district, where the owner, Winfield Scott Stratton, had already taken out five or six million; the Gold Dollar, the Prince Albert, the Beacon, the Blue Bell, the Anaconda; so many, so much money it was beyond imagination. It seemed incredible, looking at that barren crater in the blinding sunlight, that the sterile land could have yielded up such riches.

It was well after noon by the time they reached the mountaintop. With great foresight, Ward had ordered a picnic lunch to be packed into a hamper and put in the back of the buggy. They spread the food on a bed of sun-steeped pine needles and settled down to a meal of barbecued ribs, cold potato salad, and beans, washed down with pure, icy-cold water from a mountain spring that seeped to the surface not far away. To top off their repast there was melon, and they threw the rinds some distance away and watched in stillness as the chipmunks squabbled over the juicy pulp that was left.

When he was finished, Ward stretched out on the ground. Within minutes, he was asleep, his eyes shaded by the gently moving shadows of the pine above them. Serena packed the remains of their meal away, then sat beside him, hugging her close-drawn knees. For a time she watched the play of the chipmunks and the fluttering explorations of a butterfly. It was so quiet the snapping sound of a grasshopper was loud and clear. The smell of the pine needles rose around her. In this sheltered spot the sun was warm, tempered by the gentle coolness of a breeze. The sweet languor of the afternoon crept in upon her. By slow and careful degrees, she stretched out her cramped legs and eased herself backward, first to one elbow, then to full length upon the ground. She watched the high-flying clouds for long moments, noting their shadings of gray as they rose up over the mountain. The sun still shone, however. Lifting her arm, she covered her eyes.

She came awake with a start. Warm lips covered hers, and there was a loose, cool sensation of exposed skin at her throat. With slow stiffness from lying in one position so long, she uncovered her eyes and let her hand come to rest on Ward's shoulder. Pleasure as gentle and somnolent as the afternoon welled inside her, and she let her mouth mold itself to his, accepting the invasion of her senses with soft and melting sweetness.

Ward's questing fingers encountered the belt at the waist of her walking costume. Sewn directly to the material of the skirt, it could not be undone. The hooks which allowed her to remove the dress were at the side. He sighed, and with slow reluctance, raised his head, settling to one elbow above her. The gold flecks were bright in the depths of his eyes as he stared down at her, and the hint of a smile tugged at one corner of his mouth.

"I knew," he said, "that buying clothes for you was a mistake."

The urge to aid him, to unfasten the hooks that confined her, was so strong that she curled her fingers into fists to

126

keep from acting upon it. Lowering her lashes, she turned her head away.

"What is it, Serena? The bright light of day? We both know you have no faults to be revealed. Is it this open space then? There aren't many in Cripple Creek with the energy to climb heights for the view, not on a working day. Besides, we are hidden here, and if there should be someone, there will be plenty of advance notice as he comes up the hill below us."

"It—it isn't that."

"If you are worried about your dress, it looks as if the best thing you can do to save it would be to see it doesn't get in my way. And if that isn't the problem, if it is my touch you object to, then you should know by now how to endure it."

She lay still, unable to formulate an answer. There was in his voice the ring of an ultimatum, and yet she was still not sure his need for her was so great that he meant to take her there on the mountainside.

"Of course, if you don't mind a few rips and tears, or being tumbled with your skirts above your head, then I don't."

"Ward, no," she breathed, catching at his hand as he slid it over the curve of her hip, reaching to drag her skirts upward. The light in his eyes was implacable. There was a pale line around his mouth, but his face was grim and the tendons of his wrist beneath her hand were as taut as steel.

"Well, Serena?" he inquired, his voice tight.

It was almost as if he regretted the threat, but having spoken, would not retreat from his position. Would he go through with it? Would he really tear her clothes from her if she did not comply with his wishes? Somehow, she did not want to think so, did not want to find out. It would be easier to do as he said, easier because the chance he meant every hard and hurtful word was too great to risk.

She swallowed hard against the press of pain in her throat, pain whose source she was unsure of. "To make certain of my willingness again?"

"It seems the only way."

"You may be right," she whispered. Still holding his hand, she pulled herself to a sitting position. Only then, when she was certain he did not intend to force her cooperation, did she release him. Lifting her arms, she removed her toque and set it carefully to one side. With her face averted, she twisted to undo the hooks that closed the side seam of her dress, and rising to her knees, dragged it off over her head. Her shirt-

127

waist came next, followed by her petticoats. She unbuttoned her corset cover and slipped it off over her arms. Wearing only her corset and drawers, holding her chemiselike corset cover to her breasts, she glanced at Ward. He lay watching her, an unfathomable look on his face. He had made no effort to undress.

"Well?" she inquired with a lift of her chin.

"Well?" he drawled.

To be so nearly naked while he was still clothed brought a flush of embarrassment to Serena's cheekbones. Why it should be so, she could not have said; she should have been used to it by now, since she had been parading in front of him for weeks in less. It was probably sham modesty brought on by the novelty of wearing underclothing, though she recognized the unreasonableness of being more disturbed by being only partially undressed instead of completely so. It was nearly as unreasonable as having her embarrassment turn to irritated anger.

"What are you waiting for?" she demanded.

"Are you in a hurry? I didn't know you were so anxious."

"You know very well I'm not!"

"Yes, I suppose so. A pity."

Two could play at that game. With the lift of an eyebrow, Serena reached for her petticoat. "Of course, if you have changed your mind—"

"No. I was just considering the possibility that you might perform the same service for me as you have for yourself."

"You mean—undress you?"

"That was the idea."

"You must be mad!" Serena dropped the petticoat and straightened her corset cover with a snap, pushing an arm into the cap sleeve.

Ward came erect with a swift, fluid movement. His hands fastened on the corset cover, stripping it from her grasp. "Yes," he grated, "I think I must be."

His eyes, dark with frustrated desire, burned into hers. Reaching for her, he pulled her against his chest. His arms clamped hard around her, pressing her breasts to the stinging wool and cold metal buttons of his jacket. His mouth took hers in brooding possession, as with unrelenting pressure he lowered her to the bed of resilient pine needles once more. He loomed over her, his weight stilling her movements, forcing her to lie quiescent as he slipped the buttons that held the waist of her drawers and stripped them from her. He removed his own clothing with a few quick, almost vicious moves, then drew her beneath him.

With a sense of shock, Serena realized she still wore her corset with its ribbon garters holding up her silk stockings. The hard muscles of Ward's thighs glided over her, intertwining with her silken limbs, sending a shiver along her nerves. The sensation was so strong, so strange and unexpected, that she was caught in a startling and incredible surge of wantonness. The hard fingers of his hand cupped the voluptuous fullness of her breast where it was pushed upward by the constraining corset. Serena lifted a hand to his shoulder, spreading her fingers over the powerful muscles. She was aware of a quickening inside her, of the weakening of her opposition.

He tasted the corner of her mouth, trailing kisses with the feel of fire along her cheek to the curve of her jawline. He paused at the tender hollow of her throat, then dropped lower to the mound of her breast that trembled to the thudding of her heartbeat. His hand smoothed the slim, satin-covered indentation of her waist, sliding down and beneath the taut-stretched ribbon garter. Her skin seemed to glow, though the brilliance of the sunlit day was receding, leaving dimness behind her tightly closed eyelids. She heard the rush of the wind in the trees overhead, felt it brush her skin. She knew a feeling of intense life, of fullness waiting to encompass and hold, and then she felt the deep thrusting strength of him inside her. Her senses expanded, floating, surging with a primitive rhythm old beyond human thought. She felt free and yet earthbound, swept up by the plunging ardor that weighted her to the ground, soaring even as she was gathered close for one final, shuddering fall.

Ward brushed away the tendrils that had escaped from her knotted hair to blow across her face. He cupped her cheek, brushing his lips across her eyes. With a sigh that seemed to shudder through his frame, he eased from her. Serena heard the rustle of his clothing as he pulled on his trousers. Opening her eyes to slits, she watched as he shrugged into his shirt and began to button it. His face was shadowed as he attended to that small task, and there was a frown between his eyes.

A shiver caught Serena by surprise. The sun had gone behind a bank of gray clouds. Here in the shade, there was an uncomfortable chill in the wind.

She stirred, levering herself to one elbow, reaching for her petticoats and corset cover, panting a little as she tried to regain her breath against the tight squeeze of her corsets.

They dressed in silence. Constraint crept in upon them along with a feeling of haste as the blue of the sky was invaded by a spreading cover of gray, rising up over the mountains from the southeast, and lightning flickered over the distant peaks. Serena was pulling the lace-edged jabot of her shirtwaist into place over the lapels of her jacket when Ward spoke.

"Serena—"

She looked up quickly at the note of hard reluctance in his voice.

"I've been meaning to tell you. I will be leaving for Denver in the morning."

"Denver?" Her fingers were suddenly cold and clumsy; still, she could not acknowledge surprise. She had suspected something.

"I have business to attend to there. I'll only be gone a few days."

"You will be coming back then?"

He swung toward her. "Coming back? Of course I will. You don't have to worry about that, or anything else. You will be all right where you are, above the Eldorado."

"Yes, I'm sure I will." She looked away out over the landscape with its shades of yellow-green, gray-green, and black-green.

"I'll pack tonight and leave on the early-morning train after the Eldorádo closes. I—I would take you with me, but it is going to be nothing more than a series of meetings in smoky club rooms. I thought you might prefer being relieved of my presence for a time."

His words seemed to carry a shading of evasiveness. Was there more to it than he was saying? Was it, perhaps, that he preferred to be free of her presence also? The possibility was not a comfortable one, but it had to be faced.

"I—expect I can manage," she answered.

"Yes," he said, his tone grim and his eyes dark and hard as emeralds, "so do I."

Chapter Eight

The sound of a train whistle, long, clear, and mournful, jerked Serena from sleep. It was the all-night train from Denver, coming in. Soon it would be leaving again, and Ward would be on it. Serena wrenched over in the bed, giving her pillow a thump. She didn't care. She was just a little piqued that Ward could leave her so easily. The least he could have done was come to tell her goodbye. It might be he considered what had passed between them on the mountainside the afternoon before as their farewell, but somehow, to her, it lacked the right note of regret.

What would he do, she wondered, if she dressed and walked down to the station depot to see him off? Would he be glad, or annoyed? Or worse still, would he be merely disinterested? She could not begin to guess. Sometimes she thought he cared a little for her, at others it seemed she was no more than a convenience, someone to warm his bed and relieve the tensions that built up inside him at night over the gaming tables.

No, she wouldn't go down. That would look as if she was upset that he was leaving. It might even appear that she was begging to be taken along. That would never do. She was just as happy to be left alone. She would be fine by herself, just fine. The first thing she could do would be get a little more sleep, now that the din had died away from the barroom below, and the dance halls with their tinny pianos and squeeze-box waltzes had closed for the night.

It was a good resolution, but she was still awake, listening to the early-morning traffic and the raucous braying of burros known as Rocky Mountain canaries, when she heard the departing whistle of the train for Denver.

The day passed slowly. Sanchow brought breakfast, more than enough for two, leaving it outside the door as always. He must have learned of Ward's absence as he left through the barroom, however, for when luncheon time came, he did not appear. Several times Serena went out into the hall and looked up and down, but there was no sign of the Chinaman. Only the remains of breakfast, fast drying in the arid air, sat in the hall, waiting to be retrieved.

It was an oversight, Serena told herself. Her dinner would doubtless be on time, if not earlier than usual. Sanchow would be full of apologies, bowing himself in half, fearful that he had offended, that he had lost a regular and valued client like Ward. It would do her no harm to wait that long.

Darkness fell, and still the Chinese restaurant owner had not appeared. Driven by hunger, Serena dressed herself in her gray cheviot and descended the stairs to the barroom.

"Well, look who's here!" Pearlie cried, saluting Serena with a derisive gesture of the glass of golden liquid she held as she leaned against the mahogany bar. "To what do we owe this honor?"

The crowd in the barroom was not small despite its being so near time for the evening meal. There were quite a few men at the long bar partaking of the bread and meat, cheese and peanuts laid out for customers, a custom with beginnings in New Orleans that Ward had imported. Serena averted her eyes from the sight as she moved farther into the brightly lighted room, coming to a halt beside Pearlie. One or two of the men glanced in her direction, but the rumble of voices and clank of glasses made it possible for her to speak to Pearlie without being overheard.

"I came down to ask if anyone had seen anything of Sanchow. He didn't bring my lunch, and now he is late with dinner."

"And you want your supper?"

Serena did not like the smile on the other woman's face. "That was the idea."

"I am afraid I have bad news for you. You were supposed to have had lamb chops for lunch, but that happens to be

132

Otto's favorite meal. The poor thing was so hungry he couldn't help himself. He ate every bite on the tray."

"And my dinner?" Serena asked, her lips tightening.

"Beef stew," Pearlie said with a small moue of distaste. "Otto didn't like it, so he threw it out."

"Threw it out?"

"That's what I said."

"But what am I supposed to eat?"

"The choice is entirely up to you. You will find any number of eating places in town. Don't look for Sanchow, however. Like a fool, he insisted on bringing you another bowl of stew, and Otto had to get rough to convince him you didn't want it. I am afraid Otto may have gone a bit too far. He doesn't like Chinamen, you see. He's always said Sanchow should have been run out of town where the miners got rid of the other coolies last year."

"He—he isn't dead?" Serena had come to like the smiling little yellow man. He had tried so hard to please.

"I don't think so, but I am sure he won't be cooking for a while."

"If that's true," Serena said slowly, "then there's no place I can go to eat. I have no money."

Pearlie laughed. "How tight-fisted of Ward. But I'm sure, if you are reasonable, a source of income can be arranged."

"What do you mean?" Serena had a good idea of the trend this conversation was taking, but the question had to be asked.

"I mean," Pearlie answered, her face growing hard, "that if you want to eat, you will come down out of your ivory tower and earn your way here with the rest of us. I think a number or two on stage will be a good place to start."

"You know how Ward feels about me being in the bar-room," Serena said. "Just because he isn't here doesn't mean that has changed."

Pearlie drank off the liquor she held and set the glass on the bar with a sharp bang. The glitter of triumph in her pale-blue eyes, she said, "Don't be too sure. Ward and I had a long talk last night. It's obvious that your talents are being wasted up there in his rooms. It is selfish of him to keep you to himself. When I pointed it out, he was able to see you would be much better off down here where you could have a few drinks, a good time. We need a little something to liven up the show, a new face, not to mention a new form. The Golden Horn down the street has a new girl they are advertising up and down the avenue as being straight from Paris. She never saw France, of course, but who cares so long as the miners believe it? I thought we could post a billboard outside touting you as the toast of London. Men like exotic women; look at Little Egypt."

"If you think I am going to entertain on stage, or anywhere else, you are much mistaken!"

"Am I? We'll see. I believe you will think again when you get hungry enough."

"I can always go elsewhere."

"No," Pearlie said, tilting her head to one side with a considering look. "No, I think not. The only job you would be able to find would be just like what I am offering you here at the Eldorado. We may as well have the pleasure of introducing you as anyone. And if I were to let you go, Ward would be sure to think I had turned you out. I couldn't allow that."

"I don't see how you can stop me." Serena swung on her heel, starting toward the door.

"Otto!"

At the sharp command in the woman's voice, the big man rose from a table in one dim corner and lumbered toward Serena.

Unwilling to grapple with the Eldorado's bouncer, Serena came to a halt and turned slowly back to face the smugness of the other woman.

"You see?" Pearlie inquired with an unpleasant smile. "Now come, my dear. I know you will listen to reason. I think you have that much intelligence—and imagination. You can imagine, can't you, what will happen to you if I allow Otto to take you into the back room? He—is not a man to be bothered by a woman's screams. And if you should still prove stubborn, something I don't expect, mind, there are other ways. Have you ever been drugged? It can be an unpleasant sensation, unless you are willing. A woman is so helpless in that condition. While she is unconscious, anything can be done to her, anything at all. There are other measures used by some of the more hardened females who run parlor houses to keep their girls in line." A smile flickered across Pearlie's face. "I have never held with such abuse of the merchandise myself, but I know some who enjoy it, and its effectiveness in subduing temperamental females is amazing."

The glazed look in the other woman's eyes as she smiled made Serena feel a little sick. Was there really no choice

134

except to do as Pearlie suggested? There seemed none, and yet it went against the grain to yield.

"If I could bring myself to do as you say," Serena said slowly, "it would not serve. I have nothing to wear except what I am standing up in. I don't think the miners would find it much of an attraction when they can see the same thing on the street any day of the week."

"You are quite right," Pearlie agreed, letting her gaze flicker over Serena's walking costume. "I will have to lend you something of mine. With a few adjustments here and there, it should fit well enough. Or better still, is there by chance anything in your long-lost trunk that might be suitable? If so, I believe I can lay hands on it for you."

"My trunk?" Serena repeated. She could not believe she had heard right. She had counted it gone beyond recall long weeks ago.

Pearlie signaled for another drink. The glance she slanted in Serena's direction was filled with malicious amusement. "Ward, devil that he is, had them put it in the storeroom in back. Why, I couldn't say, unless he preferred to have you dressed, or undressed, to suit himself."

"You mean it's been here all along?"

"Since the day after you got here. I take it you would like to have it?"

"Yes," Serena said. "Yes, I would."

"Good. I'll have it sent up then. Come on down when you are ready. I'll send out for food." Ward's partner raised her filled glass to her lips, took a sip, then added, "I expect it will get here just about the time the first show is finished."

The contents of her trunk had been tumbled, as though someone had rummaged through it. Serena was not really surprised to discover her small hoard of money and her bag of foodstuff missing. Taking her dresses out one by one, she shook the wrinkles from their folds. It was odd how much more faded and worn they looked since she had seen them last, and how hopelessly outmoded. It was as though it had been years since she had worn them, years in which she had become a woman instead of a child.

The only thing that appeared the same was her mother's ivory silk ballgown. With reverent care, she lifted it from the trunk and spread it over the foot of the bed. Removing the matching slippers with their gilt heels, she set them beside it. With these, she placed her locket and her necklace and earrings of gold and seed pearls. Finally she laid a fan of

135

painted silk with carved ivory sticks on the shining bodice. How much more value these things had now that she had lost everything else. To have them returned to her after so long gave her a feeling of completeness and comfort, as if she had been lost, rather than her belongings.

How. had Ward dared to keep them from her? No matter how miserable she might have looked in her undersized clothing, he had no right. The man took too much upon himself, making her his kept woman, dictating where she should go and what she should wear. Perhaps it was a good thing she was getting out from under his thumb.

He might have told her, might have explained that he was bored with her company instead of leaving it to Pearlie. Was it possible it was Ward's idea that she still be kept at the Eldorado instead of making her own way? Maybe he wanted her conveniently at hand, even if he no longer required exclusive access to her person? Much good it might do him!

Yesterday afternoon on the mountain, hadn't she suspected this was coming? He had behaved so strangely. Something had been on his mind; it must have been this. Why couldn't he have said something then? Odd. She would have sworn Ward was not the kind of man to shirk such a task, no matter how disagreeable.

The door into the sitting room swung open, then closed with a slam. The tap of wooden heels came on the pine floors, stopping abruptly as they reached the wool rugs. Serena was jerked from her absorption. With a quick turn, she moved to the bedroom door.

It was Pearlie who came toward her. Over her arm she carried a dress in a garish shade of yellow-green trimmed with the sparkle of black spangles. A smile curled the woman's lips as she saw Serena standing in the door with one hand braced on the frame.

"Did the barman bring your trunk?"

"Yes, he did."

"Since you were so long in coming down, I thought you might still be having problems finding something to wear. I brought you this, just in case."

"That was—kind of you," Serena said, her tone dry as she gingerly accepted the costume the woman offered. The bodice, with its gaudy edging of spangles, was scooped daringly low. The skirt was raised to knee level in front, angling to the floor in the back. It was clear that no allowance had been made for the wearing of either corsets or petticoats in its

136

design. If any confirmation of this last fact was needed, Serena had only to look at Pearlie, who wore a replica of the dress in ice blue though it was trimmed in marabou rather than spangles.

"The fit may not be perfect, but it should do for tonight," Pearlie went on. "I've had a little talk with Timothy at the piano. It's all arranged for you to do a solo in honor of the occasion. Try to make it something special, won't you? Just tell Timothy what you have in mind. He can fumble his way through anything."

"A solo? You can't mean it!"

"Why not?" Pearlie inquired, smiling a little at Serena's dismay.

"I can't. I haven't the least claim to talent, even if I had time to think about what I should do."

"Neither do the other girls have talent, but they manage. All you need to do is make a loud noise to the music, smile and wink a few times, and move around on the stage enough to give the men a glimpse of what they will be trying so hard to see."

"I couldn't." Serena tried to keep her voice firm, but there was a sinking sensation in the pit of her stomach.

"You'll manage." Pearlie swung toward the door. "You will have to."

Serena stood staring at the costume in her hands long after Pearlie had slammed her way out of the room. She knew well enough what Pearlie intended. The woman wanted to embarrass her, and at the same time, present her as an available girl, a possible addition to the parlor-house roster. She had watched such tactics before when new girls came in off the street. She had watched as they smiled, leaning forward to shake their bosoms and allowing the men a clear view, or turned to swing their backsides, flipping up their skirts. Most tried to imitate their idea of a Parisian can-can. There had even been one girl who had gone so far as to do the high kicks in true French style, without her drawers. The miners had nearly brought the place down around her ears. The act had lasted only through the second night, however. A visit from the town sheriff, followed by a lucrative invitation from a combination dance hall and brothel called the Topic, had ended her stage career.

With an abrupt gesture, Serena tossed the gaudy dress on the couch and watched it slither to the floor. She would not do it. She would not appear in public in such tawdry trappings, not even if she had to make her debut in corset and petticoats, like another of the more famous chanteuses along the avenue. At least such undergarments were not deliberately constructed to reveal her body to all and sundry. If she had to make a fool of herself, there was no need to compound her embarrassment by doing it nearly naked.

Her mouth in a straight line, Serena turned back into the bedroom. She had taken no more than two steps when she came to an abrupt halt. Her narrowed eyes fastened on the silk ball gown that lay across the bed. There had been a time, during a brief period of prosperity, when Serena's mother had insisted she learn to play the piano and accompany herself as she sang. Her teacher had been Mrs. Walsh herself. Serena's mother had enjoyed the advantages of both a French and an English governess as she was growing up. The knowledge she had acquired she had attempted to pass on to her daughter, including an appreciation of music. The two of them, with much excitement and secret planning, had arranged concerts for Serena's father. Clad in a silk dress made from one of her mother's old gowns, with the soft ringlets of her hair caught up by a ribbon and her hands folded demurely in front of her, Serena had sang the sweet old melodies traditional to the Deep South. That had been long ago, of course. But what had pleased her father once might, with a few sophisticated touches, be acceptable to other men. It was worth the try.

A short time later, as Serena descended the stairs in her mother's gown, the idea of claiming the attention of the miners with soft, sweet airs seemed ludicrous. The rumble of men's voices rolled toward her in profane waves, along with the clink of beer mugs, the slap of cards, rattle of dice, and monotonous drone of faro and roulette dealers. Above it all rose the sharp tinkle of a piano in ragtime, punctuated by the dull clang of the brass cuspidors that lined the bar as a tobacco-chewing customer found his mark. A blue fog of smoke hung in the air from cigars and hand-rolled brown-paper cigarettes. Combined with the smell of tobacco was the scent of woodsmoke from the potbellied stove that sat in the middle of the room, the sour odor of ale and beer, and the indescribably animalistic smell of unwashed men in close quarters. Those men not taking part in the gambling lolled in their chairs, laughing, swearing, ogling the bargirls that passed among them and pinching any section of their anatomies that remained too long within reach.

Serena lifted her hand to the necklace of gold and seed pearls at her throat. How could the attention of such a boisterous crowd, in such a rude atmosphere, be caught by what she had to offer, much less be held? Nothing short of bright and brassy impudence combined with color and glitter could make them sit up and take notice.

And if they did notice, what then? The men below expected their entertainment to be loud, fast, and titillating. If she disappointed them they might well boo her off the stage, or worse. She had heard that unsatisfactory performers at the music halls and vaudeville houses along the street were pelted with rotten eggs and overripe tomatoes and cabbages. Singing for her supper was one thing, having it thrown at her was something else again. In addition, the corset she wore, though it gave her a waistline of fashionable narrowness and increased the soft curves visible above the decolletage of her dress, also compressed her lungs so tightly she could barely draw breath, much less sing. It was partially the effect, no doubt, of hurrying to get dressed, but she was beginning to think a tight corset in the thin air of the mountains was a mistake.

It could not be helped. Already the men in the barroom were turning to stare at her. There was nothing to do but descend.

At the foot of the stairs she paused. Pearlie was nowhere to be seen, and she was uncertain of just what she was supposed to do. Otto Bruin, stationed nearby, pushed away from the wall and sidled toward her. He placed one enormous hand on the newel post in what he obviously considered to be a debonair pose, and gave her a wolfish grin that exposed yellowed teeth.

"My, but ain't you purty tonight."

"Thank you," Serena replied, her tone cool as she spared no more than a glance in his direction.

He reached out to finger the cap sleeve of her gown. Jerking his head toward Ward's rooms above them, he said, "It's shore gonna be nice to have you down here with us, instead of up there all by your lonesome."

"I'm glad you think so. For myself, I doubt it will make any difference."

Twitching her sleeve from his grasp, Serena stepped away from him, then struck out across the room. She made her way through the tables, taking a path which skirted the more crowded area. As she weaved in and out, avoiding a chair

139

here and the outstretched legs of a drunken miner there, she flung a fleeting glance over her shoulder at Otto. A black scowl knifed between his small black eyes and his hands were propped on his hips as he stood staring after her. There was something so brooding and unpleasant about his stance that Serena looked quickly away again.

As she turned back, she had to sidestep to keep from colliding with a man just pulling out a chair at one of the tables near the stage. Tall and thin, in his mid-thirties, he wore a gray-striped suit with leather patches on the elbows. There was a crooked smile on his angular face, and he carried a bottle by the neck in one hand and a glass in the other.

"I'm sorry," Serena said on a gasp. "I didn't see you."

"I'm the one who should be apologizing, ma'am, for standing like a statue when I sure saw you coming."

A faint color rose to her cheekbones at the admiration shining in his hazel eyes. Excusing herself, Serena slipped past him and hurried on.

The stage of the Eldorado was located against the back wall between the staircase and the long, mirrored mahogany bar. Not large by any means, it was framed in red velvet draperies edged with gold fringe. The footlamps were coal-oil lanterns backed by reflectors. Between acts, a canvas curtain weighted by a boom and painted with a scene of snow-capped mountains encircled by advertisements for patent medicine and soap was rolled down. The piano sat at floor level at an angle to the stage so that Timothy could see what was going on. The pianist was a genial Welshman with a fair and true tenor voice who sang between shows and doubled as the announcer. In his early fifties, he had a broken nose, a weak eyelid that stayed half shut, and an appetite for warm beer. Mournful and boisterous by turns, he loved music and the ladies, not necessarily in that order.

"My, but you look beautiful tonight, Miss Serena," he greeted her without missing a note of the polka he was beating out on the piano. "It's a treat to have you down here among us, it is indeed."

The droop to his eyelid, almost like a wink, combined with his grin, made him look as if he were enjoying some droll joke. "Thank you, Timothy," Serena said, summoning a smile. "I think Pearlie told you that I was suppose to sing tonight?"

"That she did, sweetness."

"I have an idea of what I would like to do."

140

When he had heard her out, Timothy looked dubious. "You're sure that's what you want? You're taking a mighty big chance, you know, love."

"Who is taking a chance?"

The words, charmingly accented, were spoken by a woman who had strolled up behind them, placing a hand with casual familiarity on Timothy's shoulder. It was the girl called Spanish Connie, the nearest the Eldorado had to a star for its nightly shows. Serena had watched her many times as she performed her turn upon the stage, dancing with fire and fury, or circulating with drinks about the gaming tables. She had little to do with the other girls, holding herself aloof from them. Most of the time she seemed to be involved in a running feud with them, one she extended to Pearlie herself on occasion. The costume she wore was of severe, form-fitting black velvet with a full, circular skirt that was caught up on one hip to reveal the lining, consisting of row upon row of fluted scarlet ruffles, and a shocking length of shapely leg encased in a black fishnet stocking. Her hair was parted in the middle, worn loose to float like a dark cloud upon her shoulders. Her dark eyes were surrounded by black, gleaming lashes and arching brows. The only other color about her was the flash of gold earrings in her ears and the brilliant carmine of her painted lips. Her sultry beauty and tempestuous manner made her a favorite among the miners, a factor that, with her ability to hold the attention of the crowd, made her place secure. It also allowed her to be discriminating in the men she allowed to escort her out the back door of the Eldorado, something of which she took full advantage. The abrupt and arbitrary way she made her choices was not popular, but few dared dispute it, just as few of the girls with whom she worked dared trespass upon her privileges. The reason was not hard to find. The high slit of her skirt opening as she danced exposed a sharp, jewel-handled stiletto thrust into a lace-edged black garter above her knee.

Timothy glanced over his shoulder at the Spanish girl. "Serena here thinks she can flutter her fan, give the boys a few old ballads, and they will be satisfied."

The girl called Spanish Connie sent Serena a slow, considering look that began with the shiny ringlets piled on top of her head with one cascading over her shoulder and ended with the satin slippers peeping from the hem of her gown. Speaking as though Serena was not there, she said to the piano player, "You think they will not be, my friend?"

141

"I have my doubts. But what's more to the point, Pearlie left word she was to sing something lively and jump around, show what she's got. If Serena here goes against her, there's no telling what she might do."

"Bah! What does Pearlie know? She would like for me to do the same. Dress like the others, giggle and be stupid and coy like the others so she can stroll around like a peacock, the only one who is not acting silly."

"Peacocks who stroll around with their tails spread, Connie, my heart, are of the male persuasion."

"What does it matter?" the girl said, dismissing the subject with a wave of her hand. "You know what I mean."

"I think I do, but where does that leave Serena?" Timothy had come to the end of the polka. He let his hands wander over the keys of the piano, providing easy background music.

"I'm not sure," Spanish Connie said, tipping her head to one side. "She looks beautiful, very pure and virginal."

"Like a lady," Timothy said with a nod of agreement.

"Exactly so, one who is unawakened. One for which a man might pay much, even all he has, to call his own. Not, you understand, just because she is pretty to look upon. It will be a thing of the mind, the true seat of desire. It will be because of the memories she will inspire."

"But Connie, my love, men come in here to forget, not to remember."

"They must be made to stop and think on the past. We will lower the lights. The stage will be dark except for, perhaps, a few candles. You will play softly with a sweetness that falls gently on the ear. Serena will move slowly into the candlelight—no, she will light the candles herself. She will spread her fan and cast down her eyes, and then she will sing—what will you sing, Serena?"

To be included in the conversation was so unexpected that Serena stumbled over her answer. "I—I could sing 'Black Is the Color of My True Love's Hair.' Or 'Barbara Allen.'"

"Yes, and you can sing slowly, most slowly and with sadness, the song that comes from your South, 'Dixie'?"

"Yes," Serena said, a warm smile curving her mouth. "I could do that."

"But 'Dixie' is a march," Timothy protested.

Spanish Connie flicked his ear with her nails. "It is also a song of memories, and many, many of the miners come from that area that was once so rich and is now so poor."

"We'll be lucky if anybody lets her open her mouth," Timothy snorted. "You know this ain't what the boys will be expecting. They want to have a kick-up-their-heels good time, not have somebody remind them of their sweethearts and mothers, or a war that was lost."

"You are wrong, my friend. Everyone likes at times to feel a little sad. And then afterward, when I come out to clap my hands and dance the flamenco for them, to banish their woe and make them think of the delights of wickedness instead of goodness, they will be so grateful!"

"Ah, Connie my girl, there's a devil in you."

The Spanish girl smiled, shaking her hair back with a gesture that accented the exquisite lines of her throat. "I fear so, my friend, but what would you? There's a devil in all of us."

"Even Serena?" Timothy said with a wink and a nod in her direction.

"Especially Serena," Spanish Connie said, her dark eyes wide. "Because she does not yet know he is there."

The other girl's air of superiority did not sit well with Serena. Nevertheless, she could not help but be grateful for her aid. Smiling grimly, the Spanish girl whisked her backstage, and sent for a brass candelabra and a teakwood stand to be brought from the parlor house as stage props. With sharp words and sheer presence, she held the other girls at bay, quelling both their feline curiosity and indignation at the special treatment being accorded Serena.

From the sidelines Serena watched as the show began with a number to the tune of "The Old Gray Mare," one that had the girls prancing about the stage pretending to be harnessed to a freight wagon, dodging the whip that one of the barmen, a man with waxed and curled mustachios, popped with gusto about their hips. The men in the audience laughed at the antics. Their guffaws rang louder still as the "team" turned on the driver and each girl brought out her own small ribbon-bedecked whip to retaliate in kind, chasing the luckless man from the stage.

Timothy, to slow the pace a bit, sang a medley of Irish tunes. Halfway through the last, he gave a nod to a barman, who began to lower the house lights. A mutter of protest arose from the card tables, growing louder as the last tenor note died away. Timothy gave a flourish upon the piano and began Serena's introduction. Serena, clasping her hands together on an upsurge of panic, caught snatches of what he was saying. "Belle of the Old South, fresh from an engage-

143

ment in New Orleans, the Queen City at the mouth of the Mississippi, where she bedazzled the opera crowds! The Incomparable, Serena!"

The curtain creaked upward to show the darkened apron of the stage. Beside her, Spanish Connie struck a lucifer and lit a taper. Thrusting it into Serena's hand, the girl gave Serena a small push.

As she moved into view of the miners, the hubbub began to die away, except for one slurred voice that kept calling, "Bring on the girlies, bring on the girlies!"

Timothy played the introduction to the song she would sing, a soft, pensive melody in a minor key. As Serena touched the taper to the candles in the brass candelabra, the flames trembled with her uneven breathing. Glowing like tiny fires in the dark stillness of her eyes, the light cast a warm and golden glow over the lovely lines of her pale face and shoulders. It gleamed along the gold and pearls of her necklace below the black ribbon of her locket, and shimmered in the silken folds of her gown. Carefully timing her movements to the music, Serena finished her task, blew out the taper, and slowly spread the painted silk of the fan that hung from a cord at her wrist. On cue, her voice rose clear and sweet in the old love song.

"'Black, black, black is the color of my true love's hair...his eyes, they are so wondrous fair—'"

"What is this? What's going on? Turn up the lights at once! Get her down from there!" It was Pearlie, making her way from the back door of the barroom, pushing through the tables, stumbling in the semidarkness. At the sound of her petulant anger, other voices joined hers, demanding light, and the girls. *"Bring out the girlies—"*

Above this growing noise there were whistles and calls for quiet. Serena's voice grew unsteady, threatening to break.

It was at that moment that a man at one of the closer tables pushed back his chair and got to his feet. He stepped between Pearlie and the stage, effectively blocking her progress. Though he did not touch her, she stopped as though she had been jerked to a halt. The man inclined his head in a short bow.

"I would rather you didn't stop the show," he said. "I would like to hear her sing."

His words were not loud, and yet they seemed to carry. Pearlie's reply was lost in the babble around her, but her look of stupefaction was enough. From where they stood si-

144

lence began to spread, moving outward like the ripples in a pond.

The man who had come to her rescue was the same one she had nearly collided with earlier. Turning from Pearlie as though he had forgotten she was there, he made his way back to his seat without removing his gaze from Serena there upon the stage. It was gratitude for his intervention, and amazement for its success, that made her send him a warm smile. The look that sprang into his eyes was so diffident and at the same time so admiring and quietly approving that it gave her confidence. Unconsciously, she found her gaze turning in his direction again and again. As she directed her songs to the one man who seemed to appreciate them, she failed to notice the air of rapt attention that had fallen upon her audience, the aching quiet into which her clear and carrying words fell. The miners followed her every movement as if memorizing the details of hair and dress, watching her graceful gestures, taking a collective indrawn breath as she lifted her skirts to take a step, showing the merest glimpse of finely turned ankle and gilt-heeled slippers, then letting it out as the fair sight was covered once more. Her first inkling of her effect came when halfway through the first stanza of "Dixie," the men began to remove their hats, hold them over their hearts, and come to their feet in respect for the song and the singer. For some reason she could not explain, the sight brought the fullness of tears to her throat. It was with their richness threading her voice that she came at last to an end.

The whistles, the applause and yells roared against the ceiling. Near the stage a man smacked his lips and nudged the miner beside him in the ribs. In a voice loud enough to be heard clearly he said, "That's the gal for me. Just like falling into a bed of roses."

His companion snorted. "You're crazy in the head, you drunk galoot. Didn't you see them gold heels on them slippers she was wearing? She's too rich for my blood, or yours either. You couldn't afford her if you high-graded for a month!"

High-grading meant to take gold-rich ore out of the mines on the sly in lunch pails, pockets, and pants cuffs; to get rich on the side. It was a compliment in its own way. Thinking of Pearlie's probable reaction to such an attitude from the miners, Serena could not help but be pleased. She was less happy to hear the description applied to her by the miner taken up and repeated by others.

"Gold Heels," the first man said with a laugh. "She's some fancy piece all right. Gold Heels. That's just the name for her."

Sinking into a low curtsy in recognition of the applause, Serena heard the name running like wildfire over the room. It seemed that Ward had been right that night on the prairie so many weeks ago. The miners were quick to bestow a name on anyone who failed to provide one for himself.

Rising, moving from the stage, Serena vowed she would never answer to this new title, no matter how common it became. She had never asked for this kind of notoriety. She had never asked for it, nor for the uncertain future to which it led. In spite of Pearlie and Otto, even in spite of Ward, there must be a way out. There must be.

Chapter Nine

Otto was waiting for her where the steps leading from the stage descended into the barroom. He held a covered tray in his enormous hands, and there was a crafty look in his eyes.

"I've got your supper here. Pearlie said as how it would be all right with her if you wanted to eat it upstairs."

"Thank you. I would prefer that," Serena said, reaching for the tray.

Otto did not let go. "I'll tote it for you. I ain't got nothing else to do just now."

"I can manage for myself."

"Nah, I want to do it. Besides, Pearlie said I could keep you company."

Retaining her grip on the tray, Serena said carefully, "I appreciate her thoughtfulness, and yours, but I would just as soon be alone."

"Can't allow that," Otto said with a shake of his big head. "No telling what you was to get up to, if I did. I'll just go along with you, like I was told."

Serena did not like the way he was looking at her, nor the wet sheen on his loose lips. Still, it appeared she had no choice except to make do with his escort if she wanted to eat.

"Very well." With her lashes lowered and the high color of anger flushing her cheekbones, she preceded Otto across the room and up the stairs. She indicated a place on the table in her sitting room where she wanted him to set the tray, then seated herself behind it.

"Now this is something like it," Otto commented as he flung himself down on the oriental couch across from her.

"Have you eaten?" she asked with stiff politeness.

"Yeh, I et long time ago."

The formalities observed, Serena took the napkin that covered the food and placed it in her lap, then picked up her fork and knife. The meal, consisting of steak with hash-brown potatoes, eggs, and butter-fried bread, was delectable, very nearly worth what it had cost her. She would have enjoyed it more if she had not had an audience, of course. Try as she might, she could not ignore the big man lolling across from her, watching her with all the greedy hunger of an animal watching its prey. His gaze lingered on the bodice of her dress as if he were trying to penetrate the material to her flesh underneath. Every few minutes he would shift in his seat uncomfortably, tugging at his crotch as if he itched. Now and then he would wipe his hand over his mouth, rubbing it down over his thick neck to pull at his collar.

At last Serena pushed back her plate, though she kept her water glass in her hand. Taking a sip, she swallowed, glancing at Otto. "I suppose I am to put in an appearance downstairs again tonight?"

"Pearlie didn't say." He pushed himself upright and surged to his feet to lumber around the table toward her. Stretching out his hand, he snatched the glass from her fingers and set it to one side, sloshing water over the brim. "She sure don't expect to see you no time soon."

Serena jumped to her feet, brushing at the water that had splashed onto the silk of her dress. "What are you doing?" she exclaimed.

"I'm doing what I've been wanting to do for a long time," he growled, pushing her chair from his path so that it crashed backward to the floor. "Something I been wanting to do ever since I saw you that night down in the Springs."

"You wouldn't. Lay one hand on me and you'll be out of a job, if Ward doesn't kill you!" Despite her brave words, she could not prevent herself from backing away from his steady, arm-swinging advance.

"Huh. You ain't Dunbar's fancy piece any more. He finally got tired and put you out, shoved you downstairs with the rest of the girls."

"That's not true."

148

"I know better. I know, 'cause Pearlie said it, and she always knows what Dunbar's thinking. She said nobody was going to care now if I got under your skirts, and that's just what I mean to do, right here and now."

"That's what you think," Serena said, her voice hard. Whirling, she darted around the table, threading her way through the couches and ottomans that crowded the small room.

With a curse, Otto stumbled after her, kicking a table, shoving aside the chair she pushed into his path.

The outside door was her objective, and she circled toward it, slipping quickly behind the sandalwood table that sat at the end of a couch. The brass vase of peacock feathers on its surface teetered as she brushed against it. Sending a fleeting glance at Otto, she saw him charging toward her like a rutting animal. Without hesitation, she picked up the vase and threw it at his head.

It struck in a whirling rain of iridescent feathers. A gash appeared on his forehead, and a red wash of blood flowed into his eyes. Growling, he wiped at it with his sleeve.

Serena did not stop to watch. She skirted the elephant-foot table with its bowl of waxed fruit, dived for the door, dragged it open, and flung herself out into the hall. Behind her, Otto bellowed in rage. She heard the shuddering thud of his footsteps as he came after her. With her heart pounding in her chest, she ran. It was as though she could feel the hot, fetid breath of the bouncer on the back of her neck. The stairs seemed so far away, far too distant for her to reach.

And then she was upon them. The banister was under her hand. Her breath rasped in her throat. Below, a pale blur of faces turned toward her, indistinct in the gray pall of smoke.

There came a thumping crash as Otto leaped down the stairs behind her, taking them three at the time. Cruel fingers sank into her shoulder and she was pulled to a halt, wrenched off balance so that she fell against the barrel chest of the apelike man.

"No!" she cried, pushing away with all her strength. She swung her hand with pure revulsion, catching him a ringing, stinging blow on his wire-whiskered jaw. He dragged her to him, digging his fingers into her arms, giving her a hard shake that snapped her head forward on her neck. His foul breath was in her face. She felt his long arm encircle her, flattening the slender curves of her body against his paunchy, short-legged frame. She heard his grunt of pleasure, saw his yellow-toothed grin and the dilating of his eyes as he brought his face closer to hers, felt his hard fingers fumble at the silk that covered her breast. In sick rage, she twisted, trying to bring her arms up, to loosen his straining grip. The next moment, the hand that mauled her was jerked away.

"Let her go. Now."

The voice that spoke was neither loud nor harsh; still, it carried the unmistakable stamp of authority, the ring of power. Otto stiffened, a look of uncertainty coming into his face. He seemed reluctant to look at the tall, sandy-haired man in a gray suit that held his arm.

"I said, let her go."

The strength went out of Otto. "Mr. Benedict," he whined, "you ain't got no call to do this."

"It would be a shame to call in the sheriff, but we can do it that way if you prefer. I will press charges myself."

Otto released her so quickly that Serena swayed. There was a grayness before her eyes, and the sickness of reaction rose in her throat. Instantly, the man called Benedict was beside her, the same man who had forced Pearlie to let her sing. Without another glance for Otto and his muttered curses, he supported her down the last stair treads.

But Serena heard. "Next time," Otto grated under his breath, "next time you won't get away."

"Would you like something to drink?" the man beside her said, his low voice shaded with concern.

Serena shook her head. "No, no thank you. If I could have a little fresh air?"

"Certainly."

It was miraculous the way a path was cleared for them as they made for the door. The usual noise and clatter had quieted to scarcely more than a whisper. Someone swung open the heavy outside panel with its red and blue leaded glass panes. The man beside her spoke a word of thanks, and then they were out in the fresh and windy darkness.

Serena gulped great breaths of the pure air. Her nausea passed only to be replaced by an urgent need to get away from the Eldorado. With no clear idea of where she was going, she started to walk. The effects of the overheated room she had just left were whipped away by the wind. She clasped her arms around her, shivering a little, but she did not stop. The man who had come to her aid for the second time that night kept pace with her. In the back of her mind she was grateful for his presence, grateful also that he did not try to speak or detain her in any way. The cutting edge of the wind grazed her cheeks and tugged at her hair. It irritated her eyes, making them stream tears. It flattened her skirts against her, fluttering and snapping their fullness like a flag. Still she walked.

Though there were lights and music along the street, they were muffled and distant, behind doors that were tightly shut against the raw weather. There were few people on the street, most preferring to stay inside where there was warmth and cheer. Somewhere a dog barked and a burro brayed. The sullen thrump of machinery came and went with the force of the wind, resounding like a giant heartbeat.

At a touch on her shoulder, Serena flinched, her eyes wide as she swung to face the man beside her. He drew his hand back at once.

"Here," he said, stripping off his coat. "Wear this."

When she did not move, he came close to drape the wool jacket about her shoulders. The warmth left from his body enfolded her, along with the scent of pipe tobacco and the faint fragrance of Macassar hair oil.

"You—you will be cold." It was as if she was truly aware of him for the first time. She sensed, rather than saw, when he shook his head.

"I'm used to it."

"I appreciate what you did just now. Most men wouldn't have bothered, not with someone like—"

"Someone like what? Any man would have been glad to help you."

That his words were sincere she could not doubt. Touched in spite of herself she said, "I don't know you."

"Forgive me," he said. "I should have introduced myself sooner. I'm Nathan Benedict."

Nathan Benedict, the Croesus of Cripple Creek, Ward's friend, the millionaire who had loaned him his private railroad car.

"You have been kind to me more than once this evening, Mr. Benedict. I am truly grateful."

She thought he made a movement toward her, but if so he checked it at once. "No more grateful than I am for your company."

Abruptly Serena became aware of moisture against her face. Its touch was cold and faintly stinging. "Rain," she said, holding out her hand.

"No," Nathan Benedict contradicted her. "Look there."

151

Turning to follow the direction he indicated with one out-flung arm, she looked down the alleyway between two buildings toward Bennet Avenue where the only streetlamps in the town shone with a golden light. In their glowing nimbus something swirled, something fine and powdery and white. For long moments Serena watched.

"Do you see it?" he asked.

"Yes," she whispered. "It's snowing."

The snow fell with soft persistence through the night and into the next day. It sifted from a pale-gray sky, closing in, obscuring the steep slopes of the rocky bowl in which the town nestled. It drifted in the streets, piling against the sides of the buildings, stacking lightly behind their wooden false fronts. Feathery, crystalline, it mounded in the doorways and on the windowsills, shifting, whirling away again in the wind.

After her late night, and with the closed-in dimness of the snowfall, Serena slept late. When she awoke, she could not bring herself to make the effort to rise. There was no reason for it. It was so cold in the room and so warm beneath the covers. Beyond the windows, the world was gray-white and still, so hushed she thought she could hear the brush of snowflakes against the glass panes.

She stretched, shivering a little as she felt the cold reaches of the mattress around the section warmed by her body. The bed, with its crimson brocade hangings, was so large and so empty. Turning her head, she considered the place where Ward usually slept. She smoothed her hand over the un-dented pillow. It was strange how easy it was to become used to sleeping with a man, to easing against his body, basking in its furnace heat. There was a certain danger in such actions, of course, one she had learned to weigh carefully. Ward was a light sleeper. Drawing close to him was enough to cause him to wake, and turning, close her in his arms. Though generous with his warmth, he often exacted a price. She could hardly complain; the exercise did have the effect of heating her blood.

With a wry smile curving her lips, she huddled back into her warm spot. She did not miss him, certainly not. It had been pleasant to have the bed to herself, to drift peacefully off to sleep, knowing Ward would not be coming upstairs in the small hours of the morning, throwing back the covers, reaching for her. She did not mind being alone in the least.

152

She looked forward to being able to do as she pleased, when she pleased.

She closed her eyes, courting sleep once more. It did no good. If Ward were there, he would get up and build a fire in the stove to take the chill from the room before she emerged from under the quilts. There were advantages, she had to admit, to living with a man.

Gritting her teeth, she flung back the covers and slid from the bed. In a flurry of movement, she ran to the wardrobe and dragged it open, whipped out Ward's heavy quilted dressing gown and swung it around her, then found his woolen slippers, thrusting her feet into them. Shivering with an exaggerated moan, she dived into the sitting room. She piled kindling and chunks of pine wood into the stove, doused the whole with coal oil, and put a match to it, jumping back as the flames leaped high, roaring up the smokestack.

She had forgotten to open the damper. With a muttered imprecation, she attended to that chore, wiping the tears from the smoke that boiled in the room from her smarting eyes.

The fire was soon roaring with such a resinous popping and crackling that she had to shut the stove door. For a time she crouched in front of the heat, then as the temperature of the room became bearable, she began to move about, getting into her clothes, making the bed, brushing her hair. Apparently someone had let the fire go out in the boiler downstairs. The water she used to wash her face, all that would come up the pipe, was so cold that slivers of ice ran from the spout into the china washbasin. By the time she had finished her morning ablutions, her complexion was glowing.

She picked her toothbrush from the glass which held it and began to look around for the Arnica tooth soap. She had just found it, or rather half of the bar, since Ward had divided it into two neat sections, taking half for himself, when she heard the tap of heels along the outside hall. It was Pearlie, no doubt, come to gloat over her victory last night. With a grimace, Serena left the bathroom, hurrying toward the sitting-room door. Quickly and quietly, she moved the table and settee that she had pushed against the panel to bar entry. She had no key to these rooms, something she had discovered to her dismay the night before. Nonetheless, she had no desire to have Pearlie know that she had been frightened to stay alone without the means of locking herself in.

It was Spanish Connie who stood outside. *"Buenos días,"* she said, the corners of her eyes crinkling as she smiled. "I hope I am not too early. I saw the smoke from your fire and knew you were up."

"No," Serena said, surprise making her inarticulate for a moment. "I mean, no, it isn't too early. Come in." Standing back, Serena allowed the Spanish girl to enter, then closed the door behind her.

Spanish Connie wore a walking costume of black faille piped with taupe satin. On her head was a round hat of black felt banded with taupe ribbon and finished with a bewitching veil of the same color scattered with black beauty spots.

"How comfortable you are here. I am wild with envy." The other girl moved to the peacock feathers that had been returned to their brass vase on the sandalwood table, flicking them with the tips of long, slender fingers. "One sees the handiwork of our delightful lady proprietor, Madam Pearlie, of course."

"Yes," Serena answered. "I wish I could offer you something to drink or eat, but I have nothing in these rooms."

"I know. That is why I have come. I thought you might like to go shopping."

"How can I? Otto will stop me."

The Spanish girl smiled. "Not this morning. The cat is away, and the mice—they are not on duty. The barroom is empty. The back door is not even locked."

"I would love—" Serena began impulsively, then stopped. "But I have no money."

"Did Ward leave you nothing? How thoughtless of him."

"He thought that Sanchow would be bringing my food."

"Even so, it is ridiculous. Without money, you may as well be a prisoner! Ah—forgive me."

"It isn't your fault. I do appreciate your thoughtfulness. It was nice of you to try to help me."

Shrugging a little, the Spanish girl moved away a few steps. "It is nothing. But don't sound so—so defeated. We will not give up yet. Does Ward keep no funds here, no small cache put back for the emergency, no jingling change, no tiny sacks of gold dust or nuggets? Does he leave behind no valuables?"

"I don't know. In any case, I couldn't steal from him."

"Who mentioned stealing? I am not suggesting that you become a thief, but surely you have done much in these last weeks that deserves payment?"

154

"I don't expect to be paid. That would make me nothing more than a—" Serena stopped abruptly.

The Spanish girl swung around. "Yes, nothing more than a whore. That is silly talk. If men and women still lived in Eden, what is between them would always be good and natural, freely shared. Since they are not, it is a thing to be bartered, whether for cash in hand or for a wedding band and the food and shelter it symbolizes for a woman and her children. This is the way of the world, the way it will stay, until a woman, with her own brain and skill, can earn as much money as a man."

"Possibly," Serena answered, "but most people don't look at it in that light, and they are the ones who make the rules."

"That may be, but are you willing to go hungry, to remain at the mercy of a woman like Pearlie, for the sake of a rule made by someone who has never been in your position, and that someone a man?"

Seeing the doubtful look that crept into Serena's gray-blue eyes, Spanish Connie went on. "You are a person with needs and rights of your own. I have watched Otto guard you, keeping you here for the pleasure of another man. What consideration do you owe to one who has denied you freedom, keeping you barefoot and near-naked for his entertainment?"

"You don't understand," Serena protested.

The other girl flung her a quick glance over her shoulder. "Understanding I have, yes; it's the feeling between you and your man that I don't know, nor do I want to know. The question I am interested in now is, will you come with me?"

There was money, Serena knew, now that she thought of it. Ward hated to carry silver in his pockets, disliking its rattle and clink. "I think," she said, taking a deep breath, "that I will."

The snow had stopped when they reached the street. All that fell was the dry flakes blown from the rooftops of buildings by the biting wind. It was cold, bitterly so. Smoke from the many fires in the town swirled around them. The glass display windows of store buildings were fogged over and edged with fernlike patterns of frost. The dung dropped into the snow from the few horses that lined the hitching rails steamed. The breath of the two women fogged as they moved quickly along the street, leaving their mouths in blown puffs as they spoke.

They had not gone more than a half block before the Spanish girl begged Serena to call her Consuelo. It was her name,

155

she insisted; she did not answer to that given to her by the miners. With that agreed upon, they discussed where they would go first. There was a length of scarlet satin at the May Store Consuelo had noticed the day before. She wanted to buy it and carry it to her dressmaker. Then there was a tonic she had promised to pick up for a friend from the drugstore. The girl, her friend, had swallowed pennyroyal oil to induce an abortion. The stuff had nearly poisoned her, and she was in need of building up. After that, they would stop by the general store for Serena's purchases. She did not want to run all over town hugging greasy bacon and cheese to her chest, did she?

At the May Store, the clerk took down the satin Consuelo indicated. With a smooth manner and an oily smile, he pointed out its fine quality, though his overwarm gaze was on the Spanish girl as he spoke, rather than the material.

As Consuelo told him she would take it, giving the yardage she would need, he nodded. Taking up the scissors hanging on a piece of twine behind the counter, he said, "You are from the Eldorado, aren't you?"

The Spanish girl inclined her head and moved a short distance away to look at a spool of machine-made lace.

"I caught your act once or twice. You're mighty good." Undaunted by the cool reception of his compliment, he glanced at Serena, then back to the Spanish girl. "You know, you and your friend look enough alike to be sisters?"

"I can't say I've noticed the resemblance," Consuelo said.

"It's there, until a man looks you right in the face. It's the black hair, I reckon, and the way you both carry yourselves, straight-up-and-damn-your-eyes."

Consuelo looked at Serena with mischief brimming in her eyes. With a sly wink she murmured, "You are too kind."

The man folded the material he had cut from the bolt of satin, tore off a sheet of brown wrapping paper, and began to do up the bundle with twine. "Not as kind as I would like to be."

"I beg your pardon?"

"I said I would like to be kinder to you," he repeated, handing the bundle to Consuelo, but retaining his grasp as she reached for it. "I could see my way to forgetting what you owe me on this here red satin, if you was to say the right words."

"And what words are those?"

To Serena, watching this exchange, it seemed the Spanish girl's voice dropped to a lower note, became almost caressing.

The man swallowed. "We could discuss that when I deliver this here package to you this evening, say after ten o'clock?"

Abruptly Consuelo's fingers tightened and she jerked the bundle from his grasp. Digging into her purse, she took out a handful of bills and flung them down on the counter. "Never have I been so insulted. Pig! If you think the price of this cheap satin is worth a night in a woman's company, then I suggest you go to see one of the crib girls!"

Turning on her heel, she gathered Serena with one outstretched arm and swept from the store.

"Bastard," the Spanish girl muttered through her teeth. "Pig of a bastard. It is men like him who make me sorry I am a woman. I could die of hating him and his kind. Smiling like so, reaching out to touch always, thinking that you let them into your bed for any favor, no matter how small. It would not surprise me to learn it was just such an animal who murdered Boots last night!"

In her agitation, the other girl walked so fast that Serena had to extend her stride to keep up. "Boots?" she inquired.

"A girl from one of the cribs down toward Poverty Gulch. She wore a pair of jackboots everywhere, even to bed sometimes. She said they kept her feet warm. She had a man friend who made it his business to see she didn't lack for customers. He checked on her—or checked up on her—every morning about dawn. When he got there this morning, she was dead. She had been beaten and strangled."

"How terrible. That's the second girl who has been killed in the last few weeks."

A hard smile curled Consuelo's mouth. "Second, third, fourth, what does it matter? Nobody will do anything."

"You sound so—so bitter."

"And why not? Women in our profession have a lot to be bitter about. We cannot earn a decent wage any other way, and yet we have no place in society, no value. Nobody cares if we die. But just let one of us cause trouble, and the police are on us like a terrier on a rat. It's enough to make women like me put on bloomers and join the suffragettes, except women in Colorado were given the vote a year ago. The only trouble is, the laws that get voted in apply only to respectable women."

"Surely things can't be that bad? Isn't the sheriff looking into the killing?"

"They're looking, so they say. They questioned Boots's friend. It seems he was in an all-night poker game with three good witnesses to speak for him."

With snow crunching under their feet, they proceeded along Bennet Avenue, passing a barber shop also advertising baths in huge block letters. Steam rolled from the door as a man issued forth, nearly colliding with them. He tipped his hat, then as Serena smiled, meeting his eyes, flushed and hurried away. Farther along, they neared a tall brick building, one of the few in town. It was the stock exchange. A group of men lounged in the upstairs windows, watching the passersby. As Serena glanced up, one man lifted a hand in greeting. Though a portion of the window was obscured by fog, she thought the man was Nathan Benedict. She inclined her head with a slight smile before hurrying past.

With their errand at the dressmaker completed, they turned back toward Myers Avenue. Fitful sunlight glinted from the overcast sky, shining on the snow with blinding brilliance. The arctic chill began to leave the air; the melting snow dripped from the eaves of buildings with the uncertain sound of beginning rain. More people were out and about now. They passed a laundress with red, raw hands carrying a basket of fresh wash. A bearded man with staring eyes and damp clothes reeled by them. A young girl with her hair flying and her high shoes unbuttoned chased a cat down the street, followed closely by a team of yapping dogs pulling, willy-nilly, a wagon with an advertisement for a haberdashery emblazoned on the side. Behind them came a man cursing and yelling as he tried to regain control of his dog team.

By contrast to the brightness outside, the interior of the general store seemed dim and cavelike. In one corner, a pot-bellied stove glowed red around the midsection. The heat brought forth the aroma of leather from the horse collars and harness that hung from the ceiling beams. It intensified the dry, nose-tingling smells of spices and coffee beans on the shelves, the scent of toilet water and cake soap from the paper wrappings on the counter, and the sourness of the pickle barrel near the door.

Serena, her mouth watering, bought bacon and beans,

cheese and crackers, oil sausage, flour, salt, and baking powder. She looked longingly at the dried dates and raisins in their wooden boxes, and the bags of green coffee beans. No matter how she tried, she could not stretch the money she had found to cover such luxuries, nor could she afford the enameled pot that caught her eye. The skillet she had found still in her trunk would have to serve not only as a frying pan, but as a boiler for the beans.

As Serena and Consuelo, carrying their purchases, came out onto the street once more, the Spanish girl sent Serena a sidelong glance. "I see I am not the only one to attract an admirer," she said.

"What?" Serena shifted the burlap feed bag that held her food to a more comfortable position in her arms.

"Not only did the nice man back there scurry around in his storeroom to find a bag to hold what you had bought, he presented you with a free pickle! A conquest, there can be no doubt of it."

Serena grimaced. "At least he didn't expect to—to be kind to me in return."

Laughing, they failed to see the tall gaunt man on the sidewalk. Their first indication of his presence was the thundering sound of voice.

"Serena!"

The harsh command, the intonation that invited all within earshot to see and hear, could not be mistaken. Serena came to an abrupt halt.

"Elder Greer—"

"Yes, it is I. I looked to snatch one brand from the burning, and lo, I have found another! You don't look happy to see me, but that is to be expected. You can't want people you have known to see you walking the streets in the company of lewd women, yourself the kept mistress of a gambler."

"Who is this person?" Consuelo demanded, anger flashing in her dark eyes.

"He is a Mormon, of those known also as Latter-Day Saints."

"I should have known," the Spanish girl said with a contemptuous shrug. "Come, Serena. His kind are always raving about something."

The elder stepped in front of Consuelo, barring her passage. "She will not go just yet. I have to talk to her."

The other girl eyed his menacing pose with a curl of her

lip. "Say what you must, old man, but say it quickly. And lower your voice. Draw any more attention than you already have, I will say to one and all that you are trying to molest Serena and myself."

Fury worked its way across the elder's features, but he did not quite dare put the Spanish girl's threat to the test. Turning to Serena, he said, "You are new to these wicked ways. Give them up and come back with me to the wagon train. I promise I will hold nothing against you, but will take you back into my bosom. All that has passed will be forgotten."

"I couldn't," Serena said.

"That's what you tell me now, but when your gambler tires of you, you will change your mind. The wagon train is encamped on Fountain Creek. There has been illness among us again, not typhoid but a bloody flux. The delays have made our supplies short. We have decided to rest where we are for the winter while the men find work to earn the money for more provisions. Any time between now and the spring you will find a welcome."

"Thank you, but no," Serena answered.

"Why are you thanking this man?" Consuelo asked, her voice rising. "It is an insult!"

The Mormon elder ignored the other woman. "There is another thing. My wife Lessie came down with flux. Because of her sickness, the child she was carrying came early and was stillborn. The death grieved her so much that she went out of her head. As soon as she could get up from the bed, she ran away. I have searched these many weeks for her, both down in Colorado Springs and here. I was told she was seen with a man, a fancy drummer who was on his way up here to Cripple Creek to sell his patent medicines to the drugstores. If that's so, she is in hiding. I'm asking now, since you and she were friends, have you seen her?"

Lessie, quiet, childlike Lessie, leaving the wagon train, going off with a man. "What did you do to her?" Serena asked, her voice hard.

The elder looked away, avoiding her clear, blue-gray gaze. "Nothing. Nothing that wasn't my right. I'm asking again. Have you seen her?"

"No, I haven't seen Lessie. But if I had, I wouldn't tell you. Not after the way you have treated her, and allowed her to be treated."

"She is my wife. It is a sin and an abomination for her to

consort with other men. She will be damned to the eternal fires."

"Will she? In what way is what she is doing now any different from what she was doing with you? You say she is your wife, but how can that be when the laws of this country allow a man only one? Legally, she is no more than your concubine. If she chooses to be the woman of another man, how can you condemn her?"

"Bravo, my Serena!" Consuelo said with a sharp clap of her hands. "Now let us go."

"That's not so," the elder sputtered. "According to Mormon teaching it is my right to have more than one wife."

"Is it also the right of the women to have more than one husband? No? I thought not. It sounds a mighty convenient teaching to me, for the Mormon men." Stepping around the elder, Serena set out along the wooden sidewalk with Consuelo behind her.

"You think this is the end, but it is not!" Elder Greer shouted after her. "I have been called to minister to women like you. I have been called to bring the Word to this Sodom and Gomorrah, to save the souls of the lewd temptresses who live on this street, to deliver them to salvation and the glory of heaven. You won't escape me, do you hear me? I will save you! You will be mine yet!"

It was all Serena could do not to run to put a greater distance between herself and the fanatical shouting. It was Consuelo that broke the tension that held her. As they climbed the rising slope of Myers Avenue she snorted. "Bastard! That's just what the women of this town need, a preacher after them, on top of a killer. I am not at all certain which is worse!"

"I hope he doesn't find Lessie," Serena said, a frown drawing her brows together.

"This Lessie, you knew her well?"

"She was a good friend," Serena answered, and went on to explain the circumstances.

Consuelo pursed her full red lips. "What does she look like?"

"You think you can find her?"

"I do not know. There are thousands of people in this town, twenty-five, thirty thousand, maybe more. Still, if she has run away with a drummer as the preacher said, she may come finally to Myers Avenue, and if she does, it may be I will hear of her. I can ask around."

161

"It would be wonderful beyond anything if you could find her," Serena said, impulsively placing her hand on the other girl's arm.

The Spanish girl smiled. "It will be nothing. If I can help you, then perhaps sometime you will help another. This is the way people live."

"Not all people," Serena said, and looked quickly away.

Chapter Ten

Consuelo, who shared a room with another girl at the parlor house next door, left Serena at the entrance to the Eldorado. Serena stared after her. The Spanish girl was so pleasant, such easy company, at least with her. Did she like the way she lived, did she dislike it? It was impossible to tell, just as it was impossible to remember when she was with her that Consuelo entertained men in her room. Watching her go with her back straight and her head held high, it was beyond belief to think that Consuelo undressed a half-dozen times each night, and in the lamplit dimness of her room, lay down naked upon her bed, and for the sake of money, allowed men intimacies with her body.

With a shake of her head, Serena turned to push open the door of the Eldorado and step inside. She stood for a moment, letting her eyes adjust after the blinding light outside. The barroom was dark and cold, since the fire in the stove had been allowed to go out in the early hours of the morning. The sour odors of spilled liquor and the contents of the cuspidors that were set at intervals along the bar hung in the air. So murky was the light it was a moment before Serena noticed Pearlie standing on the stairs.

"Well!" Pearlie said, as Serena turned in her direction. "So you came back. After the way you and Nathan Benedict left here, I wasn't sure you would."

"I'm sorry to disappoint you. I came back last night, you know, but you were otherwise occupied at the time."

The woman gave a negligent shrug. "If that's so, then more fool you. I saw how Benedict looked at you. He's a rich man, richer than most ever dream of being. If you played your cards right you could have a snug position and an income for life, on top of the things that he could give you. He has a reputation for generosity. There would be jewels, furs, everything you ever imagined you might have."

"I only just met the man."

"That doesn't matter. Things happen quickly out here. You needn't look so skeptical. It really is a great opportunity for you. Why, he might even marry you. Stranger things have happened. That would serve Ward right, wouldn't it?"

"I don't know what you mean," Serena answered, shifting the bundle she carried.

"Don't be stupid! Ward ruined you, didn't he? Oh, I know he made amends in his own way, but you do realize he has done all he is going to do? There won't be a wedding ring for you from Ward Dunbar, and that's the only way he can make it right, isn't it?"

"He doesn't have to make it right, as you call it." The woman's intention was so obvious it was irritating.

"How sweet of you. I wouldn't be so generous in your place. He would pay for what he had done to me, one way or another."

"Maybe," Serena answered, preparing to ascend the stairs, "but the only way my favoring Nathan Benedict would hurt Ward would be if he cared for me, and, Pearlie, you have already assured me he doesn't."

Pearlie stepped aside. "You would also deprive Ward of your company."

"And leave the way open for you to—how was it you put it—console him? I grant you that might be a form of punishment, though somehow I don't think it would give me much satisfaction." Hefting her bag a little, Serena brushed past the other woman.

A flush of anger stained Pearlie's face, then she tried another tack. "From the looks of things, you have been spending quite a lot of money. Did Benedict give it to you?"

"That's none of your business."

"No, but Ward might make it his."

"Let him," Serena answered, and did not look back as she

reached the upper hallway and turned down it toward her rooms.

Now that she had food, she could not be starved into submission, but there was still the threat of Otto. The big man might be wary of mistreating her after his encounter with Nathan Benedict; still, she could not depend upon it. The best thing she could do might be to put in an appearance below, just as she had the night before. There would be no excuse then for Otto to come to her rooms. She had not forgotten the threat he had made. This way, so long as they were in public view, any impulse he might have in that direction would have to be contained. In the topsy-turvy world of Myers Avenue, it was the nights, while she was in the barroom, that she was safest.

During the early hours of the day, while she slept, there were always the overstuffed chairs and ottomans to use as a barricade. When Ward returned, she would ask for a key to the outside door. He had one, she knew. Of course there might be no necessity. It was all too likely that she would have to look for other accommodations when Ward returned. She would have to wait on that time, wait and see.

Serena set her purchases down on a table in the sitting room and looked around her. A swift inspection of the bedroom showed that also to be just as she had left it. And yet, Pearlie had come from these rooms; there was no other reason for her to be on the stairs, and if further proof was needed, there was the smell of her patchouli perfume lingering in the still, close atmosphere.

What had she been doing up here? What was she after? Was it curiosity that had prompted her visit, or something else? Serena had no way of knowing.

Serena had forgotten to provide herself with a knife to slice the slab of bacon she had bought. Her inspection of Ward's desk turned up a penknife, however, and using this she was able to cut off several chunks. In the grease left from frying these, she cooked a combination of biscuits and flapjacks. Because of the altitude, more than her skill or ingredients, they rose up thick and fluffy. Wrapped around the bacon, they were the most delicious food she had ever tasted. She ate every crumb and licked the last sheen of fat from her fingers.

With her hunger satisfied for a time, she fried more bacon, and leaving it in the pan with the drippings for seasoning, she put a double handful of beans on to simmer for her supper.

While they boiled, she brought out her tin plate, fork, and cup from her trunk. Rinsing them, she dried everything and set a single place for herself at the sitting-room table.

By midafternoon snow clouds had closed down around the town once more. Inside, it grew dark and the lamps had to be lit. The snow, so thick it was like fog, blew in upon them. Serena, keeping an eye on her beans, replenishing the water in them now and again, looked over the smaller tables in the sitting room. Choosing one, she set it near the nickel-plated stove. She draped a linen towel over the top to protect the finish, then placed her food upon it. Nothing she had chosen would spoil; the bacon was well cured and smoked, the cheese, she felt sure, would not be around long enough to mold. If she should find it necessary in the few days before Ward's return to buy something that might turn, such as a quart of milk, there was no problem; she had only to open the window and set the can outside on the sill. In a short time it would probably be frozen solid, but it could always thaw.

While the beans were finishing their last hour of cooking, Serena tested the water in the bathroom. The boiler had still not been stoked for her. The water was like ice, and Serena, letting it run over her hand, was surprised it had not frozen in the pipes. No doubt it was only the heat in the rooms, both upstairs and down, that kept it from doing so.

Undaunted by this setback, she marched out of the rooms and down the stairs. Behind the stage there was a storeroom where cases of liquor were kept, along with supplies for washing the many glasses used every night and keeping the barroom semi-clean. There she found what she wanted, a heavy tin bucket. With a triumphant set to her shoulders, she carried it back up the stairs. By the time she had finished eating, there was hot water to wash her dishes in, and a short time later, hot water for her bath.

As she performed her ablutions, a hurried job in the chill bathroom, Serena wondered what Ward would think of her new arrangement. He might not like having his rooms filled with the smell of food, or putting up with the clutter where he sat of an evening. He would have no trouble, she was sure, persuading Sanchow to resume serving his meals once more. It was virtually certain that the Chinaman could provide greater variety for the menu; still, it was worth something to be able to eat when a person wanted to, instead of when the food arrived.

She had no idea why she was concerning herself with such

matters. In all likelihood, how, when, and where Ward ate would not concern her.

Her second appearance on the stage of the Eldorado was much like the first. Timothy was at the piano, banging out a rollicking rendition of "The Man Who Broke the Bank at Monte Carlo" as she came downstairs. He tipped her a sly wink as he broke into song. Consuelo, with a full-length cloak of black velvet wrapped tightly around her as she sat at a table near the stage steps, called over the music, beckoning to her. The Spanish girl indicated a chair, then flicked a fingernail against the glass that sat in front of her.

"Would you like a brandy? It will keep out the chill."

Serena smiled, shaking her head. "I'm not cold."

"You should be," Consuelo said with a realistic shiver. "I am frozen. I hate the snow, snow, snow. One day, when I have made all the money I want, I will go back to Mexico. I will buy myself a husband, eat all I want, and lie in the sun all day."

"You will grow fat and lazy," Serena teased.

"Yes, that is what I want. You smile. Don't you believe me? I tell you I do. My father was an Englishman, my mother Spanish. He left her when I was a baby. She worked in the cribs in silver-mining towns like Aspen and Leadville, taking men into her bed while I hid underneath. But there was never enough money, always there was a man to take it, or an official to pay. One day, when I was twelve, a man came when my mother was not there. Since then, I have worked, and I have learned much. I have never let a man get close to me, close enough to talk sweet, then beat me and take what I have earned. I have saved, even when I was hungry, never spending more than was necessary so that I can have the future I have described to you."

"Consuelo," Serena breathed, but the other woman went on as if she did not hear.

"Soon I will have enough to build a house of my own, and then it will not be long. Only a few years more, and I will be rich, rich enough to eat as I please, make love as I please. And never, never will I live in the mountains where the snow falls nine months out of the year."

"A house? You mean a home?"

"No, my innocent. I mean a parlor house."

"Like Pearlie's?"

"Pearlie? Bah! She knows nothing of what a parlor house should be. She runs it not with her head but with what is between her legs. She is stupid and greedy and miserly. She opens her doors to all men, reaching for their money before she gives them what they want, and therefore her place is no more than a bordello. It has no distinction, no class."

Serena watched the Spanish girl sip her brandy. "What are you saying? Isn't that what a parlor house is, a bordello?"

"No, and no again!" Consuelo said, laughing. "If you would know what a parlor house should be, you should see the Old Homestead. You should watch how the madam handles her clients. Her establishment is of the most exclusive; no man may enter, no matter who he is, without an appointment. Before such a thing can be made, he must first speak to the madam. He must give his name and address and provide references, the names of men already known to her. He must be willing to discuss his finances, and show himself able to afford fifty to a hundred dollars for his hours of pleasure."

"A hundred dollars?" Serena exclaimed. That was more than most men made in a month.

Consuelo shrugged. "It is often more, much more. The men who go to the Old Homestead are not miners and shopkeepers; they are the men who have made fortunes in mining stocks and gold claims, real estate, and railroad shares. For most, their wealth came easily. Why should they not pay it out in the same way?"

"Even so—"

"These men aren't paying merely for the body of a woman, you understand. They are paying for membership in a club, a most exclusive club. If they are acceptable to the madam, once she has checked them out, then they will be admitted to a house where all is luxury, where there is good food and wine, liquor and cigars, where lovely young ladies entertain on the piano, or sing and dance while other musicians play. They are paying for someone to listen to them and ask intelligent questions, to amuse them and make them feel relaxed, important, at home. And then, when the gentleman so desires, there is an adventure into the delight of the senses. He may choose which woman he will, so long as she has not promised her time to another, and when with her he may suggest what will please him most, even that which his wife refuses."

"I don't think," Serena said, her face pale, "that I want to hear any more."

"Why, Serena? You need no longer pretend to virtue, the virtue that men expect while they retain their vices."

168

Serena stared at her a long moment, then, thinking of Elder Greer, gave an abrupt nod.

"Where was I? Ah, yes. At the Old Homestead, if a man is undecided which lady he prefers, there is the viewing room."

"The what?"

"The viewing room, a most genteel practice, I assure you. In most places, the girls parade around either in their underclothes or as near naked as makes no difference. Not so, at a well-run parlor house. While downstairs in the entertainment rooms, they are fully, even magnificently, dressed. Upstairs it is very different, of course. They wear as much or as little as the man they are with pleases. But first he must choose one of their number, and that is where the viewing room proves its advantage. There the women naturally wear nothing whatever."

Serena lifted a brow. "Yes, that sounds very genteel."

Consuelo laughed. "Well, at least it's modest."

"Oh, yes?"

"The girls who are not occupied enter the room and disrobe. The gentleman who has requested the showing, and perhaps one or two others who are merely curious, troop upstairs and peer into the room through a special window."

"I fail to see the modesty in that, since the girls must know perfectly well why they are there."

"Oh, but yes, and so they either let down their hair and, turning what they consider to be their best feature toward the window, stand around like statues of Eve, or else they do their best to appear unconcerned."

"You sound," Serena said carefully, "as though you had been in such a room."

"No, never. But often and often I have wished, when some man commanded me to take off my clothes before him, that I had at least that much protection from his stares."

How easily the other girl spoke of such things. Would the time come, Serena wondered, when she would find herself in such a position, parading before men, doing her utmost to attract their interest, or else trying desperately to seem uncaring? She would not think about it. Surely she could not be forced into such a life against her will. Still, much could change in the space of a few weeks or months. A year ago she would not have dreamed that she would be where she was at this moment, the kept woman of a gambler, parading in her mother's finery for the entertainment of a crowd of crude miners.

In an effort to turn the direction of her thoughts, Serena said, "Regardless of how much the girls may be paid, if the Old Homestead is so exclusive, there must be a limit to what they can earn."

"There are near a dozen millionaires in the district, and their numbers are increasing every day. Of men who are not quite so wealthy, but still comfortably well off, there are scores more, all certain they deserve the best. The madam of such a place as the Old Homestead, which is the position I crave, is more often than not the first choice of the gentlemen. In this way she scrapes off the cream, plus she receives a portion of the earnings of the other girls. Moreover, there are gifts from her admirers, jewelry from Cartier's, magnificent furnishings, gowns from the marvelous stores in the East, or even from Worth in Paris. Furs, carriages, and a thousand small treasures are hers. Then there is the possibility that one of her admirers may become permanently attached to her. In that case, he may bestow a house upon her, land, even mining claims in order to wean her away from the parlor house. It is even possible that if he is enraptured enough with her charms, he will offer marriage."

"Surely not?"

"No? You must have heard of Baby Doe Tabor?"

"I don't think so."

"She was a young married woman who came out to the state some twenty years ago, during the first gold rush. Her husband made money for a time, then he went bust and took to drink and playing around with other women. Baby Doe found out, and she took a lover for herself. Eventually she divorced her husband, an act which put her beyond the pale, made her, in the eyes of respectable women, little more than a whore. With her lover, she went to Leadville, and there she met the silver-mining king, Horace Tabor. She caught the great man's fancy; he paid off her lover, and Baby Doe became his mistress. In time, Tabor divorced his wife and married his kept woman."

"She was never a parlor girl," Serena pointed out.

"I will grant you that. Still, it isn't impossible, not out here where women are scarce and the strict rules of civilization, even civilization itself, seems far away. A number of the girls have married. But I only mention it in passing. That isn't what I want."

170

"Isn't it?" There was such an air of strength about Consuelo. It was as if she, and she alone, controlled her destiny. Watching her, Serena knew a fleeting taste of envy.

"No. As I said before, I mean to make what I can in the next few years, then take my savings, go where no one knows me, and begin over again. If I married a rich man and stayed here, I would be always that woman from Myers Avenue, never trusted, never accepted. No, I prefer my independence to such false respectability."

The Spanish girl fell silent as Pearlie entered at the back door of the barroom. The red-haired woman hesitated, then with a frown drawing her brows together over her pale-blue eyes, she came toward them, the taffeta skirts of her costume rasping about her ankles.

"Well," she said, a hard note in her voice. "Is this all you girls have to do? Sit here and gossip? You should be circulating."

Timothy brought the chorus of his song to a flourishing finish. Before Consuelo could speak, he said, "Don't shoo my girls off now, Pearlie, me darling. Show starts in two minutes."

Pearlie compressed her lips into a thin line. "Very well," she flung over her shoulder at the Welshman behind her. "Serena, I had an interesting inquiry about you a little while ago."

"Oh?" Serena said, her tone colorless.

"What kind of inquiry?" Consuelo asked sharply.

"Just the kind you think." Pearlie allowed herself an unpleasant smile. "Not that it was the only one by any means. There have been men clamoring at my door all day to know when our delectable Serena is going to be available. But this particular inquiry I spoke of was special."

"Are we to learn what it is all about, or are we to guess?"

"I fail to see, Consuelo, how this concerns you, but if you will stop interrupting, I will most certainly tell Serena of her conquest. The man who is so interested in your exact status here at the Eldorado is none other than Nathan Benedict. I take it he has been in the East on business for some weeks, and had never seen you in here before, until last night. He was disappointed to hear you had been Ward's girl, but he recovered quickly, fast enough, at all events, to tell me that he wished to reserve your time tonight, and to ask as to the availability of a room at the parlor house."

"You—you can't mean it," Serena whispered.

171

"I can, and I do. I told him you were still staying in Ward's rooms, but he seemed to feel that it would be wrong of him to have a tryst with you there. I was obliged to promise him my back parlor, and against the possibility that he might need it, one of the front bedrooms upstairs."

"You led him to think that I—that I might be agreeable?" Serena could not keep the dismay from her voice.

"All you have to do is talk to him, listen to his offer. Who knows? You may be more agreeable than you think when you have heard him out."

"It's impossible. I can't!"

"Oh, but you can," Pearlie said, a dangerous undercurrent in her voice. "And you most certainly will. I will see to that."

"So that's what you are up to," Consuelo said, her eyes narrowing. "That's what you intended from the start, to get Serena into the parlor house before Ward comes back."

Spots of color appeared on Pearlie's cheekbones. "Be silent!"

"Not I! You think Ward is so fastidious that if he finds Serena has been next door he will wash his hands of her. It won't matter then how she got there, or why."

"Ridiculous," Pearlie snapped. "You are only jealous because Nathan Benedict took you upstairs once or twice this summer. You see your big chance with him slipping away, and you would spoil Serena's chances if you could; I saw that last night when he led Serena outside."

"That isn't true," Consuelo said, rising to her feet.

Serena stared from one woman to the other, her mind in turmoil. Who was right, Consuelo, or Pearlie? With a sick feeling in the pit of her stomach, she recognized it was most probable both were. Where that left her, she could not be certain. Did it mean that Pearlie was acting without Ward's approval, that she had lied when she had said that he was tired of her and wanted her to find her own way, or was the accusation Consuelo had made a ruse to discourage Pearlie from going through with the plan that would deprive the Spanish girl of Benedict's patronage? Either way, it made no difference. If she met with Nathan Benedict it would be here, with people all around them, not in a private parlor in a house of prostitution. He would most certainly have no use for the front bedroom he had ordered.

Pearlie stared at Consuelo. "Take care what you are about, you greaser tramp," she hissed, "or you will find yourself looking for another place."

172

"Ladies," Timothy said, beginning the bass roll that prefaced the nightly entertainment. "Ladies, no time for quarrels now. It's showtime!"

The first act on the bill was an arrangement sung by the chorus of girls of "The Sidewalks of New York." It was followed by a provocative dance involving parasols and the gradual disappearance of the skirts the girls were wearing. Serena was to be next. She stood waiting in the dark area at the side of the stage, a space too cramped and small to be called wings. Her gaze was on the girls twirling their parasols behind them in mock demureness, when a man, a barman in a white apron, spoke at her elbow.

"Excuse me. Timothy sent this to you. He said tell you it was good for a dry throat."

"What is it? Not some of his warm beer?"

"No, ma'am, just sarsaparilla with a touch of brandy."

Serena accepted it with a doubtful look. It sounded an unpleasant concoction, and it was. She tasted it with a grimace. From where she stood she could see Timothy at his piano below the stage. Catching her gaze, he sent her a wink and nod. He was only trying to be helpful, to bolster her spirits. Smiling at the Welshman, she lifted her glass and, with a deep breath, drank down the contents.

Her stint upon the stage went easily enough. There was a bad moment when, looking out over the audience, she saw the tall shape of Nathan Benedict at the back of the room. She glanced away without a sign of recognition, shielding her face with a flirtatious gesture of her fan. She was aware of disappointment where Ward's friend was concerned. She had expected more of him than this. His connivance with Pearlie, his headlong rush to secure a room to which to take her, seemed a betrayal after his pretense of quiet understanding the night before. She did not know what she would say when she came face to face with him again, but she had a strong inclination to see that he did not get off lightly.

The roar of the men, the whistles and shouting for an encore could not be ignored. Another Stephen Foster ballad did not satisfy them, nor did yet another. It seemed, in fact, that nothing would. Serena was sweeping into her final curtsy when giddiness seized her. She swayed a little as she rose. It was the tension of appearing in public, she told herself, or else the strain of breathing deeply enough to sing against the pinch of her corsets. She had not noticed the problem the night before, but then the room had not been so crowded or so filled with smoke. She must get off the stage at once, and out into the fresh air.

Before she could move, a man in the first row of tables leaned toward the stage and threw something toward her. It hit her skirts and fell onto the stage with a metallic clank, rolling to a stop at her feet. It was money, a twenty-dollar gold piece. In an instant the air was filled with flying silver and gold. It struck her bodice and her arms, thudded on the silk of her gown, clanking, clattering, a rain of wealth that glittered in the light of the footlamps. Serena retreated before it. It was a compliment, she knew, these riches thrown at her feet, and yet she felt nothing but horror. Smiling valiantly, she curtsied once more, bowed, and then ran from the stage.

"Well done!" Consuelo whispered, giving Serena a brief hug as she brushed past her, ready to make her entrance for her torrid Spanish dance. "Don't worry. A barman will collect the money for you."

Serena murmured her thanks, but did not stop. Behind the backdrop to the rear of the stage, amid the ropes and pulleys that controlled the raising and lowering of the curtain and other scenic booms, there was a door that led into the storeroom. On the other side of that room was a wide outside door used for unloading the drays and freight wagons, a place where she could reach fresh air without going through the noisy clutching crowd.

It was dark in the storeroom and cold. The smell of dust and spilled beer was strong. Groping her way past kegs and barrels, Serena felt disoriented, increasingly dizzy. She had to reach the door.

The rough wood panel was under her hand. She felt down it for the knob. Behind her, she heard a scraping sound, followed by a thump and a curse. Her heart leaped in her chest. Frantically, she ran her hand over the door. It seemed to be moving under her fingers, receding and coming closer. From far away she could hear the flamenco music of Consuelo's dance. It was overlaid by a rushing in her ears and the soft thud of the blood pounding in her veins.

Then the doorknob was under her hand. She tried to turn it, but she had no strength. She could only cling to it for support, a sob in her throat. A footstep sounded behind her. She felt the animal heat of a body. She smelled the acrid stench of sweat, then hard hands clutched her arms, digging into her flesh.

A scream, piercing, desperate, echoed in the dark chambers of her mind, then faded away to soft silence. She never knew it did not reach her lips.

Chapter Eleven

"Serena?"

She lay still, scarcely breathing. Her bones felt locked in place, though the rest of her body was without feeling. The voice that called seemed to come from far away. There was an anxious sound in the quiet, masculine timbre, but no particular hope.

"Serena? Open your eyes, dear girl. Please, I am so sorry."

That voice, so familiar. If she could only— Her eyelids felt glued tight. Her mind groped, prodding her sluggish memory. Nathan. Nathan Benedict. In disappointment, she let her mind sink back once more into darkness.

"Here. Drink this, Serena. Drink."

The cold rim of a glass was against her lips. Liquid wet her mouth and trickled down her cheek.

"Stupid fool of a woman, to think I would want you like this. If there is permanent harm, I swear I will—"

Slowly, as if there was a great distance between her brain and her mouth, Serena opened her lips to take a little of the medicine offered her. Immediately she coughed, choking on fiery liquor. A strong arm beneath her shoulders raised her higher. Her head was against a man's chest.

"Another sip, please, Serena."

She tried, and this time was successful. Regardless, she could not seem to open her eyes or support herself. The strains of the "Beer Barrel Polka" sounded in the distance, punctuated by a woman's shrill laughter.

"Wake up, Serena. You've got to wake up."

She was lowered once more, then she felt the friction of her hands being chafed. It seemed important to do as she was bid, no matter the effort required. Suddenly a shiver ran over her. She was cold. There was icy dampness on her face, and she seemed to feel the brush of open air as from an open window. A crackling sound came like wrapping paper, then she felt the cool smoothness of satin, the softness of fur beneath her chin.

By slow degrees, Serena opened her eyes. She was lying on a chaise longe of the type known as a fainting couch. It had been drawn up before an open window, and cold wind laden with the breath of snow lifted the panels of Brussels lace that hung in the frame. She seemed to be covered by the glossy, brownish-black pelts of beaver made up in a cape. Kneeling beside her on the floor was Nathan Benedict, his eyes searching her face in a look of mingled relief and regret.

"What—happened?"

Her voice came out as something less than a whisper, and she had to repeat the question.

"You were drugged," Nathan said. "Laudanum, I think."

Serena stared up into his face. "In the sarsaparilla?"

"I expect so, if that is what you had."

With a suddenness that made her eyes widen, Serena remembered. Pearlie and this man, the room at the parlor house. "Where am I?"

"At Pearlie's place, I'm afraid. I am sorry, more sorry than I can say, Serena. I asked her for a place where I could speak to you in private, no more. I never expected this, never wanted it. You must believe me."

His hazel eyes were shaded with pain, though their gaze was steady. In the angular lines of his face there was something firm and dependable, aligned to a fine simplicity that could not harbor deceit.

"Do you believe me?" he asked, his voice quiet.

"Yes," she whispered.

"Thank God," he breathed, and bending his head, pressed her fingers that he held to his lips. After a moment, he looked up once more. "I—do you think you can walk?"

"I can try."

"You've been here a long time, three hours at least. When I first walked in here and saw you, you were so pale I thought

177

you were dead. Your laces had to be loosened so you could breathe."

Serena had not noticed, but since he spoke of it, the looseness of her dress, the ease with which she could expand her chest, made it obvious. "That's all right," she said slowly.

"If you will allow me, I will help you fasten your clothing and we will get out of this place."

Serena gave a nod, and tried to sit up. In the end, he had to help her. The movement made her feel groggy. She sat clutching the fur in her lap, her eyes closed as she turned her back to him. He was slipping the tiny buttons of her mother's ivory silk into place when there came a noise at the outside door and a draft of cold air eddied in the room.

The sliding panel that closed the parlor off from the hall slammed into its recess with a crash. In the ceiling, the lusters of the red hobnail hanging lamp jangled with the reverberation. Serena jerked, startled, and her eyes flew open as she twisted toward the door.

Ward stood in the opening. The heavy coat he wore was caked with ice. As he reached up to pull his wide-brimmed hat from his head, snow cascaded from it, sifting to the floor.

"Well," he drawled, tossing the hat onto a table beside Nathan's homburg with a gesture of contempt. "Isn't this a pretty picture? Claim jumping, Nathan?"

"Ward," Nathan said, getting to his feet. "It isn't what you think."

For an answer Ward strode forward. When he was less than two feet from Nathan, he drew back his fist and drove it into his friend's face. Nathan fell back against the couch. As Ward reached for him again, he held up his hand without attempting to protect himself.

"Ward, no," Serena cried, reaching out to him, trying to catch his arm.

He flung her off, and so weak was she that she slipped from the couch to huddle on the floor. There was a flurry in the doorway, and in whirl of skirts, Consuelo came into the room.

"Por Dios!" she exclaimed. Her face flushed, she rushed at Ward, dragging at his arm with both hands, jerking him around. "You fool of a bastard! Can't you see nothing is between them? May you be damned, Ward Dunbar, if you don't know Nathan better than that!"

An uncertain look came into Ward's face as he stared at

178

the Spanish girl, glancing from her to his friend, and then to where Serena sat on the floor.

"I don't blame you for being ready to kill over this," Consuelo went on, "but I thought you had better sense than to believe what Pearlie says."

Ward swung back to face her. "Pearlie may have told me what was going on, but I saw what Nathan was doing, and I saw the look on his face."

The Spanish girl glared at him with bitter contempt. "And why not, as far as that goes, since you went away and left Serena to the tender mercy of that she-dog who is your partner? What man would not want to protect such as she, your so beautiful Serena? But no, Nathan did not seek to take advantage of her weakness. I know, because until a half hour ago, when I left to dance in the final show, I was here with him. He sent for me to help him loosen Serena's laces. I don't know what you saw, but I know you are wrong."

"He saw me fastening the buttons of Serena's dress for her," Nathan said, coming to his feet, straightening his coat and tie. Without a glance in Ward's direction, he leaned to help Serena, lifting her back onto the couch.

Serena thanked him in a low tone. She slanted a look at Ward. The slow rise of anger was beginning to rout the gray fog that enveloped her, and yet she felt detached. The black scowl that drew his thick brows together, the suspicion that clouded his green gaze, only added to her growing sense of ill-usage.

"And that?" Ward asked, indicating the gleaming fur that lay at Serena's feet.

"I bought it for her," Nathan admitted. "The cape she was wearing wasn't suitable for this climate, and I saw no reason to let her catch pneumonia. I bought her this too, something else it seemed she needed."

Nathan bent to pick up a mahogany box lying on the table beside the couch. He flipped the top open to reveal a small pistol nestled in a bed of green velvet. With a chased silver barrel and an inlaid pearl handle, it was a fine example of the gunsmith's art, as beautiful as it was deadly. Turning, he gave the box into Serena's hands, then swung back to face Ward.

"I suppose you mean something by that?" Ward ripped open the buckles that held his coat down the front with angry jerks.

"I do, though it has nothing to do with you."

179

"What then?"

"I think it will be better if I let Serena tell you, and it appears the best thing I can do now is to leave you to thrash this thing out between you. That is, if that's what Serena wants?"

The look he turned in her direction was questioning. After a moment, Serena nodded. "You have been exceedingly kind to me," she said, a soft expression in her blue-gray eyes. "I won't forget it."

"If there is ever anything you need," Nathan said, a ragged edge to his voice, "you have only to call on me." He sent Ward a look that conveyed the essence of a challenge. Turning stiffly, he strode through the open doorway. A moment later, they heard the snap of the latch as he left the parlor house.

There was a deep silence. It was Consuelo who broke it. Stepping to the marble-topped table, she picked up Nathan's homburg he had left behind on the polished surface.

"He—he left his hat. I'll see if I can catch him."

"While you are at it, you can give him this, too," Ward said. Stooping swiftly, he picked up the fur cape and thrust it at the Spanish girl.

A frown flitted across Consuelo's face as she took the fur in her hands. "Yes," she said, then leveled a hard glance at Ward. "Serena has suffered much through no fault of her own since you have been away. You will remember it?"

"I fail to see how it concerns you."

Consuelo made a slight movement of her shoulders. "So do I, but it is so. This, also, you will remember." Without waiting for his reply, she whirled and went quickly out the door.

With slow, even steps, Ward moved to stand over Serena. "It appears," he said, a brooding tone in his voice, "that you have gained not one champion, but two."

"Do you object?" Serena asked.

"How can I, when you have obviously needed defending? I didn't realize you were so helpless."

Serena sent him a look of cold dislike. "There are some things difficult to fight."

"Such as?"

"Starvation, and laudanum."

The words hung between them. The blank look on Ward's face became a frown. "I think you had better explain."

"I'll be happy to do that," Serena snapped. Above them

came a laugh that ended in a smothered shriek. "But not—not here."

With the box containing the pistol still clutched in one hand, she pushed to her feet. A feeling of lightheadedness assailed her, and she stood still for an instant with her eyes closed.

Ward caught her elbow, his touch warm and firm. "Are you all right?"

She shook him off, and for an answer, took a few steps toward the doorway.

Standing aside, Ward said, "Your dress is still unbuttoned."

"It doesn't matter," Serena answered, and holding to her precarious dignity, moved from the room.

The hallway was empty, though the rumble of voices and the crackle of a fire came from the room at the far end. A peculiarity of the parlor house, though a practical one, was the staircase that led upward from the back of the central hall, instead of rising directly from the front entrance. It made it possible for men to come and go without being seen by those in the front entertainment rooms. The back door near the stairs was also convenient. Serena, discovering this exit with its lace curtain over the glass inset in the frame, was gratified by the arrangement. The curtain flapped in the draft as she pulled the panel open.

The cold struck her with numbing force. Though the snow had stopped, deep drifts covered the ground. Serena could see the tracks left by Nathan and Consuelo. They were headed in the opposite direction from where she needed to go, fading into the darkness that had a blue tint from the light of the moon, half hidden behind a dark swath of cloud.

At a sound behind her, Serena took a deep breath and plunged out into the night. She would not stay at the parlor house, not another minute.

The snow sifted into her slippers, wetting the silk. It caked on the hem of her dress, freezing to it, making it so heavy she had to tuck the pistol box under her arm and pick it up in both hands, holding it well above her knees. Dry flakes blown from the roof above her by the night wind drifted down, slipping across her bare shoulders, wafting into the crevice between her breasts. Shivering, clenching her teeth to keep them from chattering, she began to run. Behind her came the crunch of swift footsteps in the icy night.

"Where do you think you are going?" Ward demanded. His

181

hand closed on her forearm, dragging her to a halt, swinging her around so quickly she fell against him.

It was then that the clouds left the face of the moon. The clear, brazen light poured down. It fell on Serena's face, giving her pure features the look of marble, leaving her eyes in mysterious shadow. It sculpted the upswept darkness of her hair in silver, and glittered on the snowflakes that spangled her shoulders.

Ward's hold tightened. He did not wait for an answer. With a soft sound as if he had been struck, he lowered his head and took the cool sweetness of her lips.

The warmth of his arms enfolded her. She slid her hands beneath the open edges of his overcoat, seduced by the heat of his body and a sudden, overpowering need to be held close, and closer still. Here was safety and an odd sense of comfort so strong that it brought an ache to her throat. His kiss was hard and consuming, yet tender, a brand that for the moment she had no wish to deny.

On a deep-drawn breath, he raised his head. "I knew when I left I was going to miss you," he said, his voice husky as he smoothed his hands over the bare skin of her back, "but I never dreamed how much."

At his touch a shiver not entirely from the cold ran over her. She drew back slightly. "Ward," she began.

"No. No explanations, Serena. Not now. Dear God, not now."

His face was in shadow, but there was a thread of strain in his harsh words. Bending with an abrupt movement, he scooped her in his arms and strode toward the back door of the Eldorado.

Inside they were greeted by a ripple of silence, followed by a wave of comment, most of it ribald. "Didn't take him long to lay her by her golden heels! Looks like pretty little Gold Heels may have round heels before long. There do be some that can afford her! Wish it was me! You need any help there, Dunbar, you let me know—"

At one side of the room, Pearlie sat before a green-baize-covered table dealing faro. Her face slowly drained of color as she saw Ward with Serena. With the cards still in her hands, she got slowly to her feet. A gray-bearded miner with a wad of tobacco bulging in his cheek looked up from laboriously counting the hearts on the card he had been dealt. Reaching out, he clamped a gnarled hand on Pearlie's arm. "Where are you going there, honey? We got us a game to finish here. There ain't no call for you to get het up. Dunbar's back and he's got his gold-heeled canary where he wants her. Far as I can see, it ain't no skin off your nose, nor mine neither. Deal!"

Serena scanned Ward's face, so near as he held her against him while he weaved among the tables. The gold flecks were bright in his green eyes, and there was a corded muscle in his jaw. If he noticed Pearlie, if he heard what was said or realized its import, he gave no sign. Serena, with no small difficulty, set herself to follow his example.

The fire had gone out in the sitting-room stove. Though some heat rose into these upstairs regions from the barroom below, it was still so cold the windows were thick with frost that shone in the moonlight behind them. Seeing it, feeling the chill after the warmth downstairs, Serena felt a shudder ripple over her. It was followed by another, and yet another until her whole body was shaking. With a muttered curse, Ward shouldered into the bedroom. Not troubling with a fire or the lighting of a lamp, he set Serena on her feet. Taking the mahogany box she still held from her nerveless grasp, he tossed it to the bureau, then, swinging her around, began to unhook the rest of the buttons at the back of her dress. His movements quick and sure; he stripped it off over her head, removed her wet slippers, and, throwing back the covers of the bed, bundled her unceremoniously between the sheets.

He was not long in joining her, pausing only to kick off his boots and throw the weight of his overcoat across the foot of the bed. Turning to her, he pulled the heavy quilts over their heads and gathered her close against him. Time stretched as they lay still, shaken by the thudding of their heartbeats, listening to the faint, faraway sound of Timothy's piano below them.

By slow degrees Serena's trembling ceased. She became aware of Ward's hands on her hair, probing the soft mass for the pins that held her ringlets in place, spreading the loosened curls upon the pillow. He pressed the heat of his lips to her forehead and drew his fingers along the curve of her cheek to the sensitive line of her neck. Tilting her chin upward with his thumb, he brought his mouth down on hers, questing, firm, still with a gentleness that was an indication of the control he kept upon himself.

Was he angry with her despite the words he had spoken in the darkness outside? Or did he hold her with such luke-

183

warm passion because he felt nothing stronger? A vague discontent stirred in Serena's mind, and she moved her lips experimentally on his. He went still for a moment, but the clasp of his arms remained protective.

Driven by some emotion beyond her understanding, Serena turned her hands to press the palms against his chest. Tentatively, she toyed with the buttons of his shirt. Almost by accident, the top one slipped from its hole. Greatly daring, she let her fingers move to the next.

It was not a betrayal of her principles, what she was doing. He had made such a request before, true enough, but rather than complying with his wishes, she was merely using them for her own ends. To gratify his desire was no more than sensible. Though being his kept woman gave her no joy, it was better than being put up for the highest bidder, as had so nearly happened with Nathan Benedict, or parceled out to the miners.

His shirt was undone and also the top buttons of the woolen union suit underneath he had donned against the cold. Her fingers encountered the buckle of his belt, and she tugged at it with her one free hand. It was a long moment before she could manage to get it unfastened. Ward did not help her, he only lay at ease, brushing his fingertips over the soft curves of her breast above the low neckline of her chemise.

Her movements slowed as she reached the buttons at the front of his twill trousers. It was not that they were difficult; it was simply that it was increasingly evident that he was far from indifferent to her ministrations. The lower buttons of his union suit were a task requiring even more delicacy. In the end, it was impossible to keep the backs of her fingers from pressing against him. She ceased, finally, to try.

In that instant, his arms tightened and he crushed her to him. Deep inside she felt a leaping gladness. She twined her arms around his neck, holding tightly, allowing her breasts to be flattened upon the board hardness of his chest. Their mouths clung hungrily, twisting, turning with the sweet savor of desire on their tongues.

Their breathing quickened. Serena could feel the hard thudding of Ward's heart against her. There was a section of his heated body that was bare to the touch, and with a longing that was frightening, she wanted to remove the barrier that kept the entire length of their naked skin from joining. The touch of his fingers at the buttons of her chemise

184

sent a thrill of excitement along her nerves. She moved to aid him, shrugging from the cambric chemise, turning so he could reach the strings of her corset. She unhooked her petticoats, pushing them down over her hips as he struggled out of his own clothes under the confining heaviness of the covers.

Once more they came together, rocking, sighing in sensuous enjoyment of unimpeded contact. Ward slid his hands down over her hips, drawing her closer against him. He inhaled the fragrance of her hair, his lips burning on her neck and shoulders, trailing with the feel of fire to the throbbing mound of her breast. Serena arched her back with her eyes tightly shut, granting him free access. Enthralled by the sensations that coursed through her, she spread her hands over the muscles of his back. She had no will to resist the close binding intimacy of his touch, no recognition of why she should.

The rapture grew, a mindless thing. It was as if they sought in each other the opiate of passion. Hardness and softness, male and female, they clung, merging, fusing with closed eyes and pounding blood, seeking to dull the pain of the past with the pleasure of the present. It was an endless thing, a ravishing rapture that flowed between them, filling, rising to a crescendo, bursting, flooding, then falling away to bring ease of mind and body. In that temporary exhaustion of care, warm in the chill blackness of the night, they slept.

One minute Serena was asleep, the next she was awake, though her chest still rose and fell with a deeply even cadence and her lashes rested like fans on her cheeks. It was morning. Even behind her closed lids, she could sense the white brilliance of sunlight reflecting on snow from the direction of the windows. She was not alone in the bed. She could feel the press of Ward's lean thighs against her, and that was not all. His hand cupped her breast and his warm breath stirred her hair. His arm tightened around her waist. He fitted her to him, and it was as if they had never parted during the night. The tumult swelled around them. The metal springs beneath the feather mattress creaked in protest, and frigid air found its way under the quilts. When at last Ward began to ease from her, she caught his arm, holding him in place close against her.

He was still for a time, caressing the slim indentation of her waist. Serena was almost dozing once more when he shifted, raising himself to one elbow. She felt him tug her hair from underneath her, easing the tension on the long

185

tresses. Her eyelids quivered as she realized he was studying her. As the quiet continued, she imagined that his touch on her shoulder was less gentle, that a brooding quality pervaded the atmosphere between them, ousting their brief physical rapport.

"Gold Heels," he said softly, trying the words on his tongue, tasting the bitterness of them. "Gold Heels—"

Serena's eyes flew open. She twisted to stare up at him, a chill settling in the region of her heart as she saw the speculation that narrowed his green gaze. "You don't understand," she faltered.

"Don't I? I wish I didn't. You are so lovely, Serena, so much the embodiment of every man's dream of beauty, of what is fine and good. The thought of you here alone haunted me while I was in Denver. I cursed myself for leaving you behind, and the minute I finished what I had come to do, I caught a train back to the Springs. I was too impatient to wait for the night train. I took the Colorado Midland to Florissant. I should have been in Cripple Creek by dark last night, but I hadn't counted on the snow. We were after midnight getting in, and when I reached the Eldorado, what did I find? Men lined up outside in the streets, waiting to get in to see the new toast of Myers Avenue, a girl called Gold Heels, men who refused to go away even though Pearlie had announced that Gold Heels would not be appearing because she was making a special command performance for a rich client. You can never begin to understand what I felt when I found out it was you they were talking about, that you were Gold Heels."

"I didn't ask for the name," Serena said, a shadow of pain in her blue-gray eyes as she searched his bronzed features. "It was because of my slippers, the ones that belonged to my mother. The miners mistook the gilt for the real thing."

"Not surprising," he said, irony in the smile that tugged the corner of his mouth. "I seem to have been in danger of doing the same. What bothers me is why you were downstairs in the first place. You must have been so sick of these rooms, so desperate for night lights, that you could hardly wait until I was out of sight."

"No," she answered with a quick shake of her head. "I had to go, there was no other choice."

"You said that once before. Starvation was the excuse you gave, wasn't it? That doesn't make sense, not with Sanchow coming in three times a day."

186

"That's just it. He didn't come. Or at least he did, twice, but the food never reached me." With quick words that tumbled over themselves, she told him of what had become of the trays and the Chinaman who had brought them. As she came to Pearlie's ultimatum, a look seeped into his face that was so dark, so coldly dangerous, that she stumbled to a halt.

"So you sang for your supper?" he said, the sound of quiet menace in his tone. "And then what?"

Irritation rose inside Serena at this catechism. What right did he have to question her, to make her feel this unearned guilt? She edged away from him, turning to her stomach and rolling to the opposite side to support herself on one elbow. The quilts slid from her shoulders, though she hardly noticed.

"What do you mean?" she demanded.

"Exactly what you think I mean."

"You are neither my guardian nor my husband. By what right do you presume to ask?"

"The right of might," he grated, reaching to close his fingers on her shoulders. "Are you going to tell me?"

"Are you going to pretend it matters?" Serena snapped. The memory of Pearlie's words, her assertion that Ward was tired of his new playmate and was ready for her to earn her own way, gave her words a biting edge of sarcasm.

"It matters," he said through his teeth. "So much that if you value your neck you will— What is this?"

The grip of his hand loosened. A frown snapped his brows together as he stared at her shoulder, at the purple bruises and tiny halfmoon cuts caused by Otto's digging fingers.

"The price of a tray of food," Serena answered, her tone brittle. "The cost would have been much higher if your friend Benedict hadn't managed to convince Otto that I should not be obliged to pay twice for the same meal."

"Otto did this?"

"How was he to guess you would mind? You told Pearlie it was time I joined the other girls, and she gave him to understand that she would be grateful if he—he broke me in right."

"My God," Ward breathed.

"As you say. At least you can understand why I feel a certain gratitude toward Nathan Benedict, though not to the point, I can assure you, of being happy to be drugged and thrown into his arms. It's possible, however, that if you had been gone a few more days I might have had cause to change my mind."

187

Ward stared at her, the gold flecks glittering in his eyes and a white line about his mouth. Abruptly he rolled from her and threw back the covers. Without a word he began to pull on his clothes, stepping into his trousers, jerking on his shirt, stamping his boots on. He ran his fingers through his hair and, still stuffing his shirt into his pants, shouldered out of the room, moving with long strides across the sitting room.

"Ward, where are you going?" Serena called. The slamming of the outer door was her only answer.

What was he going to do? The look on his face had been murderous. Serena hesitated only a moment before she scrambled from the bed. Snatching up her petticoats and underwear, she stepped to the wardrobe and pulled down the first dress that came to hand. She did not know if it was Otto's conduct or Pearlie's that had incensed him, but it must have been one or the other. The implications, either way, left her with a tight feeling in her chest.

Serena was twisting her hair into a knot when a sound penetrated the thin walls of the building. She stopped, holding her breath to listen. It was a woman screaming. The sound came from behind the Eldorado, in the direction of the parlor house.

Pushing the pins into place as she ran, Serena left the room and hurried out into the hallway. At its end, just above the stairway, there was a window that overlooked the side of the parlor house, giving a better view than from the back. The frost that coated it prevented her from looking out. With swift care, she twisted the lock that held the window shut and pushed up the stiff sash.

By leaning to one side, she could see the delivery yard. Ward had crossed its sloping, snow-packed surface and was just disappearing from sight behind the storeroom. Pearlie was standing ankle deep in the snow, outlined cruelly in the harsh morning light. She wore a wrapper of cherry satin over a chemise and drawers of the same material inset with long lozenges of openwork lace through which her skin gleamed. The overbright henna red of her hair was spread upon her shoulders, and her face was contorted with fear and rage.

"Ward!" she screamed. "Come back! Come back and let me explain. You can't do this to me! I won't stand for it. I'll kill myself before I do! Do you hear me? I'll kill myself! Ward!"

The last word was a cry of torment, a despairing wail. As

Serena watched, Pearlie went down on her knees in the snow. Holding her face in her hands, she gave way to racking sobs as she crouched, weaving back and forth like an animal in pain.

At the sound of footsteps below, Serena turned from the window. When Ward reached the foot of the stairs, she was standing at the top with one hand on the banister. She lifted her chin in an unconscious gesture of defense as she met his eyes, but she could not bring herself to speak.

He moved toward her with slow steps, pausing halfway up the stairs. "You will be glad to know," he said, his voice even, "that Otto will never set foot in the Eldorado again."

"Yes," Serena said, though the word was not as strong as she could have wished.

"As for Pearlie, the partnership has been severed. After today, she will have nothing more to do with the Eldorado, or anyone in it."

"I see."

"I realize that is no compensation for what has been done to you, but it will, I think, serve to make you understand that it was no will of mine that you leave my rooms or my bed. I am not tired of you, Serena, and I'm beginning to wonder if I ever will be. As for your earning your way, I have the feeling I will be able to keep you busy enough on that score. There is no need for you to exert yourself on the Eldorado's stage again."

"If that's so," Serena said slowly, "then why were you so strange about going to Denver? Why were you so determined to leave me here?"

"If I was strange," he answered, a wry smile in his eyes, "it was because I didn't want to go. As for why I left you, it was to be certain I could."

Serena looked away. "It seems you proved your point."

"Yes," he agreed, moving slowly up the stairs toward her, "though at a price higher than I am likely to risk again."

"Yes, you lost a partner." Serena stepped away, refusing to accept his meaning.

He came to a halt beside her, his hands slipping around her waist to draw her nearer. "Will you have it in plain words? You are necessary to me, more necessary than food, or drink, or rest on a freezing night, and I don't intend to share you with any man."

The quick, hard kiss he pressed to her lips before he

189

turned, guiding her back toward their rooms, was a seal to what was, in some ways, a vow. The sense of it was plain enough, and yet there had been no word of love. She did not expect or require it, but there had been a moment when she had thought it might come. It was ridiculous. What use had a gambler for such a soft emotion? He wanted her in his bed, close to hand, and he resented any interference with his desire. That was all.

"Get your cloak and we'll find something to eat," Ward said, pausing outside the door of the sitting room.

"There's no need, unless you are especially hungry. I can make bacon and flapjacks, but I'm afraid there's no butter or syrup."

She pushed open the door and stepped inside, indicating the table beside the stove that held her meager supply of food.

"What is this?" Ward stood in the center of the room, his hands resting on his hips.

"I didn't relish starving, so I bought myself a few things to eat. I—had no money so I took yours."

He turned from surveying the neatly laid-out cheese and crackers and bacon, the bags of flour and beans. "You what?"

"I took your money," Serena repeated, her pewter-blue gaze clear. "The change you had in the back of the wardrobe."

"And you managed to get all this?"

He didn't sound angry. Serena sent him a small, uncertain smile. "I would have liked to buy eggs and coffee, and a coffee pot, but there wasn't enough."

"Is that all?"

"Yes. No, I could use butter and syrup, as I said, and if I had a dutch oven I could make biscuits and pot roast—"

"Hold on! Good heavens, Serena! I feel guilty enough for leaving you alone and destitute without your making it sound as if you haven't had a decent meal since I've been gone."

"Oh, I don't need all that for myself, but if I'm going to cook for you—"

"You are not. That is," he went on as the light died out of her face, "I don't expect you to do that, not with the little you have to work with here." A smile softened the lean lines of his face. "I'll admit it would be nice not to have to go out looking for breakfast, or to have somebody banging on the

190

door interrupting our sleep, or whatever we're doing. But that's enough. I'll check on Sanchow. If he's up to it, he can bring in our evening meal, and if not, I'll make other arrangements."

Serena could see no fault in that plan. "All right."

"Right now, as long as we are dressed, I think I would like to have that coffee, and whatever we can find to go with it. I didn't stop to eat last night, and frankly, I'm starving."

Serena nodded, and with a curiously light feeling that bordered on happiness, swung from him, hurrying to fetch her cape. As she pulled the old gray mantle about her shoulders, Ward slanted a quick look at it, then with an impassive expression, held the door for her to pass from the room ahead of him.

They ate at a German restaurant, consuming hot coffee and warm apple fritters, with side dishes of ham and eggs, all prepared by a German hausfrau with her sleeves rolled well above her pink, dimpled elbows. Replete, they set out for the general store, where they purchased all Serena had outlined, plus a number of other items. They were returning along Myers Avenue when a girl came running toward them along the sidewalk, dressed in a long cloak that flapped open in her haste, revealing the chemise and drawers that were all she wore beneath it.

It was one of the girls from the Eldorado. Usually brassy and loud, her face was pale and her hair a rat's-nest tangle. Her voice was a rasp in her throat as she came near them.

"Mr. Dunbar, oh, Mr. Dunbar. You've got to come. Come quick!"

"What is it?"

"It's Pearlie. She's done gone and swallowed a whole box of morphine tablets."

"How do you know?"

"I saw her doin' it. You've got to do something quick or she'll die."

"I don't suppose she happened to mention that she would like to see me before she—passes on?"

"Oh, she did! Yes, she did. She said she wanted to beg you to forgive her before it was too late."

"It's already too late," Ward said, his voice hard. "If Pearlie let you watch her take her overdose, then she fully meant for you to save her. I suggest that you get a doctor for her; that's who she needs, not me."

191

"You're a cruel man to do this to Pearlie," the girl said, tears starting into her eyes.

"And she's a fool to think she can do this to me—nearly as big a one as you are for standing here wasting time."

The girl stared at him with hate in her eyes, then with a sound between a snort and a wail, she turned and ran off in the other direction.

Chapter Twelve

Pearlie did not die. A doctor came, dosed her with an emetic and a purgative, then stripped her to the skin and rubbed her with snow followed by alcohol. Taking advantage of her feeble state, he shut out the other girls of the parlor house for the purpose of giving Pearlie a thorough and probing examination which required the removal of his own clothing. Having made certain that she was sufficiently stimulated, he rendered a statement for his services and went away, leaving Pearlie raging weakly on her pillow.

At least, that was the way it happened according to Consuelo. The Spanish girl visited Serena within a week of Ward's return. It was the first time Serena had seen her since that night. Consuelo had not returned to the Eldorado, nor to the parlor house, though she still had friends at the latter place. There was a quiet glow about the other girl as she told Serena where she had been staying. She had become the mistress of Nathan Benedict. When he had left Serena with Ward that night, he had taken Consuelo to the Continental Hotel. The next day he had leased a small house for her, not a crib but an elegant little four-room house with a front porch, fish-scale woodwork on the sharp gables, and real beveled glass in the front door. They had been down to the Springs, the two of them in his private railroad car, where he had allowed her a free hand in purchasing furnishings. He was generous and kind, was Nathan Benedict, and the Spanish girl had never been so happy, except that sometimes at night, when he held her in his arms, he called her Serena.

"Oh, Consuelo," Serena whispered. "I'm so sorry."

The other girl shook her head, a smile wavering on her lips. "It isn't your fault, and really, I don't mind. You—you must come and see me sometime. I will serve you tea from a china cup, real china."

"I would like that," Serena said, "though I would rather not come when Nathan—Mr. Benedict—is there."

"That's easy," Consuelo said, her rich brown eyes dark. "He only comes at night."

Serena thought it best not to repeat what the Spanish girl had said to Ward. It was not that she actually expected him to be jealous, but he had not been on very good terms with his friend since the night he had found Nathan with Serena.

On the other hand, things between Ward and herself had never gone more smoothly. He spent most of his time with her when he was not downstairs at the gaming tables. They talked of a thousand things, and at night when the stove burned itself out and they retreated from the cold under the covers, they laughed and made love in equal portions. The days and weeks went by, and winter closed in. Serena, complaining of the long days with nothing to do, persuaded Ward to let her buy materials, and needles, and thread, to stitch a dress or two and to make over some of her old things.

"Must you?" he asked. "I will be glad to buy you another dress, even a dozen more, for wearing in public. But I would rather see you in your wrapper, or nothing at all, when I am here alone with you."

"I don't doubt it. So convenient," she said, sending him a roguish glance, "but also drafty. And I'm of the opinion the effect would be lost entirely if I were to borrow your union suit."

"Yes, I can see how it might." He gave a mock sigh. "At least I had you where I wanted you for a while."

"I haven't forgotten."

"I know, and it bothers me. I expect any night to come in and find my wardrobe empty."

"I'm not such an idiot as to play into your hands like that! You would enjoy it far too much."

"It's possible. But you, Serena, did you hate it? Was it that bad?"

194

She looked away from him, shielding her expression with her lashes. "Not so long as I thought my things were lost."

"Your trunk was misplaced for twenty-four hours, if not lost. By the time it turned up after a round trip to Denver, it seemed best to let the situation stay as it was."

"Best! For whom?" The blue-gray gaze she turned in his direction was hard.

"For me. That's the answer you expected, isn't it? But also for you. I wasn't sure that if you had clothes to wear you wouldn't set out looking for one of those gold millionaires you mentioned."

"I have clothes now, including a walking costume you bought me that is quite respectable. What makes you think I won't do the same thing any day?" Anger at his unflattering estimation of her character lent a challenge to her words.

"I don't think it," he said, his voice rough, "but I can promise you I will do my best to see that you don't have the opportunity."

"And how do you propose to do that?"

"By keeping you so busy," he said, his tone low as he moved toward her, "that you have no time or thought for that project. Shall I show you how?"

Despite the abrupt conclusion of their conversation, the subject was not ended between them. It surfaced again before another week had passed. The situation between Serena and Ward had not changed materially. She did not appear upon the stage again, nor wear the gilt-heeled slippers that had been nearly ruined by the snow. She was no longer constricted to the upstairs of the Eldorado, however. Nearly every night she descended to the barroom. Sometimes she stood talking to Timothy or approached the other girls, a new group since Ward had forbidden Pearlie's parlor-house girls to solicit customers in the Eldorado, for a few minutes of quiet conversation. When not occupied in that way, she stayed close to Ward at the gaming tables for luck, or assumed in a quiet way the role of hostess for the private poker games that sometimes convened in the sitting room. She discovered by degrees that her presence had a quieting effect upon the miners in the barroom. They were unfailingly polite to her, stepping aside for her to pass, pulling out a chair for her to sit, quelling any rowdy who might look to be getting out of hand. Still, Ward never left her without his protection. He was always nearby, keeping an eye on her, calling to her to come and stand at his shoulder, or take the chair beside him so he could hold her hand or toy with the shining ringlets that fell over her shoulder.

It was unusual, then, for him to disappear one night; more unusual still for him to remain out of the room for a long length of time. Serena had not seen him leave. The last she had noticed, he had been talking to Nathan Benedict, and then she had been called backstage where one of the dancers had twisted her ankle.

It felt peculiar, being in the barroom without Ward near at hand. Not that she was molested in any way, but she was aware of being watched, of sly glances and guffawing laughter from a corner as at some lewd joke, of a man with blood-shot eyes and silica dust in his eyebrows and hair averting his gaze when she glanced in his direction.

Without hurrying, Serena worked her way around the room to the staircase. So as to prevent any impression of retreat, she climbed the treads with slow grace, pausing now and then to look over the railing.

In the hallway outside her rooms, she came to a halt. From inside could be heard the sound of low voices. This was where Ward had gone, then. She did not want to intrude on what must be a private conversation; still less did she relish the idea of returning to the barroom.

Making a decision proved unnecessary. Before she could move the sitting-room door was flung open. Ward, his face dark and his green eyes glittering, stared at Serena a long moment, then stood aside for Nathan to pass from the room.

"You will let me know what you decide?" Nathan asked, turning back.

"I'll do that," Ward grated.

Lifting his hat to Serena before fitting it on his head, the other man bade them both a good night, then with a lingering look in Serena's direction, walked away down the hall.

Serena stepped through the door Ward still held. "I didn't know you were up here," she said over her shoulder.

"There was a matter Nathan wanted to discuss." He shut the door and turned with his hand on the knob. "One that, for obvious reasons, he wanted kept quiet."

There was a jeering note in his voice, a scathing inflection that seemed to suggest Serena should understand what he was saying.

"Oh?"

"Come, you can do better than that. You should be more surprised, or at least you should act it."

196

"I don't know what you are talking about. Your business affairs are no concern of mine." Serena turned to face him, a puzzled frown between her winged brows.

"As you know very well, in this case they very much concern you."

"If I am supposed to answer that, I'm sorry. I haven't the least idea what you mean."

Ward stared at her. "That really is too much to ask me to believe. I have good reason to know that you haven't spoken to Nathan in private since I came back, but I thought there might have been a letter, a smuggled note or some such romantic foolishness."

"There's been nothing like that. I don't know what you are accusing me of, but whatever it is, I don't like it."

There was an arrested look in Ward's eyes. "If Nathan is willing to stake so much on such an off chance, he must be more smitten than I realized. I wish I had known."

"Known what? What are you talking about?"

"Here in this room a few minutes ago, Nathan offered to sign over to me his interest in one of the most promising mining claims in the area, plus a block of shares, a large block, in the corporation that controls his other holdings. The value of what he was willing to give adds up to thousands of dollars, possibly even hundreds of thousands."

"Just like that?"

"Not quite. As you must have guessed, he wants something from me in return."

The heavily ironic timbre of his voice grated along Serena's nerves. "And that is?"

"He wants me to—to formally sever my relationship with you."

"He—what?" Serena felt a coldness that had nothing to do with the chill of the night. She stared at Ward, unable to believe what she had heard.

"If you are telling the truth, he offered me, without any concrete expectation of having you for himself, a large sum of money to relinquish you. That looks to me as if he feels that you have some attachment to me, though not so much but that he has hopes of winning you, if I can just be persuaded to give you a push in his direction."

Serena swallowed. "I see. And what did you say?"

"I said, my dear Serena, that I would have to think about it."

"What is there to think about?" Serena asked, whirling

197

from him, moving to stand with her hands held out to the nickel-coated grate of the stove with the red glow of coals behind it. "With so much money involved, you don't dare refuse."

"Don't I? You would be surprised what I would dare, for the right reasons."

In her distress, Serena barely heard him. "Then there is your friendship. You wouldn't want to destroy that for the sake of—of—"

"Of a beautiful woman we both want? It wouldn't be the first time friends had parted company for such a reason. But neither of those things counts in this. What matters is how you feel. Are you making excuses for me, to make it easy for me to turn you over to him? This is your big chance, Serena. Here is your mining millionaire ready to drop into your lap. All you have to do is say that's what you want."

"You would let me go, just like that?"

"If you tell me you want Nathan and his money it shouldn't be too difficult."

Serena looked away from him across the room. "I understood Nathan already had a woman, Consuelo."

"That will be her problem."

"I don't think I would like being the cause of her losing so much."

"There is that, of course."

"As for Nathan, I'm not certain I like the idea of being—bought."

"A valid objection."

He was not going to help her. Straightening, swinging around, she found him watching her through narrowed green eyes. She managed a small smile. "Moreover, I doubt that he would appreciate anything which came to him so easily. Add to that my reluctance to have you think you know me too well, and I believe Mr. Benedict's answer must be—no. That is, of course, if you are positive his offer doesn't tempt you beyond your power to resist?"

"You really intend to refuse?"

She was aware of the intensity of his stare, the shading of disbelief in his voice. "I believe I must."

"Knowing you are unlikely to get a better offer?"

"Are you suggesting I am holding out for marriage? I assure you, I know how futile that is."

"Serena—" he began, then stopped.

"Yes?" She met his eyes, her blue-gray gaze unflinching.

There was a suspended look in his face, as if there was something he wanted to ask, but was not certain he would like the answer.

"It doesn't matter," he said finally. "Nothing matters except this." He took her in his arms, drawing her close against him, holding her as though he meant never to let her go. His kiss was deep and cherishing, unending even as he sank to one knee upon the thick carpet before the hot glow of the stove, pulling her down with him. With trancelike slowness, they undressed each other, and, stretched upon the sybaritic warmth and softness of the rug woven in ancient Persia, they moved together in fearful harmony. Tasting, exploring, they endured the torment of holding the final crest of pleasure at bay, until it could be held no more, then with piercing, aching apprehension they plunged toward satiation.

Afterward Serena lay staring at the wavering shadows cast by the coal-oil lamp that burned on the table. The proposition put to Ward by Nathan Benedict, though admittedly no compliment to a woman of principle, was flattering in its way. As much as she might dislike the idea of having a value put upon herself, it must be taken into account that Nathan Benedict had not meant for her to be informed of the offer; that much was obvious since he had seen fit to discuss the matter with Ward in private. Doubtless if he had thought she could be swayed by money alone, he would have made her a handsome offer and swept her out from under Ward's nose without regard for how his friend might feel. That he had chosen the way he had to go about it indicated not only that he did not think so, but that he, as Ward had suggested, considered she had some feeling for the man with whom she was living. That was Nathan's mistake, of course. By the same token, didn't his offer indicate that he was fairly certain Ward had no such affection for her?

Was it possible? Could he call her beautiful, say how he had missed her, make love to her with such caring gentleness, and feel nothing stronger than lust? It disturbed her to think so. Not that she wanted Ward to love her. It made no great difference, after all. But if he should come to care for her, it would be a fitting punishment for what he had done, a fine revenge. She closed her eyes, trying to dismiss that train of thought. A petty thing, vengeance. But so satisfying.

"Are you certain this is where she is living?" Serena voiced the anxious question as she came to a halt in the middle of the frozen ruts of the road. Before her sat a one-room house with a single door and one sagging window. Built of green lumber at no distant date, its board siding was warped and twisted, leaving gaps for the wind and rain to enter, and the roof was canted at a strange, hip-shot angle. There was no name painted upon it, no red curtains, and yet it was without doubt one of the notorious Poverty Gulch cribs where women too independent, too unattractive, too old or diseased for the dance halls and parlor houses solicited customers.

"I am sure," Consuelo answered, "or at least, I am sure there is a girl who lives here that matches the description you gave. She has hair like white silk and is well shaped, though she is a little childish. She speaks often of a babe that died, but never of a husband. And there is a man who comes often to visit, usually in the morning."

Serena took a deep breath. "If it is Lessie, I don't know what I'm going to say."

"You will think of something."

"I am more grateful than I can tell you for finding her for me."

The Spanish girl gave a small shrug. "It was nothing. I am only sorry it took so long. She doesn't have many friends, this Lessie. She keeps much to herself, never goes out. Even her food is brought by the man who visits. For this reason it took time for me to hear of her."

"I expect she is afraid of being seen, afraid Elder Greer will find her," Serena said unhappily.

"I can't blame her for that," Consuelo answered, her tone dry. "I would not want that one to find me either."

"She may not want to see me," Serena said.

"There is only one way to find out," Consuelo stepped to the rock that served as a step, and gave a sharp knock on the loose slats of the door.

As they waited, Serena glanced at the other girl. Until today, she had not spoken to Consuelo since Nathan Benedict had made his offer to Ward. It might be the result of her own feeling of awkwardness, but she thought there was a change in the other girl's manner toward her. It was nothing obvious. Cynicism and quick action were in Consuelo's nature, as much a part of her as her pride and unobtrusive helpfulness. And yet there was a brittleness about her and an edge to her voice that made Serena wonder. Surely Nathan could not have been so unwise as to tell his present mistress that he was inclined to replace her? Such honesty would have been too cruel.

The door in front of them opened a crack. A whispery voice issued from inside. "What do you want?"

"Lessie?" Serena inquired, her tone doubtful.

"Serena!"

The door swung wide. Lessie, her face shining with wonder, reached out to take Serena's hand, dragging her inside. She looked as though she would protest as Consuelo followed close behind, but relented as Serena, keeping an arm about the girl's waist, made a quick introduction. The Spanish girl spoke a few cool words of acknowledgment, then, in answer to Lessie's frantic signals, pushed the door shut.

"How are you, Lessie?" Serena asked.

"Fine, but I have so much to tell you." The white-haired girl sat on the end of the unmade bed, waving Serena to a seat beside her. There was a chair with uneven legs and a sunken cowhide seat, but after one look at it, Consuelo elected to lean against the wall.

"All right, begin," Serena said when they were settled.

Lessie smoothed the gown of pink outing she wore over her knees and clasped her fingers together. "First, I was sick and my baby was born, only Beatrice killed it. They told me it died, but I know better. I heard it crying; that must have meant it was alive. I told Agatha, but she slapped me. She said I was silly and stupid, that Beatrice wouldn't do such a thing. Then she told Elder Greer that I was out of my head, and he believed her. He prayed over me for days and days, and then he—he said the only way for me to stop grieving was to make another baby."

Serena, her face grim, looked at Consuelo. "I knew he was a bastard," the Spanish girl said, her voice dispassionate.

"Yes," Lessie said with sudden bright enthusiasm. "I didn't want to, Serena. I didn't want to at all, not with him. So I ran away."

The crosscurrents of hate and jealousy, weak wrath, backbiting, and lewd suggestion that Lessie had evoked with her simple words were vivid in Serena's memory. "That was probably the best thing you could have done," she said slowly.

"Yes, because I met Jack. He was kind to me. He bought me taffy candy and hair ribbons and let me ride on the train. For a little while we stayed at a big hotel, but there were too many people, so he found me this sweet little house to stay in where I will be safe. Don't you like it?"

201

Serena looked around at the dreary, unpainted walls plastered with newspapers and pages torn from magazines, at the sagging bed with its dingy sheets, the cracked china chamberpot with its lid covered by a garish crocheted "husher" or cozy, and the rickety washstand holding a mismatched ironstone pitcher and bowl. "It—must be nice not to have to share it with anyone."

A shadow passed over Lessie's face. "I don't mind, not when it's Jack. I wish the other men didn't have to come, but Jack says it's not a sin, and it won't be for long. He says if I let them—let them do what they want, we will soon have enough money, with what he has saved up, to go away together."

"Is that important? Is that what you want?"

"Oh, yes. I love him. I wouldn't want to live without him."

"You wouldn't want to come and live with me?" Serena was aware of Consuelo's quick glance in her direction. It was no wonder she was surprised. Until this moment, Serena had not mentioned what she intended to do when she found Lessie. She had not mentioned it because she had not known herself. How Ward would react to the other girl, she did not dare think. She would face that problem when she came to it.

"Live with you?" Lessie said, a look of wonder on her face. "I would love to, Serena; nobody has ever been as good to me as you were when you were with the wagon train. But I don't know what Jack would say. I don't think he would like it, not if it meant I couldn't have visits from the miners at night."

"I feel sure," Consuelo said deliberately, "that Ward would not like that."

"Ward?" Lessie asked, looking from one to the other.

"The—the man I live with," Serena answered, her color high.

"You have a man too? I'm so glad. You understand then what I mean."

Serena refused to look at the Spanish girl. "Not exactly."

"Oh, but anyway, I couldn't come while he was there, your man, I mean. It wouldn't be right, and I would feel out of place. And if he wouldn't like the miners, he might not like Jack either. I couldn't go anywhere where Jack couldn't come to see me. I like going to bed with Jack, though I never liked it with Elder Greer."

"Oh, Lessie." The impossibility of explaining her position

202

to the girl made Serena feel helpless. But wasn't she helpless, in truth? What could she offer Lessie that would be better than what she had? A job at the Eldorado, no matter how well intentioned, would be all too likely to lead to the same kind of situation, and the next man to take advantage of her might not go to so much trouble to make himself agreeable. This man Jack was using her, that could not be plainer. One day he would grow tired of her, and then what? Another man? An endless line of men? But, Serena asked herself, how was her own situation any different? What would become of her when Ward no longer wanted her? How could she hope to help Lessie when she could not help herself?

"Don't be sad, Serena. You can come and visit me. We can talk to each other."

"You can come and see me at the Eldorado. I'll give you the direction, and then if you ever need help you'll have somebody." Reaching out, Serena clasped the other girl's hand, giving it a quick squeeze.

"Is that where you are, at the Eldorado? I wondered what had happened to you, after we left you. We heard you were seen with a man. I—I don't think I would ever have been brave enough to leave the wagon train if it hadn't been for you."

"Oh, Lessie, you will come to see me?" Serena said, her throat tight with the guilt of knowing she was in some sense to blame for the white-haired girl being here, instead of with the Mormons where she would have been safe, if not happy.

"I wish I could, Serena, really I do, but I saw Elder Greer the other day. He's looking for me; I know he is. If he found me, he would make me come back. I—I'm glad you came to see me, but if you can find me, anybody can. I've got to be careful, more careful than ever."

Serena tried to reassure her. Even Consuelo tried, telling her of her special contacts with the women of the parlor houses and cribs. Lessie seemed relieved, but she refused to talk of leaving her house, even for a few minutes. There was nothing Serena could do except leave her there.

"Do you think she will be all right?" Frowning as she stared back over her shoulder at the bleak crib whipped by the raw winter wind, Serena put the question to Consuelo.

"Who can say?" The Spanish girl lifted her shoulders and let them fall. "It sometimes seems God looks after such as

203

she. It may be she will fare better than either of us. If not, she will assuredly have the blessing of suffering less."

For an instant Serena met the dark and deep gaze of the woman called Spanish Connie. It was she who looked away first.

The winter wore on. The high mountain snow clouds came down to smother the volcanic valley, scattering their weight of soft crystals, followed always by the brilliant sun to melt them away in an ever-recurring cycle. Often, as the early winter dark drew in, there was a commotion heard on a street corner here and there about town as Elder Greer tried to bring the men parading the streets to a recognition of their sinful ways. Shouting, exhorting over the noise of barkers from the vaudeville theaters and raucous music from the dime-a-dance halls, it was not unusual for him to share his impromptu pulpit with a tall thin man in sackcloth dolorously predicting the end of the world in just six years, at the close of the century. The unruly Saint was also known to preach before the cribs, praying with trembling fervor for the soul of the girls who stood half-naked in the windows. On one occasion he was led away by the sheriff for attempting to force his way into a parlor house.

Christmas came and went without much notice beyond a few carolers slogging their way through the muddy streets, and a bit of tinsel here and there in the store windows. Ward bought Serena a new cape with a beaver collar and a muff to match; compensation, she thought, for the fur cape from Nathan he had taken from her. She embroidered his monogram with careful stitches on a set of handkerchiefs and made a bowl of wassail. It did not seem much compared to the set of cufflinks in the shape of gold nuggets that Pearlie presented to him, but it was the best she could do. It was some consolation that Ward seemed pleased with her gift, tucking one of the embroidered squares into his pocket, while the cufflinks were shut away in the back of his wardrobe.

It was not, at all events, a happy holiday. The celebrations, small though they were, reminded Serena of Christmas a year before when her mother and father were still alive and there had been such hope for the future as they planned their westward move. The final seal was supplied late at night after the long Christmas day. A drunken brawl erupted at Pearlie's parlor house. A belligerent customer claimed he had been robbed; the girl called him a liar. Pearlie supported her girl, the man's friends took his side. A vase was thrown, someone was slapped. Other girls and their customers joined the fray. Ward was called, arriving with the sheriff in time to put out a small fire from an overturned coal brazier in the bedroom where it had all started.

In order to get Pearlie away before she antagonized the sheriff and his deputies to the point of arresting her, Ward brought her to the Eldorado. Long after peace had been restored, she stood at the bar, her hair disheveled, the pupils of her eyes huge and brilliant with the effects of belladonna-leaf compresses, waving a glass and cursing men in general and those in authority in particular. She ended by passing out, and as Ward carried her back to the parlor house, she murmured slurred and befuddled endearments against the strong column of his neck.

After New Year's, one-seated cutters and open sleighs appeared in the streets. It was counted a great treat by the men of the town to stand on the wooden sidewalks and watch the ladies from the Old Homestead, clad in silks and satins, with cartwheel hats swathed in veils and blooming with flowers on their heads, and fur lap robes tucked around them just under their bosoms, skim by behind high-stepping teams of blowing horses. The jingle of the sleigh bells made a merry sound that rang far in the cold, clear air.

Finally the last snow fell. The banks that lay in the shade, protected from the growing heat of the sun's rays, turned gray with soot and ash, and grew hard-caked, like ancient glaciers. The hillsides took on a haze of green. Rock squirrels darted here and there. At night the dogs kept up a constant barking, and the alleyways on the edge of town echoed to strange thuds and huffing grunts as the black bears came down out of the heights to forage in the rubbish heaps. Bear hides, the basis of next winter's lap robes, appeared, pegged to the sides of buildings, their rancid and sickly-sweet smell of death hanging in the air. One morning they woke to find wild roses and tiny pink geraniums blooming on the scarred slopes between buildings, and tiny, jewel-throated hummingbirds beating the air with their wings. Summer was upon them.

Serena stood at the back door of the Eldorado, enjoying the delicate perfume of the roses wafted toward her. The warm wind brought with it also the clean smell of spruce and pine from the crater rim above the town. It reminded Serena of the day she and Ward had driven up Mt. Pisgah and their picnic on the sun-kissed slope. He had made love to her that day, a farewell before he left her. It seemed so long ago, and yet like yesterday. They had been such strangers then, not that they knew each other so much better now, but at least there was little constraint between them. In the last weeks of winter and early spring Ward had seemed more relaxed. She herself had come to trust him, to feel secure as the days passed and he showed no sign of boredom with her company. That was not the only reason for her tranquillity, of course.

Serena compressed her lips together, closing her eyes, then forced herself to composure. She was tranquil at times; at others she was far from it. Her body had adjusted with placid resignation to the physical changes necessary for the child growing inside her; it was her mind that was in turmoil.

She had not told Ward. First she had waited to be sure, then she had put it off because of the death of one of the parlor-house girl's from a bungled abortion performed upon herself with the nib of a pen. To announce her own condition so soon after the tragedy seemed the wrong thing to do. She wanted no one suggesting that ridding herself of the baby was the best course. Now, in her third month, she thought it was nearly too late for such measures. Rather than tell Ward at this late date, she had a perverse desire for him to see it for himself.

How could he not have noticed the changes in her body? True, her morning sickness had taken the form of no more than a general malaise accompanied by a slight nauseous reaction to odors at all hours of the day. Her waist was still slim and her stomach flat, but the changes were there for anyone who cared enough to see them.

That was the question. Did he care enough? Did he think of her so little that such a thing could pass unrecognized? It was difficult to believe that he could live with her for months, lie with her at night, hold her in his arms, and never guess.

Sometimes she caught him watching her, a somber light in his green eyes. Often at such times he would smile and pull her down onto his lap. Others, he would get up and stride from the room, descending to the barroom or stalking out into the street to come back hours later, chilled and wind-blown. She learned not to question him. It was not that he became angry or abusive; it was the look of blank anguish in his eyes as he turned to her, and his grim silence, that persuaded her it was useless.

The sound of a man whistling caught her attention. From

around the side of the building came a stooped and bearded Negro man. He nodded at the sight of her, and broke off in mid-tune to give a chuckling sound to the pair of gray burros that followed behind him on lead ropes.

"Morning, ma'am," he said. "I was told to deliver these misbegotten beasties back here. Whereabouts do you want me to tie 'em up?"

"Who told you to deliver them?" Her question was mildly curious, nothing more.

"Why, Mr. Dunbar, ma'am. He always takes a pair of burros with him when he goes up in the mountains. There's places they can go no horse can, or maybe will."

"Did—did Mr. Dunbar say when he meant to take them out?"

"Seems like it was in the morning bright and early, best I remember. Said he had his pack saddles all loaded, strapped up and ready."

Mechanically, Serena pointed out the rings set into the back wall of the storeroom for tying horses, then watched as the man fastened the burros and went whistling on his way once more. It seemed she was not the only one with a secret. Ward was going back into the mountains prospecting this summer, just as he had the year before, and the year before that. She shouldn't be surprised, she supposed, but she was. He had spoken not a word of it to her, had made no plans, said nothing of what she was to do in his absence, where she was to go. She had seen nothing of his pack saddles, loaded or otherwise. If he had packed food, it had not been from the supplies in her makeshift kitchen, nor had she noticed any of his clothing gone from his wardrobe.

Ward had gone out that morning after breakfast. He had not said where he was going, and though there was nothing particularly unusual in that, the more Serena thought of it, the more significant it became. He did not return for the noon meal, nor did he put in an appearance as darkness fell. Serena, making her supper on cheese and bacon wrapped in a biscuit, pictured him at the Continental Hotel, dining on steak and liver, with vegetables swimming in butter, and rich custard pies. No doubt he was with Nathan or some of his other wealthy acquaintances. More than likely their wives were present, glittering with diamonds, dripping with lace. There would be pompous speeches and champagne. The air would be thick with perfume, the smoke of Havana cigars, and the languidly ridiculous voices of the new rich trying to talk in what they imagined to be cultured tones.

Lightning flickered behind the curtains. Serena put away the remains of her meal, then, wiping her hands on a linen towel, wandered into the bedroom. She pushed back the drapes at the windows and stood staring out at the pulsing, white-gold light that played across the sky in the direction of the Sangre de Cristos. They needed a rain to lay the dust now that the snow-melt was gone. Dropping the drape, she turned toward the bathroom. She might as well get ready for bed. Whether Ward returned or not, she did not feel like making the effort to go down to the barroom.

The bath water was hot and relaxing. Serena lathered herself with slow preoccupation, using the Pears soap that had been a Christmas present from Consuelo. It wasn't the end of the world that Ward was leaving. She didn't know why the idea affected her so, unless it was his secrecy about it. Had he kept it from her because he thought she would make a scene, crying and asking him not to go? Was it simply that he had been so long a bachelor, accountable to no one, that he saw no need to inform anyone of his plans? Or was the omission more sinister? Did he intend to release her before he left? Maybe he meant to stave off any unpleasantness by waiting until the last minute to let her go, trusting that she would have found a new niche for herself by the time he returned.

If she told him she was going to have his child, would it make a difference? Despite the length of time she had lived with Ward, she could not be sure. He was a self-sufficient man, self-contained. The life he was living did not satisfy him; that much was obvious. If he were happy he would not need these yearly treks into the wilderness. He went to look for gold, or so he said, but if that was truly his aim he could have investigated some of the mining claims right here in the Cripple Creek district that he had won at the gaming tables. No, Ward was not content as a gambler, and yet he sought to justify his choice of occupation. Why? Was it the money? Did it serve as a recompense for what he had lost? Or was the making of it the only challenge left to him, the only way he could hope to regain, in some sense, the prestige that had once been his by birthright?

After so long, she should have been more sure of his feelings toward her. She did know that he liked to be near her, that he enjoyed the use of her body and considered her beautiful, but that was all. Sometimes it seemed that should be enough. Was it a fault within herself, or in Ward, that it wasn't?

What would she do if she was no longer wanted? Where would she go? There was no place in Cripple Creek, or elsewhere, for women in her condition who had no husband, no home. She would be able to work for a short time, but that only if she could find a job. She supposed Elder Greer, and his kind, would say whatever happened to her was just punishment. Strange, but she did not feel guilty. She only felt a vast weariness aligned to a smoldering anger at her own helplessness.

With sudden energy that sent water slopping over the sides of the tub, Serena came to her feet and stepped out onto the rug. She dried herself with careless efficiency, then pushed her arms into her wrapper. Flushed and overheated from the hot water, she left the cambric robe hanging open for coolness as she moved from the bathroom.

Lightning still flickered, sending its glow into the darkness of the bedroom. Releasing her hair that had been piled on top of her head to keep it out of the water, letting it cascade down her back, she stepped to the window. The fiery bolts crackled down the sky, dancing over the mountain tops. Thunder rumbled, shuddering between the high walls that surrounded the town, its echos rolling off into the distance. Looping the draperies to one side, Serena stood staring out. There was something appealing in the wild, elemental forces abroad in the night. It made her pulse beat faster, gave her a sense of excitement, of portent, that was edged also with dread.

At a sound behind her, like a soft, indrawn breath, she turned. The dark shape of a man stood in the doorway. She went still, scarcely breathing. A brilliant flash of lightning illuminated her there, outlining the dark mass of her hair with silver, shining with blue fire in her eyes, sculpting the slender lines of her arms and the proud globes of her perfectly formed breasts in translucent marble. Its flare also lit the room enough to identify the intruder who had entered under the cover of the storm.

"Ward," Serena breathed.

"I hope you weren't expecting anyone else, not dressed like that." He lounged toward her, the sound of lazy humor in his voice, though she could have sworn that an instant earlier his face had been a hard mask of pain.

"I didn't hear you come in."

"My good fortune."

As he neared, one hand outstretched in the darkness, Serena dropped the curtain she held with an abrupt movement, and snatched the edges of her wrapper together. Reaching for her belt, tying it with quick jerks, she stepped away from him. The white glare of lightning filled the room once more, with the bass roar of thunder that vibrated in the walls around them. Ward's words were nearly lost in the rumbling sound.

"I didn't mean to startle you."

"You didn't, at least not more than a moment."

He was silent for the time it took for her to cross to the bathroom and return with the low-burning lamp. "I never saw you upset by a storm before."

"It isn't the storm," she said without looking in his direction.

"I take it there is something else bothering you, then. What is it?"

Serena hesitated. "Nothing. It's nothing."

He shrugged out of his coat, his green gaze steady upon her. When he began to unbutton his shirt, Serena swung to the dresser, taking up his silver-backed brush. With fingers that shook a little, she dragged it through the tangled skein of her hair, tugging at it as she drew the long length forward over her shoulder. A knot of apprehension in her stomach, she watched as he flung his shirt to one side and approached to stand close behind her. He lifted his hand, closing the strong brown fingers around the brush she held, taking it from her grasp. His touch gentle, oddly soothing, he began to draw it through her hair, smoothing the silken black strands, gathering them in his hands before letting them ripple down her back. His face was absorbed, pensive. Serena hardly dared breathe. In the quiet she could hear the soft sputter of the coal oil lamp as the flame shivered on its wick.

"I'll be leaving tomorrow."

The words hovered in the air, emphasized by the boom of thunder. Serena swallowed. "I know."

"I thought you might." Ward leaned to place the brush on the dresser.

"I saw your pack animals."

He gave a slow nod. "I suppose I should have told you, only I wasn't sure until yesterday that I was going this summer."

"Why not?" Serena asked, her gaze going quickly to his face reflected in the shaving mirror.

"A number of reasons. You, for one. Pearlie, for another. I'm worried about her. She drinks too much, and I'm told she can't sleep without her nightly dose of morphine. That stuff should be outlawed, instead of available on any drugstore shelf."

"She's a grown woman. There's nothing you can do."

A wan smile crossed his face. "There is, if I could just bring myself to do it."

"You mean—live with her?" Serena swung slowly to face him.

"That, or make a clean break. I sometimes wonder if making myself responsible for her wasn't a greater cruelty than leaving her to make her own way would have been."

"She saved your life."

"For what it's worth," he agreed. Sighing, he rubbed the back of his neck, as if his head ached.

It was foolish of her to make his excuses for him, especially where Pearlie was concerned. Moving to the bed, Serena began to turn back the covers. "Will you be gone long?"

"A few weeks. I'll be back long before the snow flies."

"And what," she said deliberately, her voice as calm as she could make it, "am I supposed to do in the meantime?"

"What do you mean? Did you want to come with me?"

He had thrown himself down on a chair to pull off his boots. Serena glanced at him then looked away again. "No, certainly not."

"Too bad. I might have enjoyed the company," he said.

"I'm sure."

He sent her a measuring glance. "If you won't come, then I suppose you will have to stay here until I get back. I'll lay in another supply of penny dreadfuls and leave you plenty of money for food. You'll have nothing to do except lie around and read, get fat and lazy."

Serena sent him a sharp glance, but his expression held nothing more than quizzical humor. "It sounds enticing."

"So it does. If I think about it too much, I may decide not to go."

"I doubt that," Serena said, smiling before she sobered. "Is there—would it be possible for me to have a key?"

"To these rooms? It depends."

"On what?"

211

"On whether or not you mean to lock me out," he answered, drawing off his last boot and setting the pair to one side.

She tilted her head to one side. "It's an idea."

Getting to his feet, Ward moved toward her. "I didn't think much of it." He took the pillow she was fluffing from her hands and drew her into his arms. "But tell me the truth, are you afraid to stay here alone?"

Otto was gone. Pearlie had been relegated to the parlor house. She would have food and safety. "No, not really, not if you don't stay away too long."

"I think," he said, a serious light in the green of his eyes, "that I can promise that."

His lips were warm and firm, his arms a haven. He pushed the fingers of one hand through the soft mass of her hair, cradling her head, while with the other he loosened the tie beneath her breasts. His questing fingers slid under her wrapper, smoothing upward to cup the swelling fullness of her breast. With ravishing gentleness he caressed the thrusting rose nipples so they contracted under his hand.

Releasing her with slow reluctance, he reached to douse the light, then in the lightning's fitful glow, brushed the wrapper from her shoulders and let fall his trousers. Flesh to flesh, they sought the bed, he lowering her beside him with iron muscles. His mouth moved on hers. He invaded her senses with relentless sweetness, stirring her to the slow rise of abandon, urging her toward a distant delight. She turned toward him in a response of her own will, a fatalistic and secretive farewell.

There was about him the ozone freshness of the night and also its dark excitement. Entranced, she touched the crisp vitality of his hair as his kiss seared the delicate hollow of her throat, dropping lower to the warm valley between her breasts. She felt the tantalizing flick of his tongue as he shifted to one soft mound, scaling the peak. His hand glided over the sensitive skin of her abdomen to the flatness of her belly, lingering, or so it seemed, on that silken surface. Her stomach muscles tightened in anticipation and alarm, a defense against the dissolving rapture that threatened.

It could not be denied. No tender curve, no exquisite hollow was left unexplored, no barricade of modesty unbreached. The night pulsed with molten fire, and that same burning essence flowed in her veins. There was a fullness in her loins. She felt the hardness of Ward's thigh against her and the rigid strength of his desire. She wanted to encompass and hold, to take him deep inside her. With pent breath she clung, suspended in the paralyzing ecstasy of her need.

Sensing her distress, he raised himself above her, entering her quickly, pressing deep. Snared by his own extremity, his arms clenched upon her and his breathing grew ragged. Serena moved against him and was caught in a spreading, splintering conflagration.

It was a consuming caldron, fury and flame, a blood-red heat. It was a suffocating, demanding thing, a devouring inferno that swept over them and left them spent and panting.

In the still, exhausted aftermath, Serena lay, her body intertwined with Ward's. The night was dark and quiet. The lightning was done, the thunder had rolled away. The promise of the storm had been false. There had been no relieving rain.

PART TWO

Chapter Thirteen

The summer in the high mountains was such a fleeting season that little of it was allowed to go to waste. There were baseball games at the new park on the outskirts of Cripple Creek, horse racing at the rough track at the small town of Gillett, and rodeos at the ranching properties on the edge of the district. Tent meetings, Chautauqua assemblies, prize fights, political rallies, all with food spread on groaning tables, occupied those with social natures, and for the younger crowd there was square dancing, and in some cases there were parties of a formality to be classed as balls. There were wild-flower-gathering expeditions, junkets on the hundred-thousand-dollar carriage toll road up Pikes Peak, and drives to gawk at the summer visitors staying at the magnificent hotels and rooming houses in the small, Alpine-flavored towns that lined Ute Pass.

The Fourth of July was a grand day with a wonderful parade that included the firefighting hose companies, and the bands from every club and lodge in the district, marching down streets decked with red, white, and blue bunting and streamers. But one of the most favored events was the flower parade, not the least reason being that it featured the prettiest and most vivacious young women in the town.

Held in August, the parade consisted of carriages, wagons, and two-wheeled bicycles with the bodies and wheels covered with flowers and greenery. The young ladies wore their lightest and most fragile pastel organdies and voiles, and flower-bedecked hats of white straw. Veils of organza and airy parasols were also much in evidence, as were gentlemen in white suits, or white trousers with dark jackets and white ties, as escorts for the frail drivers.

Serena watched the festivities of the flower parade from the street in front of the Eldorado. Beside her was Consuelo, a useful and amusing companion, since the Spanish girl was able to separate the dashing young society matrons and the daughters of the mine owners from the fair cyprians of Myers Avenue. It was not always an easy task, especially since the most high-spirited and eligible men might be seen riding or walking at the side of any equipage. If there was good reason to suppose that the escorts were to a man far from sober, it only added to the gaiety and exuberance of the day.

A matron who made her winter home in Colorado Springs wheeled by in a spider phaeton decorated with smilax, geraniums, and sweet peas, and pulled by four white horses. The girls from the Old Homestead sat enthroned in a victoria on burgundy velvet seats strewn with pink roses. A mine owner's wife, sitting with her two homely daughters in a surrey smothered in marigolds, the most blatantly golden yellow blossoms available, drew comment for the overpowering fragrance that had the occupants looking a trifle green. Close behind them came an equestrienne seated upon a saddle blanket covered with purple asters, setting off a habit of billowing lavender twill.

Pearlie was an entrant in the parade. Her carriage was decked with orange poppies. In solitary splendor, she lolled on the seat wearing a dress of white printed with orange-and-blue flowers, and with a live, brilliantly plumed parrot sitting on her shoulder. The man who was driving her, dressed in white with a top hat of iridescent green, was Otto. Serena stared at him without surprise. After Ward had fired him, the big man had worked in the mines for a few short weeks, entered a few none too successful boxing matches, and finally wound up as Pearlie's right-hand man at the parlor house. So long as he stayed well away from the Eldorado, she had no complaint.

Hardly had the sensation Pearlie and Otto created died away than the cyclists came into view. Dressed in white, with white straw boaters on their heads and their cycles trimmed with daisies, they were a dazzling sight in the bright sunlight.

"Look," Serena said, craning this way and that to see over the milling crowd. "Isn't that Lessie?"

It was indeed Elder Greer's third wife, riding a bicycle as if she had never covered ground any other way. A plump young man ran along beside her, trying valiantly to keep a white Chinese parasol over her head. Catching a glimpse of Serena, Lessie waved, and nearly collided with a horse trough that loomed in her path.

"I heard the Mormon wagon train had gone on. I guess this proves it," Serena commented with an amused glance at Consuelo.

"I don't know," the Spanish girl replied. "I haven't seen or heard anything from your crazy Saint, but someone told me they thought he let his family go on ahead while he stayed, working as a carpenter down in the Springs."

"Why would he do that?"

"Who knows?" The other girl twitched a shoulder. "He's lost two of his four women, hasn't he? Maybe he means to stay around until he has you both back in his, ah, bosom?"

"Don't say such a thing, even in joking!" Serena exclaimed with a mock shudder.

"Or maybe he feels he has a sacred duty to bring the word to the women of Myers Avenue, along with various and sundry other delights?"

"If that's so, he has been neglecting it."

Those last words, uttered so lightly, returned to haunt Serena. Before the month was out, the elder had taken up a stand in front of the Eldorado. Shaking his fist, he railed against an establishment dedicated to the gods of mammon and to Beelzebub, citing faro, poker, and roulette as temptations of the devil.

In the weeks since Ward had been gone, Serena had continued her habit of spending an hour or two each evening in the barroom. The barkeeper and other barmen had adopted a protective attitude toward her, whether because of her advancing condition or due to instructions from Ward she could not say. From time to time there had arisen a situation that the men were at a loss to handle; the drunken disappearance of Timothy for the better part of a week, the sickness of one of the girls in the show, the delivery of a shipment of inferior whiskey instead of the good stock ordered. In each case, Serena supplied the solution, taking Timothy's place at the piano, rearranging the show, refusing payment on the bad liquor. It was Timothy who, in lieu of Ward's former partner, was supposed to see to it that the Eldorado wasn't robbed of profits during Ward's absence. Since the job seemed more than the Welshman could handle without finding respite in a shot glass instead of his usual beer mug, the responsibility gradually devolved upon Serena. It was to her they came then, when the disturbance began outside the Eldorado's doors.

"What are we going to do about that soap-box preacher, Miss Serena, ma'am? He's running off business, that's what he's doing, besides stirring up an awful row. It's enough to take the head off a man's beer, the way he's carrying on."

"I don't know what can be done about it," Serena said unhappily. "He's not breaking any law."

"He's slandering a fine woman, namely you, ma'am," the barkeeper said, his face reddening. "The boys could just take him by the arms, gentle-like, and walk him back into the alley—"

"I don't think that's a good idea," Serena said hastily.

"I don't see why not, dang me if I do. The way I've got it figured, that feller needs a lesson in manners, and Mr. Dunbar would be plumb upset if some of us didn't give it to him."

"That's kind of you," Serena answered, "but it isn't necessary. What that man says can't hurt me."

"It sure hurts me to hear it," the man behind the bar said, giving his polishing cloth a vicious snap.

"Maybe he'll move on soon."

"If he don't, he's sure looking for trouble, and he's just liable to find it!"

In the end, no action had to be taken. The elder was not only turning business away from the Eldorado, he was affecting the clientele at Pearlie's. It wasn't long before Otto appeared on the sidewalk outside and tapped Elder Greer on the shoulder. What he said to him was unknown, but the elder deserted his post and was seen to enter the building next door. No more was seen or heard from him for the rest of the night.

Serena let a week or so pass. The thought of Lessie, so enthralled with her triumphal progress on the flower-bedecked bicycle, was constantly with her. Did she know that Elder Greer had not left the area? Had she gone back into hiding? Serena hated to think of Elder Greer's finding Lessie. His will was so strong, he was so sure of himself and his rights. For all the girl's newfound independence, Serena did not think Lessie would be able to withstand the elder's methods of persuasion. It would be far better if he had no chance to see and talk to her. Surely he would give up and go away eventually if he could get no satisfaction from either her or Lessie.

After another day or two of worrying, Serena decided the only way to make certain Lessie stayed out of sight was to go and see her. Flinging a shawl around her shoulders, Serena set out along the street. It was still early, not quite dinnertime. The blast of a mine whistle, signaling the end of a shift, was like a shriek. A train chugged its way up the slope, curving toward the mining town of Victor, trailing its black smoke like a plume. The western sky above the mountains was pink and lavender blue, while the opposite slope was tipped with the last gold rays of the setting sun. The air was cool here at this height as the sun went down, even in Indian summer. It caught in the lungs with a sharp ache. The street was dry and dusty. There wasn't a blade of green grass anywhere, only the sere, rattling mats of yellow gamma dotted with fat white heads of milkweed. This late in the year, everything was as dry as tinder.

She was getting so clumsy. She wasn't that large yet, but she felt enormous. Breathless from the quick walk, she stopped a minute outside the door of the crib before lifting her hand to knock.

There was no answer. Had Lessie gone out? Serena stood listening. Nothing moved inside; the only sound was the distant voices of a group of boys playing stickball farther along Poverty Gulch.

"Lessie?"

Serena knocked again. When still no answer came, she tried the knob. She might leave a note, provided Lessie owned such a thing as a lead pencil.

The door gave under her hand. "Is anybody here?"

It was dim with the approach of evening inside the one-roomed cabin. The sound of flies buzzing was loud in the stillness, and an unpleasant sickly smell hung in the close air. The single chair had been overturned. The pitcher from the washstand lay broken on the floor. Clothes were strewn everywhere, most of them torn to rags. In the corner, the bed sagged, with the mattress drooping off its frame. To Serena, standing amid the violent disorder, it looked as if someone had deliberately torn the place apart. The destruction was

221

so complete it gave her an uneasy feeling, raising gooseflesh along her arms.

It did not look as if Lessie would be returning; there was nothing left for her here. Serena turned to go. It was at that moment she noticed the swarm of bluebottle flies between the bed and the wall.

Lessie lay crumpled on the floor, her white hair clotted with dried, blackened blood, and her pale eyes glazed and staring. Her face was purple and lacerated with deep cuts, and her tongue protruded between her teeth. There were great black bruises on her neck, and also on her naked shoulders and breasts. She had a rag around her waist, all that was left of a nightgown. Her thighs and hips, covered with bloody gashes as from a knife, were crawling with avid, humming flies.

Serena dragged breath into her lungs on a choking gasp. Shivering uncontrollably, with tears starting from her eyes and her hands pressed to her mouth, she stepped closer.

There could be no doubt. Lessie was dead, had been for some time. There was nothing she could do to help her, nothing anyone could do. Whirling, Serena ran from the house out into the cool freshness of the evening and the pure, untainted air.

Since she had discovered the body, Serena was questioned by the sheriff and his deputies. Their faces grave, they took down the particulars of Lessie's short life, including the name, supplied by Consuelo, of the drummer who had been keeping her. It was a distressing affair, they said, an occurrence that was becoming much too common. Cripple Creek would be getting a bad name if they didn't watch out, people would be thinking it was a dangerous place to live. They couldn't have that. Promising a full inquiry without delay, they went away, though as Consuelo put it so succinctly, they looked as if they had found a worm in their soup, one that should have had sense enough not to get itself cooked.

The funeral was held the next day. It was a warm, clear afternoon. Serena stood with her skirts catching on the dry weeds of the cemetery, staring at the raw, rocky earth mounded beside the grave. She could smell the fresh wood scent of the new pine casket, overlaid by the fragrance of flowers. The red and white roses, calla lilies, and carnations brought in by train lay wilting in the dry air and burning sun, too vivid reminders of the flower parade such a short

222

time ago. Lessie had been so happy that day, happier, possibly, than she had ever been in her life.

Serena was not alone. Consuelo was with her, and also Nathan Benedict. There was the drummer, looking uncomfortable in a striped suit and spats, and with a daisy in his buttonhole, standing well back, half hidden by the horse-drawn black hearse with its bobbing plumes on the roof. A few other men were clustered on the other side of the grave as if for company, rough-looking miners, a ranch hand or two. Beyond them waited a group of musicians provided by the undertaker, sweating in their woolen uniforms as they played a soft, dirgelike hymn.

There was one other. Standing at the head of the open grave, a Bible in his hands, was Elder Greer. With his head thrown back and an ecstatic look on his features, he intoned the service with power and zeal. He had not been invited to perform this rite. He had simply appeared in his black, and claiming the dead as his own, began to pray for the repose of her restless soul. The prayer became an oration on the sanctity of marriage, which turned into a sermon on the conduct of women.

Serena wanted to protest. The urge to cry out, to scream for him to stop, swelled in her chest. The look of pious grief yet sublime justification on his face made her gorge rise. The only thing that held her silent was the knowledge that nothing he said could affect Lessie any longer, that the most heated of his remarks were directed at her.

Staring out over the town spread below, she stood it as long as she could. When she began to feel that she would have to fly at the elder and claw his face, or go mad, she swung around and marched toward Nathan's carriage waiting behind the hearse. She had gone no more than a half-dozen paces when Nathan fell into step beside her, taking her arm to steady her on the uneven ground. By the time he had handed her up into the town carriage, Consuelo had joined them.

That Serena was the target of the Mormon needed no further proof. With the most important segment of his audience fading away, he brought the liturgy to an end and called for prayer. Before the coachman could turn the team, the first handful of earth had been sifted onto the casket; the band had formed in marching order and began to troop ba~k toward town.

223

"Do you want to wait?" Nathan asked, his thin face set in lines of concern as he looked down at Serena.

"No," she answered. She could not bear the idea of being forced to exchange solemn pleasantries with the man who called himself Lessie's husband.

With a firm nod, Nathan gave the order to proceed, and they fell in behind the musicians. Serena twisted in her seat to stare back at the barren hill where the gravediggers were busy, watched over by the old man with his white hair and jutting beard. She did not cry until the band ahead of them began to caper, striking up a tune that had surfaced in one of the dance halls on Myers: "There'll Be a Hot Time in the Old Town Tonight."

The carriage pulled up in front of the Eldorado. Consuelo reached to touch Serena's hand.

"I wish you would reconsider and come back with me to my house," the Spanish girl said, her voice anxious.

"No, I'll be fine. It was good of you, both of you, to come to the funeral with me."

Nathan cleared his throat. "I wish I—we could do more. I worry about you here alone. I don't know what Ward's thinking of, going off and leaving you here like this so long."

"If you are referring to my condition, he doesn't know," Serena said with a wry smile.

"Doesn't know? You mean you didn't tell him?"

Serena shook her head.

"He won't like that, and I can't say I blame him. Why didn't you let him know?"

Nathan's voice was so stern that Serena slanted him a look of surprise. "A number of reasons. I didn't want to interfere with his plans."

"Balderdash!"

"But no," Consuelo said with a quick lift of her chin. "I understand perfectly. If he would not stay for you alone, why should he be given the opportunity to stay for the child? Should it be more important to him than you?"

A smile creased Nathan's angular face. "Defeated," he said. "You women always stick together."

"And why not," Consuelo demanded, "when you men are forever ranged against us?"

"Not I," he answered, a disclaimer so firm that both women had to laugh. For a single instant Serena, looking across Consuelo as they sat three abreast on the carriage seat, met Nathan's hazel eyes. The warmth in their depths was a reminder of his offer to Ward of mining shares in return for the chance to win her. How Ward had phrased his answer, whether declining the offer for himself alone, or conveying also her rejection, Serena did not know. The subject had never been mentioned between Nathan and herself. No slightest hint of it had been allowed to surface, and yet it hovered unspoken in the air whenever they were together.

"When is Ward to return?" Consuelo asked, turning so that the wide brim of her cartwheel hat blocked Nathan's view of Serena.

"I'm not sure. He said before the snows."

"He'd better hurry along. Already the aspens have turned and are beginning to fall," Consuelo said.

"He certainly had," Nathan agreed. "All jokes aside, it isn't right for you to be by yourself now, not with this maniac going around killing women."

"I'm not alone, at least not at night. But I hate the idea of whoever is commiting these terrible crimes getting away with them. I know the authorities, for their own reasons, are looking into the deaths. Still, there ought to be something we could do. I get so angry when I think of how helpless these women are who are being killed, women like Lessie. They have no protection, none whatever!"

"You are right, of course," Nathan said slowly. "I've been thinking about offering a reward for information. Most of the people out near the section where your friend lived aren't too anxious to talk to the sheriff, but they might be persuaded to come forward if the price was right."

"That's a wonderful idea," Serena said.

"Yes," Consuelo said dryly, "it should certainly brand you as the friend of the crib girls."

"That doesn't matter," Nathan said with barely a glance in her direction.

"You may think differently when the good ladies of the town cut you in public."

"Fortunately, I am not interested in good ladies, only beautiful ones, such as you two," he answered.

"Next you will be endowing a home for destitute Ladies of the Lamplight!"

"It's an idea," Nathan told his amused mistress before he turned to Serena. "Will you promise me, Serena, that you will come to me if anything goes wrong?"

Consuelo, a frown between her dark eyes, divided a look between the man at her side and Serena before her lips curved

225

in a smile tinged with sadness. "Yes, Serena," she seconded, "will you come?"

"There, see what you've done," Serena said as tears rose to her eyes once more at their kindness. "Though really, I couldn't impose."

"Not even if I begged you?" Nathan said, a whimsical note in his voice.

"Anyway," Serena said, smiling valiantly as she applied her handkerchief to her nose, "I'm sure it won't be necessary."

She had reason to be less positive before the day was out. In her rooms, she removed her hat and the shawl that concealed the fact that her dress of gray cheviot was unbuttoned along the side seam. She had moved to the wardrobe to put the toque away when she noticed a paper lying on the floor in the corner nearest Ward's desk. There was also a corner of a book protruding from under the rolltop.

Stepping to that massive piece of furniture, Serena pushed the top up. The well-fitted tambour moved easily, retreating into the back section. That was the only thing that was right about it. Inside, the account books and papers were tumbled this way and that, letters, bills of lading, business cards, and receipts wadded indiscriminately together. The upper level of pigeonholes had been emptied and their contents piled helter-skelter with the rest. On top of that had been dumped the contents of the inner drawers, and a collection of pens, extra nibs, pen wipers, stamps, tacks, paper holders, and string. An exclamation on her lips, Serena hesitated. She could attempt to restore some kind of order, but without knowing exactly what she was doing, such a task would be useless. She had watched Ward at work, sitting over the books of the Eldorado, totting up the profits, but she had never pried into the papers. Lacking any idea of what was supposed to be there, it was also impossible to tell what was missing.

Closing the desk with a thoughtful look in her eyes, Serena moved to the wardrobe. The store of money Ward had given her was slowly dwindling, but what was left was still where she had hidden it, in the toe of her gilt-heeled slippers. She did not delude herself that her small hoard would have been missed by a determined thief. That, plus the fact that the other drawers and shelves in the room appeared undisturbed, was enough for her to dismiss the idea of robbery as the motive for someone rummaging through Ward's desk. No, there had been something someone had wanted, a particular something. On at least one occasion Pearlie had made herself free of these rooms. It was only logical to suppose she had done so again, more especially since Serena had left them locked and there was no sign the door had been forced.

The first time, because of a lack of proof and her own insecurity, she had let the incident pass; this time she would not. She was tired of being treated as if her needs and feelings were of no consequence. Rather than sit brooding on the awful thing that had been done to Lessie, she would see what Pearlie had to say for herself.

The housekeeper at the parlor house opened the door. Colorless, self-effacing, she was a new installation since the girls had complained of cleaning up after such a constant flow of chewing, spitting, smoking, beer-guzzling men.

Madam Pearlie was not in, Serena was told in a fading voice, and was not expected back for some time, several hours at least. As to where she was, it wasn't the housekeeper's place to say. Serena could leave a message if she was of a mind. No, there were no writing materials available.

It was then that a plump, candy-box brunette passed through the hall. One of the girls who had danced on the stage at the Eldorado before Ward separated the two establishments, her name was Cora. She recognized Serena on sight.

"Who are you looking for, honey? Pearlie? She's down yonder smoking up a pipe dream."

"You mean—" Serena began, glancing back in the general direction of the girl's casual wave.

"Sure, the doctor's place, that shack right along there. You know. Don't look much like a pleasure palace, does it?" The brunette gave a flippant chuckle.

"Thank you," Serena said.

"Don't mention it, honey. Whatever the problem is, I'm on your side, mainly because it ain't Pearlie's. Be seeing you." With a lifted eyebrow in the direction of the open-mouthed housekeeper, she flounced away.

The housekeeper, her mouth snapping tightly shut with disapproval, relieved her feelings by closing the door upon Serena without another word.

The shack pointed out to Serena was down the hill from the Eldorado and almost directly behind it. Ramshackle, looking as if a strong wind would send it crashing to the ground, it stood alone, shrinking away from its nearest neighbors, a livery stable and a blacksmith shop. Serena had seen

Pearlie making her way in that direction more than once, as well as a number of other women and a few men. She had been told it was a doctor's office, though there was an odd tone in the voice of those who mentioned it and Serena had seen for herself that his patients were drawn mainly from the cribs and parlor houses. It had crossed her mind more than once that she ought to consult a physician, but somehow she had shied away from the thought of being attended by this particular man.

She could wait until Pearlie returned to the parlor house, but the housekeeper had seemed to think it would not be any time soon. She had no idea what course of treatment Pearlie might be undergoing to take so long, but she was in no mood to wait.

The door to the doctor's office was closed and locked, though Serena thought she saw the curtain move at a side window. She knocked and waited. After what seemed an interminable time, a man came to the door. With a cheerful smile that had wariness behind it, he ushered her into a small anteroom in the one-story building.

"Yes, and what may I do for you this evening?" he asked, rubbing his hands together. As he spoke there came a soft moan from the back room. He sent a fleeting glance over his shoulder, but his smile did not waver.

"I am looking for someone," Serena answered.

"We are all looking for someone or something," the doctor, a small man with a full head of hair and a small mustache, replied. "Who sent you to me?"

"No one, really. I wanted to see Pearlie—" Serena stopped, aware suddenly that she did not know Pearlie's last name, or even if, when she had taken the pseudonym, she had troubled to give herself one.

"Ah, yes, Pearlie. A magnificent female, but so lost. May I assume she told you of my little place here?"

"No, it was Cora at her parlor house, if you must know." Serena replied, unable to see why it mattered but willing to humor the man.

"Ah, yes, a delicious morsel, so cooperative. Come in then, by all means. We will see what we can do for you."

"I only want to see Pearlie," Serena repeated as her arm was taken and she was steered rapidly toward the door at the end of the room.

"And so you shall, so you shall. One would never have guessed your predilections ran in that direction, especially not to look at you, but I am not one to deny or question another's desires. Come in, my dear girl, come in."

As he finished speaking, he half-pushed, half-dragged Serena into the back room. At the sharp sound of the door closing behind her Serena swung around, but the doctor smiled and, closing his delicate fingers firmly around her arm, propelled her forward.

The room was not large. The rugs in the brilliant hues of the Orient that covered the walls as well as the floor made it seem smaller and more close. Low couches were set here and there, each with a small table beside it holding a nargileh, or Far Eastern water pipe, of ebony, silver, and brass. Upon these divans three women reclined, among them Pearlie with her auburn hair spread around her. Brass coal braziers glowed in the four corners of the space, adding their smoke to the blue haze that hung in the air, adding also their heat, a necessary element since the women who lay in such attitudes of abandon were completely naked.

"Here is a place for you here, my love," the physician said in a soothing tone. "Make yourself comfortable, just as you like, and I'll bring you a pipe."

A pipe, a pipedream. This place she had come to was no doctor's infirmary. The women sprawling upon the couches were smoking opium. This was an opium den.

Serena had heard of such places. Now and then the sheriff raided one and hauled all who were caught in them off to jail. They were places of iniquity far worse than the parlor houses, or so it seemed from the editorials let loose in outrage against them. The opium enslaved the user's senses, made the person a slave to the fatal gum that filled the pipes, sapping the will so that the user became the tool of the person who supplied the mind-rotting substance. There were tales of women ruined because of an addiction they could not control, and from the look of the caress the doctor gave the flank of the young woman lying face down in a stupor on the couch near the door, it was not difficult to imagine the path such destruction could take.

The instant the door closed behind the doctor, Serena stepped to the couch where Pearlie lay. She put a hand on the woman's shoulder and gave her a quick shake.

"Pearlie? Pearlie!"

With excruciating slowness, the fine auburn lashes of the woman lifted. "Oh," she said without surprise. "It's you."

"Yes," Serena said grimly. "Are you awake?"

"I don't know. Am I?"

The beatific smile the other woman gave Serena made it seem doubtful, but since she was here, she could only try to get some sense out of Pearlie. It might well be a better opportunity to do so than she was likely to have at any other time.

"I want to know if you were in my room this afternoon, if you went through Ward's desk while I was out?"

"Ward's desk? Half mine. We were partners. He had no right, no right at all. I'll pay him back."

"What did you take? I know you took something." As Pearlie's eyes began slowly to close once more, Serena shook her again.

Pearlie giggled. "Take? The deed, silly. What else would I want?"

"The deed? But—why?"

As abruptly as the woman had begun to laugh, her face dissolved into a look of woe. "He doesn't want me as his partner any more, all because of that girl. What did I do? What did I ever do to make the men I love leave me?"

"The deed," Serena prompted, her voice less harsh.

"If I can't have the Eldorado, why should he? Ward made a mistake, you know, a stupid mistake for a lawyer. He paid me for my half of the place, but he didn't make me sign—anything. The deed is still in my name. That means I can sell my half. If he doesn't come back, I can sell his half, too."

"If he doesn't come back?" Serena straightened, staring at the moist face, the staring eyes, and flushed body of the other woman.

"There was an old prospector came down out of the mountains last week. Said the Indians told him a man who looked like Ward had an accident, fell from a ledge."

"He—was hurt?"

"He may be dead. He's probably dead. That would be just what he would do to me. Everyone does it to me. I never mean to make them die; I never mean to!"

Pearlie's voice was so strident, her movements as she began to toss on the couch so violent, that Serena did not hear the doctor enter once more. When he spoke at her side, she started, turning to stare at him.

"Here we are, my love, just what you need. Let me help you off with your shawl and loosen your dress. Perhaps after a while you will like me to come and sit beside you?"

"I need you, doctor," Pearlie said, suddenly opening her

eyes wide. Serena, taking advantage of the moment, snatched her shawl back up around her shoulders and stepped around the couch out of the man's reach.

"Not as much as this lady who is new to us. I know she voiced a preference for your company, but it seems such a shame. I'm afraid she has found the company of men rough and hurtful. I think I should show her it needn't always be that way."

"You like her better than me," Pearlie accused, her tone rising.

"No, no. I'll admit she's attractive, even as she is, and I quite look forward to initiating her into the mysteries of the pipe, but like her better? How could I?"

"Doctor," Serena said, interrupting in a firm tone, pushing the smoking pipe, an ornate affair of chased gold and pink quartz, back at him across the couch, "there's been a mistake. I didn't come here for this."

"You're upset now. Soon you will be calm," he answered, gently refusing the pipe. "You must lie down. Soon I will come to you and you will be more relaxed than you dreamed possible. I will show you delights unimagined."

"Show me!" Pearlie pleaded, snatching at his arm, reaching higher, pulling him off balance in her desperate strength.

As the doctor's feet went out from under him, Serena threw the pipe down on the low table and fled. The key was in the front door. Turning it, she flung the panel open. If she was followed she did not know. She did not look back. Eyes wide and unseeing, she ran from the house with its somnolent degradation. She ran from the comatose women unaware in their debasement. She ran from Pearlie, from her shameless, naked lust, her vicious need for revenge and piteous lack of understanding. She ran from the mind-dulling smoky gloom and from the man with the stroking, persuasive hands who called himself a doctor. But most of all she ran from herself, from the tearing anguish that came with the thought of Ward's death, from the shattering recognition of the love she felt for the gambler who owned the Eldorado.

Chapter Fourteen

It snowed in Cripple Creek in late September. Sleet and snow fell in October. In November it came down again, a white blanket that drapped itself over Pike's Peak to the east and turned the ranges of the Sangre de Cristos and the Continental Divide to cones of frosted ice. Still Ward did not return.

The inquiry into Lessie's death turned up next to nothing. When found, she had been dead more than twenty-four hours, placing her death the night before. A man had been seen coming from her crib around ten o'clock, though in the dark it had been hard to get a good look at him. No description was available beyond the fact that he had not been dressed like a miner. Despite the reward posted by Nathan, no new information surfaced. The incident was unfortunate, but the police had no choice other than to consider it closed. This was especially true in light of the fact that no new attacks against the women of the tenderloin occurred.

The newspaper of the town had been inclined at first to treat the case as cause for alarm. Featuring headlines that called for the capture and conviction of the mass murderer, they gave much space to the gruesome details of the crime. The murderer was dubbed Colorado's Jack the Ripper, despite the fact that all three women had died from strangulation. There was even some speculation that the mysterious killer who had terrorized London only seven years before had immigrated to the United States and taken up his grisly trade once more. In both cases, London and Cripple Creek, it was pointed out, the victims were prostitutes plying their trade.

Gradually interest waned. As the weeks passed and the reward money remained unclaimed, other news took over the front page. The coverage of a mining accident, a broken cable that let a bucket hoist carrying four miners fall three hundred feet, taking all to their deaths, ousted the murders even from the back pages of the dailies.

Serena did not see Pearlie for some time after that day at the opium den. The thought of the deed to the barroom in the woman's hands troubled her, but there seemed little she could do about it. The danger of Pearlie's attempting to sell her supposed half interest was slight as long as the chance remained Ward might return and call her to account. And if for some reason he did not return, what became of the Eldorado was of little concern. Serena well knew she had no claim to anything Ward owned, and as far as she was aware, he had no direct heirs. If Ward was dead, Pearlie was welcome to the Eldorado.

Pearlie had never been denied access to the barroom. She had stopped coming of her own accord after the rift with Ward over her treatment of Serena. Now as the fall turned more to winter, she began to put in an appearance. More often than not, she was far gone in drink. At times she turned maudlin, crying, going on and on to whoever would listen about the death of her husband and Ward's part in it. Just as often, she would laugh with an edge of hysteria, joking with Serena of how Ward had deserted them both. Occasionally, her mood grew spiteful and she would stand at the bar with her foot propped on the rail like a man, criticizing, carping, telling everyone what she would do, how she would change the running of the place when it was hers. She did not speak again of her right to sell, but she did drop the hint that she expected to have a large sum of money in the not too distant future. With these allusions usually went a few derisive remarks about the looks on the faces of certain Natchez matrons when they saw her again.

One person who had been denied entrance to the Eldorado was Otto Bruin. Since it was he who usually came looking for Pearlie to carry her back to the parlor house, keeping him out became a problem. The first time it was tried, the barman who made the attempt was knocked sprawling, his jaw broken. Serena barred his way on one occasion, but the feel of his

233

hands on her flesh as he set her aside made it an experience she was not anxious to repeat, nor did she care to risk having the barroom torn apart as the miners tried to come to her aid. It reached the point where it was better to give in gracefully than court destruction and ultimate defeat. Otto, as well as Pearlie, came and went as he pleased. It seemed to Serena as time wore on that it pleased them to come more often and stay longer.

The situation amused Pearlie. Whether she kept Otto at her side because she knew he affected Serena with shivering disgust or because she enjoyed his slavish attention in the same way parlor-house girls enjoyed their pampered French poodles was something no one but Pearlie knew. It was certain she took perverted pleasure in the havoc he could cause, often urging him on to start fistfights, or giving him a loose rein when his attention was snared by a pretty face or a lissome body.

Serena was only happy that her growing size made it possible for her to retreat more and more to her room. A stout door with a lock and key made her feel reasonably secure, though sometimes she thought she heard the shuffling footsteps of the apelike man in the hallway outside in the early hours of the morning. That Otto Bruin went no farther she attributed to two causes; first, her continued position as a favorite of the miners, Gold Heels, the lady of the Eldorado, and second to lack of proof that Ward was alive or dead.

It was a day in the first week of December. The last snow had melted in the places where the sun struck, but there were still streaks of white in the lee of fences and buildings. The sky had been clear and overcast by turns all day. Toward evening the sun came out once more in bright gladness, though there was a gray bank to the northwest that heralded more bad weather.

Serena, tiring of the overheated confinement of her rooms, left the bed where she had retreated for comfort and began to get dressed. Now that she was so near her time, she had only one outfit, a kind of shirt and dressing sacque she had made from her old dresses. It didn't look too bad as long as it was covered by the fur-trimmed cape Ward had given her. It didn't look too good either, she told herself wryly, but at this point she had ceased to care.

Exercise was what she needed to clear the cobwebs from her mind, perhaps a brisk walk. Well, maybe an ambling stroll; it was all the same thing. She had seen no one lately.

not even Consuelo. The Spanish girl had been in bed for a week with a fever and forbade Serena to visit, fearing she would catch it from her.

Serena needed to get out, to take some action to banish the lethargy she had fallen into lately. It could not be good for her child, this brooding inactivity, this preoccupation with her problems, with death and the possibility of dying.

Fully recognizing that fact, she turned in the direction of the cemetery when she left the Eldorado. It had been some time since she had visited Lessie's grave. She had simply lacked the energy until now. Somewhere she had heard that it wasn't unusual for a woman to feel this driving buoyancy before her child was born. It seemed unlikely. The baby was as much affected by the fresh air as she was from the way he was thumping her in the ribs, but she had felt nothing that would indicate delivery was going to come any sooner than the middle of the month. With a shake of her head and a small smile, she pressed her fur muff to the bulge of her stomach as she moved with slow majesty along the sidewalk.

The cemetery was deserted. Making her way to the mound that marked Lessie's grave, she noticed footprints frozen in the mud leading to it. A headboard of plain white marble had been erected though it bore neither dates nor surname, only the simple legend *"Lessie."* Before it on the raw earth lay what Serena at first took to be a red paper rose, so stiff and brittle was it. On closer inspection she saw that the flower was real enough, only frozen.

A red rose, symbol of love. Who had laid it so gently there? A man, from the looks of the tracks he had left. Was it Lessie's Jack, the drummer who had given her a few brief weeks of happiness? Or was it some forlorn miner she had given herself to for a night, a night he remembered longer than she had?

No matter. Someone had loved her. The sight of that rose lying on the cold earth stabbed past Serena's carefully erected defenses. Tears rose in her eyes and flowed in warm paths down her cheeks.

Was Ward lying somewhere under the frozen ground? Was it possible that the strength and force of him could be forever stilled, that the light and intelligence could be extinguished in his green eyes? If not, then why didn't he come?

He was dead. She would never see the tender mockery of his smile again, never watch a laugh crowd into his eyes, never feel his arms about her, or tell him that she cared. Worse than these things, he would never see his child.

Enough. Grief was a luxury she could not afford. Soon her baby would be born and she had not yet decided what she would do. Arrangements would have to be made. As much as she might prefer it, she could not bring the baby into the world without help; she did not want to risk endangering it.

Lessie had lost her child, a stillborn babe. That small death had set her free of the wagon train, free of Elder Greer and his wives, but at what price? If her child had lived, would she still be with the Mormons, still alive? Still unhappy?

Lessie had not loved the father of her child, had found no pleasure in his arms. It was incredible, after what had passed between Ward and herself, that she could acknowledge both.

Or could she? Perhaps it was an illusion brought on by her condition, a determination to lend some sort of respectability, no matter how remote, to the event. Or perhaps she was merely influenced by her situation, alone, without family or close friends. She had needed to attach herself to someone, and the man who had forced her to share intimacy, the one she had lived with in close quarters, was the most likely target for her starved affections. If he were to put in an appearance tomorrow, it was likely she would feel nothing.

Serena clenched her hands inside her muff. Suddenly she was chilled. Why was she standing here tormenting herself? With one last glance at Lessie's grave she turned away. The cemetery was behind her, hidden beneath the crest of the hill, when it occurred to her that at no time had it crossed her mind that the rose could have been put there by Lessie's husband, the Mormon elder.

The lights of the Eldorado shone bright through the foglike mist of low-hanging clouds. As Serena neared she could hear the tinkle of Timothy's piano in a ragtime tune. The sight and sound were more than welcome. It had been a long walk, more, probably, than she should have attempted. Her footsteps were dragging as she neared the double doors with their colored frosted-glass panes.

As she stepped into the noisy brightness of the barroom, she shivered a little in reaction to the warmth after the cold outside. The place was fairly empty for this time of day; only a few tables were occupied. There was to be a special burlesque show tonight a few doors down the street, a sultan's harem direct from Egypt, or so the fliers said.

Pearlie stood at the bar. She pulled herself erect and swept

236

toward Serena with a hard look about her carmined lips. She was dressed in black from the aigrette held by a diamond clip in her bright auburn hair to the flounce stiff with sequins on the hem of her gown. She stopped, barring Serena's way a few feet inside the room. With her hands encased in opera-length gloves on her hips, she demanded, "Where do you think you're going?"

"To my room." The other woman's belligerent attitude made Serena uneasy, but she allowed nothing of it to show on her face.

"You don't have a room," Pearlie sneered. "Not any more."

"I'm tired, Pearlie, and I really don't feel like arguing tonight. If you will just step aside—"

"Not likely. I've stepped aside for you my last time. I'm telling you that you don't belong here any more. Ward is dead, and this place is mine to do with as I like. I've taken on a new partner, and this evening I moved into the rooms upstairs. All that's left for you to do is get out!"

"You've heard from Ward? You know he—he's not coming back?"

"If he were coming he would have been here by now." A swift desolation crossed Pearlie's features. The light-blue irises of her eyes were almost extinguished by the enlarging of her pupils with belladonna. They were overbright with the glitter of unshed tears. "He's never been this late."

"You haven't heard from him," Serena said dully.

"You don't hear from dead people! Now turn around and take yourself off. I don't want to see you again."

"Where am I supposed to go?" Serena glanced past Pearlie to where Otto was pushing back his chair from a rear table, moving toward them.

"That's no affair of mine. I just want you out of my sight. I'm sick of looking at you and your belly!" The last word was said on a gasp. Pearlie's face was white with grief and rage, and her hands were clenched into fists.

"Hey, Pearlie, what's going on?" a miner yelled from one of the closest tables. There was a low murmur of voices and Serena caught several sympathetic glances cast in her direction.

"I'm taking over the Eldorado. It's my place again, and I'm cleaning house, getting rid of the trash!"

"Wait a minute, Pearlie."

"Keep your nose out of my business, friend!" she snapped. "Otto!"

"Here, Pearlie."

"It's a good thing. Earn your pay. Get her out of here."

"Now, Pearlie—" the miner said.

The woman flung around. "Ward's gone and I don't have any use for his leavings. If you want her, you're welcome. If not, keep out of this unless you want to deal with Otto!"

"That won't be necessary," Serena said with a lift of her chin. "I'll go. If you'll just let me get my belongings—"

Pearlie swung back. "I threw everything of yours I could find into that old trunk. I don't think you're in any shape to lug it around, and I'm not in any mood to wait for you to pack it all nice and neat. You can send for it, but I'm warning you, if it's still here two days from now I'm burning it!"

"You can't do that."

"Can't I? Otto!"

The young miner got to his feet. Serena looked from him to the bulky prizefighter who had stepped around Pearlie, moving toward her with his teeth bared in a grin and his long arms swinging. Compared to Otto, the boy was no more than a stripling. He would be hurt for nothing.

"All right, Pearlie," Serena said, keeping her voice steady with a strong effort. "Call off your dog. You may be right. I've stayed here long enough." She turned away, reaching blindly for the door handle. Somehow she got it open. Before it closed behind her she heard a doleful male voice.

"It ain't gonna be the same around here without Gold Heels."

She felt numb. It had happened so quickly. She should have known it was coming. She might have, if she hadn't been so reluctant to admit Ward was not coming back.

Pearlie in black, proud, flamboyant black. Who was the new partner? Someone who meant to give her free rein, apparently, since she had moved into Ward's old rooms. Could it be Otto, a reward for faithfulness? Would that brutish species of a man sleep in the bed where she and Ward had lain together? Would he and Pearlie sport there? What a foul desecration it would be.

Surely not. Pearlie was not stupid. She would not put so much power into such a man's hands. She valued her freedom too much to give anyone such a hold over her. There was no real reason for her to take a partner, especially after Ward had paid her off. She should have more than enough money to run the place by herself. Except that she had not been noticeably concerned with business lately, and expenses;

238

food, liquor, musicians, doctor bills, and various payments under the table could run high for the parlor house.

What difference did it make? It was herself she should be thinking of. What was she to do? She had no money; she had left the little that remained of her hoard in her rooms when she went out. The hotels and rooming houses required payment in advance, especially for women alone, without baggage, and that was if they would accept her. Still, she had to have shelter. The poor unfortunates who tried to spend the night in the alleys and back doorways of the town at this season were usually found frozen in the morning with their hair and lashes stiff with frost.

Serena suppressed a shudder at the thought, huddling into her cloak. She looked up at the night sky that hovered so close overhead. Something cold and stinging touched her cheek. It was snowing, the icy flakes spiraling down out of the darkness.

Serena began to move, walking aimlessly along the sidewalk. Her footsteps echoed, a hard, hollow sound in the cold. She passed a two-story dance hall. Through the windows she could see the men enjoying their two-bit whirl on the floor. The lively music stopped and there was a rush to the bar for the drink that went with the taxi dance. On the top floor, the lamplight inside the cubicles opening onto the three-sided balcony cast the wavering shadows of those occupied inside onto the thin curtains that covered the openings.

Farther along she caught the hot oil, cornmeal, and spice smell of Mexican cooking. The thought of a hot bowl of chili con carne made her mouth water. She had not eaten since noon. That, with her long walk, must account for the weakness in her knees.

She must not fall. The sidewalks were so uneven in the dark. There were steps as the street rose, ramshackle things with warped boards that sagged in the middle and had only half enough nails on the ends. The coating of fast-thickening snow did not help matters, nor did the fact that she could not see where she was putting her feet over the bulge in front of her.

Whistles and cheers, the clatter of applauding and wail of flutes and drums indicated she was nearing the burlesque theater where the sultan's harem was performing. It was brightly lit, surrounded by buggies, buckboards, and saddle horses. A sheriff's deputy standing with his arms locked behind him in an on-duty stance nodded to her, though he did not speak. Serena knew a brief urge to appeal to the man, but resisted it. Where could he take her except to jail? She could not stand that, and she had heard enough of the corrupt ways of the local bigwigs to fear she would be no better off. Kindness was not something she could expect, nor could she depend on being left free of molestation. Failing that, she might be locked into a frigid cell and forgotten. That was not what she needed.

There was only one place she could go. She had known it all along. As much as she hated the thought of imposing, there was no other choice.

The noise of the theater died away behind her. A vending cart met and passed her by in the street, trailing after it the aroma of warm, buttered popcorn. A dog howled, the mournful sound far-floating in the night. The saloons grew farther apart and stopped altogether. The last parlor house with a red silk shade over the door was passed. The sound of merry-making died away, leaving a hushed quiet. The sidewalk ended and Serena stepped into soft, quiet snow.

She had gone no more than a few yards when she noticed it, the sound of footsteps with the heavy thud of booted heels on the boards of the sidewalk behind her. A miner, hurrying home to a wife holding supper and waiting to scold for the smell of liquor on his breath, she told herself. There were many such who lived in hastily thrown-together houses on the outskirts of town. It was only a little way to where she turned toward Consuelo's house. When she reached that point the man would pass on by.

The sudden cessation of the hollow thuds as the man also left the sidewalk sent a chill of horror over her. Only a little way, she repeated, only a little way.

On the lee side of the houses lining the sidestreet there was no snow as yet. The fine granite gravel crunched underfoot. Serena stumbled in the shallow washes where rain had swept the pulverized granite into the rutted roadbed. Little light penetrated through the windows along here from the frugal coal-oil lanterns burning inside. Many houses were entirely dark, the owners already in bed. The snow was getting thicker. There was no feeling in her fingers, despite the fur muff she held against her, and her toes were the same. She would have chilblains without doubt, and would be lucky if she escaped frostbite.

At a grating noise somewhere to the rear along the dark street where she had just come, Serena started violently. She tried to hurry, but stumbled again in her clumsiness, staggering off balance. When she straightened again there was a pulled feeling in her lower abdomen.

In the dark all the houses looked the same. She would recognize Consuelo's with its front porch and beveled door glass when she saw it, but she could not be certain how far she had come, or how much farther along it was.

Her heart was pounding, and there was an ache in her side. The thin air with its slicing edge of ice cut into her lungs. She threw a quick look back over her shoulder, but could see nothing. She was reminded wrenchingly of the time she had been followed in Colorado Springs. She had not felt so helpless then as she did now; her body had not been so huge and unwieldy. She had been stopped by Otto that night. Was it he who trailed her now, ready to complete in grisly fashion what he had begun so long ago? Ward had come then to protect her, whirling down upon them, a cutting carriage whip in his hand. He would not come now, not this time, not ever again.

There, wasn't that Consuelo's house with the fish-scale woodwork on the gables? Serena's heart sank inside her at the sight of it. There was a phaeton with flickering sidelamps standing outside the neat iron fence, and smoke rose from the chimney, but the windows were dark. That told its own story; Consuelo must be entertaining, earning her keep. How long would it be before she heard a summons? Would she bother to answer it?

The foot treads were coming closer, a steady scraping of long strides that quickly covered ground. She thought of running to the nearest house with a light, of screaming and banging on the door. Would they let her in? Would they come in time?

A shadow moved under the porch of Consuelo's house. With a strangled cry Serena swerved in that direction. The shadow materialized into a man wearing an inverness coat and astrakhan hat, moving with purpose toward his carriage. He looked up as she came nearer.

"Serena," he exclaimed. "What in the world—?"

"Nathan," she said, "Oh, Nathan!"

He reached out to catch her as she fell into his arms. "My dear, you're trembling! Tell me what's wrong."

"A man. Following me," she gasped. Nathan's arms around her were awkward, but comforting. By degrees, her terror faded.

241

"I don't see anyone."

It was true. The short distance they could penetrate the snowy darkness was empty of shape or movement. Only the ghostly silhouettes of houses with their fuzzy nimbus of light at the windows took shape against the night.

"There," he said, giving her shoulders a pat. "You must have imagined it, and no wonder. What are you doing out this time of night walking the streets, and in this weather?"

The concern in his voice was like balm. In short jerky sentences Serena answered his questions.

"This is terrible. That woman should be horsewhipped. But what am I thinking of, keeping you standing here? You should be inside, where it is warm."

"I thought, that is, I hoped I might stay with Consuelo, just until I find something else."

"I'm afraid that's impossible."

Serena was aware of his deliberate choice of words, though she could not see his face. "Impossible?"

"As you probably know, Consuelo has been ill. We thought at first it was the flu, but it turned out to be scarlet fever. The house is under quarantine."

"Scarlet fever!"

"You needn't worry about her. She's strong, and already she's beginning to show signs of improvement. I've hired a nurse, and I make a habit of checking on her in the morning and at night, although even I can't get past the door."

"She's all right? You're quite sure?"

"I was told a few minutes ago that she's sleeping as peacefully as a baby. Right now, it's you we have to think about."

"I—I have no money. I hate having to ask, but if you could lend me enough for a hotel—" It was all Serena could think of. There was no other place in the whole town that might shelter someone like her.

Nathan shook his head. "They wouldn't let you in, at least none where you would be safe and comfortable; especially if I drove you to their doors, which is something I most certainly would have to do. No, I have a better idea."

Without another word, he turned and urged her toward the phaeton, helping her up on the high seat. Serena could have wished for a closed carriage, but she was so exhausted, so grateful to be able to sit down, that it didn't matter. She accepted the fur lap robe Nathan wrapped about her, the steadying arm he kept about her shoulders, with a fervent gratitude that she seemed unable to express. Closing her

242

eyes, she leaned against him as he slapped the reins on the rumps of his horses and sent the light carriage bowling along the dark deserted street.

It was several minutes before Serena could summon the will to notice where he was taking her. What roused her then was the silence. They were in open country; there were no lights anywhere around them. The snow whirled toward them, collecting in their laps, growing thick upon the buffalo lap robe, forming a yellow fog around the side lights of the carriage.

"Nathan," she said, her voice uneasy.

"We're almost there. See, there's the gate."

It was the arched entranceway of gray granite that marked the drive to his house, the gateway she had noticed on that long-ago drive with Ward to Mt. Pisgah. "But—but this is the way to your home."

"Yes. Do you mind?"

"I can't impose on you." She tried to lift her head from his shoulders, to sit up straight, but he would not allow it.

"I insist," he said, his voice low. "I've waited for a long time to see you in my house. I want to take care of you, Serena, to offer you every protection and comfort. You won't deny me that?"

What choice did she have? A fleeting memory intruded of the occasion when Nathan had offered Ward money to release her, but she dismissed it. Not only did she lack any alternative, she had no strength to protest.

"Only for tonight, then," she conceded. "Tomorrow—"

"Tomorrow is another day. We'll take it as it comes."

There was something insidious in the idea of allowing someone else to take charge, to shoulder her cares. It had not been easy since Ward had failed to put in an appearance when he was expected. The future had loomed as dark and without hope. Now that the worst had happened, she felt only a great urge to drift, uncaring of where she came to rest. Tomorrow would be different, tomorrow she would have energy and courage and faith again. But for now, she could do no more than sigh and close her eyes, letting herself be carried on toward the house where Nathan Benedict lived.

There was a lantern burning under the portico of the great white house. It illuminated the wide brick steps with their outward-curving banisters, gleamed on the knocker on the heavy paneled door, and shone with the colors of jewels in the leaded stained-glass window above it. There were flowers

243

worked in the glass, flowers that winked and glowed in the wavering lamplight from inside with the look of rubies, emeralds, sapphires, and amethysts.

Nathan half-led, half-carried Serena up the steps. The door was opened to them by a woman in black bombazine wearing a starched white apron and a white cap with streamers. She had iron-gray hair and a lined face that creased into an expression of concern.

"Here now, Mr. Benedict! Let me help you," the woman exclaimed, moving to Serena's side, ready to support her into the great hall that opened before them.

"I can manage, Mrs. Anson. You can run a hot bath for Miss Walsh, and see that a bedroom is made ready."

"You know there's always a fire lit in the green room in case of visitors."

"I think I prefer the gold room for Miss Walsh."

"But sir, that's—"

"I know that it is," Nathan interrupted.

The woman, staring across Serena, was silent an instant. "Yes, sir," she said and whisked away, her back stiff as she climbed the broad oak staircase that rose against one wall.

It was blissfully warm inside the house, a warmth that came partially from the bronze gaslight chandelier with pink morning-glory shades overhead, and partially from the blazing heart of a great fire burning under the marble mantel in the room that opened out of the hall. The mellow light was reflected in the waxed polish of the golden-oak paneling on the walls and staircase, and the sheen of the parquet floor. There was a gothic hall tree to one side, a huge affair with a carved satyr head wreathed in ivy on the pediment, a rose marble seat, and brass hooks in the shape of ram's horns. An oriental rug broke the expanse of parquet, and centered upon it was a round table holding a china bowl of Japanese design filled with coins. There hung in the air the smell of beeswax, camphor, and gutta percha from the oilskins and boots that crowded the hall tree.

To the right was a parlor, judging from the stiff formality of the horsehair settees and chairs, the crowding of tables covered with bric-a-brac, and the tightly closed curtains. Beyond it, an open door revealed a smaller room where a fire also burned, a room with a rounded alcove that indicated it had one of the twin towers of the house grafted to its sides.

The height of the arabesque-patterned steel ceilings, the size and grandeur of the rooms, affected Serena with a sense

244

of panic. She was out of place. She had no business being here, none at all.

"Can you make it up the stairs?" Nathan asked, bending over her.

Serena turned her attention to the wide flight with its oriental runner and another window of stained glass at the first landing. "I think so," she whispered.

In the end, Nathan half-carried her, his arm firm around her as he supported her weight. Serena saw the upstairs hallway with its flocked paper in green and gold and its shimmering brass gaslights through a haze of fatigue. The housekeeper met them at the open door of the bedroom. Scanning Serena's pale, blue-veined face, she took charge, recommending that Nathan order a glass of warm milk and some crackers, telling him that his own dinner was waiting if he cared to ring for it, that someone she called Dorcas would serve him. With that she shut the door upon him, and with a strong arm about Serena, led her toward the bathroom where steam rose from a zinc tub encased in walnut paneling.

The hot water brought the feeling back to Serena's icy feet, but it also took the last of her strength and will. She hardly knew when the housekeeper helped her from the tub, dried her with thick, warm Turkish towels, fluffed sweet-smelling Pozzoni talcum powder over her body, and slid a soft flannel nightgown over her head.

The bed had been turned down, the embroidered, lace-edged pillow covers whisked away, leaving the linen cases. The sheets of smooth, ironed linen had been warmed, and a hot-water pig, a fat ironstone bottle with a snoutlike handle on one end filled with hot water, had been pushed into the depths of the covers. Finding it with her feet as she stretched out, Serena sighed and closed her eyes.

"Your warm milk, miss."

With an effort, Serena drank from the glass the woman held to her lips, then lay back down.

"If there is anything you need in the night, miss, there is a buzzer on the table beside the bed. You have only to ring."

"Thank you," Serena murmured, "for everything."

"Goodnight, then, miss."

Serena thought she replied, but she could not be sure. She did not hear the closing of the door as the woman went away, leaving her alone.

What followed was a confusion of lowered voices whispering above her, of soft lights and shadowy figures coming

245

and going. It was Nathan leaning to speak to her, his face earnest, pleading, Nathan standing beside her, holding her hand while a quiet voice intoned, questioned, and she answered as bid. It was hot drinks and steam rising in the room as from the stones of hell to give her a sense of fevered heat. It was agonizing chill, racking coughing and gasping for breath while a great weight rested on her chest. And then the inflamed anguish in her upper body spread, stabbing into her vitals, pulsing in hard, knotted pain as the housekeeper hovered over her with frightened eyes, a man in a black coat came and went, and Nathan shouted outside in the hall. A long period of darkness came, varied with brief moments of dim twilight pervaded with a hovering feeling of being beyond and above herself, tethered on a loose rein, and yet a well-knotted one.

Serena came awake by slow degrees. The room was bright with the rays of the afternoon sun slanting in at the window, filtering through curtains of fine Belgium lace. Its yellow light seemed to glow in the room, intensifying the gold drapes at the windows with their graceful swags of fringe and tiebacks of bronze molded in the shape of flowers. The carpet was an Aubusson of pink, green, cream, and gold. On the walls were insets of flocked paper in gold and green, outlined with moldings painted green, gold, pink, and chocolate brown. The thick and heavy moldings ran around the steel ceiling that had been molded in a repeated daisy pattern and painted a lifelike white and yellow on a pale-green background. Hanging from the center was a chandelier of pink Bohemian glass hung with crystal lusters. In one corner was a dressing screen with a gilt framework in the French style. A cheery fire burned beneath a mantel of pink-veined marble set between the two windows on the outside wall. The walnut dresser bureau on the opposite side of the room was in the Renaissance style, with an incredibly tall mirror backed with diamond dust, a carved and scrolled pediment, and tiers of bracket shelves holding what appeared to be a varied collection of Staffordshire china dogs. The paneled bed that towered above her both at the headboard and foot was of the same design.

Serena lay in the exact center of the bed with her arms outside the covers. Centered over her chest on the turned-back sheet was a monogram of entwined initials so intricate it was impossible to decipher them. There were several layers of cover on the bed for warmth, the top one of which was a crazy quilt in silk and velvet outlined in gold silk in a herringbone stitch. The most fascinating and terrifying thing about it, however, was that the quilt lay straight and smooth across her body, perfectly flat over her waist and the bones of her hips.

Without warning, tears rose in her eyes and ran trickling into her hair. She lifted her hand to wipe them away, and found she could do so only with a great effort, that her fingers were white and thin, almost skeletal. She was staring at them, at their near-transparency, when the door swung silently inward on its hinges.

A woman stepped with brisk efficiency into the room, a woman with a vaguely familiar look, though Serena could not place the name.

"Why, you're awake, my dear. How nice," she said as she neared the bed, taking Serena's hand in a firm, warm grasp.

"Yes," Serena answered, though there was a shadow of puzzlement in her blue-gray eyes as she stared up at the other woman.

"You're looking much better. I believe there is even some color in your cheeks."

Serena ran her tongue over her dry, cracked lips. "I'm sorry," she began.

"You don't know who I am, do you? I'm Mrs. Anson, housekeeper to Mr. Nathan Benedict. You have been very ill, my dear, since the night he brought you. You have been here with us at Bristlecone for over two weeks."

"Two weeks," Serena repeated, her voice a whisper. It didn't seem possible.

"You had been out in the weather, were nearly frozen. You came down with pneumonia, and I can tell you there for a while it was a near thing. You were so weak, you see, and altogether in no condition to withstand—"

"But—but my baby—" Serena said, her eyes dark with the fear of unbearable pain.

"Oh, my dear, how stupid of me not to tell you at once, especially knowing you have not been yourself in the last few days. Your child was born a week ago. It's a boy, a fine, healthy boy."

Once more tears collected in Serena's eyes, tears of gladness. "May—may I see him?"

"What a question! Of course you may. We have set up a nursery only two doors down. I'll fetch him for you."

Despite the woman's words, it was not the housekeeper

247

who stepped into the room with a bundle in her arms a short time later. It was a young woman, little more than a girl, with red-gold hair, freckles like flecks of gold, and a shy smile that revealed the engagingly crooked teeth of a child. Like Mrs. Anson, she too wore black bombazine with a starched apron and cap.

The housekeeper came into the room behind her. "There, Mary, take the babe right up to the bed so his mother can see it. Miss Serena—I hope you don't mind me making free with your name, but Mr. Benedict said that was how I was to address you for the present—this is Mary. She has been retained as nursemaid and wetnurse for your son, you being too sick and weak to stand the strain."

Serena smiled at the girl, acknowledging the greeting even as she pushed aside the covers so her son could be placed on the bed beside her. Oblivious to everything except the warm, blanket-covered weight next to her, she unwrapped the baby with slow care. She examined his waving pink hands, his perfectly shaped head and tiny, shell-like ears, the fine, incredibly long lashes that rested on his round cheeks, and the thatch of dark hair that curled over his skull.

"I can't believe it," she whispered.

At the sound, the baby opened his eyes. Mysterious, gray-blue, they stared up at her with what seemed wondering curiosity, a reflection of her own blue-gray gaze. Abruptly he made a cooing sound, kicking at the confinement of his wrappings. Curling his long fingers with their tiny almond nails into a fist, he tried to maneuver them into his mouth.

"Isn't he precious," Mrs. Anson said, a smile on her long face and a fatuous sound in her voice. "We have all fallen in love with him; Mary, my daughter Dorcas, and myself. And if Mr. Benedict isn't half wild over him! Sits and holds him for hours, and never so much as frowns when the sweet little dear soaks through its diapers onto the trousers of his best suit!"

Serena smiled. "Can he stay with me for a time?"

"Yes, indeed. He's yours, isn't he, for all that the rest of us would like to claim him. He's such a good baby, he shouldn't give any trouble, but if he begins to fuss, you can ring for Mary, two short buzzes, and she will come and fetch him. Oh, and about Mary. I do hope you will keep her on, even though you had no say in her hiring. She's a good girl,

248

and she needs the job. Her husband and her little boy were killed not three weeks ago in a wagon accident, dragged underneath it when it overturned. Mary was thrown clear, but she lost the child she was carrying, and your baby has been a great help to her in getting over the loss, to say nothing of relieving the ache of her milk."

Serena glanced at the other girl, but she was hanging over the baby, letting him wrap his strong little fingers about one of hers, smiling as if she did not hear.

"Oh, you needn't fear that I'm blabbing out something that will hurt Mary's feelings. She doesn't hear, hasn't since she was two years old. She can tell when the baby is crying, though, from the vibrations in the air or some such. And she never takes her eyes off him, so you need not worry that he will be neglected. It's far more likely that he will be completely spoiled."

"I wouldn't mind that," Serena answered, her face sober. "It will be hard enough for him later on. But about Mary, I'm not sure how long she can stay. I—I can't afford to pay her, and I don't like the idea of Nathan's being responsible. I wonder if I—" She stopped suddenly as a cough caught in her throat.

"The doctor said you were not to try to take on the task yourself, my dear. You are still weak, more so than you imagine. You must rest and recoup your strength. In the meantime, don't worry about money matters. Don't worry about anything. It will straighten itself out by and by."

Don't worry. That was easy enough to say, but how could she help it? Serena, when the others had gone, lay staring down at her baby. Poor sweet mite. What would become of him? She could not stay here forever; already she had trespassed too long on Nathan's hospitality. But where would she go when she left, what would she do with a baby boy to care for, to feed and clothe and raise somehow to be a man?

Did he look like Ward, this child of hers? With an ache in the region of her heart she had to concede that he did, a little, about the nose and chin. Though the blue-gray of his eyes would change, taking on his permanent color in a month or so, for the moment he looked more like her than anyone else, or perhaps more like her own father.

"I'll call you Sean," she said, her voice low. "Sean Walsh. You will be my child and no one else's. My Sean." She bent to kiss the silken top of his head, and drew him close, staring out through the lace curtains that veiled the window at the clouds floating against the turquoise blue of the sky.

She was wrong, however. The child would never be called Sean Walsh, never be hers alone. Nor would she ever be Serena Walsh again.

Chapter Fifteen

It was nearing suppertime. The sun had set behind the cone of Mt. Pisgah. Mary had come for Sean, to take him away, feed him and make him ready for bed. The fire on the marble hearth had died down to a bed of glowing coals. Serena, between waking and dozing, knew she should ring to have it kindled and made up again, but she could not summon the energy. The westering sun had lent its warmth to the room, just as it had melted the last of the snow left from the storm the night she had come here, here to Bristlecone. It was still cold, of course; she could tell that from the drafts that eddied from the windows, but it was no longer raw and freezing. There was so much comfort here in this fussy, pleasant room with its warm colors, she was so much thinner and lighter, that it seemed impossible she was the same person who had been turned out into the snowstorm.

She must not get too used to such luxury. It wouldn't do for her to become as spoiled as Sean. She had her own way to make in the world, and his. Sighing, she looked around her, at the polished woods with their scent of beeswax, the soft rug and rich fabrics. No, such things would not be for her, nor for her son, not for a long time to come. She did not need them, certainly not, but how much better it would be for Sean if the wealth they represented was hers to bestow.

Useless, idle thoughts. As well to wish she could turn back

the clock, let Ward know he was to have a child before he died. As well to wish Ward could see his son, could hold him. What would he think of this child of theirs? Would he be glad or sorry, proud or indifferent?

Her reverie was interrupted by a quiet knock. At her invitation, Nathan entered and came with slow steps to stand at the foot of her bed.

"Mrs. Anson said you were better. I had to come and see for myself."

"Yes," Serena answered, surveying his face with its look of haggard sleeplessness accenting the thinness. "I'm glad you came. I've been lying here all evening thinking of how much I owe you for the good care you have been taking of me."

"Misplaced gratitude, Serena. I should be thanking you for allowing me the privilege. Are you really better?"

"I think I must be."

"I—I would never have forgiven myself if anything had happened to you, or to your baby."

"It wasn't your fault I was out in the weather that night," she protested.

"I could have found shelter for you sooner, instead of being so set on bringing you here."

"It doesn't matter, Nathan. I think I—we both—will be just fine."

"It won't be my fault if you aren't." Nathan looked away. Noticing the fire that had burned down to coals, he moved toward it. His expression serious, he set the firescreen to one side and knelt to lift wood from the log basket, laying it across the andirons.

"I—I'm not your responsibility, Nathan. I wish I could make you understand that."

"You can't," he said without looking at her, "because it isn't so."

"I don't—" Serena began before she was halted by a bout of coughing that shook the bed and left her spent.

"You shouldn't try to talk," Nathan said, setting the firescreen in place once more and dusting his hands on the handkerchief he took from his pocket. "And I know I probably shouldn't upset you. But there is something I have to say, something that concerns the subject we were discussing. No, don't interrupt. It may take me a while to get to the point, but I'll make it."

Serena, held by the look of strain in his hazel eyes and

the firm resolution in his voice, watched as he returned to stand with his hands braced on the footboard of the bed.

"When I brought you here, Serena, it wasn't out of the goodness of my heart. I brought you to Bristlecone because this was where I wanted you, where I had dreamed of seeing you for months. I thought once I had you here, you would not be able to leave until I had made my appeal, played on your sympathies, overwhelmed you with all the things I would give you, all I could do for you and the baby you were going to have without benefit of marriage. If all else failed I would make it a business proposition, your company for my money. And then you became so sick. It began to look as if you might escape me after all, though not in the way I had thought. The doctor said you were not as strong as you should be. It was his opinion that you could go into early labor at any hour. I decided to gamble. If I won, I would have you and your child the rest of your lives; if I lost, you would still belong to me, if only in name, whether alive or dead."

As her eyes widened, he gave a slow nod. "You guessed it. I brought in a preacher. I told him you had consented to the marriage, but were too ill to remember. He seemed to believe it after I gave him a shameless bribe and a quick glimpse of the bride. The ceremony was performed in this room. Mrs. Anson and her daughter were witnesses. I'm sorry, Serena, but you are Mrs. Nathan Benedict. No, I take that back. I'm not sorry for the fact, only that it had to be this way."

"It's impossible," she whispered.

"No. Since you were incapacitated, Mrs. Anson helped you sign your name. The proper documents have been duly recorded at the county seat."

"But marriage, Nathan? Surely there was no need?"

"There was every need. If I accepted your child as my own, I would earn your gratitude, gratitude that might possibly turn into something warmer someday."

"But, since you've told me the truth, what now?"

"I don't know. I still feel the same, except I want us to start from here with no subterfuge, no blackmail. It's not your gratitude I want, nor a hold on you in name only. I want you, however much or little you can give me of yourself. I won't rush you, or ask for what you can't give. And I swear I will try to give no more than you can take."

It was a magnificent offer, one most women would grab with both hands. Nathan was an attractive man, with the

253

easy manners of a gentleman. He was kind and compassionate and generous, and above all, wealthy. Most ordinary men would have considered that they were doing her a favor by marrying her, to say nothing of a man who was the object of every matchmaking mama in the district, if not the better portion of the state. Why then was she so troubled, why did she have this persistent feeling that there was more to it than she had been told?

If she wanted reasons she need look no further than the manner of this marriage. It was natural for her to feel resentment at the arrangement of it.

Serena, watching her fingers pleat the hem of the sheet, said, "What you did, no matter the reasons, has had the affect of giving my son a name, one he can be proud of. For that much I do thank you."

He made a quick gesture of negation. "I gave you something, too. Do you remember?"

"No, I don't think so."

"There's no reason you should, if you don't remember the ceremony." His smile was wry, without bitterness. Straightening, he slipped his hand into his pocket, bringing out a small box covered with ruby velvet. With easy steps he approached the bed and, seating himself on the edge, snapped open the box.

Resting on the bed of white satin was an enormous sapphire in an octagon shape surrounded by flawless diamonds. It gleamed with blue fire in the fading light, a matchless jewel set in softly shining gold.

"It's lovely," Serena breathed.

"I thought it suited you." Nathan plucked the ring from the box, and picking up her hand, slid its cool weight onto the third finger of her left hand.

"Oh, Nathan, I can't accept anything like this," Serena objected, trying to pull her fingers from his grasp.

He would not let her go. "You already have. I am only returning your property. I gave you this ring when we exchanged vows; something I bought some time ago on the off chance that an occasion like this might arise. The only reason I was carrying it around with me was that you have lost so much weight in the last week that you were in danger of losing it. Mrs. Anson found it in the sheets and gave it back to me for safekeeping."

"That doesn't change anything," Serena began, only to be stopped by coughing once again.

Nathan got to his feet. "I shouldn't have kept you talking so long. I had better go and let you rest. I hope that in a few days you will be fit enough for me to have dinner with you in here."

Serena managed a smile and a nod. As he turned away, she levered herself to one elbow. "Nathan, wait."

"Yes, Serena?" He stopped in the center of the Aubusson rug, turning back.

"My belongings at the Eldorado—Pearlie said I could send for them, only she—she said she would burn them after two days. Could you—send someone to see if there is anything left?"

"I'll go myself."

"No, really, if you'll just send a message?"

"I would rather go," he said, his face stern.

Serena subsided, easing back on her pillow. "I'm sorry to be so much trouble," she said hoarsely. Then, touched by a vague memory, she added, "I—I hope I haven't kept you from your room?"

"Not at all. This was my wife's room, or perhaps I should say my first wife's." With a brief smile that creased the sides of his thin face, he let himself out the door.

Serena lay still, staring at the recessed panel. Mrs. Nathan Benedict. There was a ring of unreality to the words. It couldn't be, and yet it was. She let her gaze drop to the ring she was wearing, a rich symbol of a mystic and binding union. It meant the end of her worries, the answer to her prayers. Why, then, wasn't she happier? Married. The wife of Nathan Benedict. And what had happened, she asked herself with deliberate care, to his mistress?

The answer to her question was not immediately forthcoming. Nathan came to see her often, but did not stay long, and it was almost as though he deliberately kept the conversation on an impersonal level. He was meticulous about asking after her health. They discussed Sean, the pounds he had gained, and whether he smiled for them or from gas pains.

He brought to her all that was left of her belongings, her bits of jewelry, a handful of books, the pistol in its mahogany case he had given her. The rest had been thrown into the fire, including her mother's ivory ball gown and the gilt-heeled slippers. No, he said, his hazel eyes hard, he had encountered no difficulty in getting the items from Pearlie.

As she began to relax in her company, he became more

expansive, talking, Serena thought, to keep her from having to strain toward conversation. He spoke of occurrences in the town and, sometimes, problems in the mines. There was labor unrest as the miners belonging to the Western Federation of Miners, fresh from their victory the year before, when they had won the eight-hour-shift day at no cut in their pay of three dollars a day, were agitating for special concessions, an old-age pension, and child-labor laws. Accidents were frequent, sometimes with the dynamite charges used to blast the granite rock into small enough pieces to be removed, sometimes with the stopers, the six-foot-long, steam-powered jack hammers called "widow makers" used to gouge the gold-bearing ore from its bed; and sometimes from sheer exuberant or drunken carelessness. Problems arose with the gold veins. They played out with unsettling capriciousness and had to be sought out with careful blasting, though they often were never found again. But one of the most troubling phenomena was water in the mine tunnels. It was a situation the mine owners were going to have to face together sometime. Miners could not work while standing up to their necks in water. There was talk of digging a drainage tunnel, but so far nothing had come of it.

Nathan himself, when pressed, admitted that he was in favor of better conditions for the miners. His mines had not been among those which were a target of the union during the strike, since he had already instigated the eight-hour day and refused to return to the nine-hour rate advocated by the other owners. But it was precisely because of the scars left from the labor war, the battles between special deputies hired by the mine owners and the state militia seeking to protect the miners, the polarization of the town of Cripple Creek, which was a populist community with sympathy for the miners, and Colorado Springs, which was elitist and therefore on the side of mine owners who, for the most part, made their homes there, that he felt unable to follow his inclinations. Where before he had dared to be a maverick, feelings were running so high now that it was dangerous to run counter to his "class," which happened to be the mine owners. It was, basically, the haves against the have-nots, as the miners sought to share in the unusual prosperity of the region.

"I hate to see the boys who work in the mines," Serena commented. "They look like little men, old before their time. Their faces are so washed-out and sad, as if they had forgotten how to laugh. I can't bear to think of Sean having to go into the mines someday, shut away from the sunlight."

"You don't have to worry," Nathan answered, his tone abrupt. "He'll never have to ride the hoist unless he wants to do it for the experience."

"What are you saying?" Serena stared at him, wondering at the almost-defiant sound of his voice.

"I mean I have had a will drawn up naming Sean as my heir, along with you, of course."

"Nathan, no!"

"Why not? I have no relatives, none who deserve so much as a penny, though there's always a new cousin or nephew crawling out of the woodwork. If by some chance I—you and I—should have direct issue, the will can be changed. Even in that event, you need not be concerned. Sean will always share equally with any children we may have."

He kept his face averted from her, as if he preferred not to see her reaction to his words. "I don't know what to say," Serena told him.

"There's no need to say anything. It's just a sensible precaution, that's all. There is no obligation."

His last words were welcome, despite her recognition that she could not help but be influenced by the magnanimity of his gesture. Did he know that? Was that why they had been spoken, to absolve himself of the accusation? Or was it simply that the obligation only existed in her own mind? She had been given a choice, yes; she could stay with him, or not. Still, it seemed that Nathan, by his quiet actions, his frequent references to the future, was going to leave her no room for an answer other than the one he wished to hear. Compared to Ward, he did not seem a particularly strong or virile personality, but there was a bedrock of unassuming power beneath his calm demeanor. The discovery was more disturbing than she cared to admit.

Serena grew stronger. She progressed from sitting up in bed to sitting in a chair at the window. From there she watched the low-hanging clouds of the cold mornings frost the trees until they looked like white ghosts of themselves, watched the gray afternoons turn to snowy nights. A cradle was moved in to stand beside the fireplace, and a rocking chair was brought. Serena rocked Sean and put him down to sleep, ringing for Mary only when he showed signs of hunger, and in the late evenings when it was time to make him ready for the night with the nursemaid.

As Serena's strength returned, so did her appetite. It was a great pleasure to learn that Nathan's chef was a Frenchman, trained at Antoine's in New Orleans, and adept at all the dishes that were her particular favorites. When she mentioned the fact in glowing terms to Nathan, along with a sudden craving for oysters Bienville and seafood gumbo filé, he looked both gratified and thoughtful. Less than a week later he appeared at the head of a procession consisting of Mary, Mrs. Anson's daughter, Dorcas, Mrs. Anson herself, and the coachman. Standing in the doorway, Nathan respectfully begged permission to place a feast before her.

A table was brought forward with two tree-of-life chairs. An asbestos pad was placed on the shining table surface to protect it from heat, and onto this was spread a fine cloth of hand-embroidered white-on-white Irish linen, rolled from off a pole where it had been stored to prevent creases. Fine napkins were folded with the monogram uppermost; china dinner plates, fishplates, bread-and-butter plates, dessert plates, soup bowls, and finger bowls were laid, followed by crystal salts, each with its own tiny spoon. Waterford crystal water glasses and three different sizes of wine glasses were set in their correct places. A silver candelabra was placed between the plates. Water was poured into the finger bowls and a slice of lemon and sprig of ivy floated upon it. That done, everyone withdrew, except the housekeeper who helped Serena into her borrowed dressing gown, then lit the candles in the silver holder. While Nathan seated Serena, the woman wheeled in a cart on which sat the first course under a domed silver cover.

"Oysters Bienville!" Serena exclaimed as the dish, steaming hot and deliciously fragrant, was set before her. "How in the world did you manage to find such a thing, and at this time of year?"

He waited until they both had been served. Picking up his small, three-pronged fork, he gave a slow smile. "They are shipped in by special train. You can have anything if you have money—and if you want it badly enough."

Serena stared at him a moment, her awareness caught by a shadow in his eyes. "There are those who would dispute that," she suggested.

"They don't, usually, have money."

The shadow was gone and his expression was droll. Serena smiled and turned her attention to the food.

The oysters were removed by gumbo filé as a soup course.

With it went crusty French bread served with butter in small round pats with a fleur-de-lis design pressed into the top. This was followed by tender grillades of beef in a dark, rich sauce with side dishes of broccoli au gratin, wild rice, and brown sugar-coated yams. With the seafood dishes there was a crisp white wine, with the main course a rich red. Finally, as the almond tarts and cream were placed upon their dessert plates, a mint-green liqueur was poured.

Though she could not do justice to so much food, Serena was lavish with her praise. She was touched by the trouble Nathan had gone to on her behalf, if not the expense. She felt a warm friendliness toward him that might or might not have been intensified by the wine. There was also between them a gentle intimacy made up of the soft candlelight, the hissing and popping of the fire beside them, the gleam of silver and crystal, the sharing of the excellent meal. It seemed to deepen as the housekeeper, her last duty performed with the pouring of the liqueur, went out, closing the door behind her. Nathan's next words served to underline the impression.

"I will be glad," he said, his gaze on the rather drab dressing gown Serena wore, "when next week comes."

"Why, I wonder?"

"Because it will be Christmas, and I will have an excuse to give you a robe and sundry other items so you won't have to keep wearing my housekeeper's things. They are well enough in their way, but they don't suit you."

"I—wish you wouldn't," Serena said quietly.

He sent her a crooked smile. "I know you do, and I intend to do it anyway."

"Nathan, don't you think it would be better if you waited until—"

"No," he answered, his voice firm, "I don't."

There was no use arguing with him, that much Serena had learned. Whatever he wanted her to have, he would buy, whatever he wanted to do for her, he would arrange to have done. She changed the subject.

"It doesn't seem possible that it's Christmastime already."

"I suppose it doesn't, not to you. Would you like a tree brought in? You wouldn't have to do a thing. Mrs. Anson and Dorcas can decorate it."

"I don't know," Serena said slowly. "You must do as you like, as you usually do. I don't really feel very festive."

"I haven't bothered since Nora, my wife, died. Somehow, I feel like it this year. It's having a family again, I guess."

She had been with Ward for the holiday season last year. Nathan and Consuelo had come and the four of them had gone to the Continental Hotel for Christmas dinner.

"What is it?" Nathan asked. "Did I say something wrong?"

"No, I—I was just thinking of last Christmas, of Ward, and Consuelo."

"Oh." He reached to take up his liqueur, staring down into the dark-green depths.

"I've been wanting to ask you about Consuelo," Serena went on, her voice strained. "Did she get over the scarlet fever? Is she all right?"

"She's fine. She was feeling a little run-down, so I sent her down to Manitou Springs to drink the waters, get her out of this altitude for a while. I had a message from her complaining there was nothing going on, so she may show up in Cripple again any day."

Serena gave a nod, smiling a little at the thought of the flamboyant Spanish Connie sipping mineral water.

"I know it isn't the usual thing for a wife to know about her husband's mistress, or at least to discuss her, but our situation is not usual. Consuelo is my friend, and I know she cares for you. I don't like the idea of her being hurt."

"If you are trying to get around to asking if I told her about our marriage, the answer is yes, I did. She wasn't happy about it, but I think she is resigned."

"She must think I went behind her back to take you from her."

"I doubt that. Consuelo has—had few illusions about our relationship. She knew how I felt about you."

"She may have had an idea of your feelings, but I don't think she had any cause to think we would marry."

"No," he agreed, taking a reflective sip of his drink.

"I'll have to go see her when she comes back, or as soon as I am able to get out of the house."

He looked up, an arrested expression on his face. "Are you sure that's wise?"

"What?" Serena stared at him, surprised by the censure in his tone.

"I mean, it's bound to be upsetting for you. Then, you may be seen and recognized."

"What does it matter if I see someone who knows me? I'm no different from Consuelo."

260

"You are my wife now, and an announcement to that effect has been sent to every newspaper in the district."

Serena sat back. "And I am to behave like a respectable married woman, shunning everyone I knew before, crossing the street when I see them coming, holding up my nose? I won't do it, Nathan. You may have married me without my consent, but I shall most certainly give you leave to divorce me, if that's what you want."

"That isn't what I meant. I thought that as you made new friends among the wives of the other mine owners you would gradually see less and less of the people from Myers Avenue."

"The mine owners' wives have never been known for accepting women like me, married or not. I understand they hold themselves on pretty high form with their trips to the East, rubbing shoulders with the Astors and the Vanderbilts, and jaunting over Europe buying up castles, and importing royalty for houseguests. Thank you, but I would as soon not join the ranks of people whose only interest is how much money their husbands have and whether it is old or new."

"A sweeping indictment, Serena, but are you sure? You enjoyed our meal tonight, and that's only a small sample of what money can bring."

"I won't be bribed, Nathan! If you want to show me what money can do, then use it to help people."

"All right, Serena. Where do you suggest I start?"

His easy capitulation took her aback, but she rallied. "By—by taking the fifteen hundred dollars you offered for information about Lessie's murderer and building a home for women with it, a place they can go when they have nowhere else to turn, a place where they can find a hot meal and a warm bed until they can get back on their feet, or at least collect their thoughts. Not a place run by pious preachers and do-gooders who think that listening to a sermon is a small price to pay for aid, but a place where women can help each other. After that, you can build an orphanage, and after that, a home for the elderly and the miners who have been hurt in accidents."

"Charity, Serena? Most people don't want it, and those that do will take advantage of anyone weak enough to give them a free handout."

"That isn't so, at least not entirely. Not so long ago I needed your help; I might even have died without it. But though I am grateful for your charity, Nathan, I am not anxious to live on it forever."

"No," he answered, "to my sorrow."

That was not quite the end of the argument. The next afternoon Nathan came to her, and with a smile on his thin face, dropped a document printed on thick white paper into her lap.

"What is it?" Serena asked, slanting a long glance at him before unfolding it.

"Something you wanted," he answered.

It apppeared to be a deed to a plot of land, a city block, in the section of the town halfway between the business and residential sections. At the sight of the purchase price, a frown drew Serena's brows together.

"I don't understand," she said.

"It's the land for your home for indigent women, and whatever else it might suit you to build on it."

"A five-thousand-dollar lot?"

"You did say that it was a good use for my money."

"I didn't mean this much of it!"

"Land is high in Cripple Creek these days. You will notice that it is in your name? I hope you don't mind if we keep it that way, and if your name appears on the building? I would just as soon not be known as the mine owner who takes care of destitute women. It could prove embarrassing."

"Building?"

"The one they started putting up this morning. It should be completed by the end of January, with the crew I've got on it."

"Oh, Nathan," Serena said, lifting her blue-gray gaze to his face. "This is marvelous. You are so kind."

For an answer, he leaned over her chair and pressed his lips to hers. They were hard and thin against the vulnerable softness of her mouth. The pressure was brief, but there was a flush on his face when he straightened.

"And you are so beautiful. You grow more lovely every time I see you."

"Please, you promised—" Serena faltered.

"So I did. More fool I," he said, and smiled, though his hazel eyes remained dark.

The land was only the first of the presents. Nathan began to bring her something every day. He was not being extravagant at all, he said when she protested. Hadn't she ever heard of the twelve days of Christmas? She should be glad she hadn't received anything as impractical as a partridge in a pear tree, or seven swans a-swimming, for heaven's sake.

He did, however, bring her a canary with a stupendous voice in a cage plated with gold, and a few trifles in silver. These last included a sewing bird to hold her embroidery silks, a scent bottle on a satin cord, a chased pen with a screw-on cap from which dangled a silk tassel, an inkwell set with separate holders for ink and blotting sand, and a card case with a supply of calling cards engraved with her new name in flowing script, and instructions for leaving them when she made visits. The next thing to arrive was a lady's phaeton by Bradley with a dark-blue body, a convertible top, and hardware of sterling silver. After that came a square piano by Steinway and Sons of New York with massive turned legs and a glass-like finish. It was intended, he said, for her to accompany herself while she sang.

"The first day of Christmas is Christmas day itself," Serena pointed out.

"For the rest of the world," Nathan answered. "For us, it can be any day I make it."

He did save a few things for the twenty-fifth of December, however. She awoke to find boxes of every shape and size, and tied with satin ribbons in every shade of the rainbow, piled ready at the foot of her morning coffee and a request from Nathan to allow him to have breakfast with her. When it was granted he appeared in a floor-length robe of royal-blue quilted satin with velvet lapels. Seeing it, Serena's smile of welcome wavered for an instant. It was the same robe, or a close copy, that she had come across in Nathan's private railroad car that night so many months ago.

Without noticing anything amiss, Nathan scanned the boxes. Choosing one, he looked at it in mock perplexity. "Now what, I wonder, do we have here? I think you had better open it and satisfy my curiosity before breakfast comes."

From the length of the box, and Nathan's previous comments, Serena had a shrewd idea of what it contained. She was not wrong. From the depths of a cloud of tissue paper she lifted a wrapper of black lace. Voluminous, it featured Watteau pleats in the back and was lined with black silk for a degree of warmth. With it was a matching nightgown of diaphanous black silk with lace inserts, and a pair of black silk slippers with high opera heels.

"Are you certain," Serena asked, one brow arched, "that this is what respectable married women wear?"

"I am indeed. That is, they do if they have the skin and

263

the coloring for it, not to mention the shape. Will you put it on?"

As he spoke, he nodded in the direction of the screen that stood in the corner. Serena glanced at it uncertainly, then back at the wrapper in her hands. The label, sewn with tiny, delicate stitches into the lining, was that of a famous Parisian salon. The temptation was too great to resist. She looked at the housekeeper hovering expectantly nearby. Throwing back the covers, she slid out of bed and padded toward the screen. Mrs. Anson picked up the box and wrapper and hurried after her.

It was only as she stood in the nightgown and wrapper, wearing the slippers while Mrs. Anson smoothed her hair with quick, deft strokes, that she realized what she had done. How easy it was to become used to luxury, to be being waited upon at every turn. How fatally easy.

When she stepped from behind the screen with her center-parted hair streaming over her shoulders and folds of lace swaying rhythmically around her, Nathan got slowly to his feet from where he sat on the foot of the bed.

"It's everything I hoped it would be," he said, his voice husky.

"It's ridiculous is what it is," Serena said with an air of frank disdain, though there was a twinkle in her eyes.

"You don't like it?"

"I love it, but it means I am going to have to thank you yet again. It does look as if you might have some consideration for my feelings!"

He assumed a grave expression. "You're absolutely right. I have a suggestion. Why don't we dispense with the thanks until after you have opened all the gifts, and then you can express your appreciation one time only? Let's see, what would be appropriate without requiring you to use the words you find objectionable? I have it: you can pour me a cup of coffee."

"Done," she said and, accepting the hand he held out to her, returned to the bed.

The high-piled boxes held duplicates of the black ensemble in cream lace, and another in deepest rose. There was a selection of French parfum in what appeared to be quart-size cut-glass bottles, and a dressing case of black leather with silver catches filled with silver-topped bottles, and a silver-backed hairbrush, comb, clothes brush, nail buffer, nail file, cuticle brush, button hook, even a personal silver toothpick.

Next came a gramophone with a morning-glory horn and a box of recorded rolls. It was followed incongruously by a full-length coat of French sable with a matching hat and shoulder throw. After that came a dozen pairs of gloves hand-stitched of French kid in white, black, brown, and assorted other colors with a glove stretcher resembling a long curling iron; a carriage cloak of black satin edged with French sable that was striped with white embroidery and lined with blue satin which, quite incidentally, had a Worth label; a detachable yoke of jet that had a most satisfying "rain" or deep fringe of small jet beads; a large opera fan of black silk and marabou that Serena eyed with something less than favor; an assortment of jet, horn, and tortoiseshell hair ornaments; and finally, a boxed set of several years' back issues of *The Delineator*, a women's fashion magazine.

Serena thought that was all, but it was not. From his pocket Nathan drew a large, velvet-covered box, and in the same manner as he had presented her ring, handed it to her. Inside was a circlet of diamonds to be worn with the ring, and also a complete parure of sapphires; a necklace, bracelet, earrings, brooch, and even a small coronet. With their octagon shapes in graduated sizes, the sparkle of gems, the glitter of diamonds and gold, it was a gift fit for an empress.

As if attuned to her thoughts, Nathan said, "They once belonged to Catherine the Great of Russia, and now they are yours."

"I—I'm overwhelmed. It's too much," she told him, looking from the treasure she held in her hand to all the rest spread out around her. "I don't know what to say."

"We had an agreement, I think." As Serena turned her head to stare at him, he indicated the cart that had been rolled into the room. "Now you pour the coffee."

As prodigal as he had been with her, Nathan was no less generous with Sean, or with his staff. He distributed largess as though his wallet had no bottom. For the baby there was a complete layette, rattles with gold trim, moving toys to watch and touch, and a hobbyhorse painted dapple-gray with a mane and tail of red yarn. There were bicycles for the women, a pair of "bloomers" with which to enjoy them, fur-trimmed cloth coats, lisle stockings, scent and powder, and rugs and lamps to add to the comfort of their rooms on the third floor of the house. For the coachman there was his own mount, he not holding with new-fangled contraptions like bicycles, plus a buffalo coat, new leather boots, a bright-red union suit, and sundry other items to make his life easier. For the stableboy there was only slightly less; for the chef considerably more.

In return Nathan was deluged with small gifts, most of them made by hand. With Mrs. Anson's connivance, Serena had made and embroidered a soft leather pouch for the tobacco Nathan always carried for his pipe.

"It isn't much in return for all you have given me," Serena said when she gave it to him.

"It's worth more this minute than anything I own, because you made it."

"But you have given me so much."

"Selfish gifts, for the pleasure of watching you when you open them," he answered with a shake of his head.

"Despite what I said earlier, I am grateful, and I do thank you, for everything." The conversation had taken place at the breakfast table. On impulse, Serena had risen and, leaning across the small table, brushed his lips with her own as Mrs. Anson stood by, a benign smile on her face. When she regained her seat, Nathan had reached for her hand, his grip so tight the diamonds on her fingers had cut into her skin.

It was late, now. The day was done; dinner was over. Mary had come for Sean some time ago. Serena wound the gramaphone with its dark-blue morning-glory horn and set a roll to turning. As the false gaiety of "The Dance of the Hours" from *La Gioconda* poured from the instrument, she turned away, moving toward the window.

Outside, the glow of the moonlight was reflected on the snow while shadows stretched long and dark. Mt. Pisgah caught the light on its slope, shining as the moon rose into the night sky. The wind swept down with a lost and mournful sound, waving the branches of the trees, loosening the dry snow so it sifted in a fine powder to the ground.

She felt restless, a sign, she supposed, that she was getting well. There was still an ache in her chest when she breathed deep, and she tired easily, but her cough was almost gone. She didn't feel particularly invalidish; she felt, in fact, like putting on her clothes and leaving the confinement of the gold bedroom.

The trouble with that was the problems waiting for her outside the door. So long as she stayed in here, keeping to her bed, she did not have to decide if she was going to stay at Bristlecone, or try to make some kind of life on her own; whether she would try to be a wife to Nathan, accepting the

266

physical intimacy that entailed, or if she was going to return his gifts, take her child, and go away.

She owed Nathan so much, even life itself perhaps, and the life of her child. She was fond of him. He had many qualities that she admired. It would not be such a bad thing. She would be lapped in luxury, petted and cosseted and prevented from lifting a finger. Instead of being Serena Walsh, she would become a rich man's wife, weak, dependent, anxious to please lest her privileges be taken from her. He would buy her things and she would repay him by accepting them. In the end, wouldn't she herself be merely another toy he had bought? Wasn't that the real purpose of all the lovely trinkets he had poured into her lap, payment for value he hoped to receive? This time the bribe was being offered to her instead of to Ward, but wasn't the principle the same? It was a bitter thought, but it seemed better to recognize and accept it before she committed herself.

The record roll came to an end. The first Serena knew of Nathan's presence was when she turned to see him removing the wax cylinder.

"Do you want to hear it again?" he asked.

At the quick shake of her head, he put the roll away in the box. "I'm glad you're still up. I wanted to talk to you."

"Oh?"

"I've been thinking. How would you like to go to Europe? We could make an extended trip, a grand tour, if you like. We could stay a few weeks in New York, then sail for England. From there we could go to France. We could visit the salons of the best couturiers, order dresses, ball gowns, coats, whatever you wanted. Then we could go on to Rome, Venice, Athens, or north to Germany and Austria, if you prefer. When we return to Paris your clothes should be ready for you to wear on the homeward voyage."

"Nathan—it sounds lovely, but I'm not sure."

"You won't have to go in rags, even if you do want to buy out Paris. I ordered several dresses, walking costumes, evening costumes, and the like, from the New York salons for you. I thought they would be here in time for Christmas, but there were delays. They should be arriving any day, along with a dressmaker to attend to the fit."

Serena could not bear to look at him, to watch his transparent enthusiasm as he spread his eager plans for her approval. It was disturbing in a way she had not heretofore experienced. The feeling it aroused in her was compassion.

Turning back toward the window, she said, "Do you remember last winter, Nathan, when you offered Ward mining shares and—and other interests if he would let me go?"

It was a moment before Nathan answered. "You know about that?"

"Ward told me. He thought I should have the chance to accept or refuse, since I had as much to gain from the arrangement as he did."

"And you refused?"

"Yes, I did. I was in love with Ward, you see, though I wasn't properly aware of it at the time. But my greatest objection was to being bought and sold, like a head of cattle, or a promising mining claim."

"What are you saying? Is that what you think I'm trying to do again?"

She swung back to face him, her blue-gray gaze unflinching on his pale face. "Aren't you? Beyond the enjoyment of giving, which I don't deny, aren't you trying to impress me with what you can give me, what you can do to make my life rich and easy and interesting?"

"If it is, it doesn't look as if I'm succeeding," he said, his voice tight.

"I'm not so sure about that," she answered, her smile wry, "but I would like the chance to make my decision without such things being pushed at me."

"I understand what you are saying, and I will try to respect it, though it won't be easy. The clothes that are coming will be my last gift until—well, until later. I hope you will accept them?"

Serena gave a reluctant nod. "I didn't mean to hurt you, or seem ungrateful. And if I truly have wronged you, I am sorry."

"It's I who should be apologizing to you. I didn't realize you were in love with Ward. I understood from Pearlie that he more or less forced himself on you. And, of course, I never dreamed he would let you know of my offer. I can see how it would appear an insult to you."

"I think Ward did it in the nature of a test, because he thought I wanted a rich husband. He was interested to see—to see how much I wanted one."

"And you showed him the money didn't matter at all," Nathan said, his tone bleak.

Serena blinked at the haze of tears that rose to her eyes. "In—in a manner of speaking."

268

A small silence fell. Nathan stood still, staring at her with narrowed eyes. Abruptly he took a step away from her, clasping his hands behind him as he walked to the fireplace and turned with his back to the low-burning flames.

"It's quite a coincidence that you should bring up this subject. I've been thinking of Ward off and on all day."

"Have you?" So had she, though there was no reason to say so.

"I've been wondering what he will think when he finds out you are married to me, now."

"What?"

Serena turned toward him, the color draining from her face.

"It can happen. Any day now he will pick up a newspaper and read the announcement, or somebody he sees at the Eldorado will tell him. Maybe he knows already. It seems unlikely that Pearlie would let him remain in ignorance for long."

"What are you saying?" Serena whispered.

"I'm trying to tell you," Nathan said, his hazel eyes dark as they rested upon her, "that Ward is alive. He returned to Cripple Creek two days ago."

Chapter Sixteen

By the first week of the new year the story was all over town. It was even seized upon by the newspapers and printed up with a blazing headline touting it as a return from the grave. Ward had been in a remote area vaguely described as southwest of South Park. His horse had lost its footing on a steep slope and fallen with its rider. Ward's leg had been broken, his shoulder sprained, and he had suffered a severe concussion. If he had not been found by a band of roaming Indians, he would have died of exposure and hunger. The Indians had taken him far back up into the mountains, and there they had nursed him back to health. The Ute Indians had been confined to reservations in Utah and southwestern Colorado by a treaty signed fourteen years before. The band that had come to Ward's aid were off the reservation illegally, and were therefore reluctant to make his presence among them known, or to deliver his messages. In any case, the summer was over before Ward had recovered enough to know where he was, or what had happened to him; it had been early winter before he was able to ride, or to convince the Indian leader that it would be worth his while to lend him a mount so he could get back to civilization.

As the days went by, Serena became more disturbed, alternating between suppressed irritation and an insupportable weariness of the spirit. She took to emerging from her room when Nathan left the house for town, or one of his mines, and wandering up and down the halls, in and out of the rooms, pausing to pick up an ornament here, a bibelot there, out of the hundreds that seemed to crowd the rooms. Mrs. Anson's daughter, Dorcas, a sullen but biddable girl with a nervous habit of twisting her hair and a need to be told at least three times before she understood an order, had a trick of screaming and dropping whatever she was carrying when she came upon Serena in her flowing wrapper. Mrs. Anson herself was apt to scowl, declaring Serena would have a relapse, when she found her in some cold corridor. She was coldly disapproving when she entered Nathan's tower-room study and saw Serena leaning over his desk, reading the premier copy of the *Cripple Creek Crusher*, the district's first newspaper, printed in gold ink, that was displayed there under the glass.

The house was large, that much could be said for it. The front door, instead of being centered in its bulk, was at one end. It could be reached from the side portico where an oval driveway ended, or from a flight of steps that ascended from the front lawn and crossed the front veranda. There was a porch swing of wicker and a number of rocking chairs on the long, open veranda with its ornate railing. It would doubtless be a pleasant place to sit and enjoy the air in the summer months, but for the present it was cold and windy, the wood floor made slippery by the ice of melting snow. The same was true for the gazebo with pierced sides and turreted cupola that graced the side yard down near the creek.

Inside the front door was the entrance hall with the staircase on the left, and directly beneath it, the door to Nathan's study. The tower that opened out from one corner was used as a library, being lined with leather-bound volumes titled in gold, and arranged in concave shelves that stretched high above her head and could be reached only by a ladder. Opening out of the study was the dining room, a morose place with mustard-yellow hangings, a dark, near-black, walnut table and sideboard, and a large picture over the black marble fireplace that included a lifelike representation of a brace of pheasants being bled for the pot. From the dining room, one could move into the butler's pantry, where food was kept warming before being served and the dirty dishes were stacked between courses. Beneath the pantry, in the basement, was the kitchen. It was connected to the pantry by a dumbwaiter which brought the food up from the nether regions. The laundry, too, was in the basement.

It was also possible to go from the dining room into the front parlor. The latter was a room of stiff formality with dark-green horsehair furnishings and green-and-gold draperies at the windows that were kept tightly closed to keep the Brussels carpet from fading. In one corner was a pump organ. The wax candles in its side holders were warped, apparently from heat, though the room was extremely cold, and it remained determinedly silent, though Serena sat pumping the peddles of the organ until she was tired.

Opening out of the parlor was the sitting room, the province, in her moments of relaxation, of the lady of the house. Here had been placed the square piano Nathan had bought for her, and her sewing bird had been clamped to one of the side tables. There was also a small secretary desk with a cane-bottomed chair, several étagères with their stepped shelves overflowing with snuffboxes, small bronzes, seashells, ivory figures, glass marbles, china-egg hand coolers, and small busts of Parian marble. Whether it was the massiveness of the piano or the overabundance of bric-a-brac, there was a suffocating lack of space in the room. Otherwise, it was a charming retreat, with curtains of wheat and cream silk, a rug of pale gold and green, and in the circular tower room opening from it a collection of ferns and potted palms that complemented the leaf-design fabric on the settee and fainting couch.

On the second floor there were five bedrooms, each with its own bath in a style similar to that in Serena's room, and above that floor were smaller bedrooms of the female servants with a bath on each end of the floor, and a retiring room with a dormer in the center. There was also a box room up there, where trunks and valises were kept when not in use, and where bits and pieces of unwanted furniture had found their way. Next to it was a linen room where were stored the thirteen dozen each of sheets, pillow covers, pillowcases, face towels, hand towels, washing clothes, and Turkish towels. In addition, there appeared to be an entire cloth warehouse of bolts of dry goods, everything from striped bed ticking to bird's-eye cloth for baby diapers.

The men in Nathan's employ did not sleep inside the house. The coachman had his quarters over the stable, while the tyrant of the kitchen had his own private cottage beyond the icehouse, the springhouse where their water originated, and the machinery that supplied gas for the lighting.

It had been just that past December that the Midland Terminal Railroad had reached Cripple Creek, pulling in to the new depot at the end of Bennet Avenue. The Florence and Canon City Railroad was a narrow-gauge, with toy cars and a teapot for an engine; the new line was standard-gauge, a full-size railroad. It effectively eliminated the stagecoach run from Florissant that daily had rattled along the road in front of Bristlecone. It also cut down on the number of freight wagons, and their dust, as Mrs. Anson pointed out, but did not do away with them entirely. It was still not too unusual to hear the jangle of harness, the clip-clop of hooves, and the grinding roar of wheels as a heavy dray loaded with supplies for some store, or the belongings of a new family, rolled past. The sound of yet another horse-drawn wagon did not make too great an impression, then, until the driver yelled and pulled the rig to a halt in front of the house.

Serena had asked for a fire to be kindled in the sitting room and was sitting before it with her feet tucked under her, reading a book purloined from Nathan's study. Her first thought was of callers, some of those Nathan had mentioned. Coming to her feet in a rush, she slipped through the parlor as Mrs. Anson moved through the hall to the door. Whisking through the dining room into the butler's pantry, she hurried up the servant's stairs at the back of the house. She was at the top before it occurred to her that she had left her slippers on the sitting-room hearth.

It did not matter. There was hardly time for her breathing to return to normal after her quick ascent of the stairs before Mrs. Anson was knocking on her door.

"The dressmaker from New York, madam," she said, her voice at its most formal. "She has arrived with the trunks. Where shall I tell the driver to put them?"

"Trunks? You mean—the clothes Mr. Benedict ordered?"

"Yes, madam."

"I don't know. Not in here, I think. Perhaps in one of the other bedrooms?"

"An excellent plan, madam. The scarlet room should serve the purpose as a sewing room. Where do you wish the lady to stay while she is with us?"

The use of the term "lady" in connection with the dressmaker was revealing. "Perhaps she had better stay in the scarlet room also, instead of on the third floor. What do you think?"

"That should suit very well," the housekeeper answered, allowing herself a smile. "Shall I send her up to you?"

"Where is she now?" Serena asked in surprise.

"Waiting in the hall, madam."

That explained much. In the hallway the dressmaker might be able to overhear their conversation, and the housekeeper was anxious to show that this was a correct household. There was also a fine definition of status here. The dressmaker was left waiting in the hall, instead of outside, like a servant, or in the parlor as a guest would have been.

"What is her name?" Serena asked.

"Mademoiselle Dominic de Buys."

The accent was atrocious, but the trace of awe in the woman's tones was plain. Serena suppressed a smile. "Yes, perhaps I had better see Mademoiselle de Buys."

The dressmaker and Serena got along with the greatest of ease. Despite the title she had given herself, the French girl was little more than a seamstress, albeit a good one, who was hired to do fittings in the homes of customers. In this case the customer was at some little distance from the Seventh Avenue salon, but it made no difference. Mademoiselle had been to Denver before for fittings, and also to Chicago and Saratoga. She had once delivered a ballgown to the capital in Washington itself, sitting up half the night with the box on her lap on the train, spending all day fitting and sewing, and sitting up half the night again so a senator's wife could have a new creation to wear. That had been for the inauguration ball for President Cleveland.

With such chatter, some of it in English, some in quick rippling French, the fittings went quickly. There was a need for something to pass the time as Serena was helped in and out of an endless succession of garments that spilled from the three enormous steamer trunks that were unloaded and carted up the stairs. There were morning gowns, tea gowns, evening gowns, walking costumes, driving costumes, riding costumes, boating costumes, and hats to match each. For more private wear there were dressing gowns, dressing sacques, petticoats in sets, each a different color, corsets in amber stitched with black, in black stitched with amber, corsets in green, in red, in pastel blue, hourglass corsets, spoonbill corsets, and Thomas patent Duchess corsets. There were wickedly abbreviated drawers in the latest mode from France of fine, near-transparent silk, silk stockings by the gross, chemises, which Mrs. Anson insisted on calling "shimmeys," and fine lace-edged handkerchiefs; nothing had been left out.

"How in the world did Mr. Benedict manage to order all this from here?" Serena asked.

"His cable merely said to supply everything that might be needed by a lady of fashion and taste, of such and such a coloring, such and such a general size. Money no object." The French girl winked. "It is easy, when one adds that last little phrase."

At the end of five days, Mademoiselle de Buys was gone, riding the train back to the East with a nice *pourboire* tucked into the top of her stocking. Serena was alone again, at loose ends once more. The house ran well enough without her. Mrs. Anson was used to seeing to Nathan's comfort, and until Serena had decided once and for all what she meant to do, whether she could or could not be a wife to Nathan Benedict, she saw no benefit in interfering with the routine. If she stayed, she would want to set her own impression on the house, but for now it did not seem either fitting or worthwhile.

The snowy weather gave way to a day of sunshine. Serena, watching Nathan wheel away from the house in his carriage with the coachman on the box, was reminded of the phaeton that had been his gift for her. It sat in the coach house beside the stables, the silver fixtures tarnishing for want of polish. She had in her wardrobe a number of morning costumes just waiting to be worn. The lightweight carriage was equipped with driving apron to keep the dust and mud spatters from her new finery. Why should she not use both the phaeton and the apron? Who would stop her?

Mrs. Anson tried. Serena should wait for Mr. Benedict. She wasn't strong enough to drive herself. She needed an escort. She should wait, at least, until she could be driven by the coachman. This was a mad start. She would be set upon and robbed of her jewelry. The horses would run away with her; they were mettlesome after being shut up in the stable with so little exercise. Serena tried to tell her that she had driven a wagon across hundreds of miles, that she felt strong, nearly as strong as she ever had, that Nathan wouldn't care what she did as long as she was happy. As a sop to the woman's fears she took the pistol Nathan had given her from its box, loaded it, and dropped it into her beaded purse. Since this seemed to alarm the housekeeper more than anything else, Serena finally turned her back on the woman in irritation and left the house.

Dressed in a gown of heliotrope and black crepe studded with jet and threaded with gold passementerie, with her French sable coat about her shoulders and her draped fur toque on her low-dressed hair, Serena felt equal to anything. She stopped for a moment on the steps, breathing the fresh, clear air; then, pulling on a pair of black kid gloves, she descended the last of the steps, on her way to the stables.

The stableboy was the only person around, since the coachman was driving Nathan. He brought the phaeton out and hitched it up without argument, and even gave the silver a quick rub with the sleeve of his flannel shirt. Handing her up to the high seat, he passed over the reins, then stood back, a skeptical look in his eyes as he peered from under his tow-colored thatch of hair. Serena thanked him as she gathered the reins in her small, capable hands, then ignored him. She let off the brake, slapped the reins on the rumps of the matched pair of grays, and gave them their office to start. Head high, she wheeled from the yard. Feathering the curves of the drive with precision, she passed through the stone gateway with exactly the same distance from the wheels on either side.

She had not lost her touch. The horses were a little fresh, trying their best to pull her arms out of their sockets, but she could handle them. The greatest danger, it appeared, was that she might split the seams of her gloves.

While she was dressing earlier, a destination for her drive had occurred to her. She would go and look over the work being done on the home for women, see what progress was being made. By the timetable Nathan had given her, it should be nearly finished. She had been longing for ages to see it. Nathan had described it to her, and accepted several suggestions she had made for improvements, promising to see they were carried out, but that was not like being able to see for herself, to get into the thick of it. She was grateful for the care she had been given in her illness, but she felt stifled. She was tired of being told she was too frail, too delicate, to do what she wanted.

The phaeton climbed a hill, rounded a curve, and gathered speed on a straight stretch of road. It crossed a bridge over the creek that ran in front of Bristlecone, climbed another hill, and Cripple Creek was revealed, spread out over the hillsides covering six hundred acres.

How it had grown in the scant two months since she had seen it last! It looked as if it had increased a third in size. Shacks, canvas tents, houses, and stores straggled along every draw and staggered up every slope. Cripple, as long-time residents, those who had been there more than a year, called it, was really booming. There had never been any doubt of it, of course, but seeing the changes brought the fact home.

The street where the home was being built had been nearly empty when Nathan had bought the land. Now it was being crowded on all sides with houses hastily thrown up of green lumber. The building that stood on the block Nathan had described to her was no different, simply because that was the only kind of wood available with any speed. Lumber could be shipped in, but it would take months.

Serena pulled up before the large, square house. It was two stories tall with four gable ends, each framed in carpenter's-gothic woodwork. It had a wide front porch that extended all the way across the front, and double doors with insets of frosted glass. It had been given a wash of white with touches of green on the trim. On a brass plaque beside the door in gothic script was the legend: *Serenity Home for Women.*

Serena wrapped the reins around the handle of the carriage whip in its holder, loosened her driving apron, gathered up her purse and climbed down. As she tethered the team to a chokecherry bush, she saw where holes were being dug and poles laid out on the ground for a fence. White pickets were what she had specified, and they were there in a bundle tied up with wire, propped against the house. Smiling a little, she picked up her skirts to mount the steps to the porch. Nathan had kept his word to the letter, without stint.

Above her the front doors swung open. A woman stepped out onto the porch, while two more stood just inside. After the brightness of the sun, it was difficult for Serena to see under the dim overhang of the roofline. It was an instant before recognition came.

"Consuelo!"

The woman turned slowly to face her. Clad in a burgundy-red walking costume piped in black, she was an elegant figure. "Hello, Serena," she said, her face set, unsmiling.

"It's—nice to see you again." Serena ascended the last of the steps, coming to a halt a few feet away from the others.

"Yes," Consuelo said, then turned to the women waiting

277

with perplexed smiles inside the doorway. "Sister Elizabeth, Sister Gloria, permit me to introduce Mrs. Nathan Benedict, the lady who is responsible for the home. Serena, these are sisters of Our Lady of Mercy. They have been chosen to administer the services of the trust Nathan has established in your name for the Serenity Home."

The Spanish girl had spoken her new name with deliberation, as if it was necessary to take the pain of hearing the syllables into herself, and yet her expression gave away nothing. Serena swung to the nuns, noticing their black habits and white veils for the first time, an indication of her distress. Greeting them, she wondered why she had not been told of this arrangement. She had expressly stated that she preferred the place to have no religious affiliation.

"You are puzzled, and who shall blame you?" the first nun, Sister Elizabeth, said in a soft voice with a Germanic inflection. "Come in, my child, and we will explain to you just how we came to be here while we enjoy a cup of tea. We have facilities for that now, though not for much more." She turned to Consuelo. "And you also, my dear?"

"Thank you, no. I must be going." The Spanish girl shifted the net bag she carried to her other hand and lifted her skirts.

"Then accept our gratitude once more for doing our shopping for us. We will remember you in our prayers."

"Thank you, sister," Consuelo repeated and turned away.

She was going to leave with this cool, distant atmosphere between them. Serena held her ground, barring Consuelo's passage. "We have much to talk about. I wish you would come and see me."

"At Bristlecone?"

The amazement in the other girl's voice was plain. Serena lifted her chin. "Yes, at Bristlecone."

"Nathan won't like it."

"For the moment, it doesn't concern him."

Consuelo tilted her head, a light in her dark eyes for the first time. "An intriguing statement. I think I must see what it means, if you are certain?"

"I'm certain."

"I'll send a message first. There's no point in embarrassing either of us any more than need be." Refusing a second request to stay, the Spanish girl moved down the steps and was soon lost to sight.

Due to the disturbed state of her mind, it was some minutes before Serena took real notice of what the nuns were saying, or the rooms they showed her. What caught her attention was the pallet on the floor in the room designated as a nursery. On it lay two babies sleeping peacefully, one sucking gently on its thumb.

"The mother of the little girl on the right came three days ago while the workmen were still in the house. The men sent word to Mr. Benedict, not knowing what else to do. He had heard of us and our predicament. Sister Gloria and I came out to serve the church with the understanding that a place had been provided for us. When we reached Cripple Creek we found that only a house for the priest was available. We had been living at the hotel, waiting for funds to be found to construct a suitable dwelling, when Mr. Benedict sent to ask us to help the poor girl. She delivered her child in this room with the help of God and our hands."

"Where is she now?"

"She is in the kitchen, I believe," Sister Gloria answered. "She was a cook's helper in Colorado Springs before she got into trouble. When she lost her job, she came up here to live with her sister. The sister died of pneumonia last week. Her husband was left with a number of children. He asked the girl to marry him, and when she refused, he became abusive. She had heard of this place, so she came. I believe she will make an excellent addition to the establishment as a cook."

"So you see, my child," Sister Elizabeth went on, "we are women in need of shelter, just as any other. But I am sure I speak for Sister Gloria when I say we could ask for no greater gift than to be allowed to stay, provided the church agrees, of course, and tend the lost souls who seek refuge here."

Serena had thought of hiring a housekeeper as a permanent figure of authority for the house. It was obvious that someone was needed to see that food was prepared, the rooms were kept clean, and some kind of order was maintained. She had not pictured babies coming into the situation so soon, but since they had, their needs had to be taken into consideration. It was possible that these two women with their kind faces and gentle voices might serve better than anyone who could be hired for a wage. Compassion was a necessary requirement for this job, and it was a commodity that could not be bought.

"I am happy to have you here," Serena said, her voice warm, "and more thankful than I can say that you came when you were needed. As for the future, we will talk about

279

it again when you have the permission of your church. But the other baby, you haven't told me about it."

"The poor little thing was brought to us last night. It was found in an alley where some unfortunate creature had given birth and left it for dead. It is a lucky thing it was found so quickly. An hour more at the temperatures here at night, and it would have been too late."

What the nun meant, but was too kind to say, was that the baby had been abandoned, left to die. What kind of woman would do such a thing? Serena asked herself, then immediately countered: What kind of society was it they lived in that made the shame of bearing a baby out of wedlock harder to bear than the guilt for letting it die?

Rummaging in her purse, Serena found her chased silver pencil and gingerly drew it out to keep the tassel on the end from becoming entangled with the trigger of her pistol.

Over tea, she made a list of all the things the sisters would need, beginning, since they were obliged to balance their cups while sitting on carpenter's sawhorses, with furniture. Promising to see to the most pressing of their needs immediately, and to visit often, she left the house. As she drove away in the phaeton she looked back, her heart swelling with pride in what she had accomplished, and with gratitude to Nathan for making it possible.

She knew that she should turn at once for home. Knowing it, she swung the heads of her horses in the opposite direction. She would just take a turn down Bennet Avenue to see what had changed, what businesses had closed down, what had started up.

The grays were restive from standing, or so she thought. They tossed their heads and walled their eyes, trying to get the bit in their teeth. Serena held them steady. Then she smelled it, a whiff of smoke. No sooner had she spotted the thick gray plume on the edge of town several blocks away than she heard the first shot of the signal for fire. By the time the third pistol crack had died away, the streets were full of people, all staring about, trying to see the source of the alarm. She let her team pick their way among them.

"Will they call out the mine hands?" a woman cried.

"They do, you'll hear the whistles," another called back.

"Where are the hose companies? They're fast enough when it comes to a race, but slow as molasses when you need them!"

"Should we go to the reservoir? It'll be safe there."

"I'm waiting till I see what all the fuss is about."

The fuss was about nothing. Before Serena reached Bennet, the people were turning away in mingled relief and disgust. It had been nothing more than a trash fire that had gotten out of hand. The message went from one person to another, and the smoke clearing away in the warm, still air confirmed it.

Some men, miners on the night shift, tramps, and drunks, still stood about in wads, while others thronged the streets, heading in the direction of the saloons on the south side of town.

Suddenly a man stepped from one of these groups. With a loping run, he caught up with the phaeton, grabbed one of the struts that held the top, and swung up onto the step.

The unexpected movement and weight caused the horses to shy, and Serena had her hands full for a moment. One glance had been enough to tell her who had accosted her. No one else had such long arms, or moved with such an apelike gait.

"Lookee here!" Otto said, a leer in his bleary black eyes. "Just lookee who we have here!"

His breath was foul, and he was more than a little drunk. His clothes looked as if he had slept in them for days, and during that time used the sleeves for a napkin, and possibly a handkerchief.

"Get down, Otto," Serena said, her tone cold.

"Ain't you high and mighty, sporting around town in your fancy carriage and furs. I seen this rig of yours setting outside that house you had your husband build. Everybody in town knows about this rig, saw it come in on the train sitting on a flatcar all to itself."

"How interesting."

"I says to myself right then I had to have a little talk with you, for old time's sake, you know."

"I have nothing to say to you. Get down!"

"Huh, not likely. Not till I've had my say. I need a job, Serena, a nice easy job like hoist operator at one of your husband's mines, 'er some such." He tried to make his tone wheedling, but it came out in a blustering whine.

"Why?" Serena said waspishly. "Did Pearlie throw you out?"

"Ain't you heard? Ward's back. He's square in the saddle at the Eldorado again, got Pearlie eating outa his hand, made her give her new partner back his money. It was him that throwed me out."

"Good for Ward."

"You talking mighty high for a gal that whelped her bastard in another man's bed. I bet I could tell Mr. Nathan Benedict a thing or two about his wife, a thing or two you'd just as soon he didn't hear. I bet you could sweet-talk him into giving ol' Otto a shift foreman job, if you was to put your mind to it."

Serena looked at him squarely, her blue-gray eyes shaded with contempt. "There's nothing you can tell Nathan he doesn't already know. Now, get down, or I'll take my carriage whip to you the way Ward did in the Springs!"

"You bitch! Think you so fine, pretending to be so good butter wouldn't melt in your goddam mouth, an' all the time you lettin' half the men in town put it to you. Ol' Otto ain't good enough. Ol' Otto can't have any! You black-haired bitch. I'll show you, I'll—"

He made a grab for the reins. As he swung by one hand, Serena snatched the whip from its holder and lashed out with it, catching him on the neck. Her second blow welted his wrist. He tried to turn his hand, to catch the lash, but Serena reversed it, and using the weighted handle, jabbed him in the chest. Her horses were trying to bolt. Ahead of her loomed a streetcorner. Serena swung her team hard to the right, sweeping around in a sharp turn.

Otto swung wide, lost his grip. With a strangled curse he fell backward to sprawl in the muddy street. Still cursing, he shook his fist after her as she bowled away.

Serena pulled in her horses gradually. It was lucky she hadn't been on the busy streets near Bennet and Myers. Of course, if she had been, Otto would never have dared jump her like that.

So Ward was back at the Eldorado? Pearlie must never have found the courage to try to sell his interest in it, then. Serena wondered what the woman had said to him about her, about why she left. She would be willing to wager it was nothing to her credit. There was no way of knowing what ideas of her Ward might have.

What had he thought when he found her gone? Did he know she was married to Nathan? From what Otto had said, he must. Did he know he had a son? Did he care?

She allowed the grays to take her toward Bennet. She turned east on that main street. Despite her distraction, she was aware of the stares that followed her. Let them stare. She had nothing to hide. Ahead of her was the three-story building of red brick trimmed with green that housed the Midland Terminal Railroad depot. She swung the phaeton in a wide turn in front of it and headed back west.

She wondered where Nathan was, and if he had seen her progression. As Mrs. Anson had said, he wouldn't like it. He shouldn't have bought her the phaeton, then. There was a seat in the back for a footman or a groom. She supposed that if she had wanted to follow the rules of propriety set down in the towns of the eastern portion of the country, she should have brought the stableboy with her in the guise of groom. If he had been there, would Otto have dared attack her? The young Irishman might have his uses, but it seemed ridiculous to place so much emphasis on the presence of someone so negligible. If it was a matter of reputation, she had none to lose. There was a certain comfort, at this stage, in that.

With her back straight and her head high, Serena made a left turn down Second Street, and a right onto Myers Avenue. Amused at her own sense of excitement, she took note of the Butte Opera House, the Central Dance Hall, and the Topic Dance Hall, all nearly deserted at this hour. The buildings, some of them built in '92 and '93, had a dry desiccated look. Serena, noticing their warped boards and sagging frames, caught herself thinking what fine fodder they would make for a fire, if one like that this afternoon ever got out of hand.

There was the Eldorado, its stained-glass door shut and the interior only dimly lit by a single lantern shining through the window. The curtains at the upstairs windows hung limp over the tightly closed sashes. On the board sidewalk in front, one or two men slouched along, workers from the stable one street over from the look of them. At Pearlie's parlor house the shades were pulled. The housekeeper was sweeping the mud from the front steps, but nothing else moved.

Several blocks along, Serena slowed. Should she turn back, make another run down Myers?

In sudden irritation with herself, she shook her head. What did she think she was doing, idling past where Ward lived like a lovesick schoolgirl? If Ward wanted to see her, he knew where to find her. If he didn't, there was no point in making a fool of herself. Hadn't Otto said everyone recognized her phaeton? What if Ward had noticed her driving by, but had stayed out of sight, letting her pass on?

The past was dead. She should have more pride than to try to revive it. If she had any sense at all she would take herself to Bristlecone and stay there. She would set herself to please Nathan, to be a good wife to him. She would stop being so independent and listen to what he tried to tell her. She would learn what was expected of a rich man's wife and do it, no matter how it irked her. She would be such an example of piety and rectitude that in time the good people of Cripple Creek would forget that Nathan had married her out of a saloon that supplied women to a parlor house, that she had been the acknowledged mistress of a gambler. She would train herself to be a fine lady, a life companion, a good mother, keeping after it until she had forgotten she had ever been anything else. She would grow old and gray, a sweet doddering old thing with white hair who had to be trundled about in an invalid's chair, spoon-fed, and reminded of which grandchild was which. And one day on her deathbed she would look around her with rheumy eyes and demand to know where was the man she loved. *Where was Ward?*

Serena's attention was drawn back to her driving as an open victoria with a coachman on the box came toward her. Sitting bolt upright on the velvet seats was a *grande dame* in gray lace and ermine, a leader of what passed for society in Cripple Creek. She owned the most prestigious house on Eaton Avenue, but in between meetings of the Ladies' Aid, the Poetry Club, and various other interests, spent her time in trying to persuade her husband to remove to the more civilized atmosphere of Colorado Springs or Denver.

Serena kept to the close right of the narrow dirt street. She put her shoulders back and readied a smile in case she should be recognized. The other woman stared at her vehicle with high arched brows and narrowed eyes that missed nothing of Serena's costume or her luxurious furs. Face frozen, she deliberately turned her head, staring at the back of her driver.

It was a cut; there could be no doubt about that. Amusement curved Serena's mouth. So much for Nathan's assumption that she would be accepted. Surprisingly, it mattered not at all. She had rather enjoyed the woman's raised eyebrows. Well, perhaps heliotrope crepe glinting with jet beads was a trifle over-ornamental for Cripple Creek. Not much, mind; the dressmaker had asserted that just such a gown had been worn by the lady who had cut the ribbon opening the Columbian Exposition. But perhaps a little. That was fine. Serena found that she enjoyed being a little *outrée*. She might even take up ostentation for a style. That would give everyone something to talk about; the girl from Myers Avenue flaunting her wealthy position.

It was strange, the effect of money. It changed people. Or maybe it didn't. Maybe like strong liquor it only served to bring out what was already there inside them.

She was tired, and her arms ached from the constant pull. She wasn't as strong as she had thought. As the sun mounted overhead, it grew warmer. The fur coat was too heavy. Shifting the reins to one hand, she slipped one arm from the sleeve, then, transferring the reins again, she freed the other. The horses must have tired finally also. They did not swerve as she completed her maneuver with her coat, but kept a straight path up the hill toward Bristlecone.

The carriage rattled over the wooden bridge that crossed the creek and swept along the straightaway. It rounded a curve and topped a hill. From the crest Serena could see the turrets of the house, though she would lose sight of them again as she reached the bottom. She was nearly home. Only a few more minutes and she would see the stone arch of the gateway.

On her left was Mt. Pisgah. As she glanced at it a cloud covered the sun, making a large dark patch of shadow on the side of the mountain. The cloud shadow moved, inching toward the carriage. For no reason Serena could think of, she shivered, and turned her gaze back to the haunches of her horses with the muscles moving in perfect unison.

Above their steady clip-clop came another sound. It was the pounding hooves of a horse being ridden fast. It was an unusual occurrence on this road. Most riders tried to pace their mounts for the steep hills ahead, between here and Florissant.

Serena glanced at the man on horseback as he flashed past her. Her head came up. Before she had time for more, Otto Bruin had pulled his horse in close to the heads of her team and leaned to grab the left bridle strap, jerking viciously at their tender mouths, hauling them to a stop with brutal force.

The look on the man's face was ugly; the smile that bared his yellow teeth held cruel triumph. Serena slipped her hand beneath the linen driving apron to touch her purse, feeling the solid outline of the pistol inside. Inwardly she cursed the gloves that made her fingers clumsy.

"What do you think you are doing?" she demanded in icy fury.

"What does it look like?" he growled over his shoulder. "Get down from there."

Serena tugged at the clasp of her purse, but she needed both hands. "I will not! You must be crazy!"

"You git your purty little ass down from there or I'll take this here knife and slit the gullets of this fine pair of horses. If I do that, I won't have to stand here and hold 'em; I can come back there and haul you down right and proper."

With a sick feeling in the pit of her stomach, Serena watched as he pulled out a large pocket knife and opened it with his teeth. He jockeyed his horse around, then with a sly look in her direction touched the blade to the neck of the near gray. Blood welled, running over the shining gray coat in a thick stream. The horse backed with a shrill whinny throwing up his head, but he could not escape the hard grip that held him.

"Don't!" Serena cried sharply. "I'll get down." Throwing back the driving apron, keeping her purse in her hand, she stretched one foot shod in fine leather down to the step, and jumped lightly to the road.

"That's right smart of you. A good horse is hard to come by."

"Spare me your attempts at humor, if you please," Serena snapped. "What is it you want?"

Instead of answering, Otto swung from the saddle. Taking the tether of her team, he picked up a fair-sized rock and, holding the leather strap to the ground, set the piece of granite on top of it. His own reins he left trailing in the dirt as a ground tether. Ducking under his horse's neck, he lurched toward her.

"You will answer to Nathan Benedict for this! Don't think I won't tell him." Serena backed away a step. The clasp was open on her purse.

"Tell 'im anything you want. It'll be too late then. I'll have tore off my piece of your tail and be long gone. That's something I been meaning to get me for a long while now, and this time there ain't nobody to stop me!"

He lunged to catch her arms, his hard, hurtful fingers gouging, pressing the jet beads on her sleeves into her skin. "Wait," Serena said, forcing a sob of horror only half pretended into her voice.

"Wait, nothing," he growled, dragging her against him.

His fetid breath was in her face, his hot, wet lips rubbery as they slid over her cheek. Serena twisted in his grasp to

286

keep her mouth clear. "Wait," she panted. "I'll give you anything you want. My jewelry. Money. I have money—"

"I don't want your money," he muttered thickly. "I want you spread out naked. I wanta—"

There was more, but Serena closed her mind to it. "I have money—" she repeated, digging her hand into her purse. Her questing fingers touched the pistol, felt the handle smooth under her hand. He was dragging her closer like a great carrion-eating bear. The side of the phaeton was at her back, and she could feel the humping motions Otto made with his hips as he dug the hard lump of his manhood into her thigh. He shifted one hand to her breast, squeezing the tender globe so that waves of pain rose to her head.

"Over there, in the grass," he blubbered against her neck.

"All—all right," she gasped, her eyes closed.

As his hold loosened for an instant, her fingers tightened on the pistol, her forefinger slipped inside the trigger guard. Without trying to pull it free of the purse, she pulled back the hammer, turned the short barrel against his chest, and pressed the trigger.

The gun exploded with a roar that echoed against the mountainsides. Otto was thrown from her as if flung by a giant hand. A red splotch appeared on his shirtfront and a look of astonishment on his face. He struck the ground with his arms outstretched and boneless. Rolling over, he came to rest face down.

The horses plunged and whinnied. The carriage backed and pulled forward before the grays settled down. The livery-stable hack of Otto's reared, dragging his reins loose, then galloped off a few yards before coming to a stand with his muscles quivering.

Serena was trembling also. Staring down at the purse in her hand, she saw a great hole in one corner. From it trailed a gray-blue ribbon of gunsmoke. The acrid smell hung in the air, catching sharply in the back of her throat. She took a few quick steps into fresh air, breathing deep. After a moment, she turned and put her purse up on the seat of the phaeton. The horses were still disturbed. With a frown of concentration between her brows, she went to their heads and stood stroking them, talking in a low, soothing voice.

Otto lay still, unmoving. Serena glanced at him, then looked away again, her face grim. The dirt of the road beneath his chest was turning dark in a spreading stain. She should do something, as much as it went against the grain.

With a final rub to the left gray's nose, she moved toward the fallen man.

She was kneeling with her hand on his shoulder when she heard hoofbeats once more. She glanced up quickly. What should she do? It seemed doubtful that Nathan's position could protect her from a charge of murder. She could plead attempted rape, but where was the evidence, the witnesses? Her past would count against her. It would seem ridiculous to speak of such an assault concerning a woman who had come from Myers Avenue, especially in connection with a man, it could be demonstrated, she had known well, if not intimately. Who would believe self-defense in such a case?

There was no time to do anything. A rider topped the hill and came bearing down upon her. As he drew closer, Serena rose to her feet. He reined to a halt in a spray of gravel, swinging from the saddle in the same fluid movement.

"Serena," Ward said, "are you all right?"

"Yes," she answered, her tone matter-of-fact.

He approached her warily, his green gaze narrowed on her pale face. "What happened here?"

"Otto stopped my carriage. He—he meant to—I shot him."

"You're not hurt?"

Serena shook her head.

"You're sure?"

Serena sent him an irritated stare. "I'm sure!"

A faint smile crossed his face. "Good. Is he dead, or did you botch the job?"

"I'm not certain. I think he's dead." Her voice was a trifle unsteady on the last word. To cover it, she cleared her throat.

"Let's see," Ward said, turning his keen gaze from her to the man lying in the road. With a hard shove, he turned Otto to his back, feeling under his shirt.

"Well?" Serena asked.

"He seems dead enough." Ward wiped his hand on his trousers.

Serena turned away, catching at the side of the phaeton. Ward got to his feet and came to stand beside her.

"Don't take it so hard. If anybody needed killing, he did."

"I—I never killed anybody before."

"I should hope not. But as I said, if you had to do it, this was a good place to start."

She thought he made a gesture, as though he meant to take her in his arms. If so, he did not complete it. Swinging away, he looked up and down the road.

"We can't stand here all day," he said, his voice rough and impatient. "The next person to come along may not take so kindly to this bit of mayhem you've committed."

"How did you—come to—happen to come along, I mean?"

"I saw you in town, saw Otto ride out right behind you. I didn't much like the look of it, so I decided to trot along behind. I might have been a little closer if that idiot at the livery stable hadn't been out in the corral. I really put the spurs to that misbegotten beast I was riding when I heard the shot."

"I see. It was good of you to be concerned," she said, her voice prim, though there was a warm gladness inside her.

Ward glanced from her to the fur coat on the seat of the shiny, silver-trimmed phaeton. "I couldn't let anything happen to the wife of my best friend."

Serena's chin came up at the lash of sarcasm in his tone. "I'm sure Nathan will thank you," she said.

"So he should," Ward snapped, "but he won't have much reason if you get yourself arrested for murder. I suggest you climb back in that fancy rig of yours and light out for home. Now!"

His gaze rested on her face a moment, then raked down over the heliotrope-and-black costume she was wearing to the great gleaming sapphire on her finger. He swung sharply away, moving toward his horse.

"What about the body?" she called after him.

"Never mind the body. Just get going."

"But we can't leave him here."

"I don't intend to," he answered, swinging into his saddle. "If you must know, I'm going to catch his horse and cart him over to the creek. I'll hide him there until dark, then there's an abandoned mine shaft I know that's nice and deep. By the time anybody finds him, if they ever do, it'll be too late to connect him with you. Now get going."

"Yes. I—thank you, Ward." Hurriedly, without looking at him, Serena stepped onto the step and swung up into the phaeton.

He guided his horse to where he sat even with her upon the carriage seat. Leaning on the saddlehorn, he said, "Save your thanks, Serena. I don't want them. I prefer a more tangible reward."

"What do you mean?" she asked on an indrawn breath.

She received no answer. Ward touched the broad-brimmed hat he wore with one finger, kicked his horse into movement, and loped off after Otto's mount grazing a short distance away.

Slowly, Serena gathered up the reins, unwinding them from the whipstock. Her lips compressed, she set the grays in motion. The sun came out from behind the cloud, shining bright and clear. A breeze fanned about her, feeling good on her flushed face. She had nearly stopped shaking, the reaction routed by the anger and puzzlement that crowded her mind.

Just before she rounded a bend and the dark green of spruce trees hid the scene behind her from sight, she turned. Otto lay sprawled in the road, his arms outflung. Off to the right, Ward had come to a halt. He sat on his horse, a still and solitary figure, staring after her.

Chapter Seventeen

Dinner was an interminable meal. Since Serena had gone out that morning, Mrs. Anson had taken it as an indication that she was ready to begin a normal pattern of living. She had elected to open up the dining room again. Serena would much have preferred a tray in her room as usual, with Nathan perhaps looking in afterward for coffee. She decided to let the arrangement stand, however. It was better than giving rise to questions concerning her motives. She was aware that she had already given enough cause in that line.

When she had reached Bristlecone at last that morning, she had refused luncheon and retreated to her room. She had tried to rest, but had been unable to compose herself enough to sleep. Pacing or standing long moments staring into the fire had not relieved her feelings, nor could she erase the image of Otto, lying sprawled in the road with his shirtfront stained red, from her mind. Nevertheless, she was perfectly capable of holding up her end of any conversation, and of enduring until the coffee was served and she could retire for the night.

Serena had not counted on Mrs. Anson's solicitous attempts to persuade her to eat. The housekeeper was fearful she had made a mistake in her suggestion they have the evening meal downstairs, and afraid also that Serena had overestimated her strength. In her concern, she glanced often at Serena's pale face above the rose crepe of her gown, and hovered over her, offering dish after dish. Serena took a little of this and a little of that, pushing it about on her plate until the course was removed. She could not bring herself to eat more than a bite, something that did not escape the house-keeper's notice.

"You aren't eating, madam. Perhaps the menu isn't to your liking? Is there anything I can bring you from the kitchen that might tempt you?"

"No, thank you, Mrs. Anson. I'm just not hungry." There was a trace of strain in Serena's tone as she answered.

Nathan looked up. "Are you feeling well, Serena?"

"Yes, fine," she answered, her lips tightening at the corners.

"I hope you didn't overtire yourself this morning. You were recovering so nicely."

"I—perhaps a little." It was better to admit that much than to have him probe for some other cause for her lack of appetite. From the corner of her eye she saw the housekeeper slip from the room. There was satisfaction in the look on her face now that Nathan's attention had been centered on his wife.

"I wish you had told me you felt like an outing. I would have been happy to drive you."

"I'm sure you would, Nathan. It was an impulse, that's all."

"I would rather you took someone with you in the future."

Serena sent him a long glance. "That hardly seems necessary."

"I'm not so sure. I'm told one of the grays was injured while you were out, cut on the neck."

"I hope it wasn't a bad injury. I really couldn't tell."

"Nothing that can't be cured with a few applications of Fleming's Healing Oil, they tell me."

"I'm glad. I—I'm not sure how it came about," Serena said, looking down at her plate, drawing up her shawl that had slipped off her shoulder. "It must have been when the fire signal sounded. There was a good bit of confusion and people crowding into the streets. At one time I was surrounded."

"I heard the shots while I was in town," Nathan said, nodding. "My point is that the same kind of rowdies who would do such a thing to a fine horse would not hesitate to commit worse acts, especially against a woman alone."

"I understand that, but I don't like having my activities curtailed."

Nathan started to speak, then thought better of it. Seeing the grim set of his mouth, Serena was reminded that he was aware of how close Ward had kept her at one time. Was consideration such as this ever to be arising between them? There seemed no help for it.

Finally he said, "I wish you would be guided by me in this, Serena. I don't ask it for selfish reasons, but out of my concern for your safety."

"Are you positive it isn't a matter of propriety?" Something inside her seemed to drive her to be contrary. She picked up her water glass and found her hand was trembling so the crystal rim clinked against her teeth.

What would Nathan say if he knew she had killed Otto? Would he say good riddance, like Ward? Or would he insist on lodging a full report with the police? It was the prospect of the last that held Serena silent. Nathan, she had discovered, was an extremely conventional man. He might seek his entertainment on Myers Avenue, he might have his mistress, or take for his wife a woman somewhat less than pure, but that did not alter his position as a man of standing in the community. He preferred that on the surface at least, his life conform to the tenets laid down by his circle of acquaintances, his peers. For now, that meant the society of the mining elite in the district and its environs. In keeping with that attitude, he might well go to the authorities, not simply to report the death, but to protest the lack of protection by the sheriff that had allowed such an attack to be made against his wife. The results would be the same; questions, embarrassment, and the specter, in spite of Nathan's influence, of prosecution. No, she could not tell him.

"I'm not certain what you mean by that question," Nathan said.

"I'm asking if you are not more concerned with what people will think to see me driving about by myself than with my safety."

"That's absurd!"

"Is it? I'm not so sure. It was brought home to me this morning that I am unlikely to be accepted by the matrons of Cripple Creek, regardless of my behavior."

"What do you mean?" He stared at her, a frown between his hazel eyes.

293

Serena told him of meeting the mine owner's wife on the road and the cut she had received.

"I am sorry if you were hurt by that woman's behavior," Nathan said, reasonably enough, "but that's no reason to doubt my motives."

"You are one of them, and I am an outsider. It's never going to be any different." To her horror, Serena felt tears rising to her eyes.

"Serena," Nathan exclaimed, putting his napkin on the table and rising to come around the corner of the table toward her. "You're upset. I didn't realize. I promise you things will change, but you can't expect it to happen overnight. You must go out and meet people, give them time to know and love you, as I do. I promise you that within a year you will be the darling of Cripple Creek, admired and feted everywhere."

He leaned over her chair, his hand on her shoulder, his thumb smoothing the creamy, blue-veined skin below her collarbone. Serena sent him a quick upward glance. "You are probably right," she said on a tight-drawn breath. "I expect I'm being silly. I—I seem to be on edge tonight."

"Understandable, I'm sure. You have been ill, and you overdid it today. We'll have to take better care of you."

"How can you say that? I've never been so cosseted and mollycoddled in my life." Serena managed a smile as she tried for a light note.

"You know I would like to do more, much more."

"Nathan, please," Serena said, aware of the deepening timbre of his voice, the increasing pressure of his fingers on her shoulder.

"You know I want you. I've made no secret of it. I promised not to try to influence you, or to rush you, but since then the situation has changed."

He was speaking of Ward's return. "Not—not really," Serena said.

"I'm no fool, Serena. Today you drove into town, and tonight your nerves are overset. The reason is not hard to find."

"I didn't go into town to see Ward, if that's what you are suggesting." That much was true, as far as it went.

"Whether you are disturbed because you saw him, or because you did not, makes no difference. It's plain he still has the power to cut up your peace. The best cure for that I know is to take you away from here. I have to travel up to Denver for a business meeting, and then east to New York. I'll be

294

gone quite a long while, even several weeks. The doctor tells me you are well, nearly normal. I want you to come with me, Serena."

Ward had never asked her to go with him when he went away. He had been more intent on proving he could do without her than on worrying about her well-being. "I don't know, Nathan," she began.

"It won't be a taxing journey. We will travel in my private railroad car in the greatest comfort—"

Serena came to her feet so suddenly that she brushed the table, splashing wine from her glass onto the white cloth. As she stared down at the spreading red stain of the burgundy, the sickness of revulsion rose inside her. Blood, soaking into the dirt just as the wine soaked into the damask. Just as it had stained the brocade coverlet on the bed that night in Nathan's private railroad car.

"Serena!" Nathan said, the dark glaze of pain in his eyes, evidence that he recognized the blunder he had made. Once, long ago, he had sent a basket of roast chicken and champagne to Ward and his lady friend aboard his private car, a lady friend who had occupied Ward's rooms over the Eldorado longer than any other. "Serena, I—"

"No, please, Nathan," Serena gasped, pushing away from the table, and from him. "I can't. Really, I can't!"

"Serena," he called again, but she was gone in a whirl of skirts, running from the room.

The fire still burned under the marble mantel in Serena's bedroom. She went toward it, dropping to her knees on the hearth rug, holding her shaking hands out to the blaze.

Poor Nathan. It wasn't his fault. He had tried so hard. She wished she could make him happy. She didn't mean to hurt him, but just now she could not help herself.

She was a murderess. It didn't matter that the man had deserved to die; she had killed him, cut short his life. Thinking of Otto, of the way he had come after her, the things he had said, Serena had tried to convince herself that it didn't matter, that he was little better than an animal, that he might even be the man who had killed the women on Myers Avenue. His huge hands, cruel in their strength, would have made it easy for him to strangle a woman, to leave her maimed and broken. There had not been a killing for some weeks now; still, if they stopped for good, she would know. If it was true, she might find justification for what she had done, and a measure of peace.

Peace. Peace of mind. That was what Nathan had offered her. She wished with sudden fervor that she could accept it. And yet, what kind of marriage would they have based on lies and deceit? She could tell him nothing, not that she had killed a man, not that she had seen Ward, not even that she had spoken to Consuelo. What kept her from it was not simply a lack of trust, or even fear of what he might do. As much as either of these was her dread of the judgment she would see in the stern lines of his thin face.

A sound caught at Serena's attention. It was the clatter of hooves on the drive with the jingle of harness and the rattle of a rig. Pushing to her feet, Serena moved to the window. Drawing aside the curtain, she peered out.

The rig was the buckboard from the carriage house, the vehicle used for a runabout by the housekeeper when she went into town to shop, or the coachman when he met the train to pick up supplies for the house and outbuildings. Neither of those two was handling the reins now, however. It was Nathan who sat on the seat, sending his horses at a swift pace down the drive, sweeping beneath the stone arch on his way to Cripple Creek.

If there had been any doubt as to Nathan's destination that night, it was soon dispelled. Late in the afternoon of the following day, Serena had a visitor. Mrs. Anson came to Serena where she sat in the sitting room, playing with Sean after giving him his bath before the fire and making him ready to be put to bed, she hoped for the night. Serena looked up from the baby, nestling against her breast with his eyelids irresistibly dropping over his gray-blue eyes.

"Yes, Mrs. Anson? What is it?"

"There is a person to see you, madam."

A person. That did not sound good. Serena nodded at Mary, sitting on a stool nearby, her rapt face rosy with firelight as she watched Sean. Holding the sleepy baby out to her, Serena got to her feet. When the nursemaid had slipped from the room, Serena turned back to the housekeeper.

"What kind of person?"

"A woman of the streets, if you ask my opinion," Mrs. Anson said with a sniff, her complexion reddening only slightly as she met Serena's eyes. "A Spanish-looking female."

"Oh." Serena turned away, standing with her hand on the white marble mantel. "Show her in, if you please."

"Yes, madam." With her back stiff, the housekeeper left the room. In a few minutes she was back, ushering Consuelo into the sitting room.

"Tea, please, Mrs. Anson," Serena said pleasantly, "and whatever you can find in the way of cakes."

The older woman signified her understanding, and swinging sharply around, took herself away.

"Consuelo," Serena said, holding out her hand, a smile curving her lips. "I'm so glad you came. I wasn't sure you would."

"Nor was I," Consuelo answered, moving forward. "That is remarkable, because I have long wanted to see the inside of this house."

"Would you like a tour? I will be happy to show it to you." Serena started toward the door as she spoke.

"No, I've seen enough," Consuelo reassured her hastily. "Some things it's just as well not to know, and really, I haven't the time."

"Come and sit down, then." Serena returned to the chair where she had been sitting, indicating a petit-point-covered Eastlake chair beside it.

"First, let me give you this." Consuelo handed over a small package tied up in brown paper that she held in her hand, adding awkwardly, "It's for the baby."

"How thoughtful! Would you like to see him? I've just sent him up to bed, but Mary can bring him down again."

"Another time, if you don't mind, Serena. I would rather not stay long. To be honest with you, I would rather not have Nathan find me here."

"Oh yes, I see." Serena undid the paper on the gift quickly. It was a small spoon of sterling silver, the size just right for a baby's tiny mouth. "How lovely, Consuelo. Thank you."

"It was nothing." Consuelo sat on the edge of her seat with her ankles crossed and her hands folded on the drawstring purse in her lap. Her sharp black gaze flicked over the tea gown of draped chiffon printed with lilacs that Serena wore with a pale-green cashmere shawl. Her own costume was her usual severe black. On her hair, dressed in a figure eight at the back of her head, was a flat little hat banded in crimson ribbon.

Serena put the spoon and its wrappings to one side. "We didn't have time to say much to each other yesterday. How have you been? I see you have recovered from your fever."

297

"As you see, I am well enough. I was never as ill as Na
than—pretended."

It was an odd choice of words. Serena did not pursue it
however. "I have often wished that you had been home th
night—that night. Do you know what I am speaking of?"

"Yes. I've been told," Consuelo answered shortly. "I an
sorry that I didn't send you word that I was coming thi
afternoon. It was a sudden decision."

"It wasn't necessary," Serena began.

"I am here not just to deliver my gift for your baby, bu
because Ward asked me to come. He wanted me to give thi
to you." Pulling open her purse, Consuelo drew out an en
velope, extending it to Serena.

"Ward?" The envelope was stiff, but thin, containing onl
a single sheet of paper.

"Yes." The Spanish girl got to her feet. "That is still no
the end of my reasons for wishing to see you, however."

Serena looked up dazedly from the sealed missive in he
hand. She watched Consuelo move to stand in the openin
to the tower room, staring at the drooping green ferns or
their teakwood stands. "What?"

"Nathan came to visit me last night. I came to you today
Serena, because I had to ask you, to find out, what you ar
doing to him?"

"I—don't know what you mean."

Consuelo swung about. "I said once that you had a devi
in you, Serena, one whose danger was great because you wer
unaware. I think you must know your devil now. I think i
is this inside you that is killing Nathan."

"What are you saying, Consuelo? I don't understand."

"Don't you? He is a tortured man, Serena. He was alway
thin, but now he is skin and bone. He bleeds for you, he crie
and it breaks my heart. Why? Why are you doing this, lac
erating his soul by allowing him to move close, then pushin
him away? Is it because of what he did, of how he made yo
come to him? Is that it? If it is vengeance you want, then i
is yours; he hates himself for deceiving you, for causing you
illness, more than you possibly could."

"Deceiving me?" Serena repeated, her voice stiff.

The Westminster chimes of the brass-and-walnut Tiffan
clock on the mantel began to sound, each soft and melodiou
note dropping into the silence.

"You didn't know," Consuelo said when the last echo ha
ceased.

"Know what? You may as well tell me." Serena's voice was unnaturally calm. Her face pale, she watched the other girl as if she had never seen her before.

"I—I can't," Consuelo said brokenly.

"If you don't, I'll only have to ask Nathan."

"He'll never forgive me."

"Whatever it is, he won't learn from me that you told me." Consuelo lifted her head. "It makes no difference. I'll know."

She stopped, then went on in jerky sentences. "Nathan was Pearlie's partner in the Eldorado until Ward came back. He bought into the place with the understanding that Pearlie would see that you left at a date and time specified by him."

"He knew I would go to you."

"And so he hired a nurse to give me laudanum, and he waited. The time, the night, was chosen quite simply because I was so conveniently ill. *Por Dios*, Serena, don't look so."

"I might have been killed. I might have lost my baby."

The Spanish girl moved in a rush to Serena's chair, going down on her knees beside it. "But you weren't, you didn't. Think, Serena, he made you his wife, gave your baby a name. He brought you here as mistress of his home, gave you furs, jewels, and a thousand other things. He has done everything he can think of to make it up to you. And he has suffered, thinking you might die, fearing for you, hoping for your love. Oh, Serena!"

Footsteps sounded outside the door. By the time the housekeeper entered with the tea tray, Consuelo was standing before the fireplace, a smile pasted on her lips. "Your Elder Greer," she was saying, her voice brittle with false gaiety. "He is much respected by certain of the women from Eaton Avenue. They are inclined to forgive him his polygamous habit in the past for the sake of his stand against the women of the red-light district, and unbeknownst to their husbands, I'm sure, make small donations to his cause from the treasuries of their clubs."

Gathering her composure, Serena pointed to the table where she wanted the tray placed before turning back to Consuelo. "How interesting. Has he made any converts yet?"

"In a manner of speaking. There was one girl that he caught outside her crib. He made her kneel in the mud while he stood over her praying with his hands clenched in her hair. They say she went quite mad after the experience and had to be locked in the town jail to prevent her from destroying herself. After a time, her family came from the Midwest and took her away."

"It looks as if I am going to have to disown him," Serena said unsteadily. "He is definitely not *my* Elder Greer."

"The man is a bastard," Consuelo said, her voice dispassionate. "If he isn't careful, somebody is going to give him a coat of tar and feathers."

"An idea with merit," Serena answered, picking up the teapot in one hand and a cup on its saucer in the other. Her face like stone, Mrs. Anson left the room, closing the door behind her.

Serena started to hand the filled cup to Consuelo, then as the liquid began to quiver, set it back down abruptly. "Sugar or cream?" she asked.

"Sugar."

Serena picked up the tongs and dropped two lumps one after the other into the tea. This time when she picked up the cup, she was able to pass it without mishap. Lashes lowered, she poured her own, added sugar, and picked up the fragile china cup to sip at the steaming brew.

"What are you going to do?" Consuelo demanded, stepping to seat herself once more in the chair she had vacated earlier, leaning toward Serena.

"Do? Why, nothing. What can I do?"

"Don't be cruel, Serena. You know what I am asking. Are you going to forgive Nathan and be a wife to him, or are you going to go on as before, giving nothing of yourself?"

"You must love him very much," Serena said, staring into the fire.

"What has that to do with anything? Please answer me."

"I don't know. I can't seem to make myself believe what he has done."

"It was a great betrayal, I know, but truly he meant it for the best."

"Did he mean it for the best when he sent you to Manitou Springs to get you out of the way? Did he mean it for the best when he came to you for comfort last night? You are so concerned for his happiness, but has he thought of yours?"

"It is you he loves, you he wants."

"I can't help that, Consuelo. I'm not responsible for how he feels. I wish I could give you my place. You should be sitting here as his wife. Not me."

"It was you he asked to marry him."

"Did he? I don't remember. I don't remember agreeing, though I suppose I must have."

"Out of compassion, Serena, can't you pretend?" Consuelo asked, a shade of desperation in her voice, one hand knotted into a fist.

"Would that suffice? Would Nathan be satisfied with so little?"

"Ah, damn your scruples, Serena! Have you no heart, no feelings?"

"Yes! Yes, Consuelo, I have, but they belong to another man!" Serena stared at the other girl, the glitter of tears in her eyes.

Consuelo sat back, her face blank. "Oh," she said. "I should have known."

Serena looked away, her throat aching. She sipped her tea which was fast growing cool. When she looked back, Consuelo had set her cup back on the tray and was rising. The Spanish girl placed the strings of her purse on her arm and began pulling on the glove she had removed while she drank her tea.

"You aren't going?" Serena said.

"Yes, I must," Consuelo answered, her voice subdued. "If I have been clumsy, I'm sorry. I never meant to hurt you. I only wanted—"

"I know," Serena said simply.

Consuelo nodded, then seemed to hesitate. "Nathan mentioned that he had asked you to travel with him to Denver and the East, but you had refused. Would you object if I went in your place, provided he will take me, of course?"

"Isn't that an extraordinary question to ask of the wife?" Serena queried, her mouth curving into a hint of smile.

"Yes, but then we are neither of us ordinary, I think," Consuelo answered, her black eyes bright.

"You may be right. No, Consuelo, I don't mind—and I wish you luck."

"Thank you, Serena."

There was grace in the Spanish girl's movements and pride in the tilt of her head as she moved toward the door. With her hand on the knob, she turned back. "After what you have said to me, I think you will be wise to read your letter, and decide with care how you will respond."

"You know what it says?" Serena asked, taking up the envelope that lay in her lap.

"Ward did not tell me, if that is what you mean. But if

you will notice, the flap is not well sealed, and I am a very curious woman, especially when there is much at stake." As Serena started to her feet, she went on, "Don't bother. I will let myself out."

A final soft farewell, and she was gone. Serena put her teacup aside. She turned the envelope over and over in her fingers. The distress in her mind was so great that she was reluctant to add yet another element to it. What had Ward to say to her, or she to say to him? What had been between them was over. There was no point in letting herself be disturbed for nothing.

Serena leaned toward the fire, ready to consign the envelope to the leaping flames. At that moment there flitted across the surface of her memory a mocking suggestion. What had been the words Ward had used? Oh, yes. *I prefer a more tangible reward—*

Flinging herself back in her chair, Serena ripped open the envelope and plucked the folded sheet from inside. It was growing dim in the room as the evening advanced. She had to turn the page toward the fireglow to read the slashing script. Her name was the only salutation. The body of the note was short. It read:

> *Guilt unproven is the equal of innocence; the difference is in knowing where the evidence lies. If you recognize this truth, you will come to the Eldorado Wednesday morning at 11:00.*

It was signed with Ward's initials.

Serena sat staring at the words until they danced before her eyes. Then, slipping from her chair, she went to one knee, reaching to place the sheet carefully on the burning logs. She did not move until it had turned to blackened ash, whirling slowly in the wafting heat, rising in ragged bits of fire up the chimney.

Chapter Eighteen

On Tuesday afternoon, Nathan left Bristlecone to catch the train for Denver. The coachman drove him into town. Serena did not offer to see him off, nor did he ask her to do so.

The purpose of his trip to the East was to inspect a new type of hoist. The old bucket hoist was obsolete, Nathan maintained. A new, safer way of lowering the men into the mines had been found. Called a cage, it worked on a similar principle, but had a superior electrical system for lowering and raising it, a practicality now that nearly the entire district had electrical power. It also had added safety features, such as a steel mesh covering to protect the miners from injury against the rough granite walls of the shaft, and a means of stopping the cage if for any reason it should begin to descend too fast. The mechanical aspects of the system fascinated Nathan, and he was determined that his Century Lode Mine was going to be the first to have it installed.

Waving goodbye from the front veranda, Serena wondered if Consuelo would be waiting when he reached the depot. She hoped so. She had thought a great deal about Consuelo's appeal. She did not think the Spanish girl actually wanted her to be warmer toward Nathan, or more intimate with him. Serena had learned long ago that the temperamental, stiletto-carrying guise Consuelo affected was no more than a defense for her compassionate, caring heart, and yet she gave her more credit for natural jealousy than to believe the Spanish girl wanted to push her into Nathan's arms. No, Consuelo was concerned for Nathan, but she was perfectly capable of seeing to the binding of his wounds, whatever their cause, herself.

The realization was a relief in its way. She did not feel charitable toward Nathan after what she had learned of his Machiavellian arrangement of their marriage. She had avoided him the past two days as much as possible. It was all she could do to be pleasant when they did meet, to restrain herself from blurting out an accusation of his crimes, without having to try to behave in a more informal manner.

In the way of all good servants, Mrs. Anson knew Nathan had asked Serena to go with him on this trip. She had hinted once or twice that Sean would be well looked after in her absence, that his mother was by no means necessary for his health and well-being. Serena had ignored the suggestions. It was not unreasonable for Mrs. Anson to be prejudiced in her Mr. Benedict's favor. She had been with him for some time, and to her, Serena was a newcomer, and one who came with no very good credentials at that. She knew that in spite of the wedding vows that had been exchanged, Mr. Benedict still slept in his old rooms, with no evidence that he sought his new wife's bed in the night. That was bound to be the madam's fault, since it was as plain as the nose on a person's face he was wild about her.

Serena had seen the sidelong glances the housekeeper had cast in her direction on mornings when she changed the beds and carried the linens away to be washed. She knew the woman had heard stories of her wicked past on Myers Avenue, and considered it beneath her to be forced to wait on such a woman. The earlier softness of her manner, when Serena had first come, had been for her as a human being sick and in pain. Now that she was well and whole again, there was no such indulgence. It might have been different if it could have been demonstrated that she was good for Nathan, that she made him happy. Quite the contrary was true. He had never looked so bad as since Serena had come. It was true the time was short, yet, since she had recovered enough to be considered ready for the marriage bed. It was still early days to pass a final judgment, but the time was coming. It was coming.

If relations between the housekeeper and herself had been less strained, Serena might have spared the woman the necessity of waiting on her at the table later that evening. As it was, she sat in solitary state in the dining room, partaking of course after course. Not that she was able to eat much of any one dish. Her stomach was knotted with agitation. Nathan was gone. Tomorrow at eleven in the morning she would present herself at the Eldorado according to Ward's instructions. Why had he set that date and time? Had he seen Nathan before he sent the note? Did Ward know he would not be in town then? What had he meant by sending her such a cryptic message? What did he want of her? Did he intend to exact his more tangible reward, and if so, what form would it take? One thing was certain; he would not have it all his own way. There were a few things she had to say to him also, a few charges he was going to be made to answer, one way or another. With such possibilities spinning in her brain, she would never be able to sleep, never in the world.

She didn't. Her hair was a mare's nest of tangles and there were dark shadows under her eyes when Dorcas entered the room with her morning coffee. Serena stifled a moan as she caught sight of herself in the mirror of the dresser. She neither looked nor felt ready to match wits with Ward Dunbar. She wouldn't go. She would send a note saying she was indisposed, saying she hated him and never wanted to see him again, saying she didn't care what he wanted, what he felt or intended.

In spite of such fine resolves, she was dressed and ready by ten o'clock. With a certain sparkling malice, she had chosen a walking costume with a gored skirt, a shirtwaist blouse with a lace-edged jabot, and a tight-fitting basque jacket. It was nearly identical to the gray cheviot Ward had bought her, the only exception being that the fabric was a rich, sea-blue velvet. The hat seated on her curls was a draped toque of the same velvet lined with satin and held in place by her brooch of sapphires and diamonds. Let Ward make of it what he would. She sincerely hoped he saw it as a studied contrast between her former penury when she was dependent on him, and her present position of wealth as Nathan's wife.

There had been a break in the cold weather here in this first week in February. The day was sunny and pleasant, not really warm, but not cold either. Serena decided against her furs; they would crush the velvet of her jacket, and with the lap robe in the carriage she would be comfortable enough.

The grays were fresh, but they had tested her mettle before. They settled down to a steady trot that quickly covered

305

the distance into town. What to do with so distinctive a vehicle as her phaeton loomed as a problem, until she decided to leave it at the livery stable with the excuse that she did not want to have her cattle standing for too long a time, as she had considerable shopping to do. Paying for the convenience was no problem. With characteristic generosity, Nathan had left a sheaf of bank notes on his desk for her before he left.

The livery stable, one street over from Myers Avenue, at an angle behind the Eldorado, was well placed for her purpose. The next question was what she was to do when she had seen her carriage wheeled out of sight. Should she take Second Street and actually walk up to Bennet and spend some time shopping? Or would it be better to slip as unobtrusively as possible across the alley between the stable and Myers to the Eldorado's back door? Perhaps it had been a mistake to use the livery stable here; perhaps she should have used the one on Bennet? It might have been less noticeable for her to wander away from the shops on that main street down in the direction of Myers, than for her to come up from Myers to purchase a few items, then turn back in the same direction.

After all, what did it matter? It was unlikely she could keep her visit a secret from everyone. She would just have to trust that word of it did not get back to Nathan. Since she was going to have to enter the Eldorado at some time, it might as well be now.

Lifting her skirts, Serena climbed the rise that led to the wagonyard of the barroom. She skirted the back storage area and stepped to the rear entrance. The knob turned under her hand and the panel swung inward on oiled hinges. Serena moved inside, pushing the door shut behind her.

The familiar cold dimness, the smells of liquor, stale tobacco smoke, and unwashed cuspidors assailed her senses. She stood still, caught in mingled excitement and dread. The same grit was under her feet, the same lamps with their smoke-blackened globes hung from the ceilings. The same glittering array of bottles and glasses sat before the mirror that backed the bar, flanked by the same yellowing likenesses of women in poses of abandon. To her right was the stage, its curtains closed, and beyond it rose the stairs that led up to Ward's rooms. Nothing had changed, nothing except herself.

Overhead came the sound of a door closing, followed by

footsteps. It would not do for her to be discovered hovering just inside, looking as if she didn't know whether to hide or run. Squaring her shoulders, she moved into the center of the room. With her gloved hands clasped tightly on her purse, a new one of corded faille, she looked around her with a great pretense of interest, turning only as she heard the footsteps reach the lower treads of the stairway.

Ward stood on the last step, one hand resting on the newel post. He looked as though he had not been long out of bed. His dark-brown hair was still damp, and there was a freshly shaven look to his bronzed face. He was without a shirt to cover the hard mahogany planes of his chest, though his gray cord trousers were freshly pressed, and there was a soft sheen on the leather of his boots. There was no sleepiness in his eyes, however. They were alert, hard, and vividly green.

"Good morning, Ward," Serena said, and was agreeably surprised to find the pitch of her voice low and composed.

He inclined his head. "Serena."

"As you can see, I received your summons."

"And you came. I always knew you were an intelligent woman."

"You overwhelm me," she answered, matching his solemn mockery.

He met her steady, blue-gray gaze for a long moment, then with deliberate, measuring intentness dropped his own to the rounded curves of her body and the costume of blue velvet that covered them. "You are looking well—and prosperous."

"That should come as no surprise, to you of all people."

A frown flitted across his face, as if he found her reply disconcerting, before he gave a nod. "I suppose not. You never made any mystery of what you wanted, did you?"

It was the opening Serena had been waiting for. "You mistake my meaning. I was referring to the sum Nathan paid you to stay hidden in the hills until he had maneuvered me safely into marriage."

His brows snapped together. "What?"

"I hope the settlement was a large one, since your absence not only came close to losing the Eldorado for you, it passed to Nathan the right to give his surname to your son."

If she had expected to see him devastated by her broadside, she was due for a disappointment. There was a moment when a tinge of gray appeared under his skin and his grip on the newel post tightened, then it was gone, and he stood straight and tall before her.

"So that's what you think?" he said softly.

"It seems an obvious conclusion."

"Even knowing that once before, when Nathan offered money, I turned it down?"

"At that time, I refused to consider it also, something you don't seem to have taken into account before accusing me."

"Why should I bother to remember past history when I have you standing before me now, the perfect example of a rich man's wife? Nathan made his proposition honorable and you took it. That much is pretty obvious too."

"Yes, I did accept it, a week before my child was born. It seemed preferable to have some kind of father for him. What is your excuse for accepting when Nathan upped the ante?" With blue fire in her eyes, Serena stared at him.

Ward ignored the question. "At least you didn't sell yourself cheaply, did you?"

"I've learned better," Serena snapped.

He lifted his brooding green gaze from the contemplation of the sapphires and diamonds that glittered in the bracelet that encircled her gloved wrist. "I don't doubt it," he answered, his voice grim.

"What I don't understand," Serena said, moving toward him with unself-conscious grace, "is why you came back. Why couldn't you have stayed dead? Why didn't you go to another town, start over, even practice law again? It should have been easy enough with Nathan's money behind you."

"I had an investment here. There was property, among other things, that I valued. I don't give up what is mine easily."

A bitter smile curved her mouth. "Bravo, Ward. You saved your saloon and lost your son!"

"There was never any hope of saving both," he answered, his voice expressionless. "I guessed that much while I lay half dead on a rocky ledge two-thirds of the way down a cliff. I knew it when I woke up and found myself in an Indian village without a name."

Serena stopped, the color draining out of her face, leaving the blue shadows like bruises under her eyes. "You knew I was going to have your baby before you left?"

"Your body was as familiar to me as my own," he answered, his voice rough. "How could I not know?"

"You knew, and said nothing. You knew, and you left me alone?"

"I had my reasons."

308

"What could they be? What could be more important—except money?"

He lifted his hand, then let it fall. "Money, gold; it always comes back to the same thing in the end, doesn't it? This is getting us nowhere. What's done is done. Our concern now is with more recent history, what happened four days ago to be exact. Or have you forgotten?"

Her lips tightened, "It isn't likely, not with you to remind me."

Though she resented his easy dismissal of her questions, she made no effort to avoid the subject. Perhaps she would receive a clear answer on one issue at least.

"That business is still unfinished," he said, a mocking smile tugging at one corner of his mouth. "If you will come upstairs, we will go into it at greater length."

"Upstairs?"

"I don't believe it's a good idea to discuss it here. You can never tell who might be listening." He stood aside for her to mount the stairs ahead of him.

Serena did not move. To be alone with him in those upstairs rooms where so much had taken place was the last thing she wanted.

"Surely you aren't afraid of me?" he queried, his voice soft.

"No," she said, sending him a dark look. It was more that she did not trust him, did not like the glint in the emerald depths of his eyes as he watched her.

"Well then?"

He was right. It could be dangerous to talk here in the open. There was no other place they could go within a reasonable distance that would not be just as compromising, if not more so. She had no choice but to pick up her skirts and move before him up the stairs.

The sitting room was more shabby than she remembered, the effect of Pearlie's occupancy, no doubt. There was a new sideboard holding crystal decanters on one wall. Otherwise it was not much changed. The splay-footed couches with their tube pillows were the same, as were the rugs, the tables, the enameled fruit, and the peacock feathers. Serena moved to touch the shimmering black-and-turquoise eye of one feather. Dust rained down from it onto the tabletop, wafting over the surface as she turned to face Ward.

"Don't look so defensive," he drawled. "I'm not going to attack you."

"I never thought you were!"

309

"Didn't you? My mistake. Would you care for something to drink, a cup of coffee or a glass of wine?"

The urge to refuse, to demand to know why he had sent for her, was strong. She suppressed it. It might well be to her advantage to establish an easier atmosphere between them. Moving to seat herself on the couch, she put her purse to one side, "Yes, I'll take a small sherry, if you have it."

He poured a pale-golden liquid into a glass and brought it to her, then returned to the sideboard, where he splashed rye whiskey into a tumbler. Serena set her sherry to one side, removed her right glove and placed it in her purse, then took up the glass once more. As she tasted the wine, she watched Ward. His hands were brown and strong as he pushed the stopper back into the decanter and picked up his tumbler. His dark-brown hair curled sleekly to the back of his neck, and it seemed the broad width of his muscled back was a darker hue than she remembered. Even when he was not facing her, she was aware of the force of his male presence. Involuntarily, her stomach muscles contracted, and a sensation like the apprehension of pain ran along her nerves.

Ward turned to face her, his gaze catching and holding hers. He lifted his glass in a toast of silent irony and drank. Serena hastily lowered her lashes, making a show of sipping her sherry.

The silence grew acutely uncomfortable. She cleared her throat. "You—you don't appear to have suffered much from your stay with the Indians."

"I was well treated," he answered. "The only hardship was being unable to get a message out from the encampment."

However stilted, the conversation must be kept going. "Your leg, it healed as it should?"

"Perfectly. Broken bones are no novelty to the Indians. And the bump on my head, in case you were going to ask, caused no great damage either. I had a headache for a while, but it healed itself without help or hindrance. I expect that's more than could be said for it if I had had the services of one of our local practitioners."

"There have been few ill effects then, for you."

"I wouldn't go so far as to say that," he objected.

"What?" He had moved to take a seat on the opposite end of the couch where she was sitting. Serena looked up, a questioning wariness in her blue-gray eyes.

"I came back to find that Pearlie had taken over my quarters, and that far from accepting the end of our partnership, had taken possession of the deed to the Eldorado and hawked a half interest in the place all over town. I found also that by some peculiar twist of circumstances, my best friend not only had snapped up the offer at a bargain, but had also gained you as his wife. I don't call that beneficial, precisely."

"Oh, come," Serena began with an impatient gesture of her wineglass.

"That's right. I was forgetting. You think I was bought out instead of being sold out."

"I know who was sold out," Serena countered, her voice tinged with bitterness, "and it wasn't you. Did you know that Nathan bought the Eldorado for the express purpose of having me put out? That he then saw to it that Consuelo, the one friend I could turn to, was unavailable so he would be the only one who could come to my aid when I had nowhere else to go? The man who is my husband is many things, both good and bad, but he knows well the value of money."

Ward stared at her, his brows drawn together in a straight line over his eyes. "I was under the impression that Nathan bought the interest Pearlie was offering in the saloon to keep anyone else from taking what he knew to be a false deed, causing trouble when I got back."

"Knowing you would reimburse him, I suppose?"

Ward gave a short nod.

"How marvelous. He achieved what he wanted, having me put out on the streets, and it didn't cost him a penny."

"Yes, marvelous," Ward repeated. The planes of his face were smooth once more, the look in his eyes closed-in and secretive.

Serena leaned forward, clenching one small hand on her knee. "Doesn't it matter to you what he did? Don't you care that Nathan lied to you and used Pearlie as his dupe to take what was yours?"

"Were you mine, Serena?"

"What difference does it make?" Serena cried, lifting her fist. "We were talking about Nathan!"

"So we were. The answer to your question is, no. No, I don't think it does matter, not even if it's true."

"I should have known!" Serena set her wineglass down with a sharp bang and sprang to her feet. Tears of rage rose into her eyes and she turned her head to keep Ward from seeing as she snatched up her purse and swung toward the door.

Ward came erect in one lithe movement, blocking her

path. Serena sidestepped, but he was before her, reaching to close his hard fingers around her forearms.

"Let me go."

He shook his head, staring down at her flushed face and tear-bright eyes. "I told you, I don't give up what is mine easily."

"I'm not yours!"

"Aren't you?"

"I won't be treated like some pawn in a game between you and Nathan. You've made it clear enough that you despise me. Why should you care where I go, or what I do?"

"I care," he said, his eyes dark and unreadable.

Serena pulled back from him, her hands braced against his chest and her lovely mouth set in a look of scorn. "How can you, when you don't mind what Nathan has done?"

"It's because I care that I can understand what made Nathan do what he did for the sake of having you. I'm even glad he went about it the way he did, since it makes what I'm about to do that much easier."

The grim tone of his voice and the strain in his face were so marked that Serena went still. She was aware of the frantic beating of her heart against her stays, and the corded muscle in the lean line of his jaw. Her fingers seemed to burn where they rested on his chest. She touched the tip of her tongue to her lips. "Ward—"

He released her so abruptly she swayed. Swinging from her, he moved to the sideboard and poured himself another drink. "I'm not going to force myself on you, if that's what you think. At least, not quite."

"What do you mean?"

"In a word, blackmail."

Serena took a deep breath, gathering her composure around her like the shreds of a garment. "I suppose," she said slowly, "that you mean to explain?"

"Certainly, if it's necessary. Somehow, I was positive you would guess my meaning."

She could. And yet, it seemed so unbelievable that she could not bring herself to face it. "By no means."

Ward drained the glass in his hand, set it on the sideboard, then turned to face her. "Four days ago you shot a man on the road between Cripple Creek and Bristlecone. To my certain knowledge, I am the only witness to your—crime."

Otto, lying in the road. The bloodied, tattered edges of the hole where the bullet had entered his body. The yellowed, waxen look of his skin studded with the bristles of his beard and excessive, animal-like body hair. Serena lifted a hand to her lips, then lowered it to clasp her fingers tightly together over her purse. She raised her blue-gray gaze, liquid with pain, to meet the brooding green light in Ward's eyes.

"I will grant you that," she said through stiff lips. "What of it?"

"There haven't been many women in this part of the country who have been hanged for murder, but there have been a few."

"I murdered no one. I shot Otto in self-defense."

"Really, Serena, I hardly think you can claim that Otto meant to kill you. I would say that was the last thing he had in mind."

"You know very well—"

"Yes," he said, cutting her short. "I know, but will the sheriff believe you, will a jury? Will they, all things considered?"

It was a polite reminder of what she knew all too well, that her background would be weighed in the balance if she should claim to have killed in protection of her honor.

"What are you getting at?"

"Oh, Serena, trusting Serena. I am offering you my silence in return for—your presence? Your time? Your compliance?"

She lifted her head. "You are saying that if I—comply with what you ask of me, you won't go to the sheriff?"

"I did warn you it was blackmail," he pointed out.

"So you did. Have you considered that it may strike the sheriff as strange that you disposed of the body, or that it took you so long to come forward?"

"As for the time, I had to overcome my feelings for you based on our past relationship, a difficult thing, even with your desertion of me for a more wealthy client and the bliss of matrimony. The body, now, I don't think I disposed of it at all. I only saw the deed done at a distance. I expect you hired some passerby to get rid of it for you, paying him well for the dirty job. If a thorough search is made of the area, no doubt the corpse will turn up somewhere."

"I could tell them you were my accomplice."

"Not without admitting your guilt. Even so, where is your proof? Can you point out the old Dragon Hole mining claim where I took the corpse? No, there is nothing to connect me with the affair at all, except as witness. It will not help your

313

case to try to involve me in the hope of discrediting my testimony."

He was so certain of himself and the position in which he had placed her. The desire to flay him, to tear and rend, to obliterate the sure and gentle mockery of his smile, rose up within her with such violence she felt dizzy. It took an extreme effort of will to open her lips and speak calmly.

"Who will believe you, a gambler? You may get in deeper than you imagine."

"You forget, I was once a lawyer. The language of the law, and its methods, are second nature to me."

She spun around on her opera heel, her heavy skirt swinging in a bell shape with the force of her agitation. She was half blind with rage, and it was a moment before she realized she was moving in the direction of the bedroom. With a sharp turn, she changed her objective, coming to a halt near the warmly glowing nickel-plated stove.

"Let me understand you," she said over her shoulder, her voice stifled. "By requiring my—compliance, you are demanding that I be unfaithful to my marriage vows, to Nathan?"

"It seems only fair, all things considered," he answered, his tone clipped, relentless. "Besides, you'll forgive me if I doubt your loyalty to a marriage that has yet to be consummated."

Serena went still. After a long moment she spoke a single word. "Consuelo."

"That's right."

"How could she?" Serena whispered.

"She seemed to think I would be interested."

Serena stared at the nickel grill, seeing the dark blue of her velvet dress reflected there, seeing her pale face, distorted in the rounded surface. Would he go through with it? Would Ward actually lodge information about the shooting with the sheriff? She could not believe he would. The mingled contempt and desire he seemed to feel for her was a strange combination. If she did not do as he said, he might well prefer to see her humiliated by being taken off to jail; he might enjoy knowing that she would not be able to keep the wealth he thought she wanted, that Nathan would be denied access to her as surely as he would himself.

"Ward—" she began, then stopped. What use were appeals? Even if she could bring herself to make them, he would not listen. What was she to do then? It seemed she had no choice.

"Yes, Serena?"

"Nothing."

She thought he made a movement toward her, then stopped, drawing back. She did not turn to look. Her anger was a cold thing inside her. Ward Dunbar thought he could do with her as he pleased. He thought he could lend her to Nathan for gain, and finding himself dissatisfied with the arrangement, use circumstances to rescind it, restoring their relationship to something approaching its original status, and all this without regard for her feelings. Compliance. That was all he required, that and her physical presence, her time. It was the bargain a man struck with a whore, a bargain without love, without tenderness, without respect. Very well. If that was what he wanted, that was what he would get.

She still wore the kid leather glove on her left hand. With silent deliberation, she began to remove the bracelet she wore over it, then the glove itself. Undoing the pearl wrist buttons, loosening the fingers, she stripped it from her hand, then tucked bracelet and glove into her purse and snapped the catch. Moving with fluid grace, she dropped the purse on a table, the table that had once held her foodstuffs, but now carried only a coating of dust.

Without looking at Ward, she raised her arms and, grasping the jet-teardrop-tipped hatpin, drew the long bodkin from the draped velvet of her toque. The hat joined the purse on the table with the hatpin thrust like a dagger into its soft folds. Face impassive, she removed the pins from her hair, letting it fall in shimmering black waves about her shoulders. She let the pins spill from her hand onto the table beside her, then turned her attention to the small buttons down the front of her velvet jacket. Unlike her old cheviot, this jacket-and-skirt costume was made in two pieces that had to be removed separately.

There came the clink of a bottle neck on the rim of a glass. Serena slanted a swift glance from under her lashes at Ward. There was a white line around his mouth, and his eyes were shuttered, but his hand was steady as he poured whiskey into his tumbler once more. As he picked up the glass and began to turn toward her, Serena looked hastily down at her buttons.

The jabot of her blouse gave her a bit of trouble until she remembered that it was held in place by a stickpin. Beneath

315

the blouse, she wore a cream chemise of tucked raw silk threaded with apricot ribbon over a corset of apricot satin with cream lace. Her petticoats, heavily ruffled about the hem, matched her chemise.

In the recesses of her mind, Serena had half expected Ward to stop her. He did not. The realization that he was going to stand and watch her undress without a word or gesture served to stiffen her wavering resolve.

Her silk drawers in the French style were extremely brief, showing the length of her white thighs. She thought she heard Ward's swift intake of breath as she stepped from the last of her petticoats, but his expression was so rigid it was impossible to be certain. In the silence she could hear the sound of the wood hissing in the stove and the slosh of rye whiskey as Ward slowly swirled the liquid in his glass.

Spurred by an impulse as demonic as that Consuelo attributed to her, Serena trailed the petticoat over the nearest chair, then with the swish of silk-clad legs, moved to stand before Ward.

"You'll have to help me with my corset," she said, her voice low.

For an instant their eyes met. Serena's gaze was steady, unsmiling, faintly challenging, his as hard and unfathomable as jade. He made no reply, but put his glass aside, and as she turned slowly to present her back, began to release her from her tightly laced prison.

When he was done, Serena stepped to the couch and sat down. Holding the corset beneath her breasts with one hand, she began to unbutton her black leather shoes.

Abruptly Ward went down on one knee. Taking her foot in his hands, he stripped the buttons from their holes and drew off her shoe. He removed the other, then, his warm touch gliding over her silk-clad legs, he unfastened her garters and gently pulled away the stockings.

His movements stilled. He rested his hands on her thighs as he knelt before her. A shadow of torment lay in the still green depths of his eyes, and then he moved, slipping his hands under the edges of her corset, spreading them, expanding the width of the stays. With firm fingers, he removed her hand from its hold and raised her arms above her head. Seeing his intention, Serena lifted her other arm, allowing him to slide the corset off over her head as he rose to his feet.

Ward flung the undergarment aside and, stretching out his hand, took Serena's fingers and pulled her upright. He encircled the narrow circumference of her waist, using his thumbs with a light pressure to massage the red marks left on her skin by the squeeze of the corset. Without hurry, he drew her against him, his chest swelling as he smoothed his hands upward over her back. He bent his head and found her lips.

His mouth held the heady taste of whiskey and the firm sweetness of desire. Serena stood disarmed in his close embrace, enthralled by the cool touch of his flesh on hers, enraptured by the sure strength of his arms that held her and the devastating tenderness of his touch. Her heightened senses crowded out thought and reason in the recognition of pleasure long denied, long despaired of.

He shifted his hold, sliding one hand beneath her hair, pushing his fingers into the silken softness to tilt her head, preventing movement. The realization of her weakness swept over Serena like a rush of cold air. It was no part of her plans to submit meekly to the dictates of Ward Dunbar, melting into a dream of unappeased hunger. If she was so affected by his touch, then the reverse must also be true.

Serena pressed the palms of her hands to his chest, pushing them upward, stretching on tiptoe to lock them behind his head. She thrust the firm points of her breasts into him, moving slowly, sliding the silk of her French drawers across the heated hardness of his pelvis.

She heard the sharp rush of his indrawn breath. He drew back slightly to consider her, a frown between his brows.

"Coals of fire, Serena?" he asked, his voice rough.

"Isn't this what you wanted?" Serena tilted her head, her gaze limpid and innocent.

"Beyond the dream of a doubt, but are you sure it's what you want?"

"I wasn't aware my wishes entered into it. You have the means to command me, and like any woman of the street, I perform."

He stiffened. "I never meant it to be like that."

"Didn't you, Ward? Then why the ultimatum?"

"I didn't think you would come to me any other way."

"No more would I. But since I am here, I may as well please you, if not myself. After all, my future is at stake."

"Be careful your ante isn't too high. In this game, the winner takes all. I can promise no mercy if you overplay your hand."

Did he mean that in pretending to passion she might suc-

317

cumb to her own emotions? "There is risk in all things," she answered. "You have to calculate the odds."

"A calculated risk will sometimes pay off, but the greatest reward comes from those that are undertaken on nothing more than a feeling."

"For myself," Serena said, her eyes dark, "I only gamble on a sure venture."

"There's no such thing," Ward said, and lowered his mouth to hers. Their lips clung in devouring fury, a fierce forging of the bond of passion. They were locked together with bruising closeness, their caresses savage, in their ardor a haunting anguish flavored with desperation. His hands slid down her back to her hips, drawing her against him as if to imprint the feel of her upon his memory.

The couch was beside him. He put one knee on it, and with muscles taut, pulled her down with him upon its smooth, resilient width. He kicked off his boots, eased from his trousers, drew off the wisp of French silk left to her. Her hair cascaded in shimmering darkness over his arm, rippling over the edge of the brocade upholstery to touch the floor. Her lashes trembled on her cheeks, her lips were parted. His hands moved on her, arousing, inflaming, invading. His mouth ravished the nectar of her lips, searing her throat, her breasts, the flat white surface of her abdomen, until it seemed no part of her body remained untouched. Bronze and ivory, the contrasting shading of their skins blended as his body covered hers. They strained together, their breath locked in their chests, fused, glowing with heat, swept by trembling.

Serena felt feverish, caught in a maelstrom fueled by her own fervor, blinded by a blood-red haze of rage and ecstasy, torn by the need to relieve her inner pain by hurting him, and the burgeoning impulse to take him deep inside her. It was wrath and joy, a violent, rending delight that turned her blood to molten honey and lodged wild and suffocating horror in her mind. She was engulfed in the fire of delirium, yet within her there was the black and bitter iciness of unthawed winter. In the tumult of the assault upon her senses, she curled her fingers into claws, raking the ridged muscles of his back with her nails, while at the same time she felt the scalding seep of tears from under her lashes, tracking slowly into her hair.

Chapter Nineteen

Serena returned to the Eldorado the next day, and the next, and a dozen times thereafter in the following weeks. Ward was stern, imperious, insatiable. As she had thought, he knew Nathan was gone from home. He wanted her and he would brook no excuse, no refusal. A hundred times, Serena came near to putting his threat to the test; a hundred times she changed her mind. To stay away, she told herself, was not only to run an unnecessary risk, it would also be granting him a reprieve. Granted, his need of her was so great that it might be a form of torture to deny him; it was a more effective punishment to go into his arms with dutiful obedience to his commands while she remained outwardly unmoved. She was not always able to sustain such detachment. Her lapses were not harmful, however, serving only to demonstrate to Ward what rapture could have been his if he had not bartered her for gain, had not seen fit to coerce her.

She felt no guilt for what she was doing. Sometimes panic hovered at the outer edge of her mind when she thought of Nathan and his return, but she had no compunction about breaking the vows she had taken with him. They had been made under false pretenses, on false assumptions. Nathan had forced her to come to him as surely as Ward, though with more guile, less honesty. What loyalty did she owe him then, what fidelity?

It could not go on like this. The passion she found in Ward's arms was tainted, unsatisfying to her, or to him. That it was also as addictive as the sticky residue of poppy flowers Pearlie smoked in her opium den was a fact she chose to ignore. Acknowledged or not, it flowed in her veins, this distilled essence of desire. It made her prone to the drift of daydreams, to a flushed and startled awareness of her own sensuality. It affected her with irritability when she was not with Ward, to a tingling feeling of exposed nerve endings. It assaulted her with sudden rushes of tenderness toward Sean, during which she would pick up her baby and hold him achingly close, pressing her face into the sweet curve of his neck, inhaling the fragrance of his small body. If anger and annoyance were close to the surface, so too was this strange exultation and a heedless inclination toward silent weeping. By contrast, when she was in Ward's presence she schooled herself to present a cool and emotionless demeanor.

Her attention to her appearance was undertaken with much the same object. Like a rare and expensive jewel, such as one of the sapphires Nathan had given her, the life she presented was no more than a surface thing, the effect of reflected light on the hidden heart, artfully revealed, skillfully hidden.

Sometimes in the need to hide her emotions, to counterfeit her coolness, it was difficult to know what she really felt. She despised Ward for the subterfuge and hateful pettiness of what he was asking of her, and at the same time, was torn with compassion for the depth of his need. The love she felt for him was a constant pain made more aching by its betrayal. And yet it was also the source of the strength she drew on to continue, the base from which sprang her terrible sense of outrage.

It was on her third visit to the Eldorado that Serena came face to face with Pearlie. The woman was waiting for her as she emerged from the back door of the barroom. Swaying slightly, with her auburn hair straggling around her ravaged face, she stared at Serena with bleary venom.

"So you're still in one piece," Pearlie greeted her.

Serena paused to smooth on her gloves, her gaze wary. "It seems that way."

"I wasn't sure you would be. I've never seen Ward so mad as when he found out you had taken up with Nathan Benedict."

"I'm sure you were careful to give him the most damaging

version of how that came about you could think of," Serena answered, her tone cold.

"I tried." A malicious smile gleamed in Pearlie's eyes.

"It did you no good as far as the Eldorado was concerned, I see. You appear to be *persona non grata* there again."

The other woman looked away, her slack lips quivering before she pressed them tight. "Ward isn't a forgiving man."

"You tried to take over his property when you thought he was dead. What you didn't keep, you sold out. I don't see how you can expect anything else."

"You were gone, married to your millionaire. Why couldn't he have let things be, turned back to me?"

"I don't think I need tell you the answer to that," Serena said.

"Because of you?"

Serena stared at her, caught by the sneer in the red-haired woman's voice. "I meant because of what you have done to him, both in the past and this last year."

"That's not it! It's not! He's obsessed with you. His meanness to me had nothing to do with the Eldorado; it was because I got rid of you. That's why he threw me out, why he told me not to come near him. That's why he hates me! It's your fault, yours!"

There were flecks of spittle on Pearlie's red lips, and a wild look in her dilated eyes. Her voice was shrill, rising to an uncontrolled shriek.

"You're mad," Serena breathed.

"Me? He's the one who's mad for wanting a cold little gold-digger like you. You're the one who's mad for coming back here, rutting with Ward like a bitch in heat, instead of playing up to your rich husband!"

The thought of Ward's hearing the commotion, coming down to find her embroiled in a shouting match with Pearlie, filled Serena with repugnance. Thus far, she had managed to leave him each time with some few shreds of pride intact; she did not care to have it appear that she was engaging in a brawl over him now.

Taking a firm grip on the purse that dangled from her wrist, she brushed past the other woman. "What I do," she said, her expression aloof, "is no concern of yours."

"That's what you think! We'll just see about that, we'll just see how hoity-toity you are when I tell your husband what you've been up to with Ward!"

Serena stopped. "You can't do that."

"Can't I? Can't I just? You wait and see what I can do. It wouldn't surprise me if Nathan Benedict tried to kill Ward!"

"No, oh no," Serena whispered.

"Yes, oh yes," Pearlie mocked her. "You'd like that, wouldn't you? You'd like having them fight over you like a pair of wolves? You'd be right there, ready to spread your legs for whoever won, no matter which! That's what you want, isn't it? That's what you really want!"

It was useless to exchange words with Pearlie. She was beyond reason. Serena picked up her skirts and, with head high and shoulders straight, walked away in the direction of the livery stable.

It was while she was waiting for her grays to be harnessed that she saw Pearlie once more. Her face twisted with a terrible look of grief and self-loathing, the woman stumbled down the incline from the parlor house, making for the weathered building where the opiate of forgetfulness was dispensed. She dragged herself up the steps and slumped against the door, beating on the closed panel with a weak fist. The door swung open, and, moaning, Pearlie fell inside.

Serena lay staring at the ceiling with one arm flung across the pillow above her head. Her eyes were wide and desolate, but dry. Her breathing was deep and uneven, threatening to dislodge the covers that lay across the swell of her bare breasts. Ward lounged beside her, one sinewy arm holding her against him. He shifted, reaching to pull the quilts higher against the chill of the room, tucking them in on either side of Serena. It was cold, enough so that their breaths fogged in the air in spite of the fire roaring in the stove in the next room. Beyond the windows, the sky was gray with the advance of the afternoon and the promise of snow.

Ward withdrew his arm beneath the covers once more, settling his hand at her waist, slowly caressing the smoothness of her skin with his palm. There was a reflective note in his voice when he spoke.

"You are a stubborn woman."

Serena closed her eyes. "How so?"

"You were made for the sharing of love, but you hold it tight inside you. You give so much, and no more, refusing to fall until you are forced to it beyond the point of resistance. You cheat me of pleasure, yes, but don't you know you also cheat yourself?"

322

"You have the use of my body, I come when you send for me. Isn't that enough?"

"You come, but you aren't here, not really. No, that is not, will never be, enough. Once I thought it would be, but no more."

"That doesn't make sense," Serena told him, knowing she lied. It made excellent sense, more than she had expected from him. She had thought that this time she would have no tears; she was wrong. They were only locked inside.

"Doesn't it?" he queried. "A few times, before last summer, I came close to complete possession, close enough to be tantalized by the richness of the prospect. I won't be satisfied until I have taken all you have to give."

She turned her head, opening her eyes to stare at him. "What you want cannot be taken. It is given in return for trust, and in exchange for a gift of the same worth. You will have to be content with what you can gain by threats."

"I can't accept that."

"Are you ready to renounce your bargain, then, since it doesn't satisfy you?"

"That would make you happy, wouldn't it?"

The tone of his voice was harsh, yet tentative. The sound sent a shaft of anguish through her. "Does it matter?"

"No," he answered, and in the word there was the whisper of a sigh.

This was the first time they had talked of anything other than surface occurrences. Serena looked away from the shuttered darkness of his green eyes and the new lines etched in the mask of his features. "What I feel may not be the deciding factor."

"Meaning?"

She sketched her exchange with his former partner in a few words, leading to the woman's threat to inform Nathan of their meetings.

Ward gave a slow shake of his head, a gesture of pity.

"Yes," Serena agreed. "Sometimes I feel sorry for her, too."

"Don't," he advised. "Too much compassion is a trap. It becomes a burden, one that makes you convict yourself of some nameless guilt if you try to put it down."

He was speaking of the past, and of his part in the destruction of Pearlie's life. Compassion and guilt; wasn't that an accurate description of what she felt for Nathan? Serena returned to the original topic.

"What are we going to do?"

"It bothers you that Nathan might find out?"

Serena swung to face him, a frown clouding her eyes. "Don't you think it should? He is my husband, in spite of everything. He would have a perfect right to be upset."

"Tell him I blackmailed you," Ward recommended.

She levered herself up higher in the bed, a mistake, since his hand dropped lower, though she scarcely noticed at the time. "You don't understand. It's not me I'm worried about, it's you. Nathan could kill you, and none would blame him."

"Your concern is touching."

"I'm glad you think so! Unfortunately, I don't find the idea of having another man's death on my conscience amusing!"

"Serena!" He pushed himself up in the bed beside her, resting against the ornate headboard. "You don't really think Nathan would do anything so melodramatic, or that I would let him if he tried? If I know Nathan, he's much more likely to look about him for some way to squeeze me out of business, and see that I am escorted out of Cripple."

"Is that supposed to be a consolation?" she demanded.

"I thought it might be, considering it was the thought of my death, rather than my departure, that you claimed troubled you."

Serena lowered her lashes, plucking at the sheet. "I'm not anxious to see you ruined for my sake either."

"I would have expected you to see it as my just deserts.

"No doubt it is," she answered, her lips tightening.

"None whatever."

The words were even. They almost sounded as if he meant them. When Serena slanted a glance at him, he was staring past her at the far wall. Suspended in surprise, she could think of nothing to say. In the distance there came a train whistle, the Midland on the trestle over Poverty Gulch, coming into town.

Ward's hand moved over her thigh, then stopped. "When will Nathan be coming home?"

"I'm not sure. In a few days, I expect. He's been gone longer now than he planned."

"Has it occurred to you that even if Pearlie tells him, he may do nothing for the simple reason that he has no real right to accuse you?"

"You mean—because of Consuelo?"

"So you know about her, that Nathan is still involved with her?"

"I know."

324

"Is that, by any chance, why you show so little remorse for making him the cuckold?"

His tone was detached, mildly curious. Serena refused to be lulled, however. "My feelings toward Nathan are no concern of yours."

"Your feelings?" he said, his grip tightening on her upper thigh. "I'm not sure you have any, for anyone."

"That isn't true!" Serena objected, her pose of coldness forgotten.

He gave her a hard stare. "No, it isn't, is it? There is your home for women, a grand gesture of charity, and an indication of how thoroughly captivated Nathan is, not that I blame him."

"You don't approve?" Somehow she had been certain he would. She had not forgotten Mrs. O'Hare and her descriptions, that day so long ago down in the Springs, of Ward's kindness and generosity.

"It is something Cripple needed, something only a woman, or a church group, could have provided without misunderstanding."

"Why do you sound so cynical, then?"

"I wonder how long it will last. For now, you remember the hardships you endured and you may offer genuine aid to women who find themselves in trouble. But how long will it be before you decide you were meant to be rich and respectable, that you would rather forget where you came from, sever all connection with the sordid past? How long will it be before your fine home is torn down to obliterate what it stands for, or else transformed into something more refined, a home for indigent gentlewomen, perhaps?"

"If you think I will do that, you know nothing about me!"

"I know people. I've watched what money does to them. I've seen it happen too many times in the last few years. The men strike it rich, and for a while nothing changes, then the fact of great wealth begins to sink in. After they get their surfeit of worldly goods comes the realization that wealth is power, that it can buy a place among the highest. They crave that place. They move to the Springs, to Denver, to New York. They travel in Europe and look up their family trees. They import castles block by block, and fashion coronets for themselves. They have original coats of arms made up to paint on the sides of their carriages. They order champagne from France, caviar from Russia, oysters fresh from the coast, and turkeys from Tennessee—"

"I'm not like that," Serena interrupted, strain threading her voice.

"No, but you will be. Nathan will want to show you off, and you will let him because it's easier than refusing, and because there has to be something to do to fill the days."

"Ward—"

"Come back to me, Serena. Bring Sean and come back to me."

Serena had never expected him to make such a request. She had thought he did not care that she was married to Nathan so long as he could have her when he wished. To be proved wrong made her feel as if she had been duped, betrayed in a way that made all her calculations inaccurate, and threatened to crumble the foundations of her new existence before she had even begun to build upon it. He wanted her to come back to him, uproot her life once more, destroy the security of her child, return to Myers Avenue and the Eldorado, and in return he promised nothing, not love, not permanence, and not, no never, marriage. In spite of all that, the longing to do as he asked was like a canker growing inside her, spreading its mind-numbing poison. The resulting confusion brought the glint of anger to her blue-gray eyes.

"Come back here?" she asked, her voice dangerously quiet. "Bring Sean and raise him over a saloon? Or maybe we wouldn't stay that long. Then what? Maybe Sean could become a faro dealer, or a pitchman, or grow up to be a grubby miner's apprentice with old eyes and a white face from never seeing the sun?"

She flung back the covers, preparing to slide out of bed. His fingers sank into her leg, holding her. "Serena, no. It wouldn't be like that."

"How would it be?" she cried, snatching his hand from her, throwing it off, leaping from the bed. "Are you going to leave me alone again while you look for your fortune? Money, gold, gold mines. I'm sick of hearing about them! I'm tired of being pulled this way and that. All I want is to be left alone!"

"I don't have to go looking for gold. I've already found it in a mining claim that I won in a poker pot."

"Don't tell me," she snapped, gathering her clothes, snatching them on. "I don't want to hear. What good is a mining claim without the capital to work it? What good is the few thousand you might get from selling it, if it doesn't get you away from here?" She made a fierce gesture around

326

her with the shirtwaist in her hand. "You sneer at the people who want to make a better life for themselves, but what's wrong with that? What's wrong with wanting something more for themselves and their children? To mingle in society and hobnob with royalty may not be what I want; still, it's better than resigning myself to Myers Avenue as an alternative!"

Ward opened his mouth, then closed it again. A grim look in his green eyes, he threw himself back flat on the bed, his hands clasped behind his head. He did not speak again, nor did he give any sign that he was aware of her struggling into her clothing beside the bed.

Serena, moving to the bureau to bring some order to her hair, sent him a quick look in the mirror that topped it. She was right, she knew she was. Why then did his black look of contained rage affect her so?"

She picked up her hat and set it on her hair, pushing the hatpin through it without a glance at the way it looked. "I had better go now," she said. "It will be snowing soon."

He did not answer. Serena scooped up her fur coat, brought this time because of the low-hanging snow clouds, and her purse. She hesitated a moment, then, swinging around, left the room, closing the door quietly behind her.

In her phaeton, she whirled through the streets. It was later than she had thought; already the dance halls and opera houses were brightly lighted. She would be lucky if she made it home before dark. She should have asked the stablehand to light the sidelamps. It wasn't that she was frightened or nervous of being on the road alone. There had been no further incidents to cause her alarm. But she was perfectly willing to admit that having her way lighted would be comforting once she got beyond the town.

She thought of Ward back at the Eldorado, then pushed the image from her mind. What consideration did she owe him? she reasoned with herself furiously. He had taken advantage of the fact that she was alone in the world, forced himself upon her against her will, kept her a prisoner for his pleasure, got her with child and left her. Then when he came back, he had demanded her compliance as the price for allowing her to retain her freedom. He was everything that was base. That he had given her shelter and protection, that he had been gentle and considerate, even tender at times, made no difference. She owed him nothing. Nothing.

Today was the only time he had mentioned his child since

the first day she had gone to him. What did it mean? Did he regret the circumstances that had given Sean another man's name? Was he seeking to redress that wrong with his request for her to come back to him with their child?

What a tangled mess everything had become. Serena, staring at the gaily lighted facade of the Gold Nugget Saloon, could see no way that she could win free of it, no way she could ever be happy again.

Ahead of her was a small crowd gathered around a speaker using a wooden TNT case for a platform. Serena had to slow to allow a loaded dray to pass the men spilling into the street before she could go around them. The voice of the lecturer, harsh, loud, etched with the acid of fanaticism, was both repellent and familiar. She flashed the man a quick look, knowing even as she did so she could not be mistaken.

The elder's hair hung in tatters about his shoulders. His beard was long and unkempt, blowing in the wind. The flesh had melted from his frame, giving him the sharp features and desiccated look of a desert ascetic. In one hand he clutched a Bible, while with the other he made vicious, stabbing gestures that caused his faded clothes to flap around him like the rags of a scarecrow. For all his wasted appearance, his eyes were still vigorously alive. They burned silver-white with zeal above the fevered, wind-burned flesh of his cheekbones, terrible eyes that looked beyond his listeners with menacing fury and contempt.

"Whore of Babylon!" he shouted, his voice cracking as he shook a fist at Serena's phaeton. "Evil woman as thou art to set up your house of iniquity among the innocent, instead of staying with your own kind, to offer succor to the wicked females of the town instead of leaving them to their just punishment, the disease and pain that are the wages of sin! You are known for what you are, Serena Walsh Benedict, corrupter of the good in men. You drag men down to their doom, forcing them to consort with the devil, he who first penetrated you with his double-pronged pole, before they can come to you! You are known, with the blackness of your sin! Adultress! Fornicator! Come now from your lover to go to your husband! Your day of reckoning is not long in coming. You will be dragged down to the dogs like Jezebel of old! Your punishment shall be meted out! You will be stripped and the white skin of your body scourged with scorpions, flayed with asps! Your end shall be as bitter as wormwood!"

White to the lips, Serena gave no sign she heard the diatribe directed at her. The impulse to whip up the grays and get quickly away was strong, but she controlled it. She skirted the men who had turned to stare at her in good form, then sent her horses along the street once more at an even trot. Behind her, the elder still shouted, his hoarse denunciation calling down wrath upon her head in such terms that it was to be wondered that he was not embarrassed to trumpet them aloud. There was nothing to be disturbed about; he could rant and scream his obscenities after her, but he could not hurt her.

Or could he? If he knew of her meetings with Ward, who else might not know? How long after Nathan's return before he was told, if not by Pearlie, then by somebody else?

Coming from her lover, going to her husband; those had been the elder's words. Was it possible that Nathan had already returned, was even now at Bristlecone, that he already knew?

The snowflakes began to fall as she passed under the stone archway over the drive. By the time she had driven her team under the portico and handed the rig over to the waiting stableboy, the cold white powder had dusted her hat and the shoulders of her fur, and settled onto her lashes.

Mrs. Anson opened the door to her and helped her out of her coat. Serena, by no means certain of the shape her hair was in, made no effort to remove her hat.

"Has Mr. Benedict returned?" she inquired, her voice as offhand as she could manage.

"Yes, madam. He has been waiting for you in his study this past half hour."

There was cold disapproval in the woman's tone. Serena ignored it. "Tell him I will join him shortly," she said in a pleasant aside, "as soon as I have made myself presentable. You may serve tea when I come down."

"Mr. Benedict has already had his tea."

"But I haven't." Serena smiled and swung away, forgetting the housekeeper the instant her back was turned in her determination to walk slowly up the stairs instead of running. Her greatest fear was that Nathan might have heard her voice, and would emerge from his study to greet her before she had time to collect herself.

A quarter of an hour later, she had bathed her face and hands, brushed her hair and pinned it into a fresh knot at the nape of her neck, and exchanged her lavender merino for a dinner gown of teal-blue silk-lined crépon with a seamless

329

corsage. Regaining her confidence with her look of severe elegance, she descended the stairs once more. She paused at the door of the study to take a deep breath, then turned the handle and swept into the room.

"Nathan, I didn't know you were back until Mrs. Anson told me. I wish you had telegraphed; I would have met you at the station, or at least been here to greet you."

He rose from his chair before the fireplace and, coming toward her, caught her shoulders and brushed a kiss across her forehead. "As lovely as ever," he said as he stepped back.

"Thank you, sir," she replied, smiling.

"I would have sent word of my arrival time, but I wasn't sure myself when I would reach Cripple."

"In all events, it's good to have you back." The words were easily spoken. It was so friendly, so cordial, and so false; still, the pretense must be kept up. Serena gently disengaged herself and moved to take the chair opposite Nathan's, indicating that she wished him to resume his seat and be comfortable.

"You've gained weight, filled out again," he commented.

"Yes, thankfully. Did you have a good trip?"

Nathan nodded. "It was smooth enough. I was glad to get back here before the snow started again."

"We had one blowing storm while you were gone, nothing major. You seem very chipper. Am I to assume you were able to get what you went after?"

Before he could answer, Dorcas came into the room bearing a tray holding a fresh pot of tea. Their conversation was delayed until she had gone out again, and Serena had filled her cup and refilled Nathan's.

Her husband took a sip of the hot brew and leaned back in his chair. "In answer to your question, I did indeed get what I went after. They tried to put me off, saying the display everybody was making such a fuss about was only a prototype, that I would have to put in my order and wait until they went into full production before I could take delivery of the hoist. I wasn't having that. Well, the upshot of the matter was, I put down my money and brought their display home with me—that is, in a manner of speaking. It will come by freight in a few days. That's what took so long, though, getting the thing dismantled, then crating it up and making it ready to ship."

As he went on, talking of the superiority of the new hoist and the mechanism for raising and lowering it, Serena could

330

feel the tension inside her subside. He didn't know. He couldn't go on in such a relaxed manner if he had any idea where she had been and what she had been doing. The realization gave her a strange feeling. Human beings were capable of infinite deceit. Here she sat, smiling, nodding in an imitation of guileless interest, all the while thinking of her lover, and there he sat, knowing he had tricked her into marrying him, more than likely thinking of the interludes aboard his private railroad car with his mistress.

Consuelo had been with him, all right. Serena had taken the time one day to drive by the house Nathan had bought for the Spanish girl. The man who drove the water wagon that supplied fresh drinking water daily had stopped on seeing Serena coming from the door and called out to ask if it was time to start delivery again. Realizing his mistake, that she was not Consuelo, he had taken a hearty laugh before volunteering the information that the lady of the house had canceled her water until she got back, that she thought it would be a while since she was going to Denver and then some city in the East.

"Tell me what you've been doing while I've been gone," Nathan said. "I see you went into town by yourself again, despite my orders to take someone with you."

She was caught off guard, but she rallied quickly. "I know, and I'm sorry," she said, taking his last comment first with a pretty show of contrition. "I hate to ask either the boy from the stables or Jack Coachman to come to the home with me. I never know what I'll find there, or how long I'll be. They don't like to wait inside where there's only women, and it was too cold today for them to wait outside for any length of time."

She had not precisely said she was at the home this evening. If he assumed that was where she was it would be unnecessary to lie.

"It seems what you need is a maid, somebody who can help you into and out of these new clothes, keep them done up for you, run your bath, and whatnot, and still be available when you need someone up beside you when you go out."

"Mrs. Anson cares for my clothes and does a beautiful job, and Dorcas is learning to perform simple tasks for me. I don't need anyone else. As for driving out with me, what earthly use would a maid be? I would just have to take care of her too, while she sat there screeching her head off, like as not."

"Nevertheless, I'm going to look around for a suitable girl."

"If you want to please me," Serena said carefully, "you'll do no such thing. I told you, I don't need any more help than Mrs. Anson and Dorcas, and Mary of course, already provide. That is, unless you think I am in need of a chaperon."

He leaned to place his cup on the tea table drawn up before them. "You know I meant nothing of the kind."

"No," Serena said, forcing a smile. "I'm sure you didn't. Let's consider the idea as dropped, shall we?"

"As you wish," he agreed, though his nod was stiff.

"I am not ungrateful for all you have given me, and all you have done for me, Nathan," she said, her voice strained, and her lashes shielding her blue-gray eyes, "but in this I would appreciate it if you will let me have my way."

"My dear Serena, when you put it that way, how can I refuse? I've given you little enough, not half what I would like; I think you know that—or you should, since I've told you often enough."

"Yes, I know," she answered, and went still, waiting for him to go on as he had before, to suggest that she become his wife in more than name.

At that moment the door opened behind them. "Dinner is served," Mrs. Anson said in her most formal manner, her expression bland as her eyes met Serena's over the back of the chair. "Set forward as you requested, Mr. Benedict."

Chapter Twenty

The evening meal that was set before them had not been touched by the chef. That gentleman had traveled with Nathan to prepare the meals on board the railroad car while en route. In New York Nathan had hired a hotel suite, and on one occasion the talented French Creole had been called on to prepare a special dinner for a group of people, a coal magnate and his wife, a man who had made a fortune in pork, and a railroad heiress and her foreign husband. After the meal, the heiress had gone back to the kitchen to congratulate the chef. The results had been that Nathan's cook had succumbed to flattery, money, and the prospect of prestige, and departed in the middle of the night for the lady's chateau in Normandy. The story of the loss, and Nathan's unsuccessful efforts to recapture his prized chef, served to get them through until dessert.

A fire had been lighted in the dining room, but there had not been sufficient time to thoroughly warm the room. It was decided to take after-dinner coffee in the comfort of the study.

The fire had been replenished. Its crackling heat was welcome, especially since they could pull their chairs close and hold their chilled fingers out to the flames. The coffee sat ready in its silver pot, though neither really wanted it. After moment, Serena poured it out anyway, and passed the steaming, pale-green demitasse to Nathan. He thanked her

333

absently, placing the small cup on the table before him while he pulled out his leather tobacco pouch and meerschaum pipe.

"Do you mind?" he inquired.

"Not at all." Serena sent him a smile, then leaned back with her own filled cup, crossing her ankles on the small petit-point footstool in front of her chair.

Nathan got his pipe going. Exhaling a puff of blue smoke, he made an encompassing gesture with the stem. "This is pleasant, sitting here together, you and I. It's good to be home again."

There seemed nothing to do but agree, though Serena felt the flutter of apprehension along her nerves. It would be expecting too much for the subject broached earlier between them not to be renewed.

"I trust we will have many years like this, many happy years."

Would they? Serena allowed herself to think of Ward's request that she come back to him. At least Nathan, for all the high-handed methods he had used to make her his wife, had been willing to commit himself to a permanent union. He was thoughtful and kind, and if there was a streak of hardness in his character nearly as steely as that in Ward, there was nothing wrong in that. It was a practical necessity for a man who had made himself a millionaire.

"I love you, Serena."

The words were simple, softly spoken. That was something else she had never heard from Ward's lips. "Nathan, I—"

"Oh, I don't expect a declaration from you in return. I just wanted there to be no misunderstanding about what I feel. I had time to do some thinking while I was back East. When I left I was upset, both with you and with myself. I pressed you too quickly, and made a bad mistake, reminding you of what I think we both would prefer was forgotten."

"You have been very patient and considerate," she objected.

"I've tried, but having you here at Bristlecone, so near and yet so distant, was more of a strain than I anticipated. That was one of the reasons I decided to carry through with my trip, even after you refused to come with me."

"I see." It was inadequate as a comment, but Serena could think of nothing else. In contrast to what he made sound a staid and contemplative journey was her knowledge that he had not been alone.

"As I said, I had time for thought in these last weeks. I

came to the conclusion that our best hope for happiness is to have everything out in the open between us. If you realize my feelings, both about your past and present, then you must see that nothing I may say inadvertently is meant to hurt you. If I admit to my own sins, it will be in the hope that you will recognize I have no wish, no need, and no right to judge you. As human beings, we are what we are, and for you and me, Serena, there need be no apologies."

"Your attitude is—more generous than I deserve," Serena said with difficulty. "There is no need to go into particulars."

"There is every need. I want you to know."

"Even if I can't promise to be equally honest?"

His smile lighted the lean angles of his face. "Are you going to pretend to some misdeed I know nothing of? If it is trivial, it won't matter; if great, I think I prefer not to know. Keep your secrets, by all means."

"That hardly seems fair to you," Serena said, staring down at the coffee growing cold in the cup she held.

"Why not, if I make the rules?"

"In any case, I doubt you have anything to confess that I don't know."

He stared at her, his hazel eyes wide, considering. She lifted her lashes slowly to meet his gaze. "Perhaps you had better explain," he said finally.

"Since you were speaking of your trip, I assume you meant to tell me Consuelo was your traveling companion."

"Yes, that's so," he answered, "though I meant to tell you that our association is over, that it was ended when we said goodbye this afternoon."

"That wasn't necessary, not for my sake." The words were spoken before she could stop them. Serena looked away from him, staring into the fire.

"The decision was Consuelo's, but I will admit I am—relieved. It was as nearly perfect as such a liaison can be, but I could not get over a feeling of guilt for betraying my marriage vows, and when I was with her, we both knew far too well that it was you I wanted."

There was a sick feeling in the pit of her stomach. She had felt no such compunction. As an antidote for the remorse that seeped in upon her, she cast about in her mind for another grievance.

"I am surprised that your vows had such a pull upon you," she said, her tone reflective, "considering that you had to pay for the privilege of saying them. As far as that goes, I suppose it's safe to conclude that you bought me, too."

"That isn't so!"

"How else would you describe your action in buying into the Eldorado, and asking Pearlie to evict me from Ward's rooms at a certain time and day?" She set her cup down on the table and got to her feet, stepping over the footstool to stand before the fireplace, one hand on the mantel.

"I did what I thought was necessary. What care would you have had when Sean was born if I had left you where you were?"

"There is that," Serena admitted, "though I doubt that was your primary reason."

"I never said it was. In fact, I thought I had made my reasons abundantly clear." He put down his pipe, his expression disturbed. In the sputtering light of the chandelier overhead, the sandy shock of his hair gleamed above the sheen of perspiration on his high forehead.

"So you have, and yet, you could have asked first."

"Would you have accepted my proposal?"

Serena stared at her hand, pale against the dark rust-pink marble of the mantel. "I'm not sure."

"You see? I couldn't take the chance you would refuse."

"Couldn't, or wouldn't?"

"It comes to the same thing."

"If you mean," Serena said, "that it comes to the fact that I am your wife, then you are right."

He stood, taking the step that brought him within arm's length of her. "I'm glad that you accept that much, at least."

"You may not always be glad," Serena answered, her voice low as she allowed her gaze to rise no higher than the knot of his narrow tie between the rounded tabs of his stiff collar.

"Impossible," he answered, smiling. He moved closer. His hands were gentle but firm as they closed on her arms. He bent his head and touched his mouth to hers. His lips were soft and smooth and faintly bitter with the taste of coffee and tobacco. It was not unpleasant. Serena willed herself to stillness, aware of a sense of waiting, of testing, inside her.

His hold tightened, his kiss grew more demanding. Panic welled suddenly upward inside her, routing her apathy, washing over her with a shudder of distress. She dragged her mouth free, turning her head as she held him off with both hands against his chest.

"Please, no," she whispered. "Not now."

336

He was still, his breathing ragged as he stared down at the pale oval of her face, with her lips like crushed petals and her eyes as dark as mountain pools. At last he stepped back.

"As you wish, Serena. I'll give you a little more time to get used to the idea, and to what I've said this evening. But my patience isn't infinite. I have no use for an unwilling wife; still, I am forced to wonder if your unwillingness couldn't be overcome with just a little effort on your part—or mine."

Swinging away, he moved stiffly to the door, almost as if he could not trust himself in the same room with her. He paused for a moment, his hazel eyes dark and devouring as he watched her, then he went out, closed the door quietly behind him.

Serena sank down on her knees before the fire. She clasped her hands together in her lap, bending over them as if in pain. The red glow of the firelight played over her, reflecting in her eyes.

"Nathan," she whispered, "I'm sorry."

It was true. She was sorry for the hurt she had caused him, sorry for the twisted snarl of their lives, sorry she could not love him. And no small part of her contrition stemmed from the recognition that he was right. It was not distaste that had made her break from him, but fear, fear of her own unwary need for comfort and acceptance. If she had tried, and if he had dared to use his strength to overcome her protests as once Ward had done, she could have gone to him. She could have given him what he wanted, and perhaps found in his arms some small ease for the desolation that clung with icy tentacles to the beating warmth of her heart.

Dorcas showed Consuelo into the nursery where Serena sat playing with Sean. He was fourteen weeks old and his smiles were cherubic. He kicked against his long gown of white flannel embroidered in blue with exuberant strength, cooing in pleasure at having his mother's complete attention, arching his eyebrows and flailing his arms in a determined attempt at communication. He had just disgraced himself, however, by wetting himself and his mother, when Consuelo appeared. Serena looked up from her loving scolding to greet the Spanish girl. Together they hung over the cradle, consoling Sean, letting him clutch and gnaw their knuckles and generally getting in the way as Mary tried to change him. It was only as his protests turned to outraged cries of hunger that they withdrew to allow the nursemaid to feed him and put him down for his morning nap.

"He's a beautiful baby," Consuelo said, her voice caressing.

Serena smiled as she led the way down the hall toward the stairs. "And Mary's so good with him. I believe she would give her life to keep him from being harmed. I'm lucky to have her."

"You are so isolated here at Bristlecone, and it's been such a cold and snowy winter, too cold to take an infant out. I wonder, has Ward seen him?"

"No—not yet."

"It's a sad thing, when a father is prevented from seeing his son."

There was an odd note in Consuelo's voice. Serena, opening the door into the sitting room, sent the other woman a quick glance. "So far as I know, Ward has expressed no desire to see Sean."

"That doesn't mean anything, as you well know. He isn't the kind of man to parade his feelings."

Serena could only agree. "That makes it so convenient for his type, doesn't it? People always credit them with all the proper feelings whether they have them or not."

Consuelo took the chair Serena indicated. "That's one way of looking at it. People might also fail to credit them with any feelings at all."

"Have you come to plead for Ward?" Serena asked. She seated herself, leaning to hold her hands out to the fire beneath the mantel.

"Far from it. He needs no help from me, or anyone. You are right, though, in thinking I have a purpose. I would not risk coming here, even knowing Nathan is in town, if there wasn't a reason."

"You know you are always welcome."

"I know you are more forbearing than any woman of normal emotions has a right to be—unless, of course, you are not jealous because you know you have nothing to fear."

"Or unless I have reason to be grateful to you?"

"Ah, Serena, you are a fool—I say this with deepest affection and sadness."

"You may be right." The look in Serena's eyes was wan.

"This may be the last time I insult you, also, my dear friend. I am going away. This visit is to say goodbye."

Serena allowed her silence to pass for the surprise she could not claim. Finally, she said, "Where are you going?"

"I think I told you once of my plan to go to Mexico? I have not changed my mind. I will go to a town neither large nor small, take a new name, call myself a widow, perhaps. The last is needful because I am to have a baby."

Serena's gaze widened. "Nathan's child?"

"But of course!"

Stretching a hand toward the other girl, Serena said, "I didn't mean—I was only surprised. Nathan has been so concerned with Sean that I find it hard to believe he would let you go, knowing you were pregnant by him."

"He doesn't know." Consuelo's voice was flat, her words hard.

"You haven't told him? But why?"

"I—I am afraid."

Serena stared at her. "I don't understand."

"It is because I doubt he would let me go that I am afraid. Nathan wants a child, a son of his own. If I stayed, I fear that when my baby is born he might take it from me. Oh, it would be with the greatest tact, and for the best of reasons, but still, I would be alone."

"But he would take care of you; there would be nothing he would not do."

"I know that. He has been more than generous already. But how long could I bear to be his—his pensioner, once you have become his true wife? I am a realist, and I know, Serena, that if our roles were reversed, if I were kept in luxury while you shared his bed, my jealousy would destroy me. I would have to return to Myers, leaving my child to his father to be raised. I don't doubt, with your forgiving nature, you would become his mother. No, far better to go away and hope that as a rich widow, some man may be persuaded to wed me and become a father to my baby."

"I can't blame you for that," Serena said slowly.

"And yet, I am troubled." Consuelo turned to stare into the fire.

"In what way?"

"Do I have the right to keep this from Nathan? Which would be the greater cruelty, to go without telling him, or to go, leaving the knowledge behind to be given to him when he can no longer act upon it?"

"You are asking my opinion?"

"No, not really," Consuelo said, shaking her head, her

339

mouth curved in a grimace meant for a smile. "If I had wanted to go away, leaving Nathan in ignorance, I would never have come here to trouble you with my secret. What I am asking is this: Will you be my messenger? Will you tell Nathan when I am gone, when I am miles away where he can no longer find me, that somewhere in a Mexican village, his child with dusky skin and dark, curling hair will play under a hot sun? Tell him the child will be loved, will know joy, will grow in pride and will know the name of his or her father. Tell him that one day, if God wills, I will send his child to him so they may meet face to face and recognize each other?"

"Consuelo, are you sure?"

"I am sure. You must not be hasty, however. It will some weeks yet before I can sell my house and make ready, before the weather will be fit for such a long journey. I will go, regardless, at the first sign of spring. The child will be born as summer wanes and fall begins. That is when you may tell him, not before. Promise me."

"I will do that," Serena answered, her eyes dark.

"It will not be a burden? You have a son; there may be other children. You are under no obligation to share their inheritance with Nathan's Spanish bastard."

"Don't say such things! How could your child possibly have less claim than Sean, who is not Nathan's own?"

Consuelo waved her words away. "It may be you think I am doing wrong. If so, say it now."

"The decision is yours," Serena answered. "I will do as you ask. I owe you that much."

A shadow dulled the blackness of her eyes. "I don't ask this for the payment of a debt, but because you will be near Nathan, close to his heart. You will know what he thinks and how he feels. You will know the words to say to explain, and to ask him to forgive me."

The Spanish girl's words trailed off into a whisper. "Yes," Serena answered in the same tone.

"You will be kind to him, Serena? You will allow him to—to be kind to you?"

Consuelo's pathetic attempt at whimsy, reminding Serena of their walk that winter day more than a year ago when the storekeeper had offered his kindness in exchange for a piece of yard goods, was her undoing. Serena swallowed with the sheen of unshed tears in her eyes. "It seems," she said, "that I will have to."

* * *

The new hoist came the next day, arriving by slow freight in the middle of a raging blizzard. The young engineer sent out to see to its installation tumbled off the train, arranged to have it unloaded and transferred to the heavy drays he had rounded up and protected from the weather on the difficult haul to the Century Lode. By the time he was done, he was in a high fever, and had to be put to bed in a downtown hotel with bronchitis.

Serena suggested he be brought to Bristlecone, but Nathan vetoed the idea. He did not intend to expose his household to sickness; moreover, it was more convenient to keep in touch with the engineer, since the hotel had one of the few telephones in the district, and he was having a line run to the Century Lode along with the electric wire. Too impatient to wait for the young man to get well, he would act as a go-between, since he had taken careful note of the installation of the machinery during his inspection before buying. With a few good men to do the heavy lifting, they would have the hoist in operation without delay.

Between the cold and the calls on his time brought on by the hoist, Nathan did not spend much of the following days at home. Many nights, either because of the snow and ice or fatigue, he even slept at the mine. Sometimes he sent a note telling Serena not to expect him, though usually he simply did not put in an appearance. On these last occasions, Mrs. Anson held dinner back as long as possible before grudgingly serving it to Serena. Not that Serena minded the waiting. It was the fact that the housekeeper did not ask her preferences as mistress of the house that annoyed her.

The lack of supervision made no difference. There had not been another summons to the Eldorado, nor had she heard anything from Ward. It was as if with her refusal to come back to him, he had put her out of his mind. He was being considerate, she told herself, he knew Nathan was back, and was bowing to her concern for security. It did nothing to fill the void within her.

It was an evening more than a week after the arrival of the hoist. Serena sat frowning over the newspaper delivered that day with the milk and butter for the kitchen while she waited in her bedroom for dinner to be announced. There had been another woman strangled and mutilated on Myers Avenue. The victim had been a taxi dancer on her way to her room after her closing number at the Topic. There were signs, according to the newspaper, that she had been molested, and thereafter followed a graphic account of the manner in which her anatomy had been carved up, all couched in guarded, oblique language designed to titillate, but not shock, a lady reader. In the opinion of the reporter, in which the county coroner concurred, the crime was the work of the same man who had struck so many times before.

Serena threw the paper aside. She shifted in her chair to sit with her clenched fist pressed against her lips. So Otto had not been the killer. The depths of her dismay were an indication of how much she had depended on his being guilty. Without that vindication for killing him, she felt doubly a murderess, regardless of his attempt to assault her.

Who could have committed these heinous crimes? Her mind was circling warily around an idea when the door from the hallway behind her swung open.

Serena jumped, swinging around. It was so unusual for anyone to enter without stopping for at least a light tap that it was a minute before she could form a greeting. "Nathan, you startled me."

"Sorry." He advanced to stand with his back to the fire and his hands clasped behind him.

"You've already bathed and changed. I didn't hear you come in."

"I've been here nearly an hour."

"Are you through at the mine, then? Is the hoist ready for operation?"

"Almost. It will take a couple of days for safety checks before we drop it down into the shaft."

"What a terrible way to put it!" Serena protested with a smile.

Nathan let it pass. "I stopped in town on the way here to see the engineer. As I was coming out of his room, I met someone you know."

"Oh?" Serena watched him, a wary light in her blue-gray eyes. The gaslight overhead shone on her blue-black hair and lent a pale-gold sheen to her shoulders above her dinner gown of blue crepe beaded with jet.

Nathan looked away as if the sight of her pained him. "It was Pearlie."

In the silence they could hear the crackle of the fire, the slow tick of a clock in the hall landing outside, and Mary crooning wordlessly to Sean two doors away.

"I'm sure," Serena said slowly, "that the two of you had a lot to talk about."

342

"You could say so. She thought I might like to know that my wife was seen coming and going from the Eldorado at odd times during my recent absence, and that the distinctive phaeton I had presented to her was left sitting for hours at a time at the livery stable convenient to the saloon."

"Are you accusing me of misconduct, Nathan, or asking why I was there?"

"I am trying to get to the bottom of what appears to be either a malicious slur, or else a serious charge against you."

Now that it had come, finally, Serena felt her agitation leave her to be replaced by a tenuous composure. "I will grant you the right to ask, but are you certain you want to know?"

"A man has the right to be certain the child who takes his name is his own."

"That didn't trouble you when Sean was born," she pointed out, her tone soft.

"There was never any chance he was mine; there was no way you could pretend he might be."

"You love Sean as your own; you made him your heir."

"But he will never be mine."

That was unanswerable. "Does it matter so much?"

"It matters."

Serena pressed her lips tight against the urge to tell him of the baby Consuelo was carrying. She could not betray the Spanish girl, and it was she who had said the time was not now.

"Well, Serena?"

"Since you must know, it's true. I was there."

"Serena, look at me. Why?"

His voice was ragged, his face pale. Serena met his hazel gaze without flinching. Her mind teemed with things she must not say, things she could not tell. At last she said, "Because he sent for me."

He stepped toward her, leaning over her to place a hand on either arm of her chair. "And that's the only reason? He sent for you and you came running? I get down on my knees and beg, and you give me nothing, while all he has to do is send for you!"

As his voice rose, Serena knew a flicker of uncertainty. Perhaps she had pushed him too far. He deserved more of an answer than she had given, no matter what it might cost her. What was it Ward had suggested she tell Nathan?

"No," she said, "it wasn't like that. I had no choice except to go. He—he was blackmailing me."

343

Nathan straightened, all expression wiped from his face by his surprise. "Blackmail? Ward?"

Serena told him of the death of Otto, of Ward's appearance, his aid in disposing of the body, and his subsequent demands that she meet him or have the sheriff brought into the matter.

"Why didn't you tell me?"

"You weren't here when I met Ward the first time. You had left for points north and east—with Consuelo."

"No, I mean about this attack on you. When I think of what might have happened—and of you sitting beside me, keeping it hidden, showing nothing—"

"I—was afraid." It was the truth, though she did not expect him to understand. In the back of her mind, she heard in the words an echo of those Consuelo had spoken. She had not trusted Nathan's instinct either.

He didn't understand. He paced up and down, running his fingers through his hair, asking again and again why she hadn't seen fit to confide in him, and yet at the same time vowing to see to it that heads rolled in the sheriff's office for letting dogs like Otto run loose to accost women.

"Things like that, and worse, happen to women on Myers Avenue every day. There doesn't seem to be anything anyone can do to stop it."

"And you went back down there alone, after I asked you not to. God, Serena, it drives me insane to think of it."

It was not merely the danger that troubled him, she knew. "It could not be helped."

"Apparently not. Ward, that—to think that I called him my friend. He won't get away with this, that much I can guarantee. When I get through, he'll wish he had never been born."

Serena sat forward. "What do you mean to do?"

"Hanging's too good for a man who would force a woman like that, no matter what went on between them before."

"Please, Nathan, you can't. If you do anything to him, he'll go to the sheriff, and everything will come out."

"Ward won't go to the sheriff, that's not his way. We'll settle this between us."

"How can you be sure he won't, a man who would take a bribe, accept money to take himself out of the way and leave me to you?"

Nathan halted to stare at her, a curious look in his hazel eyes. "Do you mean the mining stock I offered last winter? I thought you knew he turned that down."

"Then he did, but if he didn't take it this past summer, why did he stay away so long?"

"He didn't take it, because I didn't make the mistake of offering it again. As to why he stayed away, I suppose it was because of his accident, just as he said."

The color retreated from Serena's face. She sank back in her chair. When she spoke her voice was scarce above a whisper. "There was no money involved, no payoff of any kind?"

"None." He stood gazing down at her, a slow frown gathering on his high forehead.

She had wronged Ward, had refused to listen to him. When he mentioned his discovery of gold on a mining claim won at poker, she had assumed he was lying, trying to explain away the windfall she was certain he had received from Nathan. If he had not stayed away from Cripple Creek by choice, then the fact that another man had given his son a name was his tragedy as well as hers, and she had flung it in his teeth, flaying him with it. He had tried to tell her, and she wouldn't listen, wouldn't believe him. Anguish took her breath, moving deep inside her, awakening every sense she had thought dead, every feeling of betrayal and grief, shame and despair.

"The other night," Nathan said, his head tipped to one side and his eyes like agate, "I invited you to trust me, and you refused. You refused and sat here listening to my miserable confessions, knowing all the while that you were a murderess and an adulteress."

"Nathan, no! I told you then I could not be honest with you. The reason is the same; I was afraid. And you said it didn't matter, you didn't want to know."

"You hide things so easily, Serena; you lie so well. I'm beginning to wonder if you're telling the truth now, or if you are only afraid now, as always, of what I might do to Ward."

"I have one man's death on my soul. I would as soon not have another." She had said the same to Ward and he had not been impressed. Nor was Nathan.

"I think you're lying to yourself if you believe that. In any case, I said nothing about killing him. I had in mind breaking him, putting him out of business, before I put him out of this town, this state."

"You tricked me into marrying you, and gave Ward's son your name. I will admit I was grateful at the time; I still honor you for helping me when I needed it so badly, whatever your motives—but don't you think that is revenge enough?"

345

"Maybe, if I knew you went to Ward against your will, instead of conniving at your own blackmail."

Serena lifted her head. "You make it sound as if it's me you want to punish, instead of Ward."

He stared at her, his eyes bleak. "You may be right, my darling, Serena, you may be right. If I give you my word I won't lift a hand against Ward, will you come with me to Europe in two days' time?"

Serena's fingers curled around the arms of her chair. It was a threat for all that it was softly spoken. She felt as if there was a heavy weight on her chest. Her voice caught in her throat as she spoke. "Nathan—don't do this."

"Why not?" he inquired. "You seem susceptible to this kind of arrangement."

"I don't blame you for being bitter, but this isn't necessary. I would have gone with you anyway."

He closed his eyes, turning away. "Damn you, Serena," he whispered. "Now I'll never know."

"No," she answered on a sigh that was threaded with pain and compassion.

"It doesn't matter." He swung back to face her, a hard set to his mouth and his hands knotted into fists. "You will be mine. I'll make you forget Ward, forget the Eldorado and Myers Avenue, forget everything but me. And we'll start where it all began, in my private railroad car; mine, Serena."

"No." Serena came to her feet, the color draining from her face.

"Yes! Unless you would prefer starting here and now?" His gaze traveled slowly over her in a deliberate insult, something she had never received from him, not even when she sang on the stage of the Eldorado barroom.

"Mrs. Anson will be announcing dinner any moment," she said through stiff lips.

"She can wait." He moved toward her.

"You will regret this." Serena retreated a step.

"Someday, maybe, but not tonight."

"You will hate yourself tomorrow, and so will I." Serena held out her hand. "Oh, Nathan, please. I think I could love you in time. I am your wife and—and I would like to forget Ward. I would like to forget so much."

She had backed against the Renaissance dresser. He stopped before her and the tension left him. Lifting his hand, he touched the back of one finger to the tears that trembled on her lashes, carrying it to his lips where he tasted the salt.

346

"Serena, lovely Serena," he said, his voice low and strained, "you don't play fair."

"It—it isn't a fair game," she answered.

"I suppose not, from your point of view. All right, then. My first inclination may have been right. We'll go down to dinner now. I'll tell Mrs. Anson to start packing, including things for Sean and Mary. I'll see about hiring an extra car for them for the train trip. In the meantime, I have a few details to work out on the hoist. As soon as it is in operation, we will pull out. But be warned. Only death itself will prevent me from making you mine once my railroad car starts on its way toward the sea."

Chapter Twenty-one

It was impossible, the housekeeper declared. To pack the necessary clothing and other paraphernalia needed by five adults and an infant in arms for an extended period, to put the house in dust sheets, clear the larder, and complete the dozens of small tasks involved in closing the house, could not be done, not on such short notice. She would try, but no one must blame her if they were unable to leave on schedule. She and Dorcas had only one pair of hands each. Jack Coachman and the stableboy could be pressed into service, yes, though a useless lot they were, all thumbs, more apt to get underfoot than be of help. Notes must be carried to stop the drinking water and milk and butter deliveries, and there was that order to the butcher for a side of beef and a pork loin that must be canceled; the stableboy could make himself useful that way. It would be different, of course, if Mr. Benedict had intended to take his own carriage and pair; that would have meant a great deal more preparation. Since he did not, the two males of the household who were being left behind could serve as watchmen for the estate. There would be no need for special arrangements of that sort.

Serena had protested to the idea of taking Mrs. Anson and Dorcas with them. She had no need for personal servants. But who, Nathan asked reasonably, would cook and serve their meals aboard the train? Who would attend to their clothes on the Atlantic crossing, and in the grand hotels of Europe? Everyone of any consequence traveled with an entourage. Was she going to descend to the basement laundries herself to rinse out their underclothing and linens, rubbing elbows with the superior maids and valets in their uniforms? Nonsense!

Having settled that point, and mollified Mrs. Anson by listening with half an ear to her complaints and giving her a bracing endorsement of her ability to get things done, Nathan left the house for the mine. He lifted his hand to Serena, standing on the veranda, as he drove away. Watching him out of sight, Serena's mouth twisted in a wry smile. Quietly arrogant, Nathan gave his orders and expected them to be obeyed. He arranged matters to suit himself, giving little thought to the consequences for other people. What he could not change, he chose to ignore, and it was as if it did not exist. There was much kindness and goodness in him, but he could also be insensitive. If he was generous, he had also driving need to own things, to gain them by whatever means proved necessary, to take them and hold them as his own. It was a trait common to most humans, but few had the means to attain their ends. Her eyes bleak, Serena turned back into the house.

Mrs. Anson, bolstered by Nathan's confidence, was everywhere. She issued orders, directed, and scolded in grim-lipped impatience. Serena thought of offering her aid, then decided against it. It would not be appreciated, she knew, and would probably be looked on with contempt that she should so lower herself.

It was just as well. There was something Serena had to do, a job that could not be delegated. She had wished since the night before that she could be spared the necessity. She could not; still, there was no reason she should not take the simplest way out.

Moving into the parlor, Serena seated herself at the secretary desk. She took thick, cream-colored notepaper from the drawer and drew the silver inkstand toward her. Opening the inkwell, she dipped the pen and sat poised, thinking.

What words could she use to tell Ward she was going away with Nathan? How could she explain? She could not tell him she was going to protect him. Though that was a part of the agreement, it was not the whole truth. Would Ward understand her sense of obligation and duty? Would he be able to grasp the ambivalence of her desires when she was not certain she understood them herself? She could not claim to be in love with two different men, and yet Nathan's touch was not repulsive to her. He might not affect her senses to the degree that Ward did, but she felt that if she had never known Ward, she might have been content with the man who was her husband.

Was it necessary to convey this to Ward? Did he deserve such honesty? Would he care? Was there any purpose in telling him anything beyond the barest facts? She was leaving. She had told Nathan of her meetings with him, and of the tragedy and coercion behind them. She was free of him at last; he no longer had the power to hurt her. What else did he need to know?

Dipping the pen once more, Serena began to write. She signed her name, slipped the single sheet into an envelope, and sealed the flap. That done, she went in search of the stableboy to ensure that he delivered her missive when he carried the other messages for Mrs. Anson. When she caught sight of him an hour later, bobbing down the drive on his way into town, she gave a sigh of relief. It was strange, however, how that deep-drawn breath failed to ease the ache in her chest.

By midafternoon, the house was in a state of organized chaos. Shelves had been stripped of valuable ornaments and a few of them packed to be taken to give their hired rooms a personal touch. Trunks lined the upstairs hall. A steamer trunk stood open in Serena's bedroom, and her clothing was spread over every available surface. The only room not in dust sheets was the study, and in its corner tower, books had been pulled from the shelves and stacked ready to be packed in cartons. The baby, sensing the coming upheaval in his world, was crotchety, crying off and on for no reason. Between concern for her charge and fearfulness over the coming voyage, Mary was even more withdrawn than usual, responding only to Sean. Dorcas flew here and there in answer to her mother's bidding, her eyes wide with excitement. The coachman, who would have liked to consider his job done when he had tooled the baggage wagon up to the front door, grumbled as he stomped up and down the stairs, lugging boxes and cartons and shifting heavy trunks.

In the midst of such confusion, no one heard the clatter of the buggy coming up the drive. They were not aware of the visitor until the firm knock came on the front door. Even then, it was only Dorcas who heard it as she passed through

350

the hallway with an armload of books. So demoralized was she by the knowledge that the parlor, where the gentleman would ordinarily have been asked to wait, was not presentable that she left the front door wide open and the visitor standing in the hall with his hat still in his hand while she ran upstairs calling for her mother at the top of her lungs. It was Mrs. Anson who came in search of Serena.

"There is a gentleman to see you, madam," the housekeeper informed her, staring down her nose at Serena sitting in a patch of sunshine on the carpet of the nursery, trying to entertain her small son.

"Who is it?" Serena handed the baby to Mary and reached up to smooth her hair, tucking loose wisps back into her low chignon.

"Mr. Dunbar, madam. I tried to tell him Mr. Benedict was not at home, but he insisted on seeing you. I put him in the study."

Serena went still. It was the last thing she had expected. In view of their last meeting, she would not have been surprised if Ward had shrugged the whole thing off, cutting his losses, considering himself well out of a bad situation.

"Very well," she said finally, pushing to her feet. "You needn't trouble with refreshments. I doubt the—the gentleman will be staying long."

"As you wish, madam. I'll get on with what I was doing then."

Serena followed the woman from the nursery. At the head of the staircase she paused, glancing down at herself. She had donned an apron to cover her gray merino while she played with the baby. She removed this and draped it over the banister, then rolled down her sleeves, fastening the demure, lace-edged cuffs. She touched the locket, her mother's that she wore beneath the matching lace collar, and with a lift of her chin, descended the stairs.

Ward stood with his back to the door, one booted foot on the brass fender of the fireplace. As Serena entered, closing the panel behind her, he straightened and turned to face her. His green eyes were dark as he watched her come toward him, and the chiseled firmness of his mouth pressed into a hard line.

"Whatever possessed you to come here?" The question rose to her lips without plan, without preamble. She came to a halt in the center of the room, her hands clasped tightly at her waist.

"There was a time when I was welcome here, when I came often."

"But now, of all times?"

"I came because I had your letter, of course."

"It will do no good. My mind is made up." She met his gaze squarely, her blue-gray eyes clear.

"So Nathan wins, Nathan and his money? What if I told you I was rich? What if I said I would marry you as soon as you could get a divorce from Nathan?"

"Please, Ward. Don't make it more difficult than it already is."

"You don't believe me," he said, his voice flat.

"Can you think of any reason I should? If you had wanted to marry me, why didn't you say so long ago—or even the last time I saw you? Why wait until now?"

"How could I ask you to share my disgrace, or hope you would tie yourself to a man with the uncertain prospects of a gambler? And when you had married Nathan, and he had draped you in diamonds and furs, what chance did I have, except to bind you to me with fear? Once I had done that, how else could I expect to hold you?"

"It's too late. I've given my word to Nathan." What might she have said if her husband did not hold the threat of ruin over Ward's head? She would not think about it. Such speculation could serve no useful purpose and might weaken her self-control.

"It's never too late," he answered. "I don't intend to let you go, Serena."

"You can't stop me."

"Can't I?"

The quiet determination in his tone sent alarm along her veins. "I am going to Europe with Nathan. We leave tomorrow aboard his private railroad car. It will be a new start to a new life, and I will be happy with him, very happy."

"Who are you trying to convince; me or yourself? It won't happen. I've let this go far enough, too far. Nathan was once a friend of mine. I think he'll listen to reason."

"No," Serena exclaimed, her voice rising as she took a step toward him. "You can't interfere. Nathan won't stand for it."

Ward's eyes narrowed, and a frown appeared between his brows. "He'll have to."

"You don't understand!"

"Enlighten me," he drawled.

Serena twisted her fingers together. "He resents you, not

only for the past, but especially because of what has taken place since our marriage. He is satisfied, now that I've promised to go away with him, but he may change his mind if he learns you have been here, or if you antagonize him."

"I may do more than antagonize him," Ward said.

"No!"

"What are you worried about? You sound as if you think I should be afraid of him, or as though you are."

"You—you said yourself that he would be likely to ruin you if he knew about us."

"He might have been able to, once. Now, he's welcome to try. But why such concern? I would have thought you would like nothing better."

"I—prefer to fight my own battles," she told him, her voice unsteady.

"And a formidable foe you are. It would probably serve Nathan right if I let you go with him."

"That's simple. Only leave well enough alone."

He shook his head. "I can't, not while I still have hope of a cease-fire between the two of us, and eventually, a surrender."

Anger for his willful blindness boiled up inside her. She should have known he would belittle the danger, refuse to recognize it. How had she expected anything else?

"You are a fool, Ward Dunbar. I am married to Nathan. Don't you see it's over between us?"

"Never. I won't let you go. Nothing and no one will take you from me, not if you don't want to go. If you choose Nathan freely and without reservation, than I won't stop you. Only tell me you love him, and I will gladly step aside. But if you give me the least hint, knowing there is nothing to choose between our wealth, that you prefer me, then I will level the mountains of this valley crater, tear this town apart board by warped board, and peel the rails of the train tracks from their beds like so much licorice before I will let him keep you from me, or take you away."

Serena felt as if he had struck her. She could only stare up at him, the need to deny that wealth had any bearing on the matter colliding in her mind with her attempt to accept the violence of his declaration. Her blue-gray eyes widened as he took a long step toward her, reaching to grasp her arms, giving her a small shake.

"Nathan is your husband, but that tie can be broken. Either he will grant you a divorce, or I will find another way

353

to set you free. He is not the problem, Serena; you are. Which shall it be? Forgetting the wrongs I have done you and the mouthing of meaningless words like gratitude and duty, passing beyond thought, touching only on what you feel, tell me: In the darkness of the night, would you rather turn to Nathan, or to me?"

Her face twisted as the emotions inside her leaped to meet the suppressed fury that gripped him. She tried to wrench her arms from his hold, but he would not let her. The burning green of his eyes impaled her, demanding an answer.

"All right," she whispered, going still. "You then, damn you!"

She saw the flare of triumph in his hard gaze, and then she was swept against him with bruising strength, and his mouth came down to crush her lips. There was a white-hot brightness behind her eyes. She felt as though her heart would burst and her blood catch fire in her veins. She had committed herself, and the agonizing fear of it was beyond bearing.

As abruptly as he had caught her to him, he released her. His face was like a mask as he drew back. He steadied her an instant, then he swung on his heel and strode to the door, pulling it open, banging it to behind him. Serena heard his footsteps cross the hall, and the closing of the front door.

White-faced, she stood where he had left her. She raised her fingers to her stinging lips without noticing their trembling. In her head a turgid refrain repeated itself. *What have I done?* it sang. *What have I done?*

There was no immediate answer. The sun settled behind Mt. Pisgah, casting the dark shadow of the mountain across the veranda and the drive. Nathan did not return, nor was there any message. For something to do besides roaming from window to window staring out, Serena bathed and dressed for dinner, putting on the gown Mrs. Anson had left out for her, though its taupe color made her skin look sallow and she did not like the steel bugle beads that jangled in a fringe from the draped bodice. Dorcas, who had run her bath, wanted to put her hair up in curls on top of her head. It was her one talent, a way with hair. Serena refused, pulling it back in a severe knot. What did it matter how she looked?

Throwing a shawl about her shoulders against the chill, she went along to the nursery. As she moved down the hall, for some reason her thoughts were far away. In the lower South this time of year, it would be spring. The nights would be balmy and fragrant with the smell of growing things. The earth would be alive with fecundity, instead of sterile and drear and wrapped still in winter. With a shake of her head, she pushed open the nursery door.

In the light of a pale-blue fairy lamp set near the cradle, she gazed down at Sean, snared in a paralyzing tenderness by the sight of his fine lashes resting on his cheeks and his small pink hands outflung on either side of his face. Mary, already dressed for bed, roused herself from a rocker before the fire. With a shake of her head, Serena indicated she would not stay, would not wake the sleeping babe.

Moving back down the hall, she returned to her room. There would be a fire in the study, but she had no wish to go down. She had closed the memory of what had happened there earlier out of her mind and was loath to do anything that might allow it to push its way back in. She felt suspended, encased in numbness. After all she had been through, it was not an unpleasant sensation.

The dinner hour came and went. She wasn't hungry. She didn't care if she never ate again. No one disturbed her. Time passed. She considered ringing the bell and ordering a bowl of soup, if only to assert her authority, her right to consideration. She rejected the idea. She did not want the food, and it might well be a matter of indifference to her soon how insubordinate Mrs. Anson's attitude became.

The darkness outside the windows grew less dense. The moon rose, gilding the dark branches of the evergreens, shafting its rays along the ground until every unmelted snowbank, every rock and leafless twig, stood out in stark contrast. So brilliant was its light that it was several seconds before Serena noticed the firefly specks of carriage lamps on the drive. There were more than one pair of them. Following behind the first vehicle was a second with the wavering glow of lanterns hanging low, as if suspended from the bed of a wagon.

Serena was standing halfway down the stairs when Mrs. Anson opened the front door. At the sight of the strange men who stood just outside, looking uncomfortable in their dusty miner's garb, her fingers tightened on the banister. Then at the forefront she recognized the superintendent of the Century Lode, an older man named Boston. Beside him was a younger man with narrow, intelligent features and clothing less grubby than the rest. It was the latter who stepped forward.

"I'm Patterson, the engineer assigned temporarily to the Century Lode," he said to the housekeeper. "Could I see Mrs. Benedict on a matter of great urgency?"

Mrs. Anson, her face going pale, nodded in the direction of the stairs where Serena stood. With slow steps, Serena descended the treads, stopping at the bottom.

"I'm Mrs. Benedict," she said, her voice low and clear.

The young engineer hesitated. Superintendent Boston stepped to his side. "I don't know how to tell you this, ma'am. Maybe you better sit down, or something?"

"What is it, Mr. Boston?"

The older man glanced at the housekeeper, then at the engineer. It was Patterson who spoke, his grip creasing the fedora he held in his hands. "There was an accident late this evening at the mine. Mr. Benedict was rushing to get the new hoist working. I—I told him it wasn't ready, that we ought to send it down empty a few more times, but he was bent on trying it. Everything went fine on the way down, but—"

Serena swallowed. "Yes, go on."

"On the way back up, something went haywire. The drum taking up the cable started spinning backward. The safety brakes that were supposed to hold didn't. Before we could do a thing, the cage dropped six hundred feet to the bottom level with Mr. Benedict inside."

Horror brushed Serena, then subsided. Her lips stiff, she said, "Is he—"

"We cranked the cage up as fast as we could by hand, but it was too late."

Mrs. Anson cried out, throwing her apron up over her face. Serena glanced at her, then beyond the engineer and the superintendent to the men crowded in the doorway, employees of the mine, men who worked for Nathan—had worked—men who knew—had known him well. They shifted, avoiding her eyes, ducking their heads in embarrassed silence, almost as if they felt responsible.

"Where is he?"

Superintendent Boston nodded toward the open door. "The body is out there, in the wagon. I—I wouldn't look if I was you, Mrs. Benedict. It would be best if you didn't."

Serena swayed a little, then caught herself even as the engineer took a quick step forward. Mrs. Anson, her head bowed as she sobbed, moved to the hall tree, sinking down on the marble bench. Dorcas stepped out of the darkened parlor to sit beside her mother with tears running down her face.

"I don't know what to do," Serena said, a haunted look in her blue-gray eyes, one hand clutching the shawl around her shoulders.

"There's nothing to do," the engineer said. "We notified the coroner. He'll be along as soon as possible. If you'll tell us which undertaker you want, somebody'll go after him for you."

Serena gave a small shake of her head. "I don't know."

From the rear of the crowd came a low, masculine voice. The two men turned to listen, the young engineer smothering a cough that prevented Serena from hearing. The superintendent nodded in agreement, and delegated a man to ride back into town, before turning back to her.

"Do you want him brought inside, Mrs. Benedict?"

"Yes, I suppose so," Serena began, with an uncertain glance toward the upstairs bedroom where Nathan had slept.

"No. Wait for the undertaker. It will be time enough for that when he has finished."

This time the voice was clear. Serena drew in her breath. The men had parted, shuffling aside to let the superintendent, the engineer, and the man who had spoken see each other. The light from overhead penetrated beyond the group to the outer darkness of the veranda. A tall figure stood there with the cold night wind ruffling the brown waves of his hair, and his eyes glittering in his drawn face. A part of the group, his clothes were powdered with the same dust from the mine roads, as though he had come with them from the Century Lode.

It was Ward.

Serena wore black to the funeral, mourning being a basic item in the wardrobe of a lady of fashion, for whom the proper observance of the obsequies of death was a rigid requirement. Her gown was of faille banded at the hem and the wide yoke with jet passementerie. With it she wore her coat of French sable and a close-fitting velvet hat hung with black crepe. The veil was Mrs. Anson's contribution. She had brought it, smelling of camphor, from a box in the attic where it had lain since the death of Nathan's first wife. The housekeeper had offered to tack it to Serena's hat, insisting that it would be expected. Serena had not protested. It did not seem to matter enough, though she had always felt such swathings of black an affectation.

In fact, she had reason to be grateful for the concealment the veil offered at the graveside. Even in her detachment, she began to notice the sidelong glances cast in her direction, the stares that were hastily averted when she happened to glance up. Her frozen countenance and dry, burning eyes were also shielded. Moreover, she was able to look about her, to observe the crowd that stood in the cold wind on the barren hilltop of Pisgah graveyard. The most influential men of the town, with their fur-wrapped wives, shifted from one frozen foot to the other beside miners and their families, fancy women, pitchmen, gamblers, barmen, and the hangers-on of a dozen saloons who had been treated to a drink on more than one occasion by the man in the bronze casket. Consuelo, her face contorted with grief, was supported by Ward on one side and Welsh Timothy from the Eldorado on the other.

Serena was sorry for the Spanish girl's loss and pain. She would have liked to go to her, to express her sympathy, but the width of the grave separated them. In addition, she felt encased in the solemn respectability of her widow's weeds with their stiff bands of glittering jet like fossilized tears. She was not certain she could come so close to Ward without shattering the calm that was her greatest ally. How shocked everyone would be if she suddenly began to scream, accusing him of murder.

Serena raised her gloved fingers to the high jet collar that covered her throat. She swallowed against the aching pressure in her upper chest, then clasped her hands once more on the black-edged handkerchief she held. The voice of the minister droned on and on. It was not Elder Greer, thank God. The Mormon was nowhere in evidence, another cause for thankfulness. She could not have endured his insane ranting today. It was all she could manage to stand still under the sanctimonious platitudes of the man conducting the service, the preacher Mrs. Anson had assured her had been the earthly guardian of dear Mr. Benedict's soul.

The smell of the roses and carnations mounding the casket was strong in the clear, pure air. They reminded Serena of the day they had buried Lessie. Her headstone stood stark and white to one side. The man who had taken her life so brutally still lived, still walked among them, waiting to strike again. How long would such an obscenity have been tolerated if the chosen targets had been men of wealth and

358

position such as those around her—or even their wives? Consuelo had been right. There was a different set of laws for women of the lamplight. It was as though beyond Myers Avenue they had no existence. The death of such a person hardly counted to those in authority. It would be different if they learned of the murder of one of the district's richest mine owners.

So far, there had been no sign that Nathan's death was looked on as anything other than the accident it was first designated. It might be they were keeping it from her, the grieving widow. It might also be that Ward had been astute enough to commit the deed without being detected. He was an intelligent man. His one mistake may have been in telling her what he intended, putting into words his determination to set her free, one way or another.

The casket was being lowered. Mechanically, Serena stooped to take the first handful of earth, dropping it into the grave. The picks and shovels they would use to fill in the hole with the rocky, half-frozen soil that had been dynamited from the hard ground lay near by. Serena closed her eyes to shut out the sight, waiting with dull patience for the final prayer to end.

At last she could turn away. A few of the mourners, men for the most part, stepped up to offer her their condolences. These were soon done, however, the bankers and miners and stockbrokers wandering back to their tight-lipped wives. Serena was able to move toward her carriage, where Jack sat on the box in solemn patience, and the stableboy, an unaccustomed tie strangling him and his hair slicked down with pomade, stood holding the door for her.

She picked up her skirts, preparing to join Mrs. Anson and Dorcas, who were already inside on the forward seat. At that moment a rider shouted and came pounding up the hill at a gallop, his long hair flying and the swallowtails of his rusty black coat flapping. Elder Greer pulled up, taking in the situation with a wild, encompassing glance. His gaze fell on Serena, and he piled down from his horse, coming toward her at a shambling run.

Serena's head came up. The easiest thing would have been to scramble into the carriage and give the order to drive off; it would also be the most cowardly. She stood her ground, aware of the interested faces turning in her direction.

"The news was brought to me late, but the Lord was with me, and I am come in time. Praise Him! I am His instrument of chastisement, sent here to call you to account, Serena!" He held his hand uplifted over her head in a travesty of a blessing. His words, though directed at her, were for the benefit of the audience he saw before him.

"Why must you do this?" Serena asked.

He paid no attention. "You spurned a good man for a life of debauchery, married one of the finest citizens of Cripple Creek and betrayed him with your paramour! Now you have found a way to enjoy your ill-gotten gains without the yoke of a husband. For shame! You will burn in hell for your sins, O daughter of darkness. You—"

"That's enough."

The quiet words cut across the tirade like a knife. Serena swung her head to find Ward beside her. He touched her arm in reassurance, a touch that urged her to step into the waiting carriage.

"I have a mission!" the elder shouted, his voice cracking.

"This is neither the time nor the place for one of your sermons," Ward grated. "This is a time for respect for the dead."

"You might be expected to protect this fallen woman. You are under her spell. She has made you her partner in sin!"

As Serena took her seat, her dark blue-gray gaze met that of the gambler in mute distress.

"She made me nothing," Ward said, his eyes steady. He turned back to the elder. "The problem is what I've done to her; what you and I have done, Elder Greer. Don't you think you've hounded her enough?"

"If you would protect her, you are cast in the same devil's mold."

"That may be," Ward grated, "but we'll see just how close an acquaintance I have with old Nick if you say another word. My advice to you is to get back on your horse and ride toward town as fast as you rode out here."

"You are interfering with the Lord's work!" the elder declared, then backed away as Ward took a step toward him. "This won't be the end of it," he cried, shaking a fist. "It won't!"

Ward turned back to Serena. "Go on home. I'll ride along behind to be sure he doesn't make any more trouble."

"What—what about Consuelo?"

"Timothy can take her in his livery rig. I have my horse."

He did not wait for a reply but, nodding to the open-

360

mouthed stableboy to shut the door, strode off to where his mount was tied to a wrought-iron grave fence.

The elder looked after him, the stare he divided between Ward and Serena's carriage malevolent, then, turning with many backward glances and unintelligible muttering, he did as Ward had suggested.

The closed town carriage rocked on its springs as the stableboy climbed to the box beside Jack. With a jerk, it rolled away down the hill.

Serena had expected Ward to turn back toward town as soon as they reached Bristlecone. He did nothing of the kind. He dismounted and came forward in time to help Serena out and hand her up the steps. Under the veranda, she turned to him, her manner at its most formal.

"I appreciate your coming to my rescue just now."

"That fanatic is becoming a nuisance," he said, ignoring her expression of gratitude. "Something is going to have to be done about him."

"I don't see what. He isn't actually harming anyone."

"It's possible he can be persuaded to look for sinners elsewhere. As for the harm he's doing, it doesn't pay to underestimate his kind. There are people who listen to them."

"At any rate, it was kind of you to keep him away from me."

"Kind?" He gave her a mirthless smile, unconcerned for the exasperated snort sounded by Mrs. Anson just behind them, waiting for Serena to enter the house before her. "If I didn't know better, Serena, I would say you were trying to get rid of me."

"I am rather tired," she began, not quite meeting his eyes.

"I'm sorry, but we have things to talk about."

"I fail to see—"

"I'm sure you can bring them to mind if you try. And then there's the will. Nathan's attorney will be along presently. He asked me to be here for the reading, since I have an interest in a certain provision it contains."

"You?" Serena sounded as startled as she felt.

"You needn't let it worry you. As I understand it, I'm not a direct beneficiary."

As the implications of that remark struck her, Serena flushed. "Very well," she snapped. "You had better come into the house."

Nathan's attorney was thin and self-effacing, a middle-aged man whose diffident mien made it possible to overlook

361

the sharpness of his eyes. He stared around at the company assembled in the study, adjusted his pince-nez, and cleared his throat. His duty was a sad one. He apologized for intruding so quickly upon the sorrow of the occasion, but it had been his experience that it was best to get the legalities out of the way as soon as possible. He was sure they all, and Mrs Benedict in particular, were anxious to learn how they were placed, as it was difficult to plan the future otherwise.

The document, when read, was simple. It contained a substantial bequest to Mrs. Anson and her daughter, a sizable one for the Negro coachman under his full name of Jackson Lee Grant, and a remembrance to the stableboy. The sum of a million dollars was placed in trust for Sean Benedict, with his mother as joint trustee with the close personal friend of the deceased Ward Dunbar. The great house known as Bristlecone was also to become the property of the minor, Sean Benedict, along with its contents and appurtenances. Serena Walsh Benedict was to have residence privileges there for her lifetime. The management of the property would be a function of the aforesaid trust, with decisions to be made concerning its maintenance and additions to be taken jointly by Serena Benedict and Ward Dunbar, until such time as Sean Benedict reached his majority.

At this point, Serena sent Ward, lounging against the wall at the back of the room, a quick glance. He returned her a mocking bow before she gazed forward again. What had Nathan been thinking of, leaving things in such a way? Was it an attempt, in the event of his death, to square things with Ward for taking her and Sean from him, a macabre bit of matchmaking? If so, it must have been written into the will before Nathan had made his most-recent discoveries.

The remainder of the estate, the lawyer continued, including various holdings in mines, real estate, railroad stock, and other securities, all listed exhaustively, and with a combined value in excess of three million dollars, was bequeathed to Serena Walsh Benedict, her heirs and assigns, forever.

The attorney would leave a set of papers with Mrs. Benedict. If there was anything she didn't understand, or if she should require a fuller accounting at a later, less distraught time, he would be at her service. She might send for him at any time, at her convenience.

The lawyer's careful respect was an indication of how wealthy she had suddenly become. It was a burden of intolerable weight. For Nathan to leave her so much was a parody of justice. If he had never met her, never married her, he would still be alive to enjoy his millions. To have them handed to her was overwhelming; she could not have felt more guilty if she had murdered Nathan for them, if she had in truth plotted with Ward to cause his death.

None of what she felt could be expressed, however. She had to summon a smile, act the hostess over tea, express all the correct sentiments until the gathering had dispersed and the attorney was ready to take his leave. She saw Ward walk with the stooped, graying man to his buggy, their heads together in close conversation. Sighing deeply, she turned from the door and mounted the stairs to her room.

She had not spoken to Ward, not seriously. It was just as well; she had nothing to say to him. Perhaps he had divined that for himself without her having to put it into words. She supposed that someday soon they would have to have this thing out, but not now. Please God, not now.

She had left word that she did not want dinner. Mrs. Anson had not liked that; it upset her routine. How much longer would the woman stay, now that she had enough, if she was careful, to keep herself and her daughter without working?

Serena would miss Dorcas. The girl was under her mother's thumb, and she would never be bright, but she was learning to do things as Serena wished, and even to take pride in her work. She did not chatter, or pry. Her uncomplicated presence could sometimes be comforting, and if her smile was a little vacant, at least it was not a frown.

The girl helped Serena out of her black gown and undid her laces. She ran a hot bath, and while Serena lay soaking, laid out her nightclothes and mended the fire. When Serena emerged, Dorcas picked up the hairbrush and stood waiting beside the dresser bureau.

The slow brushing of her hair was soothing, easing Serena's sense of strain and fatigue. Dorcas would have gone on and on if Serena had not stopped her, but at last the lustrous strands lay over her shoulders in a shining cape, the ends curling slightly about her waist.

"Are you going to bed now, madam?"

"No, not yet. I have a lot of thinking to do, and I may read awhile. Then I may make an early night of it."

"Mama said your lamp was on all night last night, and the night before, too. She said you weren't missing Mr. Benedict, though, not like we are."

"Maybe not, but I didn't know him as long," Serena said gently. "You may go now, Dorcas."

"Can't I get you anything else?" Dorcas placed the brush on the dresser top. "Would you like a glass of warm milk? That's what Mama gives me when I feel bad."

Once laudanum had made her sleep. Was there any in the house? She dismissed the idea with a shake of her head. "No, thank you, Dorcas."

"Shall I help you off with your wrapper?"

Serena glanced down at her cream lace peignoir with its flannel backing and black ribbon tie. In the Regency style, like the gown worn underneath, the fullness of the long skirt fell from a high waist just under her breasts. The scooped neckline had a bertha collar that fell in soft lace ruffles over the wide sleeves. With so much material, it was warm without being heavy. A favorite, it had been Mrs. Anson's idea to give it the touch of black.

"I don't think so," Serena replied. "I believe I'll sit up before the fire."

"Good night, then, madam."

"Good night, Dorcas."

The door closed quietly behind the girl. Serena passed a hand over her eyes. She was exhausted, but not sleepy. She should be, but she wasn't. She hadn't slept in three days, not since they had brought Nathan home to her. She was tired and her eyes were as scratchy as if there was grit under the lids, her arms and legs felt heavy, and the bed with its covers turned back for the night looked inviting, but it was her mind that would not let her rest. It turned endlessly, remembering, sorting, judging, always returning, no matter how she tried to block it, to Ward and his vow to see Nathan, to set her free.

She was free. What now?

The evening advanced. The twilight deepened to darkness. She tried to read, but could not settle to it. She stared out the window, watching the sighing wind moving the trees. She put on the gramophone, playing all the roles one by one, cranking until her arm ached. She buffed the ovals of her nails to a sore and shining pink, then, flinging down the silver-backed buffer, sat rocking, staring into the fire. When she grew stiff from inactivity, she paced up and down the bedroom, her wrapper fluttering around her and her shadow moving across the wall, slipping silent and ghostlike around the room. The weather must be turning warmer, she told herself. The fire felt too hot, suffocating her, taking all the air.

With a soft tread, she left her room to pad along the hall. Her wrapper flowed around her, billowing in the drafts that eddied in that long open space. The hallway was empty of the boxes and trunks that had filled it four days ago. Everything had been put back in its place, Mrs. Anson's antidote for sorrow.

The house was quiet, everyone asleep. Serena stopped outside the nursery, listening. Nothing stirred. There was no sound from the back stair leading to the servants' quarters on the third floor.

Pale as a wraith, she retraced her steps, moving with assurance. She had come to know this house well. She passed the closed door of the room where Nathan had slept. It was still as he had left it, and was likely to remain that way for some time. No matter how long she lived here, or how well she knew Bristlecone, she could not feel she had the right to change his room, dispose of his possessions. She was an interloper. Nothing could change that. Nothing.

The moonlight shone behind the stained glass above the entrance door. Serena kept her wide gaze on the glowing colors as she crept down the main stairs. They had fallen across Ward's face that night, cast by the light of the chandelier in the hall. Red, blue, and gold, they had mottled his features, making him look strange, as if he had been beaten.

She could not go on like this. Perhaps a glass of warm milk would help. Making it would at least give her something to do.

She stopped. There was a faint light in the hallway below, coming from the study. It should not have been left burning. Mrs. Anson was most conscientious about that kind of thing; Serena had never known her to fail to extinguish all lights and lock all the doors and windows.

Her gaze moved to the great front entrance door. It had not been bolted. She hesitated a moment, then moved on down the stairs. Mrs. Anson had been upset. Maybe she hadn't gone to bed yet, after all? Or maybe she had retired early, leaving these tasks to Dorcas? If the girl was used to the responsibility's being her mother's she might have forgotten. Regardless, it had to be seen about. The times were too unsettled for such carelessness.

There was no one in the study. A kerosene lamp with a ball globe over the glass chimney sat on a side table. Serena

365

opened the door into the dining room. It was dark and deserted, nor was there any sound from the butler's pantry beyond.

Serena swung back to the side table and picked up the lamp to light her way down to the kitchen regions. On second thought, she turned in the direction of the hallway. She would lock the entrance door first.

Both hands were going to be needed for the heavy bolt. She set the lamp on the marble bench of the hall tree and stepped toward the door. She was just reaching for the locking mechanism when she heard a scraping sound outside. The door began to open, swinging wide so she had to step quickly out of the way.

There was no time to be frightened. One moment she was alone, the next Ward stood in the open doorway. He stopped still, but if he was surprised to be greeted at the door by an apparition in white, no sign of it appeared on his features. There was about him the freshness of the moon-drenched night. He towered over her, the width of his shoulders blotting out the darkness, his eyes holding the fire of emeralds. Behind her, the lamplight spluttered in the draft, its glow outlining the sweet curves of her body in a white-gold nimbus. The night wind swirled outward with her rose fragrance, moving the folds of her wrapper, catching her dark tresses, blowing them lightly around her arms, wafting them toward him.

"Serena," he breathed.

"What are you doing back here?" she asked, confusion in her eyes, though there was a proud tilt to her chin.

"I never left. I was just taking a look outside. Looks like we're in for a change of weather."

His words were commonplace, but not so the look in his eyes. His presence explained the burning lamp, the unlocked door.

There was strain in her voice as she spoke. "How dare you trespass on the hospitality of this house without invitation?"

"I would dare more than that, Serena love."

"I don't know what you expect to gain!"

"One thing," he answered, his face like a mask. "You."

He stepped inside, taking the door from her nerveless grasp, closing it behind him. There was in his manner, in the finality with which he shut the heavy front panel, a sense of purpose that made her retreat from him. He followed, a grim smile curving one corner of his mouth. She moistened her dry lips with the tip of her tongue. She should say something, but she could not think.

Abruptly, she whirled to run. She was captured before she had taken a second step. His arm clamped around her waist in a circle of iron. He bent and, catching her beneath the knees, lifted her high against his hard chest. She kicked, flailing at him, scratching. He accepted her blows and the tearing of her nails without flinching, as if he did not feel them. Shifting her in his arms to imprison one hand between them, he swung toward the stairs.

"Ward, no!"

He took the steps effortlessly, his only answer the tightening of his grip.

"Put me down or I'll scream."

"By all means, if an audience is what you want."

His voice was deep and steady. The determination in its low timbre sent a shiver along her spine.

"This—this is despicable, unendurable," she said, her voice lower. "I'll loathe you."

"Do you think that will matter, when I know you see me as a cold-blooded killer already?"

She had forgotten. How was it possible? In her wrath and fearful anticipation that image of him had been wiped from her mind. True or not, she could not let his words stand. "No, no I don't."

"Oh, yes. I saw the look on your face when they brought Nathan home, and I'm afraid you do."

The acid irony of his words held her immobile for the length of time it took him to reach the top of the stairs, turn down the upper hall, and stride into her room.

As he kicked the door shut and turned toward the bed, she stiffened, her fingers closing on the collar of his shirt. He paid no heed. With two quick strides, he covered the distance to the paneled bed and dropped her upon the soft, thick mattress.

Serena gave a cry as she fell. Her hold on his collar jerked him off balance for a moment before her grip was broken. The coil springs beneath the bed jounced, creaking in protest. Using their resilience, Serena flung herself away from him, rolling, sliding, uncaring of her gown and wrapper pushing upward, riding high on her thighs. He put one knee on the bed, launching himself after her. His hand closed on her wrapper. The ribbon tie was loose; with a twist she slipped out of it, leaving it in his grasp. Her triumph was short-lived.

Seeing her object, he reached with the other hand, catching the ends of her hair. She was brought up short, half on, half off the mattress.

Ward pushed to a sitting position. Without releasing her hair, he balled her wrapper in one fist and flung it into the corner. His expression watchful behind the screen of his lashes, he wound the long dark strands he held around his hand, drawing her nearer, forcing her back on the bed. The tension on her scalp was warningly taut, but not painful, though it could become so if she fought him. Her breasts rose and fell with her quickened breathing. Her soft lips were parted, and there was the shadow of apprehension she would not admit behind the defiance in her eyes.

He stretched out his fingers to push the sleeve of her gown down her arm, leaving her shoulder and the swell of a breast bare. Leaning, he brushed his lips over their warm, rounded surfaces. She drew back slightly, and he slipped his arm behind her, the corded muscles knotting until she had no choice except to sway toward him once more.

Her heart was pounding. She felt inside the quickening of a treacherous response. He sought her mouth, plundering its sweetness as he drew her closer to lie across his knees. He cupped her breast, his thumb brushing the sensitive peak to tautness. His hand drifted lower, tracing the hollow of her waist and the curve of her hip, settling on her thigh. He pushed the hem of her gown higher, baring her body below the waist. He loosened his fingers from the tangle of her hair, letting it spill over his arm as he pressed her nearer, spreading his hand over her back. The honeyed languor crept along her veins, sapping her resistance, numbing her will. His touch was gentle yet possessive, familiar yet disturbing.

It was the touch of a murderer. Serena wrenched her lips free, arching her back to twist from his hold. On a sobbing gasp, she pushed away, sliding, slithering over the silk and satin crazy quilt. She did not get far. With deliberation, he fastened his grip on her gown, yanking it upward, above her head, imprisoning her arms in its folds. His arm snaked around her waist as he stripped her naked, and with a lithe, heaving roll, he pulled her under him.

She struck out, pummeling him with her fists, and had the satisfaction of hearing his murmured curse as she split his lip against his teeth. He made no attempt to retaliate, but pinned her wrists to the bed, jerking them above her head where he spanned both with the biting steel fingers of

368

one hand. There was the taste of blood from his cut in the bruising pressure of his kiss. Her vulnerability was total, and he took thorough advantage of it, forcing her lips apart, invading her mouth with his tongue. His free hand wandered downward over her body, and she writhed in panting fury under the intimacy of his caresses.

Weighting her to the bed, he kicked off his boots and divested himself of his clothing. The ridged muscles of his thighs pressed into her, communicating the urgency of his desire. His hard fingers closed around the rose-tipped mound of her breast; the wet warmth of his mouth covered it. Serena turned her head from side to side in useless negation, not only of his plundering touch, but of the growing fullness of her loins, the burgeoning ache pervading her that could be assuaged by one thing only.

He pressed his lips to the valley between her breasts. His eyes darkly shadowed, he rose above her, parting her legs. She felt the probing hardness of his manhood, and then the jolting quiver along her nerves as he eased deep inside her.

Her lack of control was debasing; still, she could not stop the tumult that swept in upon her. She could not check the impulse to rise against him, to clutch at his shoulders as her mind slipped its bonds, swinging dizzily to the pulsing of her blood, obeying the primitive prompting to ignore all but the heated surge and flow of the joining. There was nothing but the two of them, male and female, blending, straining together toward oblivion and the sole chance of its conquest, melded in a physical union of supreme transcendence, beyond right or wrong as set forth by puny men. He was a part of her, and she of him. They tumbled on the bed, their mouths locked, their breaths mingling, the firelight gleaming rose red on the glistening play of their bodies, reflecting darkly in their eyes. Recklessly they spent themselves, uncaring of the morrow, holding it at bay as they strove together toward the bright and golden explosion, the magical balm that would ease the soreness of their hearts, move them to the sweet relieving saltiness of compassionate grief, and allow them the wound-binding surcease of dreamless sleep.

Chapter Twenty-two

A light tapping sounded, stopped. It came again, louder this time. Serena turned over onto her back. The calf of her leg encountered the bony hardness of a knee. Her lashes flew upward, and she turned her head to stare into the gold-flecked green eyes of the man beside her.

"Your maid?" Ward asked, his words a breath of sound as he nodded toward the door.

The knocking, of course. Dorcas always brought her morning coffee, but she waited until Serena rang for it. "I don't know."

With a muttered imprecation, Ward heaved himself over and flung back the covers, preparing to step naked from the bed. It was at that moment that Dorcas turned the knob and crept into the room. She opened her mouth to speak, but as her gaze fell on Ward, no words came out. She stood rooted, her gray eyes widening until they seemed to fill her face.

Ward recovered first. His curse was stronger as he whipped the covers back over himself once more.

Amusement bubbled up inside Serena, the first in months. Holding the sheet over the swelling curves of her breasts, she pushed higher on her pillows. Refusing to look at Ward where he sat pressing the quilts down across his waist, sternly repressing a smile, Serena said, "It's all right, Dorcas. What is it you wanted?"

The girl gulped. She fastened her eyes on Serena as if in a desperate effort not to stare at the man beside her. "Mama said I was to say the—the front door was unlatched all night, and that Mr. Dunbar is—is not in his room, and—and what must she do?"

"What did she have in mind, counting the silver?" Ward demanded, his tone irascible.

"Sir?"

"Never mind," Serena said soothingly. "Tell your mother everything is fine."

"Yes, ma'am. Would—would you be wanting your coffee?"

"You may as well bring it."

"Yes, ma'am." The girl bobbed a curtsy and sidled out the door. They heard the quick pad of her feet on the hall rug as she ran toward the back stairs.

Ward grimaced, letting one hand rise and fall in a futile gesture. "I never meant to embarrass you."

"No? Just what did you intend?"

"To stay around just in case."

"In case of what?"

"To protect you, if you needed it."

Serena stared at the clenched fist that rested on his knee. "You certainly found an odd way to go about it."

The corner of his mouth tugged upward. "It worked, didn't it? You're safe."

"That all depends on how you look at it," she answered, a frown forming between her eyes still dark with sleep.

"If you are expecting an apology for that, too, don't. I'm not sorry."

For some reason she did not care to analyze, Serena found that answer reasonable, even satisfactory. She looked away to the Renaissance dresser with its tall, pedimented mirror. She and Ward were reflected in its diamond-dust clarity, something Ward had already discovered, she found, as she met his gaze in the glass.

Serena transferred her stare to the black ashes of the fireplace where the fire had burned down hours ago. "Did you really think there was any danger?"

"I don't know," he said slowly. "Something about your Mormon elder bothers me. There have always been pulpit denunciations of the red-light district. What's different about Greer is his approach. It's not him so much as the kind of people he may stir up. There's a certain type of man who just might think it good fun to take a whip after a woman, especially if he had the company and approval of a crowd."

"A whip—you mean the elder's scourge of the Lord?"

"That, or a knife—or a piece of rope, or hay wire. They all qualify."

Boots, the crib girl who had been Consuelo's friend, had been strangled with hay wire. "On the other hand, such streetcorner sermons might trigger the urge for revenge in a man, if he had something against women of the lamplight, who might prefer to do the job alone."

"The possibility had occurred to me, especially since the elder singled you out for special attention."

"Who? Who could it be? I thought before Otto—before I killed him that he might be the one, but there's been another girl murdered since then."

"Otto was never that smart. This man is either cunning, or extremely lucky. He's given no one a close enough look to recognize him—except the dead women."

A shiver ran over Serena. "It's horrible to think about. Still, they happened, all those deaths. Someone has got to think about it."

Ward reached for the top quilt, pulling it up over her shoulder. "Not you, and not now. Let it go. I may be wrong; there may be no connection whatever."

He climbed out of bed and, finding his trousers, stepped into them. Shirtless and barefooted, he moved to the fireplace hearth and knelt to kindle a fire. Serena watched him, watched the play of the muscles across his broad back, the easy competence of his movements, the quick, impatient way he raked back the unruly lock of dark-brown hair that fell over his forehead. Against her will, the memory of what had taken place between them the night before stole into her mind. She was depraved; she must be. How else could she find pleasure in this man's arms? Why else would she allow perilous desire to make her forget what he was, and what he had done? What flaw was it in her character that made her respond so passionately to the touch of a man who had killed another? To what depths of degradation would it lead her, to what terrible sacrifice of dignity, pride, and hope?

"You said you wanted to talk to me," Serena said, her tone abrupt. "What about?"

He was a long time in answering as he broke brittle sticks of kindling wood in his strong hands. "I'm not sure it was a good idea."

"Why? Because you think you can get what you want without it?"

For a moment he was still, then he snapped a stick of pine with the sound of a gunshot. "Because," he said deliberately, "I don't think it will do any good."

Serena took a deep breath. "It was about Nathan's death, wasn't it?"

"Not entirely."

"I—I don't know what you expect me to think. You were there at the mine that afternoon, I know you were."

"I don't deny that. But I never got to see Nathan privately. He was busy with the hoist; it was all he wanted to talk about. There were people around. He said we would go into his office as soon as he had run that crucial test, as soon as he had gone down in his precious cage."

Another twig snapped. Ward kept his back turned to her. She frowned in concentration. "Do you expect me to believe that, after your threat to—see that Nathan freed me? And there's one other thing that troubles me," she went on recklessly. "It seems a strange coincidence that years ago in Natchez a friend of yours died under peculiar circumstances, and you wound up with his wife, while now the same pattern has repeated itself."

Ward reached to take a lucifer from the holder on the mantel, struck it, and held its yellow flame to the pitch pine. It caught, flaring into life, the light of the flames flickering over his bronzed torso. He shook out the match and tossed it onto the carefully stacked wood. Only then did he speak.

"I will have to admit you have reason for suspicion."

"Is that all you have to say?"

He got to his feet and turned slowly to face her, his feet apart and his hands on his hips. "I told you what happened. What else is there?"

"I don't know," Serena said, her tone a little wild, "but there must be something that will make me believe you."

"If there was, I would say it," he told her, his eyes dark as he surveyed the pale oval of her face and the tumbled glory of her hair trailing over her shoulders. "It looks as if this is something you will have to accept on trust."

Serena watched him, an arrested expression in her pewter-blue eyes. Trust. It was a word she had used to him not so long ago when he had spoken of complete possession, which might have been a euphemism for love.

Her mind shifted to another occasion, to a time she had

misjudged him. Abruptly she said, "Nathan told me you didn't take his bribe, the money he offered you to allow him a clear field, neither at the time, nor last summer."

His face tightened. "I owe him that much then."

"To balance that," she went on as if he had not spoken, "I must remember, is your threat to turn me over to the sheriff if I failed to give you what you wanted. How can I trust a man who could drive so callous a bargain?"

A suspended look came into his eyes, as though he were debating the advisability of the answer he wanted to make. The moment passed; however, an odd lightness remained in his expression. He moved his shoulders in a gesture of resignation. "Stalemated, then."

Before she could reply, the door opened inward, thrown wide as Mrs. Anson swept into the room. Her cold gaze took in Serena in bed with the quilt slipping from her bare shoulders, Ward standing half dressed before the fire, and the discarded clothing that lay on the rug beside the bed, or straggled over its footboard.

"I could not believe my ears when Dorcas told me," the housekeeper announced. "I was certain she had made some ridiculous mistake. I see I was wrong."

A black frown drew Ward's brows together. He glanced at Serena. "I understood this woman was housekeeper here?"

"I am," Mrs. Anson said, her bosom swelling as she took up the challenge. "I was with Mr. Benedict for ten years and kept house for him at Bristlecone for the past three. He was a dear, sweet man, and a more generous and considerate employer than you would ever hope to meet, and I am scandalized by this desecration of his home."

"I think you will do well to remember, Mrs. Anson, that he is dead."

"How can I forget? How could anyone, with him not in his grave a day? It is past belief to see his widow, the woman he loved, consorting with her lover under his roof before he is even cold!"

"The woman you are speaking of," Ward said softly, "is now your mistress."

"That may be, but I would consider myself failing in my duty if I didn't try to bring her to some sense of propriety."

"Even if it costs you your job?"

The housekeeper looked from Ward to Serena and back again. "Who are you to interfere, and what do you mean by

374

threatening me?" she demanded, her tone a trifle less assured.

"Sometimes," Ward said, his eyes narrowed, "a threat is enough."

Serena flung him a quick glance before she intervened. "If you will remember, Mrs. Anson, Mr. Dunbar is involved with the trust which holds this house in ownership for my son, and as such, he is concerned with the management."

It was obvious from the flush that rose to the woman's face that she had forgotten. That did not prevent her from giving a sniff of disdain.

"Your loyalty to Mr. Benedict is admirable," Serena went on, "but as Mr. Dunbar pointed out, you are no longer in his employ. It would distress me to have to let you go, but if you can't be happy here, that may be the best course."

"That won't be necessary," Mrs. Anson said grandly. "Thanks to poor Mr. Benedict, I have no need to slave here another day! You may consider this my notice. I will not require a character reference from you. My daughter and I will be out of the house by noon."

Behind her there was a crash. Dorcas stood in the hall beyond the open door, the coffee service of Delft blue china in shards at her feet.

A look of annoyance crossed the housekeeper's face, but she moved toward her daughter, stepping majestically over the debris. "Come, Dorcas," she said and, collecting the white-faced girl, swept off in the direction of the servants' quarters.

A rueful look crossed Ward's face. "Too bad about the coffee."

"I suppose you know this means you will get no breakfast," Serena informed him, flouncing a little as she raised herself higher in the bed.

"I'm not hungry," he answered, admiring the results of the lowered quilt.

"Or lunch!"

"You offered to cook for me once," he reminded her.

"That was before I acquired a kitchen like the catacombs of Rome."

"What do you know about the catacombs?"

"I saw them once on a stereopticon slide. Besides, I have another mouth to feed, Mary, Sean's nurse."

"I expect we can find something for today. After that, I have an idea for a replacement."

She stared at him in suspicion. "Do you now? Do I know her."

"I don't believe you've met."

"You relieve me," she answered, her tone dry. "At least I can be reasonably certain she doesn't come from the Eldorado."

"You can."

"And what am I to do for a maid?"

He raised a brow. "You sound as if you are ready to blame this on me, too. I distinctly remember you being the one to mention that ironclad battleship's leaving."

"Only to keep you from doing it for me!"

"I will admit to some responsibility, mainly because I could see that you were speechless. That being the case, I will take on the job."

"Which job?" Serena asked, disliking the gleam in his eyes, uncertain of where this conversation had led her.

"As your maid, of course."

"Of course," she said faintly.

He moved to shut the door, turning the key in the lock. "Shall I begin by helping you dress?"

Serena watched his advance with trepidation. "That's— all right. You can put your own clothes on first."

"If I did that, you might expect me to leave, and then who would protect you from your housekeeper?"

"I don't need any protection."

"That's what you think."

His words sounded very much as if he meant his stay with her to be permanent. The arrogance of it, the unmitigated arrogance! The impulse to request that he leave the house hovered on her tongue. One thing that kept it from being spoken was the suspicion that it would be futile; the other was the purposeful way he was advancing upon her.

"Ward," she began uncertainly.

"Yes, Serena?"

"May you be damned, Ward Dunbar," she told him, her fingers tightening on the sheet as she watched the slow removal of his trousers.

"It's more than likely, darling Serena," he said as he joined her in the bed. "Much more than likely."

It was the next day before Ward went into town. In his absence, Serena sent for the mine superintendent of the Century Lode. She had thought long and hard about her ownership of the mine and her other holdings. Many of her conclusions were influenced by her father's long years as a laborer, and his views on the benefits to be derived from treating workers fairly. She had combined these attitudes with much she had learned from Ward and Nathan at different times in their talks, and with her own feelings on the subject. She was ready to make a few changes, some her own, some that Nathan had intended. And then there was the problem of the hoist. It was blocking the shaft at the present time. Something was going to have to be done about it.

When Superintendent Boston arrived, she served coffee she had made herself, then, perched on the edge of her chair in her mourning, she outlined what she wanted done. First, there would be an increase in wages to three-fifty per day. Following that, she meant to institute a form of old-age pension, with provisions for those disabled in mine accidents. Then, she wanted to set a minimum age for workers in her mines at sixteen; she wanted no child laborers, not even driving the burros and mules that pulled the ore cars. Speaking of the latter, she was convinced it was the greatest cruelty to keep them underground in the dark tunnels until they became blind. She understood that it was too much effort to haul them up and down the shafts, but surely it couldn't cost any great amount to keep a lamp or two burning in their holding pens? After that, she wanted land set aside for a corral where the animals could be pastured and fed when they had outlived their usefulness, instead of being turned loose to scavenge as best they could, finally dying of starvation.

The superintendent was a kindly man. He set out to tell her about a mule in one of the mines called Big Red who had been a favorite of the miners, picking up their bad habits like dipping snuff. He would come up to a man and hold out his lower lip, waiting to have it filled from a snuffbox. He preferred Garretts, but would take anything he could get.

Even as Serena smiled at the tale, she had the feeling it was a smokescreen, something for the superintendent to say while he took time to think. At last, she put it to the test. "You haven't said what you think of the new wages and benefits."

The man turned his hat in his hands, then reached up to scratch his head before he looked at Serena. "There's no question it would all be gratefully received by the miners, Mrs. Benedict, or that the Century Lode could afford what you have set out to do. The problem is the other mine owners. They settled all this not too long back by going through a strike that nearly came to war. They fixed things up the way they wanted them, and got rid of a lot of radicals in the process. They're not going to take kindly to your stirring everything up again."

"Even if it's fair, even if they can afford it as well as I can?"

"They say if you ever give an inch, the miners'll take a mile. There's something in that, too. If the worker demands ever get so high they interfere with a mine's profits, well, there won't be any use of a businessman laying out his capital to put a mine into production, will it? Not many men can swing the stake it takes to do that job alone. And then, it takes a lot of ore being brought out of a mine, better than a ton of hard rock from most, to get a hundred dollars in gold. If you have to pay too much to have it hauled out and smelted down, why, the amount a mine owner can make won't be worth the worry and outlay. He'll just have to close down. If that happens, where will the miners be? Out of a job, that's where."

"I see that, but surely the miners wouldn't push for so much? Surely they will have the sense to understand the consequences?"

"You'd think so, wouldn't you, ma'am? But people are just not overly understanding of other people's problems when it comes to money. They never wrote that fairy tale about killing the goose that laid the golden egg for nothing."

His allegory was too apt not to be recognized. Serena nodded, a smile in her blue-gray eyes. "Nevertheless, I don't think I am being unreasonable. If the other mine owners don't want to go along, that's their choice. Not all the mines in the district have the same pay scale, do they?"

"No, ma'am."

"This is the middle of April. I think we can put the new guidelines into effect by the first of next month."

"If you're sure that's what you want. I wish you would talk to some of the other big men in Cripple Creek first. I sure wish you would do that."

"If I did," Serena said softly, "they would try to dissuade me, and I see no reason why I should allow anyone to dictate my policies. The mine—and its proceeds—belongs to me, to do with as I see fit."

378

"As you say, ma'am." The man's voice was stiff, but he said no more.

"There is one other problem: the hoist."

"I wasn't going to mention it to you, Mrs. Benedict, things being as they are, but since you brought it up, I'm sure glad."

"I—I don't suppose anyone else has tried to go down in it?"

"No, ma'am!"

"I see. What do you suggest be done about it, then?"

"I don't know, I really don't. That's just not my field. Young Patterson has been moping around the contraption, testing this and that, his face as long as a mule's. He's the man that might could tell you what went wrong, and what, if anything, can be done about setting it right."

"Could you have him come to see me?"

"Certainly, I'll be glad to do that. Later on, maybe you'd like to talk to the bookkeeper, take a gander at just where you are according to the figures?"

"I'd like that, yes."

"Fine. I expect you'd rather he came here for the time being, but later on we'd be honored to have you visit us and poke around, maybe even go down the shaft. I know it's not my place to be inviting you, you being the owner and all, but I want you to know you'll be welcome."

Serena thanked him. The superintendent got up to leave. "By the way," she said, her head tilted to one side. "Are you familiar with a mine in production around here owned by Ward Dunbar?"

"Yes, ma'am. It's a fine producer, the Eldorado II."

"As good as the Century Lode?"

"Every bit. Rumors are they've taken better than a million out since last summer, and look to have another two, or even three, by the end of the year."

"How long has it been in operation?"

"It was started—let's see, must have been the fall of '94, but didn't really get rolling until they found a good rich vein last August or September. Funny thing about that; Dunbar had given up on it and gone out looking for a better prospect when it came in. Stayed gone a long time, and came back to find himself and his backers all rolling in cash."

Serena, a little pale, nodded her comprehension, and then moved with him toward the front hallway.

In the door, the superintendent paused. "There was quite a few thought Mr. Benedict was balmy, leaving you in control of the mine and everything, ma'am, meaning no disrespect. They said the whole operation would go to pot in a month. Now me, I don't think so. I think everything's going to be just fine, provided we can weather this wage and pension business. One thing sure. The two of us are going to get along like a house afire. I do admire a person, man or woman, who can make up their mind."

He took the hand she offered in a callused grip, clamped his hat on his head, and strode from the house. Looking after him, Serena shook her head and, smiling, closed the door.

She did not have to see her own visitors from the house for long. True to his words, Ward found a new housekeeper. She arrived on the evening train two days after the departure of Mrs. Anson and Dorcas. With her was a familiar face, that of Mrs. O'Hare from the boardinghouse in Colorado Springs where Ward had taken her so many months before. The new housekeeper was Mrs. O'Hare's sister from St. Louis. Recently widowed, Mrs. Egan was childless, with no way to support herself. She had been living on her older sister's charity until Mr. Dunbar's telegraph message reached them. It would be lovely to be earning her own way. She had never been a housekeeper before, except for her own dear departed husband, of course; still, she was sure she would soon fall into the way of it. The sight of that kitchen fairly made her itch to get started; running water, would wonders never cease? And all that lovely beef and the chickens already dressed, to say nothing of that beautiful slab of nice, cold marble for rolling pastry. What would Mrs. Benedict like for dinner? They really should have the chickens; it was so warm today they might spoil, even if they had been packed in snow.

Mrs. O'Hare, having seen her sister hard at it, and enjoyed a comfortable chat with Serena and a blatant, laughing flirtation with Ward, took the Midland back to the Springs. Before she left, however, she took Serena aside.

"I've told my sister Maureen how things are between you and Ward."

"Did you? I wish you would tell me," Serena said, the look in her eyes sparkling.

"Go on with you! What I mean to say is, you needn't fear any airs and scenes from her because the two of you aren't married yet. She understands. Being a recent widow herself, she knows that some marriages were just not meant, but that

380

a decent time has to be passed anyway, before setting out on the sea of matrimony again."

"Oh, but Mrs. O'Hare—"

"Now, I will admit I had hard feelings toward you when you upped and married Nathan Benedict, instead of Ward, but that's neither here nor there. I just want to say I'm glad you've come to your senses and decided to make Ward happy. The dear Lord knows, he deserves it."

"If by that you mean marriage, he hasn't asked me, not since Nathan died."

"Give him time, child, give him time. No finer man ever lived. He'll do the right thing by you, I know he will."

There was no point in arguing, no point in telling her what she suspected her fine man had done. It was best to smile and agree, and ignore the ache in the region of her heart.

Three days later, Patterson, the engineer, put in an appearance at last. He seemed nervous and ill at ease. Serena received him in the study, where she had been going over some of Nathan's papers. At Mrs. Egan's suggestion that she serve the young gentleman tea, Serena nodded, then indicated a chair for her guest.

They exchanged a few commonplaces about the unseasonably warm weather, the way the wind was drying everything out, then moved on to the continuing growth of the mining district and the price of gold. The last subject led to the production of the Century Lode and, naturally, to the hoist that was preventing operation.

The engineer clasped his narrow hands between his knees, leaning forward in his chair with a frown. "There's something I have to tell you about the hoist and cage, Mrs. Benedict. You may not like it, but you have to be told."

Serena felt the blood leave her face. Had this man discovered the mechanism had been tampered with, did he know who had done it, and why?

He took a deep breath, glanced at her, then looked away again. "I'm sorry, Mrs. Benedict, but I have to tell you that I'm to blame for your husband's death."

In the stillness they could hear the wind outside and Mrs. Egan singing to herself in the butler's pantry as she set out the tea service.

"You?" Serena whispered.

The engineer gave a miserable nod. "I allowed Mr. Benedict to talk me into letting him go ahead with the installation of the hoist. I let myself be convinced that I could give instructions about the way it should be set up from my bed at the hotel. It was a mistake."

"You were ill, weren't you?" Serena said. Her voice sounded strange. She jumped a little as she heard the front door open and shut, followed by footsteps on the stairs. That would be Ward, returning from town. He had not stayed at the Eldorado during the late afternoon and evening since he had come to Bristlecone, though he usually went into town every morning.

"I was ill, under a doctor's care, but that's no excuse. I should have insisted on being there, insisted on seeing that everything was done properly. If I had, if I had seen to my job, nothing would have happened."

"Are you saying it was a—a mechanical problem, something you can definitely identify?"

"That's right."

He went into a detailed explanation that meant little, though it seemed to give him comfort to tell her. Serena listened with her hands clenched on the arms of her chair. When he had finished, she leaned toward him. "Are you positive that the hoist didn't fall because someone—interfered with its working?"

"Oh, no, Mrs. Benedict. That couldn't have happened, not at all. I know because I got out of bed especially to be present for the final test. I was standing not six feet away from the controls when the accident took place."

The tears rose, shimmering in her eyes, spilling over her lashes to trace down her face. Bending her head made them run faster. Serena fumbled for her handkerchief.

"Mrs. Benedict, I'm sorry," the engineer said, horror in his voice. "I didn't mean to upset you. Please?"

She blew her nose, breathing deep against the sudden sense of release. "No, no, it's all right. I—I don't blame you, Mr. Patterson, not now, or for the accident. It seems the fault must have been my husband's for being so impatient. You mustn't punish yourself for what you could not help. I know how Mr. Benedict was when he—when he wanted something."

They had their tea. Over it, they both calmed enough for Patterson to venture an opinion on salvaging the hoist. It could be done. There was no doubt the machinery would work as it was intended once it was properly put together. The

Century Lode would be the first to have this new and modern innovation, just as Nathan had planned.

When the engineer had gone, Serena sat alone. So Ward was not guilty. None of the terrible things she had thought and accused him of were true. He had not deserted her for money, he was not battening on her because she was a wealthy and available widow, had not killed Nathan. How could she have been so wrong? Had she wanted to think the worst? Was that it? Had she used her false judgment of him as a shield, to prevent herself from being hurt by the way he had treated her? The evidence had been there, or so she had thought. To have all her theories disproved gave her an odd, bereft feeling. She did not know what to think, or what she would say to Ward when she saw him.

In the event, she said little that mattered. She ascended the stairs with slow footsteps. Ward was not in his room, nor was he in hers. The door of the nursery stood open, and Serena turned in that direction.

Inside the room, she stopped. Ward stood in the evening dimness with his hands braced on the foot of the baby's cradle. He stared down at the cooing, smiling child with softness limning his features, though there was a shadow in the deep green of his eyes. He turned his head, as he became aware of her presence. Straightening, he reached to lay the tips of his fingers along Sean's rounded cheek, and pull the long dress down over his kicking feet. Ward was still an instant, then he turned away, moving toward Serena. As Sean began to cry, Mary materialized out of the shadows to pick him up, holding him close against her.

"Does she think I would harm my own child?" Ward asked, running a hand over his hair in a gesture of weariness.

"If Mary thought so, she wouldn't have stood back out of the way. She doesn't know you very well, and so she's protective."

"She won't have to worry about it any more. I'm leaving."

Serena stopped in the middle of the hall. "You're what?"

"Coming here was the wrong thing to do; I should have known better. Instead of protecting you, I just gave the gossips, and your demented elder, something more to talk about."

"Is that—the only reason?" Serena had to force the words to her lips. She had not been particularly welcoming, quite the opposite.

"No, it isn't. There are all sorts of rumors floating around

383

town about the changes you have made at the Century Lode. It's the general feeling of the mine owners that either you are being unduly influenced by me, since the reforms you are instituting are substantially the same as those I've established at my own mine, or else you are just playing at being a mine owner and there's no need to take anything you do seriously."

"Are the things I've done similar to yours? I didn't know."

"I'm aware of that, since you didn't see fit to discuss it with me."

"I didn't know you would be interested."

He shook his head. "It would be more accurate to say you were afraid I would take over, wouldn't it? But never mind. You didn't discuss it with the other mine owners either, conduct they consider irresponsible, but to be expected from a woman who takes a man into her bed so soon after her husband's death."

Serena sent him a cold look. "I had no choice."

"They don't know that. I assume they will take notice if you throw me out."

"It makes no difference to me what they think," Serena snapped.

"Maybe not now, but it will when Sean gets older, when he starts school and begins to join the other sons of the rich."

"That will be a long time yet. Just now, I don't care. It may not suit me to throw you out; it may not suit me at all!"

He stared at her, the flecks of gold in his eyes shining bright. For an instant she thought he would reach for her, drag her close into his arms. She swayed toward him.

Abruptly the light in his face was quenched. "In this case, as in the other," he said, his voice rough, "you have no choice."

He swung and walked away from her.

"Ward," she cried.

The only answer was the sound of his footsteps on the stairs, and the closing of the door.

Chapter Twenty-three

He was gone. It was incredible how empty the house had become. It seemed Ward Dunbar had made his impression on Bristlecone just as quickly and completely as he had upon her heart. Why had he left so abruptly? The question revolved in her head for two days, along with the excuses he had given. What it all came to was, he had left for the sake of her reputation. If that was so, if that was the real reason, there was an easy cure. He could have married her. No such offer had been forthcoming. Apparently he did not care enough for that, not now. She had lost the chance to become something more than his bedmate.

So be it. With so much between them, it was unlikely they could have found happiness. She was just as well off without him. She would get along fine, just fine. She was a wealthy woman, independently wealthy. She needed no one, least of all a man who hugged his secrets to his chest, suffering all manner of misconceptions to be placed at his door rather than compromise his pride.

Damn the man! How dare he leave her just when she was ready to absolve him of guilt? The least he could have done was to hear her out, let her make her apology. What did he mean by consigning her to this state of frustration? It was maddening. Sooner or later, they would have to have this out between them.

Later, rather than sooner. She did not trust herself to speak calmly just yet; she was by no means sure she could be properly contrite. Outside, it was so warm and beguiling, almost like a Southern spring. She would drive into town to Serenity House and see how it was progressing. She would spend some time with the nuns, and possibly stop to visit with Consuelo. But she would not, under any circumstances, turn in the direction of Myers Avenue and the Eldorado.

The Sisters of Mercy were delighted to see her. They displayed the new babies, three in number, who had joined the nursery. There was so much love and pride in their manner one could have been forgiven for wondering if divine dispensation might not have had something to do with their presence, rather than immorality and vice.

Serena was persuaded to stay for luncheon, and over the meal, met four of the young women who now occupied the upstairs bedrooms. One was the wife of a miner who had been killed, a woman left destitute with three small children and no relatives closer than a thousand miles away. The nuns were anxious to be certain that Serena's charitable impulses extended to providing the woman's fare back to her people. The others were not so easily helped. There were two Myers Avenue girls far gone in pregnancy who looked to be ready to swell the numbers in the nursery any day. They were grateful for the aid given them, but had every intention of returning to the dance halls when they had given birth. The last woman was in her early thirties, though she looked to be seventy. She was a victim of syphilis in the advanced stages. Partially paralyzed, and with extensive brain damage, she insisted on coming to the table. The other women avoided her, despite the assurances of the nuns that she was not contagious. The kind sisters seemed to think she might be a thought-provoking influence for the others, but if so, there was no sign of it.

Serena was not in the highest of spirits when she finally left Serenity House. There was so much human misery, and so little one person could do to relieve it. She was trying, but nothing the nuns could say in praise of her efforts thus far could make her feel that she was making any headway.

Consuelo was not at home. Serena tooled her rig around the block and started out of town. It was a disappointment to miss her friend. Consuelo must be nearly ready to depart from the district; there was no longer anything to hold her here. Serena would miss her sorely. For all her volatile temperament, there was something firm and dependable about the Spanish girl, and it appeared their situations were going to be much the same in the long days ahead. Though it was doubtless selfish of her, Serena wished Consuelo could be persuaded to stay. They would be two women without men, taking care of small children, neither of Myers Avenue any longer, nor yet of the other side of town bounded by Carr and Eaton avenues. They could support each other, form a bulwark against all the others that were ranged against them.

Serena was nearly at the bridge over the creek when she saw a buggy coming toward her from the direction of Bristlecone. A woman was on the driver's seat, a woman in black. As she recognized Consuelo, Serena reined in, waiting for the buggy to come abreast. She smiled, calling a greeting as Consuelo pulled up.

"Thanks be to *Dios* I have found you," the Spanish girl said. "I was so afraid I would be too late."

"What is it? What's the matter?"

"It's that crazy one, Pearlie. She has been wild, like a rabid animal, since Ward moved in with you. But this time she has decided that instead of trying to kill herself, she would much rather see you dead!"

"She can save herself the trouble. Ward is no longer with me." Serena met the other girl's dark eyes, though it was an effort to keep the curve of her mouth steady.

"I didn't know. I'm sorry, Serena, but I doubt it will make any difference. Things have gone too far."

"I don't understand."

"You know that the elder who shouts after you in the streets is a visitor of Pearlie's? It seems she has been listening to him, and has decided he is right; you should be punished for your wickedness. She does not depend on the good God to do it for her, however. She has acted herself to see that it will be done. She has hired men; drunks, petty thieves, bullyboys, the scum of Myers Avenue. As a part of their payoff, she gave them the run of her parlor house. One of the men bragged to the woman he was with, and she came to me because she remembered well your kindness when she was at the Eldorado, and thought this a fate you did not deserve."

"But what is it they are supposed to do? Surely the sheriff will stop them?"

"There won't be time. They are gathered now, shouting and listening to this Elder Greer as he spreads his poison on the streetcorners. Soon they will march. They chose this time

387

of day because few people are about; the day shift is in the mines, the night shift sleeping, as well as the rest of the people in that part of town. They have been told to march to Bristlecone and set fire to it over your head. Then they are to take you out and strip you, and when they have had what fun they will, give you a costume of tar and feathers and set your feet on the path out of Cripple Creek."

The color drained from Serena's face. "Dear God."

"Exactly so," the Spanish girl said, her face grim. "Of course, if you do not survive such rough treatment, as many don't who are subjected to the tar at melting heat, then that will not concern Pearlie."

"They—they can't do such a thing," Serena breathed. "Not here in broad daylight."

"They can, and they will, if we don't do something to stop them. Already, much time has been lost." A thoughtful look came into her face. "What you tell me of Ward, that is the key."

"What do you mean?"

"It occurs to me that Pearlie knows he will not be with you when the mob comes. Ward's being at Bristlecone must be the only reason she has not sent her hired men after you before now. She knows Ward would try to protect you, and she has no wish to see him come to harm."

That made sense. Serena nodded. "But what am I to do? Sean is at Bristlecone with only Mary and Mrs. Egan in the house. If I go back, it may lead the men to where they can hurt him, but if I don't, they may go there anyway."

Consuelo frowned. "It's possible Ward is the only one who can help. If we can reach him before this group of madmen set out, he will be able to persuade, or force, Pearlie to call a halt."

"Will that work?" Serena said doubtfully.

"These men may pretend to be fired by the righteous wrath of the Mormon, but it is the money and the sport that attracts them. If these things are removed, they will go about their business."

"What if Ward won't do it?" To Serena, the whole thing was without reality. She could not make herself believe it.

"Are you demented? Of course he will! He loves you, he adores you until it is a sickness with him. If anything happens to you, he will tear this town apart."

"I think I would prefer the sheriff," Serena said, her lips stiff.

"No, and no, idiot girl! Do you not realize how your name has been blackened? The sheriff may well decide it is no part of his duty to risk his life for such a one. The ladies of society are against you for daring to come among them; their husbands, the mine owners, are ready to believe anything of you. And there is Pearlie telling lies, starting whispers that you are a scheming hussy who has arranged matters so she can have her cake and eat it too, meaning that you had something unnamed to do with the death of your husband. The stories grow and grow, until half the town is ready to think you a monster, while the other half swears you are a saint, and all are none too sure that you do not have the powers over men of a witch. They love and hate you, envy and despise you, and there are few who would not be more comfortable if you were somewhere else—or dead."

"You frighten me, Consuelo."

"Good! It's time, and past. We cannot sit here talking all day. Will you go to Ward, or not?"

Serena glanced along the road that led to Bristlecone, a faraway look in her blue-gray eyes. Then she gave a decisive nod. "Let's go," she said, and began to turn her horses.

If Consuelo had been to Bristlecone and back without incident, Pearlie's hired bullies must still be in town, still be on Myers Avenue being harangued by Elder Greer. Would it be better to take the shortest route to the Eldorado, along the main streets, or to take the back streets and hope to avoid them? Consuelo turned off on the more circuitous route that would bring them to the back of the barroom, the way Serena had taken so often for her clandestine meetings with Ward.

It was a mistake. With more caution than might have been expected, the mob had also opted for the back streets. They came surging down the narrow lane, a solid wall of humanity, blocking it from side to side. Some were on horseback, some piled into wagons, while others trotted along like hunting dogs behind. They brandished their fists, and shouted obscenities, their open mouths like wounds in their bearded faces, their hats pulled low, hiding the bloodlust in their eyes.

"That's her!" came a cry. "There she is! Git 'er, boys! Don't let the bitch get away!"

Consuelo did the only thing possible. She shouted and whipped up her horses, turning down a sidestreet. Serena followed. The houses flashed past. The Eldorado was only a dozen blocks, or less, away.

Behind them came the men, yelling, cursing, clamoring, making a demented roaring that terrified the horses and caused Serena's heart to beat with sickening thuds.

And then there were horsemen on either side of her, surrounding her phaeton, reaching for the bridles of her horses, jeering as they ripped the reins from her hands. Ahead of her, Consuelo slowed, pulling in. The men began to gain on her.

"No!" Serena shouted. "Go on, Consuelo, go on!"

"I'll be back!" the Spanish girl screamed above the noise, her voice shrill with rage and fear.

Serena barely heard her. She was caught in a nightmare. Elder Greer leaned from a horse to thrust his face close to hers. His silver eyes glittered and his breath was sour as he bellowed at her, his words nearly lost in the whooping and bawling around them. "Your time is at hand, O wicked wanton! Repent and prepare for your doom!"

Hands clutched, tearing at her, pulling her this way and that on the carriage seat. Her purse was torn from her hands before she could reach her pistol, almost before she could remember it. The sleeve was ripped from her gown. Fingers tore at her bodice, shredding it in a sparkling torrent of bouncing, scattering black jet beads. She broke free, coming to her feet with the carriage whip in a white-knuckled grasp. She flailed around her with it, her teeth clenched tight as she brought it down in fierce gladness for the yelps of pain she caused. The grays reared and backed, wall-eyed with terror, and men squalled and groaned, cursing as they were trampled or their feet squashed under the wheels.

"Git 'er, ye fools!" came the yelled command, and a man lunged up over the wheel, catching the whip, wrenching it from Serena's hand. Her skirt was grabbed, jerked, and she toppled. With a despairing scream, she fell among them, into the clawing, uplifted hands. The grays bolted, dragging the empty, bouncing phaeton away down the street.

Her hat was snatched from her head, tearing a lock of hair from her scalp as the long steel hatpin held. Her hairpins loosened and were scattered, allowing her hair to slide down her back, whipping into her face as she writhed and twisted. She gasped in pain, too winded to scream as the black crepe of her widow's weeds was torn from her, and she felt herself pinched and pummeled and squeezed. Nails rasped burningly along her arms and thighs. Her breasts and hips were grasped. Her head spun as she was thrown here and there, pulled from one pair of arms to another. She felt dirty and defiled, her body a solid ache, her mind receding as she heard the chanted litany of the elder's hate, his frenzied raving of women stoned for adultery, torn and devoured by dogs, scourged with whips.

And then there was a quieting. She was set on her feet, forced to turn, pushed into a circle of men with gleaming eyes and mouths wet with anticipation. She staggered, caught herself, crossed her arms over her bare breasts. She wore only her corset and those rags of her petticoat that could not be ripped away because their fastenings were beneath her whalebone stays. She shook back her hair there in the blazing afternoon sun, and it cascaded down her back to her hips, shining and silken, vibrant in contrast to the dazed look in her shadowed eyes.

There came the shattering, explosive crack of a wielded whip. Serena jerked her head up to face Elder Greer. He stood inside the circle, a little apart from the others. There was in his face an exalted madness mixed with the ecstasy of passion.

"Now it's your turn, Serena," he said, his silver eyes gloating as they scanned her nakedness. "I have you at my mercy, like all the others. The punishment I meted out to them shall be yours, only a hundredfold greater, a chastisement without end, until you beg for mercy, or death."

The others. So he must have looked, the thought ran through Serena's mind, when he had killed the other women of Myers Avenue, when he had relieved himself upon their bodies, then murdered and mutilated them. Or had they been mutilated first, dying in a welter of their own blood and the fluids of this man's body? In the state of detached horror she had reached, the question, and the truth to which she had so suddenly penetrated, had little real meaning.

"Yea, the time is at hand," the elder intoned as he coiled the supple leather of the whip around his hands, the keen lash of her own carriage whip. "If you had come to me as my wife, you would have been spared this, but you chose the path of wickedness, and now must pay the price. Look on me and know your fate!"

The gray-haired Mormon nodded at a man on either side of her, and her arms were grasped, pulled behind her, baring her chest. The elder flung his arm back, letting the whip trail back along the ground, then a spasm crossed his face and he brought his arm up and down. The thong of the limber lash

391

reached for her, snaking over her arm and shoulder, its whir-ring crack exploding at her ear. Searing agony leaped inside her, spreading in waves. A red welt appeared, running over her shoulder and down to the swell of her breast. She bit down on her lip, bringing blood, but she made no sound. Again, she writhed under the lash, and yet again. A scream gathered in her throat. She twisted her wrists, fighting the hands that held her. A red haze appeared before her eyes, through which she could see the elder bringing the whip back once more.

Where was Consuelo? In the blinding anguish that gripped her, the soft insidious thought came seeping into her mind that of all those in Cripple Creek, the Spanish girl had more reason than any to hate her. It was possible Consuelo had never meant her to evade Pearlie's hired mob, had never intended to enlist Ward's aid. It was probable Consuelo had led her straight into the elder's hands.

The whip cracked again with the sound of a shot, but for Serena there was no pain. An outcry went up, and died abruptly away. The men around her muttered, shifting, open-ing a path to where a buggy stood rocking from its sudden halt. The sharp percussion she had heard had not been the whip, but the firing of the smoking rifle Ward cradled in his hand as he stood holding the strut, braced with one foot on the iron step of the buggy and one on the floorboard. At the reins was Consuelo, while Pearlie huddled beside her in a stained satin wrapper, and with her brassy red hair strag-gling over her face.

Ward jacked another shell into the chamber of his gun, covering the crowd, before he jumped down. "The fun's over," he drawled. "Serena?"

The hands holding her were jerked away as if she were hot to the touch. She stumbled a little as she moved to obey the command in his voice, reaching for the hand he stretched out to her.

"Wait," Elder Greer snarled, stepping in front of Serena, his fingers closing on her arm. "By what right do you inter-fere?"

"This," Ward answered, and hefted his rifle, his face like chiseled granite and his eyes murderously green as he looked from the raw red scratches and welts that crisscrossed Se-rena's body to the whip in the elder's hand.

"She is in the hands of God. I won't let you take her!"

Ward ignored the shouts that were added to the stentorian words. "It's all right with me, if you feel like dying."

Though the men directly behind the Mormon faded back, others closed in, a low growling sound coming from their throats.

Consuelo spoke then, her voice soaring. "By what right do you do this, all of you? What makes you privileged to treat Serena so? She has done nothing to you. She has harmed no one!"

"She saw to it Nathan Benedict left her a rich widow, that's what! You call that nothing?"

The voice came from the outer edge of the crowd. It had the sound of anger, but also of sane reason, an indication that Pearlie's bullies had been joined by other men of the town.

"I call it a lie!" Consuelo returned. "And who has more reason than I to know the truth, since I was her husband's mistress?"

"It was mighty convenient!"

"Is she to be blamed for that? Punished for it? It was chance, no more. As well to beat a man for winning at cards."

"What do you know about it, fool woman?"

"I know much, me!" Consuelo said, her accent thickening with her rage. "It was to me that Nathan Benedict said he was afraid the new hoist at the Century Lode was not rightly installed. I told him to wait until the engineer was well enough to check it, but Nathan was too impatient. He would try it, he said. If anything was wrong, he would find out without irritating delays. There would be no danger, he said, because the built-in safety devices would prevent the cage from falling. He did not realize they would be affected also."

The man who had spoken looked thoughtful, glancing at the men around him.

"It is all a thing of revenge, what is being done here to Serena," Consuelo went on. "A thing hatched by this one here, this parlor-house she-devil, Pearlie, and this miserable spouter-from-streetcorners, this elder of the Mormons who once wanted to make Serena his fourth wife while he had three others that still lived. Because she took the man of Pearlie, and refused to be the woman of the elder, they make her the target of their cruel malice. Would you be a party to it? Would you have the blood of an innocent woman on your hands for the sake of such a pair? Will you be ready to stand accused with their paid assassins, these dregs of the town who would sell their souls for a tumble in bed and a few

393

dollars in their fists? And you who have been hirelings, know there will be no money! For this day's work, you have already had the only wage you will receive!"

A vicious cry went up. The mood of the core of men left grouped around Serena and Ward grew uglier as they saw many of their number easing away. There were fists shaken, and teeth bared in hissing curses. Only the rifle in Ward's hands kept them at bay.

Consuelo reached to shake the shoulder of the woman on the seat beside her. "Tell, them, Pearlie. Tell your bought mob that you have changed your mind, that you will no longer pay. Tell them to go, and never to touch Serena again!"

Pearlie lifted her head, staring wildly at Ward, who seemed to look through her as he swept the gathering that jostled around him. Her pale-blue eyes were vindictive, gloating, as she looked to Serena, who stood swaying, with her pink-tipped breasts exposed to the greedy gazes around her. She glared past the elder with bitter contempt for his failure, then let the maniacal glint of her glance pass over the others.

Consuelo shook her again. Pearlie licked her lips. "It's true," she croaked. "I—I changed my mind. There'll be no money."

It was as good as an admission of guilt. The mob stood exposed for what it was, as did the Mormon elder.

"Slut," he growled, the inimical hatred of his silver eyes focused on the red-haired woman.

Ward stepped forward at that moment, catching Serena's wrist, pulling her free. The elder swung to start after her, only to be brought up short by the barrel of the rifle against his chest.

"Stay right there," Ward said softly, and began to back away. He urged Serena behind him. "Get into the buggy," he told her, never taking his eyes from the elder.

Serena did as she was bid, lifting her foot high for the smooth iron step, pulling herself upward with a great effort. For an instant, Pearlie blocked her way, then at Consuelo's hissed command, the woman shrank back. Ward came next. He stepped up, catching the strut to brace himself against the footboard, since there was no more room on the single seat. His attention was centered on the men below.

It was then that Pearlie lunged for him, a keening noise in her throat as she grabbed for the rifle. Off balance, Ward struggled with her, his foot slipping from the step. Serena twisted around as she realized what was happening, stretching to close her fingers on his leather belt even as Pearlie lay across her, prodding her with a sharp elbow in the chest, squirming as she tried to wrest the rifle from Ward.

Suddenly the rifle belched flame, and the report reverberated under the top of the buggy. Ward was flung back, his face contorted with pain, holding to the vehicle by his fingertips and Serena's grasp.

With an animal bawling, the mob started forward. Consuelo shouted at the horses, slapping them into a run. Ward swung forward, reeling, falling across Serena and Pearlie as Serena wrenched desperately at his belt. Pearlie screamed, letting the rifle go, raising her shaking hands to her face. Her eyes were lifeless, demented, as she stared at the bloodstain spreading across the front of Ward's shirt, soaking into her wrapper as he lay over her lap. The buggy jolted, leaning around a corner. As it straightened, Consuelo reached for the rifle that threatened to bounce from the moving vehicle. She set it between her knees, then put out a hand to help Serena pull Ward farther inside the buggy.

There was no time for fear. Serena slid her hand inside Ward's shirt, feeling for a heartbeat. It was there, a little fast, but strong.

He lifted his head, turning to look at her with a tight grin. "I'm still alive, if that's what you want to know."

He ended on an indrawn breath as one of the buggy wheels fell into a hole. Pearlie stopped screaming with a gasp, though her eyes were vacant. Ward pushed himself off them, going to one knee in the jouncing buggy to relieve them of his weight. His face was gray despite his attempt at humor, and blood seeped through his fingers that he held to his ribs. Behind them came the hue and cry of the mob, a chilling sound. A man stared open-mouthed as they careened past, heading downhill. A burro trotted, braying, out of their path. Nothing else moved in the town. It was as if everybody and everything had drawn back inside, taking cover until they saw what happened.

Consuelo brought the buggy to a stop in the alleyway between the Eldorado and the parlor house. Pearlie was the first one out, climbing over Serena in trembling haste, pushing past Ward, straining away as though she was afraid of him, and of what she had done. Once down, she left them at a curious, straggling run, heading for the back door of the parlor house.

Ward swung down, favoring his side. Serena came next,

and Consuelo after her. Ward reached back inside for his rifle.

"The parlor house," the Spanish girl said. "They may be less likely to tear it apart, and there will be somebody to send for the sheriff."

Ward gave a nod, his teeth clamped together so tightly the muscles stood out in his jaws. "I should have sent someone to start with."

"There was no time for explanations," Consuelo said succinctly. "Besides, the fools should have taken notice by now."

It was only a step to the door. Consuelo turned the knob and pushed inside, standing back as Ward entered with Serena at his side, half-supporting him. A girl, the candy-box brunette named Cora, was just coming down the stairs. Her eyes widened at the sight of them. She opened her mouth to exclaim, but Consuelo forestalled her.

"Get Serena something to wear. And light a lamp. Why are the shades always pulled in places like this? It's dark as night."

The girl stripped off the wrapper she was wearing over her corset, chemise, and drawers. Handing it to Serena, she said, "I have a lamp in my room where I was heating my curling tongs. I'll get it."

"Do that," Consuelo said over her shoulder as she barred the door, "and bring bandages. Then send somebody out the front way after the sheriff. Tell him—tell him there's a riot down here, a gang trying to break up Pearlie's place."

The sound of the crowd was coming closer. Hearing it, the girl leaped to obey. In seconds, the housekeeper came pounding down the stairs fully dressed, and whisked past them along the hall and out the front door.

Consuelo pulled aside the curtain over the back door. "They are heading for the Eldorado," she whispered.

At that moment, they heard a moan. It came from the recess under the stairs. Turning, they saw Pearlie crouched there with her shoulders hunched and a look of terror in her eyes. Above them on the stairs, Cora appeared with the oil lamp. Pearlie shielded her contorted face from its golden glow. "Go away," she said, making ineffectual shooing motions with her other shaking hand. "Go away. Don't touch me. You can't touch me."

Serena had slipped into the wrapper given her. Now she exchanged a brief look of amazement with Consuelo, then reached for the bandaging brought by the girl with the lamp.

She pushed a chair forward for Ward, but he refused it, leaning against the frame of the opening that led into the back parlor. There was a listening intentness on his face, and the rifle was steady in his hand.

"Set the lamp down, there where Serena can see to Ward," Consuelo said, "and then help me drag something—chairs, stools, tables, anything—in front of this door."

There was no time. Coarse yells came nearer, and the door rattled in its frame as a fist hammered on it. A cold look descended on Consulo's features. She swept down on Pearlie and dragged her to her feet, shoving her toward the door.

"Tell them we are not here!" she hissed. "Tell them you got away and came here, but you do not know which direction we ran."

"No, no, please, no," Pearlie whispered, her eyes vacant and her mouth working.

"Yes," Consuelo said, pushing her in place before the door. "Open it and speak to them, but be careful what you say, or you will be shot."

Pearlie glanced at Ward, and her face seemed to dissolve. Tears flooded her eyes and her lips trembled loosely, while her features contorted in an ugly mask of grief. He motioned with the rifle as the hammering grew louder, and slowly she turned to put her hand on the bolt.

Abruptly, her face twisted. She jerked the bolt and swung the door wide. "They're here!" she screamed. "Come and get them!"

Elder Greer was the first man over the threshold. A shot rang out, tearing its way through his flapping coat as he dived for the floor, passing on to kick splinters from the doorframe. The next man yelped and threw himself backward. The shot that followed sent the other five or six gathered outside running for cover. Ward jacked another shell in and sent it after them for good measure, then nodded to Serena. She stepped immediately to slam the door and throw the bolt once more.

Pearlie flattened herself against the wall beside the stairs, her eyes wide and staring. The brunette with the lamp retreated upward a step, her shaking hands making the flame inside the lamp's globe flutter.

The elder sat up, then pulled himself to his feet by holding to the stair banister. Ignoring the rifle bore that swung in his direction, he took a step toward Serena. From inside his coat, he took out a long-bladed skinning knife. "Now," he said, his voice hoarse. "Now, Serena."

Her face pinched and bruised, Serena looked at him. Since she had known this man, she had been assaulted, nearly raped, subjected to public humiliation, and robbed of everything she owned. She had been hounded and harassed, held up to scorn, charged with vile accusations, branded with foul names, and threatened with acts of violence. Her life had been endangered, she had been harried and attacked, chased down, her horses and carriage taken from her, her clothing shredded, and her pride and modesty stripped away as dozens of strange men had prodded and handled her. She had faced torture and death, and finally been chased into this last place of refuge, a run-down parlor house smelling of sweat and urine and stale tobacco. Her body ached from the mauling, the cuts and whipmarks she had received, and the rankling injustice of it was like a running sore. Rage boiled up inside her, bringing color to her cheeks and a militant look to her eyes.

"Now?" she breathed, her voice strained, but firm. "What do you mean? What have I done to you, except injure your towering pride?"

"You are a fornicator!" the elder thundered.

"For living with, being with, the man I love? I count this no sin."

Beside her, Ward went still, but she paid no attention.

"An adulteress!"

"How can I have betrayed a marriage that was never a true union, a marriage to which I never agreed?"

"You murdered your husband!"

"His death was an accident. He died by no man's hands, none." Ward's indrawn breath caught at her consciousness, but she went on. "No, it is you who are the murderer, you the fornicator, you the adulterer and the deserter of your family. You killed your wife Lessie with brutal enjoyment because she left you. You stalked the other pitiful women of the cribs, using their bodies with lust before you took their lives, cutting their flesh, wounding them in your insane need for revenge. Why? What has any woman ever done to you?"

"No—I am the instrument of the Lord. They were washed in the blood of the lamb as it is written, those women, made pure and clean in his sight."

"You are insane. Your mind is so twisted you don't know what you are doing."

Concern amounting almost to fear crossed the shrunken, bearded face of the elder. "You are evil," he whispered. "I have to kill you before you turn them all against me."

"You have turned them against yourself."

The Mormon stared around at a loss, his gaze touching on Consuelo, standing on the opposite side of Ward from Serena, on Pearlie and the other girl with the lamp. From outside came shouts, as if the men left were getting ready to rush the door. Ward's attention was drawn to the sound. At that moment, the elder took a step forward, then halted suddenly as the rifle in Ward's hands steadied once more on his chest.

Consuelo glanced at Ward's face, at the pale line around his mouth. She reached out to close her fingers on the elder's arm.

"If it's evil women you want, there is one for you over there, one you know. You and your partner Pearlie make a fine pair."

The Spanish girl gave him a push. Almost as if relieved, he turned from Serena, gripping his knife tighter, drawing his righteous anger around him like a mantle.

"If it wasn't for you," he said, pointing a long, bony finger at Pearlie, "the other woman would be dead now. Her soul's salvation, my scourging of her body, the physical union, would be complete. It's your fault, yours alone."

Pearlie came away from the wall, her pale-blue eyes dilated. "Are you going to kill me like all the rest? Are you? Are you?"

There was in her voice a husky fascination and the strength of a yearning challenge. It was almost as if she wanted him to kill her, as if she defied him to try.

The silver eyes of the elder glittered. "Slut!" he cried. "Do you repent of your sins?"

"No!" Pearlie screamed. "Never!"

Before anyone could move, before they realized what was happening, Elder Greer lunged for her. Pearlie spun around and stumbled up the stairs, pushing past Cora with the lamp, shrieking with excited laughter. The elder pounded after her, knocking the other girl against the banister as he took the treads two at a time.

At this second blow, Cora lost her footing. She cried out as the lamp she held tilted, went spinning out of her hand, spreading kerosene down the wool runner of the stairs. It hit the floor with a tinkling crash. The flame of the wick leaped high, blossoming yellow and orange. In an instant, the stair runner was ablaze, the air filled with the acrid, singed-hair smell of burning wool.

The girl screamed, and with legs flailing, jumped over the fire to the hall below. "Fire!" she sobbed, turning to call upward. "Hey, you girls up there, fire!"

Black smoke billowed, making their eyes water. Ward, with his hand still pressed to his side, heaved himself away from the doorframe, heading toward the stairs. Consuelo ran after him.

"You can't go up there. This place is going up like paper. I've seen it before, too many times, in other mining camps."

"I can't just stand and do nothing," he grated.

With despair, Consuelo looked to Serena. Ducking their heads against the smoke, they went after him, edging around the flames, taking the stairs at a run.

In the upper corridors was pandemonium. Women in all stages of undress ran back and forth, carrying their belongings to the windows and throwing them into the streets below, cradling kittens, rabbits, and puppies, or running here and there with sleep-dazed eyes, demanding to know what was going on.

The door of Pearlie's room was locked. From inside came a harsh screaming, followed by the rise and fall of shouted intonations and prayers. Ward jerked at the handle, but it held solidly. Backing off, he rammed the door with his shoulder.

It shuddered in its frame, but did not budge. Ward reeled away, his breathing ragged and his grip loose on his rifle as he rested against the wall. The grayness in his face was more pronounced, and the blood gushed from between his fingers over his ribs.

"Does anybody have a key to this door?" Serena asked a girl running past. The girl only stared and kept going.

"Come away, Ward," Consuelo begged. "We have to get out of here. Think of Serena, think of me, if you won't do it for yourself."

He did not answer. Pushing erect, he backed off, then kicked at the door handle once, twice, three times. It flew wide, banging against the wall.

Serena stifled a scream, her hands clamped to her mouth. The room was bathed in blood. It smeared the walls and trailed over the floor toward the bed. On the coverlet of Brussels lace, red-stained and rumpled, lay Pearlie with her legs spread wide and blood slowly dripping from the heel of her foot, hanging off the side, onto the floor. Her hair was wet and matted, and her eyes staring. Above her crouched Elder Greer, grunting, his trousers about his ankles.

"Por Dios," Consuelo whispered, turning away.

Ward dropped to one knee. The Mormon elder turned, growling, and began to come off the bed with his knife in his hand. When the white-haired, nearly naked man was squarely facing him, Ward raised his rifle, nestled the butt against his cheek, and fired.

Chapter Twenty-four

Serena moved down the stairs with assurance, pulling on her gloves of gray leather as she went. It was a bright day, after the past month of dull weather and snow flurries; the stained-glass window above the door glowed with color. So did Serena, at least in the face. Her blue-gray eyes were clear, her cheekbones flushed with pink, and her mouth was rosy and moist. She was well at last, and happy, and if a shadow sometimes crossed her face, she did not allow it to linger long. Nothing must be allowed to mar the precarious peace she had attained, not today, not any day.

The costume she wore, of soft mauve-gray crepe de chine, was not vivid by any means, but that was as it should be. She wore with it, as a symbol of her mourning, black gloves and cartwheel hat, and the collar of jet with its ten-inch "rain" that Nathan had given her. Around her shoulders, over the full leg-o'-mutton sleeves, she had draped the cape edged with beaver fur that Ward had presented to her for Christmas year before last. It was a nice compromise, she thought, though she doubted that Ward would appreciate it.

He sat waiting for her in the sunshine on the seat of the phaeton, the reins of the grays in his capable hands. He was looking much better too. They had been worried about him for a time. The gunshot wound he had taken that terrible day had broken two ribs. During what followed, when he had been forced to jump with the rest of them from the top floor of the parlor house, he had punctured a lung. The greatest dread had been pneumonia, but he had escaped that, thank God. He was still a little pale, perhaps under the bronze of his skin, but he was fit, fit enough for anything.

A smile played around Serena's mouth as her thoughts went to the night before, and what had passed between them in the great paneled bed in the gold bedroom of Bristlecone. They had shared it for the past four weeks. That was Consuelo's doing. By the time they had reached the house, Serena and Ward had been too exhausted and in too much pain to care what became of them. Mrs. Egan had pointed out Serena's room, and Consuelo had directed the miners who had brought them to dump them into the bed. There they had lain through fever and chills and the incoherence of delirium. There they had turned to each other with a touch and a smile, though there had been little more, until the night before.

Serena let her mind wander back over those weeks, and that last day of blood and fire. She could remember hearing the three shots of the fire alarm, remember half jumping, half climbing down a rope of sheets to escape the flames that engulfed the parlor house. She could recall the way she felt when she realized that a group of miners, men who remembered her as Gold Heels, had fought off what was left of Pearlie's hired bullies and were getting ready to storm the parlor house when it caught fire. The rest was vague, though she knew her grays had been caught and brought around, and that a pair of the strongest of the miners had ridden with them out to Bristlecone. The guard had been necessary not to protect them, but to keep the grays from being stolen. For by that time, the fire had spread, and a large portion of Cripple Creek was ablaze. People were laying hands on every vehicle and animal they could find to move their belongings out of danger. The Eldorado had gone up in smoke, as had much of Myers Avenue.

Ward got down as he saw Serena. She descended the steps and allowed him to hand her up into the phaeton. As he climbed to the seat beside her and took up the reins once more, he turned his head to smile down at her, surveying the oval of her face beneath the wide brim of her hat, his green gaze resting briefly on the cape she wore. With a shading of reluctance in his face, he turned his eyes forward and clucked to the horses, sending them down the drive.

Serena watched his hands as he handled the ribbons, liking the strength and competence with which he held the grays. He was competent about most things, some in particular. Yes, she owed Consuelo much.

Her indebtedness to the Spanish girl did not end with her gratitude for putting her to bed with Ward; it only started there. She was grateful for the warning Consuelo had given her of the threat against her, for her support in standing with them against the mob, and later against Elder Greer. She was thankful for the time the Spanish girl had spent at Bristlecone, helping nurse her and Ward, and for the care of Sean when Serena had been too weak to see to it herself. More than that was Consuelo's understanding of her marriage to Nathan, her lack of blame toward Serena for his death, or her inability to make him happy, and more, a thousand small things more.

"What are you thinking of?" Ward asked, his tone casual.

"Consuelo," Serena answered, tucking her hand into his arm.

"Too bad she had to leave."

"Yes, but it was her own choice, a decision made a long time ago."

For a day or two after the fire, Serena had been afraid Consuelo's exertions might bring on a miscarriage. It had not happened. A full night's sleep, and she was perfectly well, or so she said. Her ancestors had been peasants; it took more than a mob and a sliding fall from a two-story building to dislodge the seed once it had been planted. The work she had done, carrying trays, changing beds, lifting Sean, was good for her, she maintained; it kept her from thinking of Nathan, or brooding on what she would do when she reached Mexico.

Serena had tried to dissuade her from going. Consuelo only shook her head. "I know what I am doing. You have been a sister to me, and it pains me to leave you, but it will be best. Nathan's son will grow up in the warmth of the sun. I will find for him a father who will love us both without regard for the past. There will be enough money for our needs, and a portion for our desires, but not so much that it makes us proud. And if sometimes I dream of Cripple Creek and of another life, I trust that when I wake I will have forgotten. Surely God, who is good, will grant me that much."

It had been a week ago that Consuelo left. By then, Serena had been up for some time, gradually resuming the duties Consuelo had taken on. The crates and trunks that contained the belongings the Spanish girl would be taking with her to

Mexico had been carted to the station. The house Nathan had bought her had been turned over to its new owners.

Consuelo spent her last night at Bristlecone. The two women embraced on the veranda as Jack Coachman brought the town carriage around to take Consuelo to the train station. There were tears in her dark-brown eyes as she turned away. From inside the carriage, she waved, then, sitting straight and proud, she turned her face forward toward Mexico.

"Consuelo should have been the one to marry Nathan," Serena said abruptly.

"I don't believe he ever asked her."

She slanted him a quick glance, continuing despite the stiffness of his tone, "He might have, if he had never met me."

"If he had never met you, I'm not sure Consuelo would have appealed to him. It's my understanding that her resemblance to you was what he found intriguing."

"We are nothing alike, not really," Serena protested. "Consuelo has a much stronger character."

"Do you really think so?" he asked, smiling. "I would say she is louder, more obvious about it, but maybe it's just a front with her, the way she wants to appear to the world. You're quieter, but with you the vein goes deep, pure gold."

"Ward!" She turned to stare at him, amazement in her eyes.

"Did you think I didn't have sense enough to see it?"

There was no way to answer such a question. Gathering her composure and scattered thoughts, Serena reverted to her original topic. "I—I was trying to say that if Nathan hadn't married me, he would still be alive. It was my fault he rushed the installation of the hoist."

"I doubt that, but how so?"

He knew of her agreement to go to Europe with Nathan. She told him what Nathan had said, how he had meant to get the machinery into operation as soon as possible so he could get away.

"You give yourself too much credit, sweet Serena. I'm sure Nathan was anxious to take you away, but he would have been just as impatient without that. He liked having the best, whether it was a woman, a horse, a mining claim, or a hoist, and for him it was always a case of the sooner, the better."

It was true, Serena had to admit, though Ward's words awakened echoes of things just as well forgotten; Nathan's attempt to buy her, for instance, his attempt to hold Ward's ruin over her head, and his insistence on heaping her with gifts. Nonetheless, Serena felt an easing inside her as she relinquished a part of the burden of guilt she had been carrying.

"Mr. Patterson tells me the hoist and cage can be made safe if it is installed as it should be. I'm not certain it will do any good, however."

"Meaning?"

"I seem to have blotted my copybook with the other mine owners. They may decide to close me down."

"They'll have to shut me down first."

That simple declaration and the meaning behind it brought an ache to Serena's throat. "It isn't your problem," she said unsteadily.

"Anything that concerns you is my problem. Besides, I think you're doing the right thing. As for the mine owners, your best course is to smile and explain how you weren't sure the miners would go down in the new cage that killed your husband unless they were offered special incentives. If you could manage to shed a few tears at the same time, they'll go along happily. As I said before, I've instituted a raise in wages and a pension plan already. Starting next week there'll be no children allowed down the shaft, and lights put up in the stable area."

She pressed the fingers that still rested in the crook of his arm. "That should help, having them see I'm not alone in my madness."

"I'm doing it because it's humane, the right thing to do, not just to show a solid front."

"Of course," she murmured.

"You don't believe me, but then you never do."

The grim note in his voice made her turn sharply toward him. "I do believe you."

"Sometimes, when you have no other choice."

Her lips tightened. "And you are completely magnanimous, I suppose, taking every word I say for gospel?"

"Admit you believed I had a hand in killing Nathan right up until the minute Patterson told you it was impossible."

"At least I let you know I was mistaken. You are still stubbornly convinced I married Nathan for his money, and all because I was stupid enough to agree with you once when you so unflatteringly assumed that must be the reason I wanted to be a part of the gold rush!" She released his arm and moved to the far side of the seat.

"No, Serena, I haven't thought that for a long time." He sent her a quick glance, the hardness leaving his voice.

"I don't understand why it's such a terrible thing for a woman to want wealth, anyway; we have as much right to it as a man. It isn't our fault if there's no way to get it except through a male; if jobs are closed to us, or if men themselves make it too dangerous for a woman to work in the open alone. We can resign ourselves to being poor, or being prey; there is no in between!"

"I said, I don't believe you married Nathan for his money."

"What?" She stared at him, suspicious of the amusement that lurked in his green eyes.

"You spend it, give it away, spread it around to all your charities much too freely for it to mean anything to you."

"So now you think I'm a spendthrift!" She looked quickly away, though she could not keep her lips from quivering into a smile.

"I would show you what I think" he told her, a caressing timbre in the words, "but this isn't the place for it."

They had topped the hill above Cripple Creek. The town, or what was left of it, lay before them. The bowl of the crater valley was blackened and charred, an immense area of rubble that had been raked into piles like so much garbage. The fire that had started in the parlor house had eaten away a large section in the south part of the town, the main area of saloons, dance halls, vaudeville houses, and the like, before it had been brought under control that April evening. While the better people to the north were still celebrating the wiping out of such a sordid, crime-infested thieves' den four days later, another inferno had begun with a grease fire at the Portland Hotel on Bennet Avenue. This time a driving wind had spread the flames, sending them roaring through the dry wooden structures, one-room cribs and gingerbread mansions alike. What had not been consumed in the intense conflagration had been destroyed by the dynamiting crews trying to create a firebreak to halt the driving spread of the flames.

At Bristlecone they had been safe enough. Ashes and soot had dropped onto the roof from the pall of smoke that swirled around them at times, and they could see the flare of light in the sky and tongues of leaping flame, but there had been no danger. Many were the tales of hardship brought back by Jack Coachman and the stableboy when they were sent to help out if they could, and to bring back news. The weather, so warm the week before, had turned cold once more. When night fell on the Wednesday evening of the fire, more than five thousand people were homeless. Clutching the few possessions they had managed to save, sometimes odd bits and pieces like piano stools and wicker baskets, china figures and parasols, they gathered on the hillside above the town near the reservoir, huddling in the freezing wind.

Everything that could be spared from Bristlecone in the way of food and blankets was sent immediately. It did not go far. It was the mine owners living in Colorado Springs who came to the rescue. Warned of the disaster by means of the single telephone line from Cripple to the Springs, they rounded up tents by the dozens, blankets by the gross, food by the box and barrel, medicines, bandaging, and a precious consignment of baby diapers, and sent them roaring up Ute Pass on a special train. By midnight everyone had been fed and given shelter. Nor did the aid end there. There was another train, and another, until tens of thousands of dollars' worth of supplies had been unloaded and the feud between the Springs and Cripple had been buried in the outpouring of aid.

Beyond the human suffering was the financial loss. More than eighty percent of the town was destroyed in the two fires; less than twenty-five percent of it was insured. It was not going to be the end of Cripple Creek, however. Already there could be seen the fresh wood skeletons of buildings rising from the ashes. A few were nearing completion already, sturdy structures of brick with imposing facades and a more permanent look about them than the flimsy false fronts they replaced. Myers Avenue was rebuilding also, and going fancier, more ornate. By some quirk of fate, the Old Homestead parlor house was left standing, and was open for business as usual. On the whole, it seemed the fire might have been a good thing, a purging experience. There had been pain and loss, certainly, and people ruined, but in place of the shoddy gold camp with its flyblown refuse heaps there was rising a town of vigor and prosperity and cleanliness, a place of stability and a certain charm where children could be raised and life enjoyed for as long as the gold lasted.

That looked to be a long time, since geologists estimated there was nearly a billion and a half dollars' worth of the yellow stuff beneath the ground, even at a conservative estimate. In spite of the millions taken out, they had barely scratched the surface.

Serena had thought the purpose of their outing was to view the devastated town and to see the new buildings going up. When Ward rolled through the streets and swung onto the road toward the mining town of Victor, she sent him a questioning glance. If he noticed, he paid no heed, for no explanation was forthcoming.

It didn't matter, not really. It was a fine day for a drive. After the cold had come warmth once more, a part of nature's cycle. The air was fresh and sweet and clear. There was a mist of green on the slopes around them, and the trees and wild flowers were sending out new growth. A blue-and-black Steller's jay dipped overhead, lighting on a rock to give his raucous call. A chipmunk whisked across the road in front of them, then sat on his haunches to watch them pass. The sun felt good on her face, and the wind from the high passes of the Continental Divide had just enough briskness to clear the depression of the winter just past from her mind.

Serena's wandering thoughts returned to the scenes they had just witnessed. A few buildings other than the Old Homestead had been spared by the fire, the new Midland Terminal Railroad depot, a hospital, and a section of homes on the west side of town. Consuelo's house had been among the lucky ones, as had Serenity House.

"I'm sorry about the Eldorado," Serena said, slanting a glance at Ward.

"It doesn't matter."

"Will you rebuild?"

"No," he replied with a definite shake of his head. "That's over and done."

"I'm glad." It was over, in more ways than one. Consuelo gone, Nathan, Lessie, Pearlie, Elder Greer, all dead. With them went many specters of the past for Ward as well as herself. What would happen to them now?

"Do you ever think of going back to Natchez?"

"I used to, often. Not any more. There's something about this country; the air, the coolness. I don't know, it gets to you after a while. What about you? You have grandparents in Louisiana, don't you?"

"Not really. They washed their hands of my parents, and of me. If they wanted nothing to do with us two years ago, I can't believe they would care to acknowledge me now. No, there is nothing for me in Lousiana."

She had known for some time she could not go back, did not want to. Putting it into words was still a lonesome thing. It would have helped if there had been some indication from Ward in the last few days that the situation between them might become permanent. There had been none. He had been as silent on that subject as he had on the deaths of Pearlie and the elder. The charred bodies of the pair had been recovered and buried in Pisgah cemetery. Ward had sent flowers for Pearlie, she knew that much. He had not been able to attend the services, and so far as she knew, he had not visited the grave.

It was not that Serena seriously considered that he felt anything for the dead woman beyond pity and responsibility. What troubled her was that he might look on his ties to herself in much the same light.

They clip-clopped along for several minutes. At last Serena said pointedly, "If I had known we were coming this far, I would have had a lunch packed."

"It isn't far now," he answered.

Serena looked at him from under her lashes. Was it her imagination, or was his face paler, and yes, more grim? She opened her mouth to ask him straight out where he was taking her, then closed it again. If his present mood was any sign of the pleasantness of the place, she would just as soon wait upon her arrival to find out.

They had turned off the main road. The track they had taken was narrow. It led upward toward the crest of a hill. Near the top, where the rough trail ended, Ward pulled up and got down.

"We walk from here," he said, his eyes a translucent green as he stared up at her.

He helped her out of the phaeton and tethered the horses. With his hand beneath her elbow, they trudged up the remaining steep slope, their breathing labored in the thin atmosphere.

At the highest point, they stopped. Not too far away they could see the Anaconda Mine, and its outbuildings and town. Beyond lay the rolling mountains with their slopes denuded of trees, and past them the snow-capped ranges of the Sangre de Cristos.

Nearer at hand on the slope were mine tailings with their peculiar shadings of yellow and gray and orange, pulled from a shallow hole like dirt from a prairie dog's burrow. A few weathered timbers hung askew over it, and on one was tacked an uneven board painted with a faded name. This was the site of some man's claim, the place where he had pitted his luck and muscles against a dream of riches, and seen both worn out by the hard granite that lay glittering with quartz in the sun.

"Do you know what this is?" Ward asked the question with deliberation, his gesture indicating the piled rock.

"It's a mining claim."

"Yes, but which one?"

Serena stepped closer to the signboard. By narrowing her eyes, she could just make out the name. It was the Dragon Hole.

"The Dragon Hole," Serena repeated softly, then her eyes widened. "Isn't that—"

"Yes, it is. Would you like to look?"

Serena lifted her chin, her face white. "I don't think so."

"I recommend it," he said, and gave her a small push forward.

There was iron in his voice. Fear rippled along her nerves and then receded. She pulled her arm from his grasp and stepped away from him. Her blue-gray gaze direct, she stared into the gold-flecked green of his eyes. What she saw mirrored there gave her the courage to turn and step closer to the hacked-out hole in the ground.

The shaft was not deep, no more than eight feet. She could see the bottom plainly, and the solid granite that floored it. There had been some small amount of caving from the top; low piles of fine rock and dirt lay against the sides, but the walls were as solid as the floor. There was blown pine straw and spruce needles in those rocky depths, but nothing else, no crumpled form, no decomposed body, or gnawed skeleton. There was no sign that Otto Bruin had ever occupied this pit called the Dragon Hole.

Serena whirled. "Where is he? Where is Otto?"

"I have no idea. When I went back after him that night, he was feeling sorry for himself, but very much alive. I offered him the chance of a permanent occupancy here, or taking the horse I had brought to transport him here and getting out of the district as fast as he could travel. He saw the wisdom of accepting my last alternative."

"I didn't kill him?"

"Unfortunately not."

Serena looked away, a dazed expression in her eyes, then

411

she turned back. "But you said you put him here. You told me how and where and when."

"I will have to admit I made a good story of it." For all the lightness of his words, the look on his face was still dark.

"But—why?"

"Haven't you guessed? I wanted you, Serena, any way I could get you. But you were married to Nathan. I knew without being told that you would never consent to meet me behind his back, even if you cared for me, which I had reason to doubt."

"So you blackmailed me with an empty threat."

"It seemed worth the risk."

The wind ruffled his hair and flapped his shirt collar that he wore outside his corduroy coat against his lean brown cheek. It caught at her mauve-gray skirts, fluttering them, molding them against the symmetry of her body.

"You let me think I was a murderess, that I had killed a man."

"Dear God, Serena," he said, his voice rough. "Don't look so. I would spend a lifetime in recompense if I thought you would accept it. For all the pain and guilt you have known, I have suffered the same a thousand times over for what I was doing. There was pleasure in my bargain, but when I looked in your eyes and saw the contempt I deserved, I knew that even as I held you, you were lost to me."

"How could you do it, if you cared for me?"

"Cared? No word so tame can describe what I feel. I love you, Serena, and that being so, how could I not want you near me, whatever the cost?"

"But you left me again and again."

"What kind of life could I give you at the Eldorado? I had to find something else. I left you first to go to Denver to raise capital to work the mining claim. When it began to look like money thrown away, I played a long shot, prospecting in the mountains. I lost that bet, though while I was gone the claim proved out—when it was too late. And then, after Nathan died, at Bristlecone, I had to leave you because I had put you in danger. I had heard rumors that Pearlie was up to something, but not exactly what. I thought that if I showed up at the Eldorado again she would put a stop to it. I guessed wrong again, and this time I nearly lost everything; I almost lost you."

"I would rather not think of it." He had also come close to death.

"Nor would I, except for that one memorable moment when I heard you declare that you loved me. In the full knowledge that it may commit you, Serena, tell me the truth. Were the words a lie for the sake of argument, or did you mean them?"

"Oh, Ward," she breathed, the sound an ache in her throat. She took a stumbling step toward him, and then she was in his arms. He swung her around and her feet left the rocky slope. Above them the bright blue of the sky wheeled in dizzying circles.

"I do love you," Serena whispered against the warm column of his neck.

"And will you be my wife," he asked, his voice deep, "knowing that all your life through you will be plagued by devotion and adoration until you are sick unto death of hearing of my love, by always having me close beside you so you cannot move or turn without finding me there, by the necessity of sharing my bed and my constant touch?"

"It may be that I can bring myself to bear it," she answered, her blue-gray eyes warm and shining.

The kiss he set with hard and cherishing strength upon the softness of her mouth was a seal.

Serena slipped her arms around his neck, brushing her cheek against his. "Could we go home now?" she murmured. "The ground here is more rocky than can possibly be considered comfortable."

"The ground?" he asked in distraction as he removed her wide hat, the better to hold her to him.

"At Bristlecone there are any number of beds more inviting. I have a mind to hurry and see whether I am going to enjoy being plagued as much as I think. My whole life gives me little enough time to decide."

Author's Note

The Cripple Creek gold rush, the last of the great gold rushes, began in 1891. By 1899, the district, located at an elevation of 10,000 feet, boasted 475 producing mines and a half-dozen towns with a combined population of 55,000. By that year, $59,000,000 in gold had been taken from the ground, figured at slightly less than twenty dollars an ounce. There were forty-six stockbrokerage houses, forty-one assay offices, thirty-four churches, two opera houses, nineteen schools, eighty doctors, ninety-one lawyers, fourteen newspapers, and over a hundred women's clubs. In Cripple Creek township, there was a red-light district with seventy-three saloons, eight burlesque houses, a dozen or more parlor houses, several opium dens, and scores of cribs featuring girls of every nationality. And this was in spite of the fire only three years before that had virtually destroyed the town.

Labor wars, water in the mines, high production costs, and the rescinding of the gold standard caused the slowdown of mining in the early years of the twentieth century. By early 1920, Cripple Creek was dying. During the thirty-year period of its peak production, some $800,000,000 in gold (based on values at the time of mining, which would be equal to approximately $16,000,000,000 at prices quoted in today's market) was taken from the area. At least fifty men could claim to have become millionaires, some many times over.

In *Golden Fancy* I have attempted to recreate the atmosphere of the gold camp in its heyday. The representation is as authentic and factual as several months spent doing research in the district can make it. There are, however, two exceptions. The first concerns the origin of the fire that brings the book to a climax. The conflagration actually started at about one o'clock in the afternoon of April 26, 1896, on the second floor of the Central Dance Hall. Depending on the version you are prepared to believe, the cause was the overturning of either a gasoline stove or a kerosene lamp being used to heat curling tongs, during a scuffle between a girl and her male companion. The second deviation is in the use of a series of murders. To my knowledge, no such crimes occurred, though the blending of fanaticism and sex is consistent with similar incidents from ancient times to the present day.

For those who are interested in historical detail, the brief mention of the most famous of the Cripple Creek millionaires, Winfield Scott Stratton, is the only use of a real personage in the book. All other characters are fictional, though drawn with an eye to the type of person who might have been attracted to the boom towns of Colorado during the nineteenth century.

Today, there are approximately a thousand people still living in the Cripple Creek district, most of them occupied in tourist-related businesses. A few of the landmarks of the old days still stand, notably the Midland Terminal Railroad Depot, now the Cripple Creek museum, and the Old Homestead, which has been restored in the manner of a parlor house of the 1890s. These are visited during the summer months by thousands of tourists.

And yet, geologists say that eighty percent of the available gold has never been touched. It waits underground, embedded in the hard granite of the area. With the recent skyrocketing of the price of gold, there is much interest in reopening the old mines. One or two have been put into production again. There are gold-mining claims advertised in the local papers, and Cripple Creek gold stocks bought and sold by the local brokers. Cripple Creek may soon begin to boom again!

Jennifer Blake
Green Mountain Falls, Colo.
November 9, 1979